Lost in Willipaq

Lovers, Losers, and Part-time Demons

Somewhere, something incredible is waiting to be known...

Lost in Willipaq by Rob Hunter
ISBN: 978-0-6152-4069-5

For Bonnie who knows where the good scissors are

❑

Our mother was called to claim her husband's bodiless head. She picked out a handsome stone of speckled gray Vermont granite for the resting place of what was left of her late husband. "Lost in Willipaq," read the stone. Willipaq was the name of the small Maine town where David, our father, died. There was a mix up and our father's body had been cremated by mistake. They still had the head however, neatly tagged and in a box.

—Klein, the Clone from Lost in Willipaq

The tales of Lost in Willipaq have appeared in print and online in the years 2000 through 2008.

As of this writing there are as yet no Rob Hunter tote bags, umbrellas, refrigerator magnets, ties, bumper stickers, etc. The stories collected at onetinleg.com are there for free—a sad deficiency but I'm working on it.

Typically the afterlife of a tale consists of gathering dust until the writer's heirs and assigns shred it for packing nick-knacks and other writerly impedimenta. Not quite the half-life of linoleum. And what of the loves, lives, hopes and aspirations of its citizens? Must they float forever in a shimmering noösphere playing whist and watching the flights of eidolons? Boring. Hence onetinleg.com. I regularly record stories (at the local radio station) as they become available and copyright reverts back to me, in usually a year or so. The stories and MP3 downloads are distributed for free, under a Creative Commons license.

To misquote Walt Kelly's Pogo: "We have seen the future and it's not yet..." The call, dear reader, is yours. The gentlefolk listed in the acknowledgements—who have shown the rare taste and superior judgment to purchase my work—thank you for your support.

Many of the stories of Lost in Willipaq are archived online at www.onetinleg.com.

Lost in Willipaq

Rob Hunter
tales from onetinleg.com

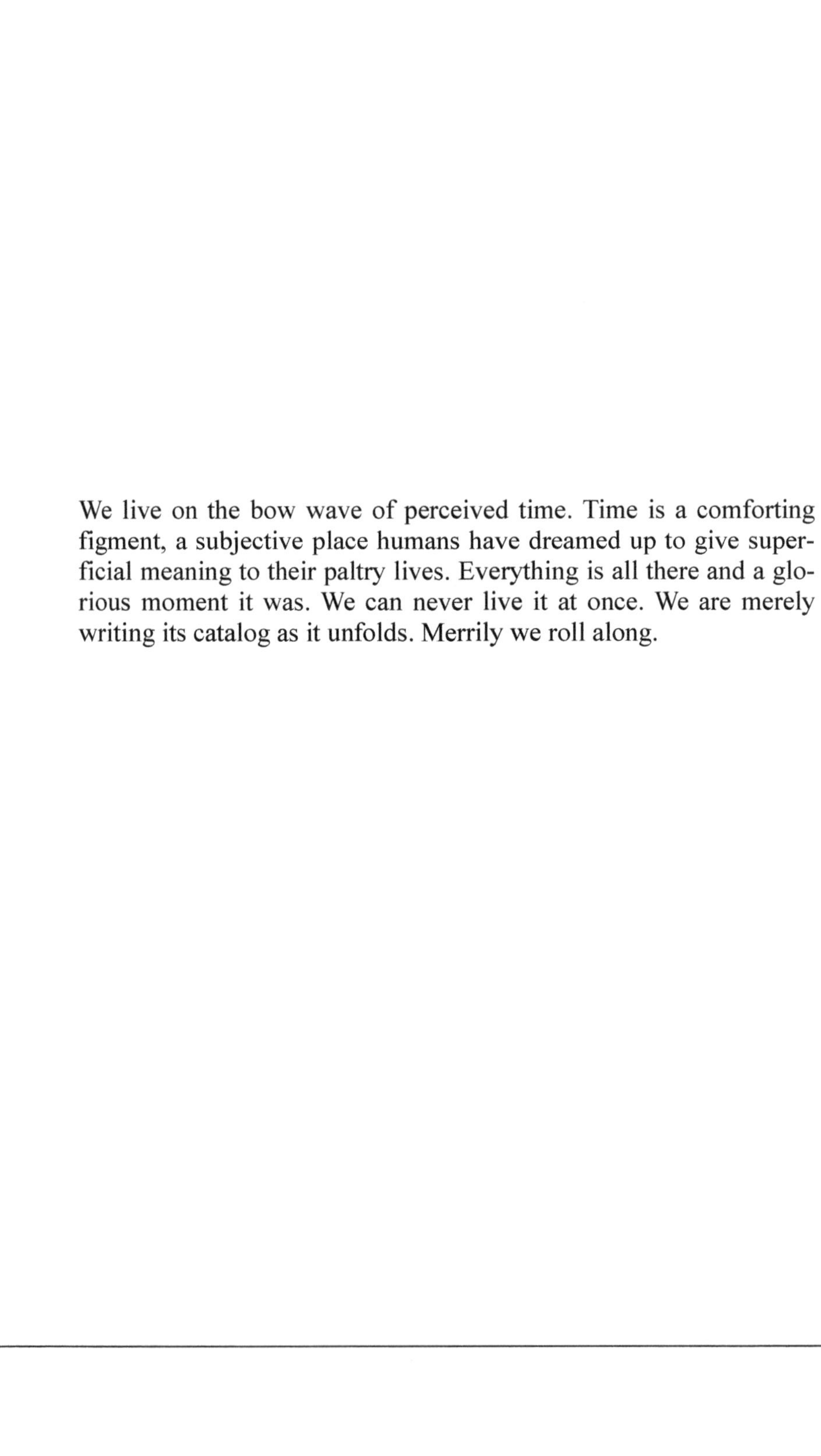

We live on the bow wave of perceived time. Time is a comforting figment, a subjective place humans have dreamed up to give superficial meaning to their paltry lives. Everything is all there and a glorious moment it was. We can never live it at once. We are merely writing its catalog as it unfolds. Merrily we roll along.

❑ The Entertainments ❑

the complete compendium: lovers, losers and part-time demons...

---

by way of explanation

A second edition of Lost in Willipaq was never in the works. Yet here it is.

Visitors to the site www.onetinleg.com (see page 76) had been promised a fresh compendium of collected tales, Platterland, in late 2007. As of this writing (Fall, 2008) the Platterland project is shifted to the back burner due to copyright considerations. Some of the stories I wanted to include will not be mine again free and clear for a year or two. I should be happy. And I am—the characters, citizens of the tales—are browsing in pastures of plenty afforded by the small press venues where I submit. In the fullness of time they will call home and Platterland will fly.

Meanwhile...

The Willipaq exegesis you have before you can rightly trace its existence to a gotcha moment when I was rewriting the script of A Special Providence prior to going into the studio to record a batch of MP3s. Yes, there is life after publication.

Providence was a story cobbled together around a synthesis of What If: an Old Testament Jehovah opts for contemporary technology to make a personal appearance/said Supreme Being will distribute largesse/the only available beholder is a gormless loser who will settle for a jelly doughnut. I had in 2002 written in, then out, a long-suffering wife with a fixation on Carl Sagan's *Cosmos*. *Cosmos*, while well-remembered by a select few had been off the air for decades. Then comes 2005 and the Science Channel brings *Cosmos* back, digitally remastered. Wow.

In addition to polishing the tales for reading aloud, there are seven new stories in Willipaq^2—*E Pluribus Human, The Red Sneaker Zones, The Song of the Rice Barge Coolie, The Year They Invented Frozen Lemonade, Scope Virgin, Dead Man in the Yard* and *The Runaway Bungalow,* a novelette.

Rob Hunter
Pembroke, Maine
October 2008

A Pass on the Tabouli

Errol Flynn reclined in a lavender-scented bath and extended a tanned hero's arm to make a fist. He suspected the studio had kept him stuffed with hormones and cloned organs for the last seventy-five years all for this one last remake. How many Kims had it been? Damned Kipling. He heard dry gears grind down the corridors of time as the British Empire spun in its grave. Kipling—Flynn wondered if camels gave him hemorrhoids, too. Perfumed bubbles danced with tiny golden flecks as he tightened his triceps. "Look at that sucker bounce," said Errol Flynn, lost in the poetry of the moment. His flexing fingers closed around a squeeze bottle of shampoo. He squeezed. Quarnk!

And now a musical version. He sank under the suds; a guy deserved a break, not an aria. "And Valentino! I never guessed that SOB had eyes for my script." One last Kim. Flynn wished he had read the fine print on the resurrection form. "My life..." said Flynn. He throttled the shampoo in a strangler's grip. A miniature globe of refracted rainbows swelled and popped. "...then, arrivederci Errol."

Quarnk! Said the shampoo.

"Kato!"

A scramble from the adjacent guesthouse.

"Yes, Errol."

"The loofa. My back." Not having his option picked up would be tantamount to a death sentence. And if Valentino got the nod... Well, it was too late now. A musical. Well, desperate situations called for desperate measures. "Kato, do we have any of that home-brew tabouli of yours left in the fridge?"

Flynn's semi-permanent house guest crossed himself. "Cat ate it. I was saving it."

"How long?"

"To long, boss; cat died."

"Any left?" The doings of tabouli past its prime were legend.

"Some—for emergencies. I tossed most of it. Those dumpster pickers from the studio commissary made off with it. The tabouli, not the frozen cat."

"What was the cat doing in the refrigerator anyway?"

"Curiosity. Whatever."

"Pack it up. La-la-la-la-la-la-la," Flynn vocalized. The faithful Kato dropped the loofa and, hands over his ears, fled to the shelter of his daytime dramas. There was that eye-catching secretary in Creative... a well-planned hustle could keep him from having to take voice lessons just to hang on to his puny life.

Quarnk! Said the shampoo. Quarnk! Quarnk!

❑

Marcia Harding struggled out of her employer's office, hastily pulling her slip down to cover her knees. A man was waiting at her desk. She recognized him from the studio commissary that morning; he had morsels of pepper and chopped tomato in his moustache: the tabouli salad guy.

"That Harry Bartlemy is such a reptile," said Marcia. A crunch of discomfited furniture and the massive flailing of varanus komodoensis, the world's largest lizard, issued from the room she had just exited. Marcia Harding did not suspect she had recently acquired unusual powers.

"You are lovelier than a kafila of fat camels..." said the tabouli salad guy.

"Well..." Marcia primped. "That's a new line."

"I am of the Ghilji. We rule the roof of the world," said the handsome stranger as he extracted a sprig of parsley from his beard. "There is an Afghan adage: 'Do you have an enemy? I have a cousin.'"

"I don't have any cousins. But I have a boss who's always trying to get into my pants."

"And who is to blame him," said Errol Flynn as Mahbub Ali, gallantly. "You are the same size?"

Marcia shrugged and flashed her visitor a smile of frank innocence. "He finds me irresistible. I had to give him a rap with Douglas Fairbanks' silver-headed Malacca walking stick. Now he's going to be crabby all afternoon. He's a lizard or something." The tabouli salad guy's beard was trimmed, perfumed, oiled and plaited with ribbons; he was ogling her. Marcia gave her pantyhose an upward yank. "Yes?" she asked.

"Ah, well... Hmm, yeess," said Errol Flynn.

"I'm sorry. You will have to do better than simply 'Yes.'" Marcia turned to check the file drawer where she hoped there was a fresh change of underwear. "You will have to state your business." From Harry Bartlemy's office came the crash of Venetian blinds being rent asunder. A dog yelped.

"Your boss seems to be having a fit in there," said Errol/Mahbub.

"Ignore him; he just wants attention. And welcome to show business by the way," said Marcia, giving her pantyhose a final adjustment and flourishing a steno pad. "The store is open. Name, please?"

"Mahbub Ali," said Errol Flynn. "I am an Afghan swashbuckler, a horse trader? Here to audition?" On her desk he plomped an overlarge floral horseshoe and a basket of figs and loquats. Errol/Mahbub scratched privately in his red pajamas. Probably fleas, damned camels. "I love you. I am sincere in this," he said, getting right to the business at hand.

Hmm, thought Marcia, a studio romance could be in the offing. She had read about these in Modern Screen. She riffled unobtrusively through her Week-at-a-Glance. April was open. "I am not easy. I want you to know this right off."

A dot sprang from Mahbub-A-Flynn's beard to the tip of Marcia's nose. "Flea," said Flynn. "Their copulations can take up to nine hours. This is a proven scientific fact."

"Wow." Marcia's eyes crossed. The dot sprang back to the beard. Marcia's eyes uncrossed. Errol/Mahbub hooked a chair with one toe, pulled it over and flopped untidily with his feet on her desk.

From Bartlemy's locked office came a noisy reptilian skulking and the whimper of a frightened poodle. The door splintered and sagged open. Bartlemy strode through, somewhat rumpled but otherwise none the worse for wear. He was preceded by a miniature poodle which sported a diamond-encrusted collar.

"You know what's funny—I thought I was an oversized Komodo dragon for a while there," said Bartlemy. "I took a Quaalude and it went away. Marcia, I have reserved us a table at Twenty-One..." Bartlemy's face went ashen. "You, sir," he held an accusatory finger under Mahbub Ali's nose. "Have you been carrying on with my secretary?" The poodle growled.

Thump. Thump. Errol Flynn as Mahbub Ali the horse trader swung his two tasseled boots to the floor. "Yeah?" He leveled a ferocious glare at the poodle. A squadron of bouncing black specs sprang from the Afghan swashbuckler's beard and launched themselves at the poodle. The poodle whined and slunk between Bartlemy's legs. "Oh, yeah?"

"Hmmph!" uttered Bartlemy, beating an undignified retreat.

Marcia's eyes glowed with admiration. "Neat trick—the fleas I mean. You do look like Errol Flynn, you know?" She picked through the fruit basket. "But if you want to get to the head of the list you'll have to better than figs and loquats," said Marcia Harding. "They will most likely be casting Rudolph Valentino this time," said Marcia. "It's a musical."

"Valentino. Ha!" Flynn/Ali struck a pose and rolled his eyes to the limits of their outer periphery to observe the young woman's reaction to this statement. "He can't carry a tune in a polder dam. Or so they say. C'mere." He pulled her close and covered her décolletage with an onslaught of passionate kisses. Marcia noticed the felt-booted mountain tribesman's breath smelled fresh as new-mown hay with an overtone of parsley.

"By-the-bye," said Flynn/Ali when they paused for a gulp of air, "what's a choice cupcake such as yourself doing working for Harry Bartlemy, a notorious philanderer?" He munched on a fig.

"I came to Astoria to make it in pictures. I was the Indiana Pork Queen."

❑

Earlier that same day, togged out as an Afghani dealer in pre-owned transportation, Errol Flynn crept up on Marcia Harding in the buffet line of the studio commissary. Unassisted, Kato's home-brew Tabouli might not be up to the task. At stake was enhanced preferment on the casting list, hence his continued existence.

"It's off," said a tall bearded man at Marcia Harding's elbow. He wore red silk pajamas and a karakul hat. "...the tabouli salad. Those who would partake of it should beware of unforeseen circumstances." Odors of patchouli and sandalwood wafted from his oiled beard. "It is a well-known scientific fact that, under the influence of tainted tabouli, one's merest utterance tends to become unruly reality." The Astoria Studio's salad bar was notorious for the disreputable state of its greens.

Marcia turned to confront the accuser of her salad choice. "You auditioning?" Marcia could not recall the studio having a mid-budget action picture in the works. "And I know the Tabouli salad is off; I eat it to keep my strength up. My boss is always trying to seduce me."

"And who is to blame him?" Errol/Mahbub eyed the young woman with a forthrightness that brought a blush to her cheeks. "Your creamy thighs aside, darling, take a pass on the tabouli; it's lethal."

"If the tabouli salad is off, how come you are eating it?"

"I eat it every day and have acquired an immunity. You gonna finish that salad?"

"You said it was tainted."

"So I did. May I suggest a tête-à-tête?" Flynn/Ali emptied a table with a swift arc of his sword arm. A snappily dressed busboy hurried up to clear. "Have a seat." He graciously held Marcia's chair and tucked a napkin under her chin. "As you are obviously naive in matters of imported condiments, it is time for a little backstory. This is common knowledge but there might be someone who needs filling in." He eyed her lap lasciviously.

Marcia crossed her legs and leaned across the table. She spoke in hushed, intimate tones. "Okay. Astoria, Queens is the movie capital of the world. We weekend on the Jersey shore. There is eternal life, almost, for stars who get their resurrectioning options renewed. Everybody knows that."

"If they had found gold instead of coal in California things might have been otherwise," said Errol/Mahbub-Ali/Flynn. "The cattle trains west are packed with bit players sent to die in the mines."

"I have heard the tales, but I never believed them." Marcia's clear blue eyes crossed in contemplation. "Well, they did fail their screen tests. But California, unthinkable!"

"A living hell, the mines. Nonetheless, whatever the human cost, cheap power from cut-rate coal has enabled our factories to run twenty-four hours a day, thus keeping impoverished children off the streets."

"You have a lovely speaking voice," said the beguiling Marcia. "Are you afraid of the talkies?"

"No, darling. Of the musicals. I can't carry a tune in a rucksack."

But that, as they say, was that morning. In the meantime, in-between time, the tainted tabouli had had leave to work its insidious ways with Marcia Harding.

❑

Mahbub Ali the horse trader, one-time Errol Flynn, and Marcia Harding, quondam Indiana Pork Queen, were entwined on her desk, between the Week-at-a-Glance and a cup of freshly sharpened pencils. Harry Bartlemy, Vice President for Creative, chose that moment to leave his inner sanctum.

"He's a bit of a jack-in-the-box, our Harry," said Errol/Mahbub, hastily re-stringing his red silk pajamas.

"Careful," said Marcia as she shimmied into a fresh set of knickers.

"Well!" said Bartlemy. "So that's how things are. I had plans for us, Marcia; we could have made beautiful music together."

Mahbub Ali leaned close to Marcia's ear and whispered, "Gary Cooper to Madeleine Carroll, The General Died at Dawn, 1936. Bartlemy is plagiarizing."

"Ohhh..." Marcia Harding frowned, an endearing petulance. Mahbub Ali took a nip at her ear.

"Ohhh!" said Marcia.

"Phooey," said Bartlemy. Giving the poodle's leash a yank, he retreated to the sanctuary of his sanctum, slamming the door behind him.

"That Harry Bartlemy is such a snake," said Marcia Harding. The words had scarcely escaped her lips before Bartlemy's poodle gave a strangled yelp and was silent.

The splintered door creaked open and a giant python thrust its head into Marcia's cubicle. "Damned doorknobs," said the snake as it spat out a broken tooth. "Call the carpenters. Get 'em changed to over to handles. After that, you're fired." Mustering as much dignity as herpetologically possible, the python gave an all-over wriggle and retraced its path back into Bartlemy's chamber. "Close the door, please. Sorry about the poodle. Instinct."

"I need some air," said Marcia.

Marcia and Mahbub Ali passed from the cloistered compound that held the Creative bungalows and out into the drizzle of a Queens springtime. Deep-bosomed odalisques from the court of the Sun King paused to peer through lorgnettes. Cowboys, Indians, Mongols, Huns and Romans, the usual crowd, strolled by.

"I must have developed a thingy—a curse—from the tainted tabouli." Marcia was inconsolable.

"You, you, you. What about me? I've got to learn how to sing or I'm yesterday's camembert. A nobody," said Errol Flynn/Mahbub Ali. "And a dead nobody at that. So what if you have turned a vice president of Creative into a giant python; get over it. You're young; you've got time."

A handsome woman of indeterminate age stood nearby sucking on a Dove bar. Her ice cream treat had a thick Swiss white chocolate coating. She was not in a good humor.

"Who is that?"

"Shhh. It's Gloria Swanson. Valentino dumped her for that big Swede, Amy Lopsin. Hiya, Gloria." The woman chucked her ice cream into a trash barrel and sauntered over. The aging star, now 108 years old, didn't look a day over

30. Albeit stooped with many contract negotiations, she still had a hit-your-brakes figure. She wore a diaphanous wrap draped with ropes of pearls.

Gloria squinted at Mahbub Ali. "Don't tell me. Kim, right? Not a chance. Rudy's going for it."

"Rudy?" asked Marcia.

"Valentino, you delirious ingénue."

Marcia wondered if her feelings should be hurt. She decided not. "I came to Astoria to make my way in the world of the movies. I was the Indiana Pork Queen."

"High hopes," Gloria was reflective. "I had high hopes, too, my dear. Of course my high hopes were realized." Marcia nodded sadly. Studio magpies gathered at the trash barrel where they pecked at Gloria's abandoned ice cream. "Yesterday's goodies," said Gloria, referring to the Dove bar. "Rudy has a marvelous singing voice; he's taking lessons. We are the best of friends."

"What? Where?" said Errol Flynn.

"The thirty-seventh remake of Kim. Rudy is up for the role of the Afghan horse trader. With his gifts, he's a shoo-in. Italians," said Gloria slyly, "they get it with their mothers' milk. Music, that is. Errol Flynn doesn't stand a chance."

"I mean where does he get his singing lessons?"

"Oh, that's a secret. He slips away every afternoon. He dumped me for that big Swede, but I still love him." She touched Marcia, who had a faraway look in her eyes, gently on the shoulder. "You didn't eat the tabouli salad, did you, dear?"

"You are beautiful," said Marcia Harding.

"20 resurrectionings, darlings." A man galloped past on a heavily lathered horse and, seeing Gloria, Mahbub Ali and Marcia closeted in deep conversation, negotiated a hazardous U-turn. "Ahh, here comes the phallic cathedral himself," said Gloria. Hooves flailed the air as the rider stood his mount on its hindquarters. "Still a hunk, that Rudy. And most of him is the original equipment, if you catch my drift." Valentino braked to a stop before them. Sally, the stallion, scattered the magpies and went nose deep in the trash barrel for Gloria's discarded ice cream. Sally, a tractable mare of many summers, had been retrofitted for long shots; the Paramount executive was not about to put at risk the life and limb of its marquee property. Sally whinnied and rolled her eyes.

“Lo, Gloria, how they hanging?” bantered Valentino. “Can’t stop to pass the time of day; I’m on the Quest. For the River that whoso bathes in it washes away all taint and speckle of sin.’ I have read the Book,” said Valentino.”

“He’s been researching the backstory for Kim,” Gloria sighed as she took the good-looking Valentino’s measure from withers to fetlock.

“Ah, the River,” said Mahbub Ali. “What river?”

“Whatever,” said Valentino. “Who’s the cupcake?” He pointedly turned from Mahbub Ali and nodded to Marcia. “How do?”

“Rudy...” said Gloria.

“Gotta go,” said Rudy. At that, he dug his heels into Sally’s flanks and charged off toward the Queensboro Bridge. The cry, “To the drawbridge! I am the drum on which God beats his message!” was carried on the wind of the original Latin Lover’s departure.

“Wrong film, but the chase is on,” sighed Gloria Swanson, “the mad, impetuous boy.”

“I thought Valentino was slipping away for a singing lesson.” Said Errol Flynn.

“He is. He’s trying to throw us off the track.” Gloria Swanson put two fingers into her mouth and gave out with an ear-splitting whistle. “Taxi!” A Checker, one of the five-seaters, screeched to a halt. Gloria gestured Marcia to a jump seat. “Your handsome Arab and I have to talk.”

“Afghani,” said Mahbub Ali. “From Kim? Kipling?”

The ancient actress rapped at the partition to attract the cabbie’s attention. “Turn left when we hit Manhattan.” She snuggled closer. “I’ve never kippled. Tell me.” Her hand was on Mahbub Ali’s thigh.

In their wake, a large snake followed as they bounced over the Queensboro Bridge.

“Nononono. Left, not right. We’re not going to the Carlyle for cocktails,” Gloria shouted. “The off ramp. Right?”

“You said left, lady.”

“Well, yes,” said Gloria Swanson as the cab veered across two lines of traffic, Sadiki bin Amin, the cab driver, being of headstrong temperament. “Now turn left. Under the bridge. See, it’s easy.” She settled back into the vinyl upholstery as Marcia relaxed her grip on the jump seat.

“Hang on” said Sadiki. “This is totally cool. I knew the lights on Broadway timed out, but this is my first crack at York Avenue.” They galloped hell-for-leather through the byways of the Manhattan's East Side. Or Sally galloped; Errol/Mahbub-Ali/Flynn, Gloria Swanson and Marcia Harding careened and wobbled. The cab veered and swerved.

"Jesus Christ," said Gloria Swanson as they hurtled diagonally through a gas station.

"A prophet much honored, blessed be his name," said Sadiki bin Amin.

"What is this, a religious picture?" asked Marcia Harding.

"Incidentally," said Sadiki, "there is a giant snake right behind us and he's gaining. Yours?"

Three heads shook an emphatic No.

"Ayee!" cried Sadiki bin Amin, his eyes riveted on the rearview mirror. The pursuing python had picked up enough time to pause under the self-serve canopy and give the hi-test pump a loving squeeze. The three passengers turned to look as a pillar of flame engulfed the former gasoline station. The python was still in hot pursuit.

"That is one fucking big snake," said Sadiki, revealing the depth of his assimilation, Oriental roots notwithstanding.

"It's only Marcia's ex-boss," said Mahbub Ali. "He's harmless if you're not a poodle."

Sally, the stallion, put on a burst of speed. Eyes wide with panic, she regretted the Dove bar and its excess calories. Valentino's mount felt the python viewed her as dinner, a not unreasonable supposition. Ahead of the careering cab, the departing leading man clung desperately to the neck of his mount as he flailed at her flanks with his heels. "To expound the Most Excellent Way is good," he shouted over his shoulder at his pursuers.

"That's in the book," said Sadiki bin Amin, who hailed from Egypt and not the Hindu Kush.

"Book?"

"God's curse on all unbelievers!" said Errol Flynn as Mahbub Ali.

"Not *that* book. Kim, by Kipling. I have been boning up on the backstory," said Sadiki. "This is a prerequisite for a hack license in New York City."

"Then Rudy's white stallion was foreordained." Gloria Swanson blanched.

"No, only retrofitted," said Sadiki. "The mysteries of the East: inscrutable, insurmountable."

“Kipling, right?” said Mahbub Ali who had not read the book even though he was in it.

“A book. With words and all. Who would have guessed?” Marcia Harding’s eyebrows curled into twin question marks. “Perhaps... then if we all read the book...?”

“We’d know how things come out but this would then be Kipling’s tale, not ours. We have our own destinies to whittle from the twig of Creation,” said Sadiki bin Amin.

Gloria rapped on the partition, “Take the 72nd Street Transverse. Rudy is making for the bridle path.” A missile flew through the air to collide with Sadiki’s windshield.

“He’s throwing rocks,” exclaimed the cabbie.

“It’s a dildo. Polyurethane.” Mahbub Ali gestured to the windshield. “See, no ding in the glass. Sonofabitch, who woulda guessed.”

“Precisely,” said Gloria Swanson. “But it’s not Rudy’s; it’s the horse’s.”

“The pedigree of the white stallion is fully established,” exclaimed the cabbie, quoting Kipling.

“Oops.” The three were knocked to the floor by one of Sadiki bin Amin’s impromptu detours.

“Sorry about that. He’s headed downtown.”

“We knew that,” replied Marcia, Gloria and Mahbub Ali in unison.

“I heard you say ‘voice lessons,’” said the cabbie. “Well, downtown you want the Kit-Kat Klub on Hudson Street; Kenny the piano player tutors solfeggio.”

“The twenty-first century is truly a panoply of marvels,” said Marcia Harding. “Consider the cinema: first the talkies, and now piano players that perform solfeggio.”

“A refugee, this Kenny escaped a contract labor gang in the California coal fields,” said Sadiki bin Amin. “This is a well-reported fact within the cinematic underground.”

The seekers, now a quartette with the avid involvement of Sadiki, rounded a tight-angle switchback onto Varick Street where the taxi skidded and took out the front of a lingerie boutique. A tinkle of broken glass punctuated the sudden silence. The Checker’s radiator steamed and sputtered in the garish light of a flashing neon sign. It said Kit-Kat Klub.

“We’re here.”

“Let’s check it out. Wait for us.” Gloria Swanson slipped the cabbie a twenty. Sadiki salaamed as the three entered the bistro on unsteady legs. An enormous python was wrapped around the jukebox. “A Rock-O-La, good taste,” observed Gloria.

“Hiya, Harry. Got here first, I see,” said Marcia Harding. The snake hissed.

A slippery-looking youngish man wearing a fez appeared from behind a beaded curtain. “Who seeks Kenny?” He rubbed his hands together nervously, an unappealing sight. From behind the curtain came the sound of a man practicing scales.

“Mahbub Ali the horse trader, if you are Kenny,” said Errol Flynn.

“I might be, depends,” said Kenny, a smooth-faced Kashmiri pundit, for indeed it was he. “I smell tabouli salad. You have brought the curse.”

“La-la-la-la-la-la-la,” vocalized the hidden man.

“Rudy, put a sock in it,” shouted Kenny over his shoulder. “The curse has come home. We got a big snake, a babe, a middle-eastern type in red pajamas and some old trout with a ton of pearls.”

“Ahh, company,” said Valentino. The beaded curtain parted and he strode into the room. “Welcome to our little soirée, Gloria. You brought friends, then?”

“They brought the curse, Rudy,” said Kenny. “Smell it? They have a cab waiting.”

“So, they hope to return. Ha-ha-ha.” Valentino’s superbly sculpted nostrils flared. “Tabouli salad!” He slapped at his gaiters with a riding crop. “It’s off. Not from the commissary?”

“Rudy...” Gloria Swanson wrung her great ropes of pearls in supplication. “I love you.” She threw herself at his neck, then slid to the floor where she lay clutching at her former lover’s gleaming gaiters.

“Oh, Gloria, Gloria. Unattractive,” said Valentino as he smoothed his jodhpurs. “Besides, the python may mistake you for a goat.” He bent to lift her and, as they embraced, their eyes met and held for one electric moment. Valentino stroked her hair as he gently kissed her eyelids. “Sorry about the Amy thing, Gloria. But she was so much younger.”

“You wouldn’t rather have experience?”

Valentino’s almond eyes misted over. “Well, now that you mention it...”

Gloria Swanson threw herself into Valentino’s arms, “Rudy...”

“Gloria...”

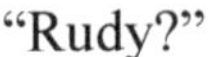

"Rudy?"

"Gloria?"

"That dildo? It was the horse's...?"

"I have a spare."

❑

As Sadiki bin Amin's taxi rattled away toward the Queens Midtown Tunnel, Mahbub Ali and Marcia leaned back into the forgiving upholstery. "Alas, we are now both addicted to the cursed compote," said Mahbub Ali. "If we stay in New York it will be the coal fields for us. This is Kismet, my petunia." The Afghan horse trader groomed his beard and, as he reached for Marcia Harding, made a quick appraisal of his career options. Valentino did have one hell of a voice.

"So you're really Errol Flynn? Really?" Marcia went walleyed with wonderment.

"In another life, perhaps. I am now Mahbub Ali the horse trader, and your humble slave. Come away with me, my sweet potato pie, and live on mutton and babaganouj. The liner Empress of Luxembourg steams to Afghanistan this very week. Screw Kim. We shall travel to where the mountains touch the sky and the tabouli salad is always fresh."

Behind them, inside the Kit-Kat Klub, Gloria Swanson and Rudolph Valentino took a respite from yet another torrid embrace.

"Sadly, there is no known antidote for tainted tabouli." Valentino gestured toward Harry Bartlemy the python who, become tabouli, had wrapped his scaly flesh around the Rock-O-La in a spiral of death. "Or its collateral damage. Sorry, buddy, you are cursed for all eternity."

There was a mighty crunch and the strains of *Venite inginocchiatevi* from The Marriage of Figaro came stuttering from the jukebox. "Tough darts, fella," said Valentino. "An encore is still gonna cost you two bits." Uncoiling his gaucho's black oxhide whip, Valentino drove the serpent from the Kit-Kat Klub and into the drizzling Manhattan April.

A Pass on the Tabouli was first published in the *Hiss Quarterly*, Spring 2006: the "Future Imperfect" issue. [www.hissquarterly.com]

Boys' Night Out

Sally Schofield was new to Sur la Mer and with the soccer mom's requisite formula family: minivan, flaxen-haired children only moderately overweight, large hairy dog, large hairy husband with pattern baldness. The invitation was for cookies and conversation. It had been Hillary Braunstein's turn to break the news.

"Did I ever tell you about David, my first husband?" The two women were seated in a suburban kitchen, an American icon: coffee and cookies and a carafe of freshly cut daisies formed a barricade across the center of a polished granite countertop, defining their spheres. The newcomer was seated near the door—an easy exit.

"Sorry? I didn't realize you had been married before." Sally's cookie was dipped, tentatively, held under the steaming surface, then removed. Well, we're cutting right to the chase, aren't we? Thought Sally. The cookie was not eaten, but studied.

No collagen here, thought Hillary Braunstein. Sally's cookie was held poised at lips too full, too young, too moist and sensuous to be anything but the genuine article.

"He wasn't..." began Sally. Had David died in the war? Unlikely. The cookie's fate hinged on Hillary's answer. The question and the cookie hung between them.

"A gated community like Sur la Mer should be the ideal place to raise a family," said Hillary.

Evidently whatever had or had not happened to David was on hold for the time being. Hillary's veering off topic was considered endearing by her friends. "You never know where Hillary is headed next," they said. Sally found it irritating.

"You know—as far from New York as you can get and still be in it," said Hillary. "Ocean bathing, surrounded by water on three sides..." She made a needless adjustment to the perfectly arranged daisies. "...and that nonpareil view of the lights on the Verrazano Bridge. At night, of course."

❑

Five blocks. The year before their move to Sur la Mer Jim Schofield had leaned into the wind and pulled his chin lower into his coat collar, shoulders hunkered up against a March wind scuddering in from the Jersey piers.

He should have stayed in Wisconsin. It was five cross-town blocks to where he parked his car—five Manhattan cross-town blocks, the better part of a mile—in the rain, sleet, snow and the pounding heat of high August.

An exquisite pain took that moment to drive a rusty cavalry saber into the pit of his stomach. That second martini at Lloyd's Bar. Or was it the third? He'd have to cut back. Jim gagged at the curb. He bent over with his head between his knees and vomited in cascading waves. He felt immediately better but his eyes were now blinded by tears. He felt for the curbing with his heel but it wasn't there; he tripped and stumbled. In a yellow arc, a medallioned taxi swerved past in a tight uptown turn, its driver leaning on the horn and screaming curses in a foreign language.

Yeah—from here on out, one drink then home. He should have stayed on the farm in Wisconsin.

❑

Sally Schofield was a pretty blond woman who still looked good in a flowered spring frock. The luxury of bare arms, not a wattle or a saddlebag on her, thought Hillary. Sturdy legs—well shaped, tanned, shaved and moisturized.

"You shave your legs." It was a statement.

Sally looked surprised and re-crossed her legs, a defensive posture. "You'll have to forgive me if I'm a little antsy. I don't do interviews well. That's what this is, isn't it? An interview, the ice-breaker, the Welcome Wagon?" This was all so very TV-Land— The Andy Griffith Show, Leave It to Beaver. Just like on cable.

"Of course, you are in denial."

"What?"

Hillary hummed a slight tune as she dithered with the daisy-painted saucers, sugar bowl and creamer that formed the cordon sanitaire between them. She reordered a stack of paper napkins. "We try to keep all this entrenous, strictly between us girls. Lycanthropism has enjoyed a, an, uh... unfavorable public image. Too much goddamned TV. That is why newcomers get the tour and the lecture. You know the drill: peasant cunning on the rampage, ozone filled air from Tesla coils and Van deGraaff generators. Great lolloping hordes of shopkeepers and railway clerks come panting up rocky switchbacks to Doctor Frankenstein's castle with their pine pitch torches—burn and destroy, kill, ravage, extirpate, their answer to the outré—quivering with dread at anything outside their daily grind."

❑

Five blocks.

The walk should have helped with the spare tire hung carelessly at his midriff, but the day's-end Martinis Jim Schofield allowed himself at Lloyd's negated all the walk's good work. The homicidal taxi had by now disappeared into the traffic at 42nd Street, its horn a descending Doppler ringing between the walls of buildings. He shuddered as he crossed an empty 39th Street against the light. Behind him the light turned to WALK and the smell of freshly savaged flesh, steaming and bloody, filled his nostrils. A red haze splattered across the insides of his eyes.

Cow slaughtering. Eight-year-old Jim Schofield rolled on the blood-wet ground with the yard dog: any other day a Wisconsin farm boy playing with Ol' Shep. At one particularly tempting chunk of offal, the yard dog snapped at him. Jim bit the dog's ear off. Jim spat—dog blood was different, somehow forbidden. He stood to throw up, then scrambled into an empty silo with his trophy as the yard dog whimpered under the swaying corpse of Barbie AB619.

His aunt Irene had stood saucer-eyed, in shock. "Jim... no." Deep in the hollow, ringing silo they pulled him clawing and howling off the cow's entrails. After that Jim was watched. The family did not speak of the business of the cow killing ever again.

From an alley stuffed with trash one of the city's derelicts beckoned to him. This was one of those alleyways of permanent twilight prowled by drunks, junkies, building supers and the homeless. The man was curled up on a ventilation grate, knees under his chin. He looked pretty well beat-up, but then they all did.

Home, he had to get home.

Jim turned to go. Another moan, weaker, brought him back. The guy was hurt, maybe by those gangs of wilding teenagers he had read about. He had to help. He steeled himself to the likelihood of mouth-to-mouth resuscitation as he crouched over the man.

The man was having trouble breathing. Jim tore at the man's clothing, exposing his chest. The man's throat was russet-ripe, a sun-swollen fruit full to bursting. As the taut skin popped, hot blood burst into Jim's mouth and dribbled past his lips to cover his face. Where it clotted and dried.

❑

"Penises," said Hillary Braunstein. "Seal penis bones. David, my first husband, cut and polished them for amulets. In Alaska. The sexually challenged wear them; Sid wears one. He rode away on his motorcycle to homestead in

Alaska—David, that is. He left me for subsistence farming and penis polishing. That was 1988. He said he was going for cigarettes."

"Oh." Sally's cookie hovered, unmoving. Sally was silent. The ball was still in Hillary's court.

"How did you two decide on Sur la Mer?" Hillary asked.

"Oh, I thought you knew. It was your husband, after all." Sally entered her comfort zone; the cookie was eaten. "Jim met Sid at one of those boys' sports nights they have after work. It was in a bar... In the city? Sid didn't tell you? After that it was every month like clockwork for about a year. All Jim could talk about was moving out here."

"Ah... yes."

❑

Sid Braunstein aimed his remote at a wide screen plasma TV. "You into baseball? I'm a Red Sox nut. Had to sign up for satellite service to get the games."

The two husbands sat out on the deck in white painted wicker chairs with cushions whose bright oversized daisies echoed the motifs of Hillary's kitchen. Sid Braunstein was a jovial, hairy man with a tightly packed body, a college jock who hadn't let himself go in middle age. His paunch looked solid enough to have genuine muscle behind it. Sid worked out. Jim surreptitiously touched the bulge at his own mid-section. Sid noticed.

"Don't let it get you down. Free weights."

"Huh?"

"Free weights. I have a mini gym in the garage. And the girls watch our diets. This," Sid held the bowl of clam dip aloft like a druid holding a chalice high to catch the first rays of a dawning solstice, "is a plenary indulgence. In durance vile here must I wake and weep and all my frowsy couch in sorrow steep, Robert Burns. It's about getting banished to the outer darkness, as it were... while the girls chat up the neighborhood amenities."

"Yeah, Burns." Jim had read Robert Burns in high school.

"Mmmm... don't know how she does it, Hillary," said Sid Braunstein. "Armed with but a simple blender and a whack of cream cheese, spices and clams, she can create ambrosia. Help yourself to another beer. We're not shy here."

"Uh, yeah..." Jim scoured his memory for Red Sox statistics.

❑

"Jim met your Sid in Manhattan," said Sally Schofield.

"A sports bar, Lloyd's on Madison Avenue," said Hillary. "Sid's baseball hangout. I know. He was on the way to the train and caught your Jim in an alleyway off 39th Street making a shambles of a homeless man. It was too late for the derelict but Sid got your husband sedated and back to the clinic." The older woman crossed and then uncrossed her legs. The legs were marvelously long, tanned and slender. "Your Jim wouldn't remember. None of them do; that's why the wives have to be in charge."

Limousine legs, thought Sally, And doesn't she love to show them off. She blushed at getting caught staring at her hostess' marvelous legs.

Too young, too pretty, thought Hillary. And dumb as a post. Let's toss her a bone. "David did come back, eventually, but by then it was too late." Hillary waited while Sally reflected on this last tidbit.

"Oh..." A neat change of subject. But she was the one who brought it up, the missing first husband, thought Sally.

"I know this because he sent a postcard once. One postcard: "Dogs run free, why not we?"

"There are huge national parks in Alaska," said Sally.

Maybe not so dumb. "He was tired of feeling confined? He needed room to roam. All this was before Sur la Mer, of course. The mere suggestion of a gated community would have driven him right up the wall."

She's doing the legs thing again, thought Sally. She couldn't pull her eyes away fast enough.

Gotcha, thought Hillary.

❑

"There is a forgetfulness—a mild aphasia, you might call it. The lacunae are sometimes... ahh, embarrassing. Like this?" Sid pulled what might have been a medallion from inside his aloha shirt. A polished disc reflected opalescent gemstone hues. It was fastened around his neck by a leather thong.

"Hmm... nice? What is a lacunae?"

"Sort of like an alcoholic blackout. Not the blackout itself, but the hole where your missing time went. A lacuna, singular—Latin, first declension, assigned gender feminine—appropriate as the girls cover up for us."

Sid held the dangle in front of Jim's nose. He gave it a gentle tap so it swung like a pendulum. He's trying to hypnotize me, thought Jim.

“From the penis bone of a seal.” Sid dropped the amulet back inside his shirt. “David, Hillary’s first husband, made it in Alaska. David made a run for it but he came back. Before he left he bit me. But like I said, he came back. Overland. He must have followed the railroad tracks. There were news reports. His trail pointed right here. Anyone with the brains God gave a tree could have figured things out.” Sid upended his can of beer and reached for a replacement. “Thank God for narrow-minded chauvinism. Nobody would have believed it even if they had caught on. Which they didn’t. Derek Lowe and Pedro Martinez. The Sox have a decent bullpen at last.”

❑

“David left on a motorcycle; we don’t allow motorcycles here in Sur la Mer. One of the rules. Here, have another.” Hillary pushed the platter of cookies across the center line back to Sally’s side. “We went the Lysistrata route—Aristophanes? Withholding sex, that got their attention. First we tried threats and confrontations about those things they will keep on dragging home to bury in the yard—the boys can’t recall anything of their midnight rambles or so they say. Dear, please don’t let your mouth hang open like that.”

“But... Jim?”

The woman is a born ingénue, thought Hillary. “And the answer was right there all the time. We simply had to get some protection.”

Sally thought of condoms and Allstate, the good hands people. “You already have the gates. What’s left, guard dogs and sentries?”

“From the government. Our husbands were threatened, therefore Section 4—CFR 17.11 could be brought into play.”

“Seventeen-eleven. That’s not the convenience store...”

“No, that’s the U.S. Fish and Wildlife Service. The Endangered Species Act of 1973.”

“Oh. Yes...?”

“We are an aging population here in Sur la Mer. You have children,” said Hillary. It was a statement, not a question.

“Yes.”

“In the play, Lysistrata, and it’s a comedy, the women go on a sex strike. They got fed up with their husbands always charging off to war. We supplement the husbands’ treatments with herbs.”

“Isn’t that dangerous?” Sally had seen a TV report on the perils of self-diagnosis. “There was that diet drug—ephedrine...?”

There was a squeak from the legs of a high-backed colonial reproduction chair as Hillary stood and collected the cookies and the cups. "For thirty years the doctors slapped hormone treatments to women and called it 'enhancement.' We pointed this out—their maleness would be 'enhanced.' It's only fair," said Hillary Braunstein. "And we got the cancer and the strokes. I figure if a woman loves her husband..." She absently dumped the plate of cookies into the garbage disposal. "We don't compost," she offered by way of an explanation. "Makes the ground too easy to dig in. I have an herb garden."

Hillary walked out of the room. They would view the garden.

"Yes, I'd love to," said Sally.

❑

"Here, help yourself..." Sid Braunstein passed the bowl of clam dip. "Ambrosial. The girls, God bless 'em," said Sid. "They have the top hand and they appreciate that. We acquiesce. Since the Lysistrata thing."

"Lysistrata," said Jim Schofield.

"Lysistrata. Don't ask; Hillary will tell Sally and Sally will tell you—that's how it works. Durance vile on the patio. Heh heh. Beer and chips beats bread and water."

"Lysistrata. Isn't that a play by Aristo..."

"Yep. The girls needed a rest. And the hormone treatments did it. No more unchaperoned midnight impromptus; we all get hairy and horny at the same time. Impotence puts a strain on the best of marriages." Sid gave Jim a nudge with his elbow. "Come home with a wet willie and the girls like to know where it's been... Heh heh."

❑

At the back door Hillary slipped into a pair of garden clogs. "Since you are the new girl you get to patrol the wire. Fence maintenance. It's only three nights a month and not too demanding. Here's a set of rubber Wellies. I think they'll fit you, Sally. They were David's; he had small feet."

"How did you meet your second husband?"

"We even had a skateboard park built. For the kids?" Hillary had changed the subject. Again. "Turns out we can't have kids. None of us. Something about the treatments. Oh, you mean Sid. Well, David and I were living in Jersey at the time; Sid was a veterinarian with a midtown clinic. On Madison Avenue. All very upscale and glitzy. The doctors couldn't find anything wrong with David. One of them made a chance remark..."

"Is this what all the secrecy is about?"

"My, Sally, but you are fast on you feet. Excellent. See, David was a werewolf. We have made some, ahh, understandably tentative, feelers to the government as to endangered species status for the husbands. But so far..."

"Then Sid is...?"

"And so is Jim. And that is why you and I are here today going on a tour of my dumb, totally useless herb garden while our husbands swill beer and natter man-talk on the deck. Ow!" A blue spark arced from a wire fence to Hillary Braunstein's finger. "It's only 24 volts but still packs a wallop if you forget your rubber Wellies."

"You have an electrified fence!" Sally was aghast.

"The picket wire. That's what we call it, from the days when Marshall Dillon gave the trailbosses til sundown to get their unruly cowhands out of Dodge. We do the same only in reverse. The husbands tend to roam."

"Dodge?"

"Ah, the generational difference. Gunsmoke—an old TV show. Marshall Dillon strung barbed wire around the perimeter of the town. To keep the cows off the streets?" Hillary held a finger poised near the wire. It was strung tight between self-anchoring metal posts and twisted onto yellow plastic insulators. "It shouldn't be much longer and we can turn the damned thing off."

"Was. You said David was. And Jim..."

"No, dear, there's no cure; don't get your hopes up. Sid put him down. An overdose of morphine, quite painless. David couldn't change back but David was a rare case. Sid and I had discovered feelings for one another. And David bit him before running away to Alaska, so Sid was a goner. Even with belladonna poultices."

"Hence the herb garden?"

"Sharp girl. Even with his medical knowledge, Sid was caught short. Belladonna is a specific for werewolf bite. Lacking belladonna, Sid improvised with the available members of the family Deadly Nightshade: potatoes and tomatoes. French fries and ketchup. We were the talk of the Madison Avenue Burger King that night."

❑

"So just how did you come to Sur la Mer," asked Jim Schofield.

"Well, as it happens I'm a veterinarian and Hillary came to see me about David. See, he killed the newspaper delivery boy."

Jim froze on the edge his chair. The blue corn taco chip in his hand dripped clam and sour cream dip onto his slacks.

"Strike a nerve, did I? Hey... get a handle on that. Ruin your crease." Sid pulled a paper serviette from a stack folded into a decorative wire holder. "Any trouble back in Manhattan? Beyond chasing cars and peeing on policemen's legs?"

As Sid leaned to wipe the fallen splotch of dip from Jim's pants he spoke urgently as if they might be overheard. "You know the kind; folks usually end up here on the run from some mess they have to get away from. Not the full of the moon, that's all bullshit. Hundreds of thousands of years ago, the moon was closer, much closer to the Earth. And the months were shorter. There is a hormonal rhythm. Antibodies in the blood release a timed catalyst that triggers a hormonal shift. Really fast and nasty. But you would know all about that. That derelict I caught you with in the alley? There, that should do it." Sid wadded up the napkin and dropped it on the floor. He leaned back and fondled his remote. "Once a month the girls fire up the electric fence and lock the gates."

❑

A weak arc of crackling blue curved from the fence wire to Hillary's outstretched finger. "It all depends on where you stand." She played the spark like a yo-yo, pulling her finger in and out. "There's a formula—inductive capacitance, something like that. See, no shock."

"You like touching the fence, don't you?" said Sally. The electric blue followed Hillary's finger but never seemed to make contact.

"Like I said, I just moved a little. It's all in where you put your feet. And the rubber Wellies, too. Give it a try.

"No thanks."

"Whatever. Being a soccer mom... I almost envy you, Sally: the ballet lessons, soccer practice, fencing, Boy Scouts. When the men developed their—ahh, problem—and we applied hormone treatments, they became sterile and lost all interest in sex, and I mean totally. No more Mom's Taxi; our kids aged and went off to school. You will have the only children in Sur la Mer. Of course if you get caught outside the wire after curfew, you'll have to fend for yourself. But it's only two days each month. And they're horny as hell." Hillary smiled a wide, suggestive smile.

❑

Sid reached to scoop up a mighty dollop of clam dip with a taco chip. "Like I might have said, lycanthropism is, or has been for most of us here, transmitted through the bite of an affected individual. I'd say you are a natural." Sid gave Jim a meaningful look.

"Meaning...?" Jim remembered his aunt's eyes when they caught up with him in the silo.

"Meaning some folks are born with the talent. We call it a talent. It is, you know, a talent. But there's nobody to show off for. Neat party trick except you don't get invited back." He stuffed the dip-freighted chip into his mouth. A blob clung to his nose. "Yep, you're a natural."

Jim uncomfortably shifted his weight on the patio cushion.

"Childhood memories? Got the fidgets?"

"Yes." Sid appeared happy with that and Jim decided not to belabor the point.

"I envy you. Hormonal," said Sid Braunstein as he reached for another Coors. "You gotta hand it to them, the girls, they got it all doped out..." Sid was enjoying a mild beer buzz. "...Vatican II, the rhythm system as applied to lycanthropy. Really cool stuff and Hillary figured it all out for herself. Got the idea from the hormone replacement therapies—you know, after the birth control pills scare? I just did the grunt work, contracted with the manufacturing laboratories and all."

❑

Hillary led Sally down a manicured path of white polished pebbles. "It's not easy being different. Ever try to slip a werewolf past a condo board? They even hire private eyes; would you believe it? OK, so the men are normal most of the time. And no amount of electrolysis would explain away the—ahh... artifacts. Things they bring home to bury. They're just like big kids, really. But who knew when they would get all hairy and feral?"

Sally slipped in the oversized rubber boots. "Oops. Sorry." A wounded mandragora officinarum hung dejectedly where it had been snapped off. White milky sap oozed.

"Careful. This little patch represents two years of work. The occasional organ—a little something for later—that we could have put up with. But the yards were a mess. Who's to know how a man's mind works? Oh, yes—the condo boards. After the twelfth try I was ready to chuck it all and buy outright. Always some old bat in a bouffant wig and her pet poodle humping Sid's pants leg. We formed a non-profit corporation. Investment capital was lean after the dot-com bust and we picked the whole place up for chump change."

"It must have cost millions."

"A million-five, actually. Sid was a celebrity veterinarian. He performed surgery on Meg Ryan's pussy. Twice. That's one of Sid's jokes. We had references. There's nothing a condo board won't ask; they leave you stripped and drained. One time I said I wanted to grow patio tomatoes on the roof, for emergencies but I didn't tell them that. Remember the French fries and ketchup? Well, it was like I peed in the communion chalice."

"Oh, are you Catholics? With a name like Braunstein, I just naturally assumed..." Sally fell silent. The insides of the borrowed boots were sweaty and her face felt flushed.

"Tomato red."

"Huh?"

"Tomato red is the color I would have turned if I had made a gaffe like that one. You are forgiven; it is really quite attractive on you, Sally. Tomato red, I mean. Tomatoes are called the 'wolf apple,' by the way. At least that's their name in Latin: lycopersicon esculentum—the 'wolf peach,' rightly."

Sally looked at the herb garden. "I don't see any tomatoes."

"No, no tomatoes. Ketchup is more concentrated. We buy it by the case at the Pick 'N' Pay."

❑

"Clap for the Wolfman; he's goin' rate your record high..." The TV was off and an Oldies' CD now blared from Sid Braunstein's patio boom box.

"The Guess Who. A favorite," said Sid. "Clap—clap for the Wolf-man..." Sid laughed heartily; he did not look like a man who laughed a lot. His eyes bulged and his face turned beet red. "Sorry. Sorree. Woo, hee. Whoop-whoop, hack hack hack." Spit flew as Sid bent double over the bowl of clam dip. He recovered still choking from the unaccustomed laughing fit. "Snorted... beer... up my nose. Ahh... hmm. Actually, sexually transmitted diseases are not the problem here in Sur la Mer they are out in the normal world—the civilians, we call 'em. Leptospirosis, distemper and rabies, though..." He grew thoughtful, pulling on his beer. "Gotta lay off the rabbits and the squirrels. Cats, too. Stick to your own kind, that's my motto. Disease-wise, the baddest actors are always the species jumpers. Gotta keep it in your pants—if you're wearing any, that is. Pants cramp your style when you're chasing a cat up a tree."

Sid beamed. Jim beamed back, this was another laugh line—clap for the wolfman, yuck, yuck. Jim Schofield smiled and felt more at ease. He wondered how Sally's interview was going. Sid ignored Jim and fiddled with his TV remote. The game was back on again.

❑

Sally and Hillary had reached the garden's far perimeter where a large cement toad crouched under a spreading ornamental yew tree. The toad was the size of a Harley-Davidson motorcycle fallen on its side.

"Don't you just love him," said Hillary. "He has a very knowing look when the light is right."

"Very... large," said Sally.

"Big is good," said Hillary. "He came with the place. And he's sitting on some of the boys' more incriminating, ahh... trophies."

Sally had lagged behind. She was scraping at a suspicious clump adhered to her foot.

"Step in something? Let's have a look-see."

Sally held up the afflicted rubber Wellie.

"Nope. Just dog poop," said Hillary. "Wipe it on the grass. It's easy to tell the difference when you've raked up enough of the stuff—the boys get a high fiber diet. They tend to fat so we watch what we feed them."

Sally sat on the toad to clean her boots.

"I called up the agricultural extension service. Bet you didn't know New York City had county agents. Anyway, that is how I met Everett Castelnuovo. There's something about a man in uniform. He was very attentive. At first I thought he had the hots for me but he smelled a research paper. You know, publish-or-perish, something for a scientific journal. Sur la Mer was going to put him on the map, career-wise."

"He wore a uniform?"

"Well, a sleeve patch and a twill serge bomber jacket. He was quite handsome, a Mark Trail type filtered through Chiquita Banana what with the bolero and all."

"Was."

"He came in over the picket wire on a bad night, intruder-wise. The boys' night out."

"Oh."

"I'm expecting his replacement any day. From the Fish and Wildlife Service, an expert on 'chemical ecology,' whatever that is." Hillary toyed with a sprig of bittersweet nightshade that had been broken off by another misstep. She looked accusingly at Sally and held the wounded herb under her nose. "Solanum dulcamara the potato family, would you believe?"

"You mentioned Lysistrata?" said Sally, trying for a diversion.

"Going without was as hard for us as it was for them. But we were willing to sacrifice for the greater good. Now that we have them back, they are totally limp, but at least we have them home nights. Most nights..."

❑

"Ahh... YES!" A crowd roar issued from the TV's stereo speakers. Sid looked expectantly at his company.

Jim felt he should contribute something. "Hey... how's about that Manny Ramirez?"

"37 homers and 104 RBIs last season, but that's not why we're here. We are self-policing." Sid zapped the set with his remote and the screen went black. "This is important. I'm supposed to be vetting you on life in a gated community. You're here for a reason, you know. In Sur la Mer? Hey, that's good."

"Huh?"

"Vetting. I made a pun. I didn't mean to, veterinarian—my profession and all. Have to tell Hillary about it; she'll get a chuckle. Basically I'm not a humorous guy."

"Oh, I wouldn't..."

"Yes, you would. Baseball and animal autopsies are my areas of competence, period. No standup. Anyway, I thought Hillary was having an affair. Some guy from the government. Now Hillary, I just love her to bits. I was hurt, chagrined, humiliated, all of the above. And I lurked. I caught him coming over the picket wire one night. He was packing a sensitive microphone — you know, the kind with a tripod and a parabolic reflector—a laptop, night vision goggles, the works. I buried him in the mandragora patch. When I was back to normal, I confronted my wife. Boy, did I get an earful! The girls had to dig him up and plant him under the garden toad. Seems I had made a mistake."

❑

"But here we were talking about having the husbands declared a threatened species..." Hillary had been idly poking with her toe at a mounded planting of atropa belladonna. A human toe was exposed. "Oh, shit.Simply shit!" She knelt and brushed away shredded cedar bark. A severed foot protruded from the mulch. It had been gnawed. Hillary poked the toe and its foot back under cover and patted the shredded bark flat. "Well! I thought he was late returning my call. A steep curve in their learning processes, these government men. Your tax dollars at work. Everett's replacement, the man from the Fish and Wildlife Service. He brought it on himself—I told him to call first. He should have checked his voice mail."

Hillary directed Sally's attention to a particularly attractive grouping of daisy-like flowers. "*Arnica montana*, of the aster family, actually. The popular name is 'wolfsbane,' good for headaches. I think I feel one coming on."

Boys' Night Out was first published in the Summer 2005 issue of *OnSpec—The Canadian Magazine of the Fantastic*

I Want to Share Your Wheat

"I want to share your wheat."

The creature on the desktop looked like a drunk gray mouse who had taken a wrong turn headed home from a party. He had pointy gray ears topped off with some kind of headgear that looked like an upside-down colander wrapped up with strings of those triangular flags that festoon the lots of used car dealerships. He was wearing green tights. "I *said* I want to share your wheat," said the visitor.

It was a sunny January morning at our coastal Maine cottage, and I had just settled down at the keyboard. Over the last three months I'd cranked out kilobytes of turgid, wordy prose decorated by two-dimensional characters that not even I cared about.

Then the visitation. "My *wheat*. You want to share *my* wheat. Right. You are a manifestation of mental collapse brought on by the frustration and despair I am currently enjoying. Get lost."

When I'd quit my job in October and settled in to write my novel, it had been all green lights and blue skies, lollipops and rainbows. Bonnie, my wife, had her job—and Blue Cross for us both—at the nearby rural elementary school. We had five cords of wood in the shed, and had been up to date on the credit cards. No longer—the bills were piling up.

"I want to share your wheat," repeated the visitor, dipping its head in my direction. The colander bobbed, the flags flapped. Its voice was that of a whiny know-it-all, straight out of Bart Simpson, Dr. Phil, or the endless threnody of soap operas and game shows on the cable channels. I watch a lot of TV, so sue me. One morning as we shoveled her car out from under a waist-deep drift of snow Bonnie had said, "If you'd spend more time writing and less time with reruns of Hollywood Squares, you'd have a Pulitzer by now." A word to the wise, etc.: Bonnie was our sole source of income. And she was right on the mark if overly optimistic on my creative abilities. I chucked the remote and unplugged the TV. No soap—opera or otherwise. And no Great American Novel. Nevertheless, thanks to my shoveling abilities, my wife was never late for work. I spent my days alone, staring at an empty computer screen.

"Ahem." The mouse was waiting for a reply. He put a foot on the M key and held it down. The screen filled up with endlessly scrolling lines of Ms. "*You* written much lately?" he asked.

"You are a psychosis; go away. *You* are an interruption I don't need about now."

"They told me you might be difficult. I am a mouse demon, your regional representative from Sminthian Apollo. *Please* may I share your wheat?" Leaving me to figure things out, the mouse became engrossed with a pad of Post-Its and ambled back and forth across my desktop, idly tacking them up in no obvious pattern. Demon or not, it was nice to have a break in my daily exercise in futility. And he *had* said 'Please.'"

While the mouse was strolling and sticking, I called up an Internet search engine and typed in "Sminthian." An article on Homer's Iliad and a reference to Apollo the Mouse-god popped on the screen.

"You people have quite a history. Can you speak Greek?"

"I speak what I speak. At the moment, I am fluent in your local patois."

"I'm so very happy for you," I said. "I keep my wheat out back with the swords and the spare plowshares." He didn't get it.

"Thank you very much." And he disappeared. No sulphur, no brimstone, just went. The Post-Its reassembled themselves into a pad. I cleared the Ms and continued with my writing. The screen filled with ampersands.

❑

"Uh, we have a problem." He was back.

"*We*? We 'have a problem'? So glad you've included yourself in my delusion."

"Alas, someone has made off with your wheat. All you have in your back room is a washer-dryer combo and a sack of rock salt. I don't share salt; I share wheat. You lied to me." The demon sat down next to my cup of pencils and drew a paisley handkerchief from his green tights. His shoulders heaved with overdone sobs as he slid into a method actor slump and tried to look dejected. "You never did have the swords and the plowshares, did you? All the time it was just the washer-dryer combo and the rock salt. Is this one of your 'jokes?' We do not make jokes where I come from."

He put kerchief to nose and, for an eight-inch figment, executed a mighty honk. "If you will simply tell me where you keep your wheat, so that I may share it, we may get on with things."

"Things? You mean if I give you my wheat, you'll barter me a Pulitzer Prize for my soul?"

"A Pulitzer falls in the category of three wishes and frog kissing—kinky stuff like that. I'm about sharing wheat. You know, ritual hospitality and all that.

When I grant a boon to such as you, it's usually for a Volvo station wagon. Volvo wagons are my specialty. After wheat." He honked again, refolded the handkerchief, and stuffed it back in his tights. "And I am not a delusion. I am a mouse demon. We bring plague or healing; your choice." He held his hands behind his back. "Left or right? Choose please. I have other calls to make."

"I am going certifiable or you are an early sign of senile dementia. Am I correct in this?"

"Come on, pick a hand."

I eyed him warily and the demon delivered an edgy, well, demonic, laugh. Bart Simpson, kid from hell, had just stuffed a load of toads down his sister Lisa's back. He brought his hands forward; both were empty.

"The hands thing is my little joke. You don't get a choice."

Hmmm... Maybe I did get a choice. I became cagey, recalling Rumplestiltskin. "OK. No Pulitzer, no wheat—where does *that* fit in this agenda of yours: my extirpation final and messy, or something a tad more user-friendly? Hey, you could spin my book into gold and just disappear. Either choice suits me fine. How's about I guess your name and win a prize?"

"My name is Prosper," said the demon. "How's about I guess yours?"

"Sorry, no prize; I already know my name. See?" I typed my name. No matter which keys I hit, I only got ampersands. "So you're a demon—big deal. Listen, if you're peddling Volvos, I don't need a car. You're sure you don't buy souls where you're from?"

"Could be, but first, I must share wheat. But I can tell you where your cat went. The gray shorthair, half Burmese?"

My wife and I had searched for the cat for over a week, slowly driving around our little town, stopping, calling. We figured a coyote got him. He was a champion mouser; we mourned, and then made do with traps. The demon was leading me, so I went for it. "Okay. Where's the cat?"

"Consider this your freebie. After this we're really dealing. There is a dead cat under your house. Your cat. I evoked his spirit. He ate poison bait at the neighbor's last August."

"Clayton Dudman?"

"C. Enright Dudman the Third is correct. He was spiking coyotes and got your cat instead. The cat asks you to forgive him for not coming home. He was dead at the time, and couldn't make it. He now enjoys life on a happier plane."

"Where the deer and the antelope roam?"

"And seldom is heard a discouraging word, yes, *yes*. So pleased you still study the classics in your time. Yes, the cat is in Paradise. As are we mice," he added brushing a piece of invisible lint from his green union suit.

"Meaning Paradise is where you come from?" Prosper took a deep bow. "That colander you have on your head doesn't do much to inspire trust in a supranatural agency."

"The Helmet of Cleptath is mine by right of single combat, a mighty battle over the cheese of the gods. My opponent and I fought each other to exhaustion. Everybody was talking about it. With the Helmet I can compress time and distance; anywhere and anywhen are to me as a trip to the donut shop is to you."

"It's a colander."

"Yes, some might name it thus, in its former, humble existence."

"And the festoons of pennants?"

"Festoons? Oh, these cute little flags. Festive, aren't they? They're from a used car dealership, Eddie Bartleby's in Bangor, my last stop. They wouldn't share their wheat, either. Eddie Bartleby made a joke. I did not like that. Now, they are a crater surrounded by smoldering wreckage and yellow police tape. And the single combat, by the way, was with Artemis, Sister of Apollo. We were draining curds together."

"Look, Prosper," I said with an inspired piece of improvisation, "why don't you check in Clayton Dudman's barn? I'll bet he has a lot of wheat all bagged up. And yours for the asking." I recalled Clayton laced his storage grain with anticoagulants to knock off mice and rats. Clayton was big on poisons.

"That's right neighborly of you," said Prosper. And he disappeared again.

❏

The next morning when I went to boot up the computer, Prosper was there by the cup of pencils. "Thank you for sharing your wheat," he said, "but I have sad news. Clayton Dudman has died of a heart attack. Myocardial infarction, to be precise. Quite apoplectic, that fellow: he should really have had it seen to. I told him that you had said he would share his wheat, and he insisted all the wheat in his barn really belonged to you. Right up to the end. A sturdy fellow, that Clayton."

"Uh, just what have you done with the wheat?"

"I took it all home and shared the gift of wheat, as you shared with me. And for this, you shall be blessed with a boon."

"A boon. Huh. One wish, huh? Well, times are hard all over. And your folk—the wheat eaters?"

"Mouse demons all," said Prosper. "Anticoagulants are as ketchup to us. The other chaps loved the poisoned wheat, too. It was they voted you your boon. I, myself, am in the service of Apollo, god of poetry and envelope flap literature. Ketchup and the arts are antithetical. Gifted with the colander I wrestled from Artemis, I shall teach you the enchantments to put just under where it says, 'fold and moisten to seal,' and as Prosper, I shall name thee Caliban and teach you to sing. That's a Shakespearean reference. Surely one who knows 'Home on the Range' is conversant with the Bard."

"Sing? Oh, you mean write. Write like Shakespeare? Wow. Write what?"

"As a token of our esteem for all the poisoned wheat, we've secured for you a contract writing advertising blurbs for the inside envelope flaps of credit card bills. We are mouse demons, and our powers are limited."

"Uh, don't I sign something? A contract with Satan?"

"There are some names we don't utter, buddy. We're the good guys. The paperwork is complete, no signature necessary. The cat has given his soul for you. He is happy in Pussy Paradise. And C. Enright Dudman the Third has evened the score for poisoning the cat. Enjoy the writing job."

❑

Well, that was five years ago, and my writing career has blossomed. Under the doors and into the mailboxes of North America, not a month goes by without every over-spending, under-funded householder reading my work. Perhaps you've seen my latest—*Discount Cruises and Free CD player-radio combo offer with Platinum Card upgrade*?

I Want to Share Your Wheat
was first published in the September/October 2002 issue of
Demensions—Doorways to Science Fiction and Fantasy

The Perfect Homburg

Be careful what you wish for.

And when you make that wish, speak up and enunciate clearly. Want rapture? You could go home with a rupture. Think about it.

Anyway, I had sold my soul to the Devil for gainful employment, not an unusual kind of wish for a writer. Except it wasn't the Devil, it was Apollo, the god of poetry and envelope flap literature. Well, not really Apollo, but one of his representatives: Prosper Epilegomenes, a mouse demon. Whatever, I got the job.

An easterly ocean gale was cannonading the shores of Willipaq, Maine. It slammed down the chimney and blew my wood stove from bright coals to a full flame. *Woo-woo-woo*, the chimney whistled like a kid blowing a tune across the lip of a giant soda bottle. *Not to worry*, I reassured myself. There was a blacktopped town road between me and the fury of the North Atlantic.

Woo-woo-woo. "Mother Carey's chickens," said a familiar voice. "Watch the north wind rise." A diminutive green figure stood before my airtight, thrusting his rear end into the heat like a life-long Mainer.

I grumped, rolled over, and plomped another pillow over my head. "It's an east wind. Nor'easter—" I came up short. It was the demon. "Oh. Prosper." If he was here, he had a problem. And if the mouse had a problem, I had a problem.

"Oh, Prosper. That is shiningly unenthusiastic," said the demon. "Flat. A minimal infusion of joy would be nice: '*Oohhh...Pros*per!' Like that." The demon sniffled and wiggled his backside closer to the stove. "Jim, Jim, I am saddened. You greet me more with apprehension than with joy. Ahh, wood heat. Can't beat it." He wrung out a pair of tiny green mittens.

"What?" I said. After all these years it was unlikely my personal representative from Sminthian Apollo had dropped in out of the storm to blow his nose and keep me company.

"*What* what? Just servicing your account, my old and rare. It is truly a dark and stormy afternoon," said Prosper. "Do you bowl?"

"That's why I'm the writer," I said. "And, no, I don't bowl."

My name is Jim Everhardy, and the mouse demon had granted my wish: to be read by millions. I now write the advertising blurbs on the envelope flaps of credit card bills. Not the Great American Novel, but it beats writing inventory codes for Wal-Mart. I had done last night's supper dishes, done laundry and hung it out by the stove on our accordion-fold wood racks. I had run the dust mop over the floors and shook it out into the wind, then flopped for a nap on the window seat. I am a house husband—no shabby occupation here in Downeast Maine where opportunities for employment are few and far between. My wife has the real job.

Prosper opened the glass fire door and stuck his head inside.

Woo-woo-woo.

A shower of sparks smoldered on the braided rug, Bonnie's pride and joy.

"Oops. Sorry about that." He closed the door and ran around stamping out tiny fires. The smoldering continued. "Nice fire, but we have some escapers. Got water?" asked the demon.

"In the kitchen," I replied. "There's a bucket under the sink."

Prosper hustled off.

The mouse demon returned with a bucket of water and doused the rug. I had not moved.

I had learned to keep my expectations under control when dealing with the lesser deities. Minor deities reward at minor levels: cheap T-shirts, herds of cattle, the usual stuff. But when they punish, it's major. Believe me, I know. From Prosper's last visit I had gotten the literary equivalent of cheap T-shirts, but the money was good. We thus far had the driveway paved plus a brand new washing machine. I liked things the way they were.

"Ah, but I'm here to change all that," said the demon. "You're too good a man to fritter away on envelopes. I've got something really big lined up. You are going to be a *contender*."

Prosper was taller than a mouse, but not by much. Five years back, during the first visitation, he had strutted on my desktop, pointy gray ears topped off with an upside-down colander which he called the Helmet of Cleptath, a magic hat. According to the mouse, he had wrestled the colander away from Apollo's sister in a fight over cheese, the cheese of the gods. From the helmet dangled strings of those triangular flags you see at gas station giveaways and pizza joints. Then as now, Prosper wore green tights. Flags fluttered as he spoke.

"And here we are, you and I, nattering away like old school chums at a class reunion."

I didn't recall nattering. Typically, he was doing all the talking. He had popped back into my life like those unwanted barrages of advertising that

regularly clogged my e-mail.

"Spam! Jim Everhardy, really! That makes me sound like one of those pesky spammers who plague your dinner hour."

Prosper was reading my mind. He was here to make me a proposition I couldn't refuse.

"Of course I am, Jim old turnip, reading your mind, that is. And to characterize me as junk mail cuts me to the quick. *Account Executive*. I like that much better. Consider me your account executive. 'A title on the door rates a carpet on the floor.' That's a gem of literature from one of your advertising greats." He did a quick two-step on a residual smoldering coal and ground his heel into my wife's prized rug. It was ruined.

"I only wanted to be an author," I whined.

"You wished for success in writing. That is different." He flicked lint from a lapel and studied his manicure.

"Consider the pickle," said Prosper, " in its progression from a humble garden vegetable to picklehood. Spiced, diced, plucked, peeled, steeped and cooked in a jar, yes? For now, you are a cucumber—not much going on, just waiting."

I considered the cucumber.

"Let's cut to the cheese," said Prosper. "I am decidedly subfusc and awash in a sea of despair. Clothes may make the man but hats make the demon. Artemis wants the hat back. The Helmet of Cleptath."

"Your funky colander?" I asked with sugary innocence.

The demon threw his arms into the air and then clutched at his heart. I had hit a nerve. Prosper's little shoulders heaved as he wept. He was overdoing it. *What the hell*, I figured. Mice emote.

"Pliny the Elder says I am a fool to seek mortal assistance. But I have faith in you, Jim. Are you acquainted with the exemplary acting skills of Walter Pidgeon?"

I recalled him as an old-time leading man, a movie star when I was a kid.

"It was classic movie night in the demons' pantry. Artemis slipped in to catch the second feature. And there he was, Walter Pidgeon, wearing a homburg. On the screen, I mean. Her Worshipfulness lost it, plop, right there on the linoleum. And Sean Connery—when he wears a homburg, it really twists her knickers. She became a regular at our movie nights. Having management hanging around puts a crimp in our otherwise freewheeling high spirits, if you get my drift."

"She was baiting you to get your colander, the Helmet of Cleptath, back?"

"Yes. She's got a new attitude and she's wearing a homburg hat. A sort of homage to Connery and Pidgeon."

"Well, good. Of all the Olympians I figured Artemis to be strong on sexual identity."

"You betcha, buddy. Struts buck naked through the firmament, with the Homburg on her head and her head in the clouds. You'd think a homburg hat would be sufficient for any goddess. But now she wants her old hat back, too. From me."

Prosper indicated the beribboned colander on his head. "The Helmet of Cleptath." The sobbing began anew. Prosper pulled a tiny kerchief out of his sleeve.

"We have been challenged," said the demon, getting his blubbering under control. "Now, a challenge in Paradise is, by definition, unusual, perfection and all. But, be that as it may, the Divine Artemis has got a feather up her royal ass over losing her hat to a mouse. She challenged me to miniature golf. In Paradise, personal differences have been traditionally settled by miniature golf. I hate golf of any size. My weapon of choice was duckpins. As the challenged, I got first call.

"Pliny the Elder is her second. I would you were mine. There's a Volvo wagon in it for you. The celestial playoffs will be at Dinwiddie's Chuck-A-Bowl Lanes in Taunton, Massachusetts. It has been bruited about that the Kennedy lads trooped their dates to Taunton for a rousing frame or two. Of course, this is hearsay. You will also show me how to wire the Helmet for two-way communication. Police and fire calls, you know, keeping in touch…"

"If we win."

"Of course we'll win. Trust me."

"And if we lose?"

"You die. I volunteered you. I have your signature on file. Remember?"

I remembered. Don't sign anything you haven't read. And if you do, keep all the copies. I was at the mercy of a mouse.

"Death is neutral," said Prosper reassuringly. "Either you are or you aren't. The means thereto are usually nasty and frequently spectacular. You should feel special. Most lives are lived like tire fires at the town dump. Years of smoldering, then a plume of gas ignites for a flashy finish when there is nobody around to notice."

I tried feeling special.

"The guys and I got our heads together and we thought we'd call on you. You owe us one," said the demon.

"Pliny wouldn't help? As your adversary's second, isn't he supposed to negotiate any difficulties, iron out the paperwork, so to speak?"

"Conflict of interests. Gaius Plinius Secundus, naturalist, bon vivant, general, senator, etc., etc., was pledged to Artemis. We needed a fallback strategy. That's you. If you should lose, and of course, you *won't...*" Prosper slipped in unconvincingly "...a hubcap from a '38 Dodge sedan should do the trick. We'll just negotiate a swap."

Over my dead body. *My body*, probably smoldering like the rug. Prosper babbled on as he expanded my vocabulary of affliction.

"Artemis is wild for chrome. See, Valentine, Feng Shui and I were watching Antiques Road Show and... "

"Hold on. A chrome hubcap? This is what my life, my hopes and aspirations, all I have worked and struggled for, are worth? You will trade her a hubcap for the hat after I am toast?"

"That's about right," said the demon cheerily. "Meet the gang."

Four new mouse demons popped up like unwanted advertising. "I am in uncertain waters, careerwise, so I got the fellows here together for some brainstorming. Jim Everhardy, meet Valentine, Tantrum, Elapse, Feng Shui."

"Hello, Flopsy. Hello, Mopsy. Cottontail, how do you do? And…Feng Shui?"

"The very same," said Prosper. A diffident demon in a red fez took a bow from the end of the line.

"You see, at my performance review, a Certain Personage was disappointed that you chose skills with ephemera over His Volvo wagon. Volvo wagons are a hot item, and I'm supposed to be pushing them. Gracewise for demons, a disappointed Personage is no fun to be around. We needed a human to take the heat. You. See, what I mean is Apollo's still fulminating over Feng Shui's realignment of the poles. Feng Shui's arrangements differ slightly in the Southern Hemisphere. All those koalas and kangaroos hopping out of a Certain Personage's jubilee cake… Apollo had hoped for a stripper. Well, you've got to run before you can strut. Trust me."

Trust the mouse demon, if I ever wanted to write the Great American Novel. And stay alive.

"I cased the location for you, Everhardy. I hung out at Dinwiddie's watching big, burly bowlers contend. They slammed the crap out of the place, splinters everywhere. The pinsetters were a-hopping, on the run and sweating buckets all night. Candlepin bowling runs very fast. You're going to have to hustle to keep up."

"Let's review just where we are up till now. You need me to bowl for the home team. And Artemis, Sister of Apollo, your patron, is more powerful than you, a mere mouse demon?"

"And sexier, pal." The demon blew his nose with a honk. "You mock me when I am down. Watch that mere stuff. *The Unknown Man*—that's the film where Walter Pidgeon wore a Homburg."

"It was."

"Indeed, it was. We have videos in Paradise, thanks to Pliny the Elder. Pliny begged an indulgence from the Higher Power. Ol' Pliny hovers at the mail-room for the latest Baywatch. For myself, I favor the classic films. And The Sopranos, of course."

"Oh, of course."

❑

Time passed.

I just love it when I read that. It usually means the author is running out of toner. Anyway, time didn't pass. Not for me. We were out of doors and the wind was whipping up the trapdoor of the comfy red flannel union suit I wear when I am at home and being creative. A neon sign flashed "Chuck-A-Bowl." We were at the far end of a strip mall somewhere in exurbia. Flopsy, Mopsy, Cottontail and Feng Shui were nowhere to be seen.

Prosper pulled at the cuff of my union suit. "Now, let's get our story straight. What we want from her is…"

"*We*? What's this 'we want'? Hey, *you* want."

"Don't get snippy with me. I want the homburg. Next to it the Helmet of Cleptath is old hat, no pun intended. Barring that, I have a fallback strategy. I have one for you, too. If you survive." His eyes got a dreamy, far away look that suggested trouble. "I have an opening writing inventory control codes for Wal-Mart…"

I shuddered. "No, the envelope flaps are fine."

Prosper studied cloud formations as a stratocumulus was ripped to shreds by the passage of a commercial jetliner. "A '38 Dodge."

"Huh?" I squinted up at the plane. No resemblance.

"A little faster on the uptake, Everhardy my doughty scrivener. Our fallback strategy, the chrome hubcap, remember? Dodge, nineteen-thirty-eight. An automobile. Prewar. On Antiques Road Show. They had the goddess kvelling for it. Honestly, Everhardy, do I have to draw you a map with every little utterance?"

There was the clearing of a heavenly throat. A radiant woman strode toward Dinwiddie's Chuck-A-Bowl. She was naked under an unfastened mink coat that flew open at each step.

"Shrewd, nude and lewd. Here comes the divine presence Herself, all greased and ready to kick some mortal ass," said Prosper.

Mortal ass. I noticed the demon's equation left Prosper, Flopsy, Mopsy, Cottontail and Feng Shui safe above the high water mark, *après nous le déluge*-wise.

"I am here."

Her eyes blazed up at us from the lowest point of a curtain call curtsey. Artemis eyed the guttering neon. "This is truly the Land of Milk and Caviar," she said of Taunton, Massachusetts, and blessed their efforts. Marring her beauty, Artemis' lip had a curl to it, a slight inflection that made her look haughty and supercilious, like a banker about to break wind. She narrowed her eyes and wrinkled her nose, making an arch of the freckles across its bridge.

"Mink becomes my legend most," said Herself.

The coat wriggled.

"Strikes and spares it is, then? Well, me boyos, bring on your balls. I'm fair itching to have a go," said the goddess.

If she had an itch it wasn't psoriasis. My eyes rolled over her body, memorizing. No rashes present. Her itchy balls analogy did chime a familiar chord, though. I reached to scratch.

Prosper waved me a caution sign—crotch scratching might be misinterpreted.

"She has that effect on most men. Jim Everhardy, meet the Divine Artemis, Sister of Apollo."

The goddess extended a perfectly formed arm to offer a handshake. "Divine Artemis, how do you do. Yes, I am beautiful, am I not?"

My hand was left hanging in mid air as hers was withdrawn to groom an eyebrow. "And you are rolling your eyes. Don't do that."

Artemis again held out her hand. "Artemis, candlepin ace of the Olympian pantheon, sister of Apollo. Likewise the Fata Morgana, Lady of the Wild Things, Diana of Ephesus, et cetera, et cetera."

"Jim Everhardy. How do you do?" was the best I could come up with. We shook hands.

"So much for bonding, let's bowl," said the Lady of the Wild Things. She spun on a heavenly heel and the coat swirled to cover her. "Shall we go indoors?"

An invitation from a goddess, who could refuse?

With all that mink blocking my view, I checked the coat. Thirty pairs of beady little eyes stared back. The pelts were alive. Tails twitched. Artemis' coat was giving me the once-over.

Artemis had noted my interest. "Ranch mink have little to look forward to but a lot of sex, hormone-laced burger meat and then coathood. These guys are wild. Even so, I like to see they get out every now and again."

Once we were inside, Artemis made a gesture, the effortless articulation of a perfectly proportioned wrist that indicated noblesse oblige, and we all were grateful. The minks jumped ship and headed for the crispy snacks spread out in the Chuck-A-Bowl's refreshments area. The Divine Personage's coat melted and flowed to the floor as the boys scrambled for the Cheetos and pickled eggs.

I felt thankful to be alive and in her presence. And appreciative for the peek. Now that the coat had bailed out, I stared.

"Yes, I do look splendid in a hat," the Lady observed.

I agreed wholeheartedly.

Artemis got right down to the business at hand. She seemed to have brought along a basket full of bowling gear.

Prosper whispered hoarsely up at me. "Jim, watch the minks. Make sure they don't get nasty. They are feral creatures. To them I may be just another mouse."

"I get it. The Helmet of Cleptath is turned off or whatever. You are powerless."

“Only for the duration of the tournament, Jim my old and rare. Hold down the fort. I’m off to get Her Wonderfulness pissed with me and hopefully off her game with rage.”

“Leaving me to win by brawn and native wit.”

“That’s why I chose you,” said Prosper, “muscle power.”

I was not cheered.

Putting on a greasy lounge lizard persona not at all becoming to a demon in the service of Sminthian Apollo, Prosper insinuated himself up to the goddess.

“Hey, Divine One, where are all your statues now?”

The Divine One was polishing a set of candlepins, popping them with her bowling towel. “My statues?”

The mouse demon struck a cocky pose atop a bowling ball.

“Ah, my statues.” The Lady of the Wild Things, Ephesian Diana, et cetera, et cetera, sniffled and held the Number Five candlepin high above her, studying its curves against the Chuck-A-Bowl’s fluorescent lighting.

“Where did I go wrong? To hide my tears I tell myself I yet smell the fumes of belladonna that once wafted forth on the polished cobbles of the night. Did you know I was once worshipped at Ephesus?” This was a rhetorical question. The goddess let fall a single, perfect tear.

Artemis patted at her eyes with the bowling towel. “From among the heart-wrenching utterances of rude devotion and abject submission I brought into my exile a favorite not so humble—a sixty-cubit image of ivory and hammered gold. I have always been fond of its fierce golden gaze and its boasted thousand breasts.” She turned coyly to give Prosper a poke with her middle finger. “It bankrupted a satrapy in Asia Minor.”

“All those tits,” said Prosper cozily. I waited for the thunderclap of divine justice.

“I understood them as an allegory of nurture,” said Artemis. Her hauteur was returning. “Besides, there were only five-hundred-fifty. Neat, but not gaudy.”

The goddess tilted the homburg back on her beehive hairdo. “And yet I am remembered, if only in the shape of a bowling pin.”

The Divine Artemis was, indeed, a whole lot of female.

“An invocation for our games,” said Artemis, “one of my favorites and I hope it’s yours, too.” She took a deep bow revealing not much more than we had already enjoyed. She was now a piano bar hostess working the house.

Her arms were extended and she held the pose. “You *will* join me, won’t you?”

Thirty sets of fierce mink eyes glared at us from the bar, waiting. Of course we would.

Artemis sang.

“There was a man, Joe Bangles, and he did a dance.
He changed his pants
Once a year.
Ooh, ooh, ooh...
Mister Joe Bangles, dance...

Kicked off his shoes, he couldn’t lose,
He had no clues.
Ooh, ooh, ooh.
The pants were new, the shirt was, too.
Your mind is weak, so shuck those sneaks.
I bless this alley, please don’t dally.”

Artemis sat splat down on the floor as Pliny the Elder passed her the rosin bag. This might be a part of the ceremony. I sat, too, and removed my shoes and socks. She dusted the soles of her feet. Prosper offered me a rosin bag and I waved him off. He gave me a wink that suggested this was the correct option.

“Mister Joe Bangles?” I had to ask. The goddess paused her lounge singer routine to explain.

“The original,” said the goddess. “Robert Graves—a poet, I believe, who wrote this little number just for me:

“I am the turning of the wheel.
I am a salmon in the pool.
A spotted snake from whom mice quake
And share Apollo’s belly-ache.
Ooh, ooh, ooh, dance, Joe Bangles...

“Okay, Pliny, let’s kick some mouse ass,” said Artemis as she closed out the prayer and bounced to her feet. “Let’s get those pin spotters hopping.”

She chucked a ball with an underhanded throw that would have done her proud in women’s international league softball. The ball flew through the air, hit the lane 40 feet down and smashed the pins flat, scattering them to the left and right.

"Well, that one cleared out the deadwood." She glanced meaningfully at Prosper and me. "Lucky for you guys we're just warming up."

"She's supposed to bowl the ball, not throw it," Prosper whispered. "But she makes the rules."

"Shouldn't you object?" I whispered back.

"*You* object."

I shut up. Subject closed. My turn, I guessed. I lost the ball in my backswing. It went flying behind us where the minks cleared the bar, diving for safety.

"Whoops," I said.

"Sweaty palms? Queried the goddess. "Here, use my towel." Pliny the Elder leaned close to Artemis. She nodded and spoke to me. "The worthy Pliny informs me you are inexperienced at candlepin bowling. Perhaps we should take a brew break. But first, let's get you a handicap."

I looked desperately to Prosper.

"She means she will give you a couple of pins advantage 'cause you're new at this."

Pliny again whispered to the goddess.

"I shall give you pins seven and ten," said Artemis. "Hit or miss, they won't count."

Sounded good to me, but Prosper was shaking his head. "Tell her you will go straight up. By the rules we need six strings to establish an average for a new bowler's handicap. She's parsing out a Las Vegas standoff. Pliny is trying to disqualify us."

After three frames the score stood at them 90, us zero. The goddess had been rolling consecutive strikes.

"Let's have that brewski break." Prosper beckoned me as he sauntered over to the refreshments area. "Hie thee here, tapster, some nut brown ale for me and my homunculus."

The tapster slid us a bowl of salted cashews. This was followed down the bar by two chilled, foaming mugs.

"Ahem." Prosper cleared his throat.

The bartender, who seemed not to notice that he was selling drinks to an eight-inch tall mouse in an Errol Flynn suit, looked mildly startled and vacant, like a senior citizen who had forgotten this was meatloaf day at Meals on Wheels.

“Sorry, sir.” He brought us two coasters and placed them under the mugs.

“No offence taken,” said Prosper. The bartender appeared relieved.

Minor Lovegrove and Lydia, his missus, were bowling in the next alley. They had joined us at the bar for some light refreshment. Their embroidered satin team shirts bore the family crest, a tree with a heart carved into the bark.

“How do?” said Prosper. The Lovegroves nodded and smiled with the same vacant, unconcerned look as the bartender. Nothing out of the ordinary here, just a mouse and a man wearing red flannel underwear bowling with a naked lady and an old coot wrapped in a bed sheet.

Prosper produced a small plastic squeeze bottle from beneath his cloak. He pressed it into my hand.

“Put some of this on your balls. You get three this frame.”

“I beg your pardon?”

“The bowling balls, you ninny. Grease the track. A fast alley will give you the edge we need.”

Unnoticed, Pliny the Elder had snuck up on us to eavesdrop. The bartender brought another mug of beer and a coaster.

“I know. You want to get back to Paradise and your soft porn,” said Prosper.

Pliny sighed.

“We’ll try to get you back as soon as possible.”

“Her Effulgence really, *really* wants to win this one,” said Pliny.

“When a building is about to fall down, all the mice desert it. Your own Natural History, Book VIII. Right, Pliny?”

Artemis’ second turned to Prosper with an appreciative bow. “*Ruinis inminentibus musculi praemigrant, aranei cum telis primi cadunt*, Prosper. May I assume you’re quoting my own work at me to signify you are in this fiasco to the bitter end?”

“*Oleo tranquillari*… You said that in Book II.”

“Ah, yes. Oil as a sovereign balsam in troubled situations. You, Sir Mouse, are slick as a greased hooker in the Forum Boarum. I catch your drift.” Pliny’s eyes brightened. He would soon be back in Paradise with his beloved Baywatch tapes.

I nudged Prosper. “What the hell is going on?”

"Shut up and bowl," replied the mouse demon.

I approached the line and scuffled my bare, un-rosined feet on the alley, testing the purchase. Nothing but purchase. I could not slide. Rosin residue from the goddess' pitches gripped me tight to the floor. With each step I had to peel the soles of my feet up like a deep sea diver walking through a kelp bed.

Prosper saw my problem. "Bring your ball and let's get back up to the bar. We'll get you cleaned off."

I picked a house ball from the return trough and sauntered to the bar where the minks had gotten into the pearl onions and maraschino cherries. With the smearing as they rolled about, spraying their musk, the scene looked like a slaughter of eyeballs painted by a crack addict. The bartender was oblivious, happily polishing Manhattan glasses with a bar towel.

"Wipe your feet, Everhardy. Then run like hell, stop and let go of the ball when I tell you. You might stop short and go buns over teakettle, so hold onto your nose. For luck," he added. Prosper gave his colander a quarter turn and focused his eyes on the acoustical tiling of the Chuck-A-Bowl's hung ceiling as he mumbled an exhortation in what sounded like an ancient language.

A mink bit me on the ass and I hurtled forward.

"Foul line! Stop!" shouted the mouse demon. I stopped and slid right up to the line, remembering to let go of the ball. Leftover rosin grabbed at my feet. I ground to a precipitous halt and clutched my nose as I careened head first onto the polished maple floor. The 2½ pound candlepin ball shot forward in a fireball curve. I noticed it pick up speed as I slid right up to, but not over, the foul line.

When the ball connected, the number seven and ten pins dodged while the others fell. The ball rebounded from the bumpers and returned to take them down, too.

We won.

And then we had to face the wrath of the goddess. And me with a bloody nose.

Artemis, the Lady of the Wild Things, Ephesian Diana, etc., etc., was whistling up her minks and packing to leave. She seemed in a good mood, for a disappointed Personage.

She handed me a large basket. "If you are here to cut a deal, you are too late. Here, hold my snakes and thrysis. Initiates may see my mysteries elsewhere. You really should get that nose looked after. Behold! Ecce Bocce: a bowling alley. What a shabby field of honor! The fields of my epistemology are awash with mice, beer and salted nuts."

She wriggled her shoulders. "I am a figure of religious fervor. Heat and reflection don't mix. You think you have a role to play in eternity. Well, you don't. As you go through life, Jim Everhardy, remember the parting words of the Lady of the Wild Things: Shut up and bowl. And be careful what you wish for."

I hadn't wished for anything. This time at least. I spoke up. "Uhn…"

"Speak up, you ninny," thundered Artemis. No more Ms. Nice Guy.

"I was just minding my own business... "

"No excuse. Not valid. Shut up. You were sucked into Prosper's machinations by a vortex of avarice."

"Yes, ma'am."

"I find you guilty of betting on a doctored sporting event. I told Pliny to tip you off about the greased ball stunt."

"Then you suckered us."

"You fell for it. You are therefore guilty as charged."

"But we won."

There was a smattering of applause from the Lovegroves in the neighboring alley. Artemis stared them to silence.

"Madam…" Pliny was edging in for a word. "If I might get a word in, edgewise as it were?"

"Not even sideways, you doddering old letch. Keep your noble Roman mouth zippered if you ever want to see another Baywatch."

Pliny persisted. "They did win. You cheated; they cheated. So it would appear you are even-up. And screw Baywatch. It's only silicone."

"You, Gaius Plinius Secundus, are sentenced to spend what remains of your eternity viewing Little House on the Prairie!"

At this, the senior statesman and preeminent natural scholar went ballistic. Screaming, "An indulgence, Madam!" Pliny reached beneath his purple-bordered toga and, in a fit of pique, drew forth a hubcap and skimmed it at Artemis' head.

Ahh, Prosper's fallback strategy. I closed my eyes and sent a silent prayer winging heavenward.

"The coveted '38 Dodge, chrome and all!" shouted Artemis. "And intact, too. Museum quality. The old hidden hubcap trick, not unheard of in dirty bowling. Leave it to a scientist. Ball greaser!"

One superbly formed arm shot forth and caught the hurtling hubcap in mid flight. "Aha! How's that for a Frisbee goal?" The other arm made a rather theatrical gesture of triumph.

"You don't get it, do you?" said the goddess. "It doesn't matter if you won or lost. I want all the hats. And whatever Lola wants…"

She snatched the beribboned colander off Prosper's head and tossed it aloft along with her homburg and the '38 Dodge hubcap. Dots of light reflected from polished chrome sparkled and bobbed on the ceiling.

"You can't knock perfection," said Artemis, sister of Apollo, as she juggled the three hats, "and the homburg is perfect."

As a finale, she took the hats gracefully out of aerobatic rotation, bouncing them one by one off the back of a heel.

"I shall keep the homburg." The supercilious curl returned to Artemis' celestial lip, this time with an evil tic she didn't even attempt to get under control. "But I am willing to share," said the goddess with a self-congratulatory chuckle.

"Prosper, here's your new hat." Artemis tossed the chrome hubcap at the mouse demon. "I'll be keeping my colander, too. Everhardy, begone, you belie your name. Pliny, get likewise lost. I banish you to the 21st Century. Prosper, I want words with you. Stay."

❑

Well, that's about the story. I sometimes wonder how Prosper fared at the hands of the Divine Artemis. I have adjusted to writing inventory control codes for Wal-Mart. Bonnie and I also have a semi-permanent houseguest.

Ask me about the shelf life of a live mink. Go ahead. Ask me how Pliny and I got home.

Thanks, we had to hoof it. We passed the hat and washed dishes to get up enough cash and made the last leg by bus. The minks tracked us, Pliny and me, all the way. I tried to visualize polecats, ferrets, weasels, the wild cousins of the goddess' coat, lining the road and cheering the lads on, north and eastward, up the New England coastline. The Divine Artemis' coat must have raided one hell of a lot of garbage cans on the road to Willipaq, Maine. On the bright side, they have since cleared our neighborhood of mice and rats. Like I might have said, negotiating with the gods is playing house rules against house odds.

Pliny, my wife and I make macaroni and cheese and watch Baywatch reruns nightly as our penance. Pliny *did* wangle us a plenary indulgence from Little House on the Prairie. Somewhere in this exchange, I ended up with the '38 Dodge chrome hubcap cum disco mirror ball. Don't ask. I have tried to get the hubcap off, but every time I try, the computer crashes.

And so it is I am writing again, in the time I free up by being good at writing inventory control codes. Be careful what you wish for, even if it's only for a better mousetrap. I love my wife, we put up with Pliny, and I wear my hub-cap all the time.

The Perfect Homburg was first published
in the March/April 2003 issue of *Demensions—Doorways to Science Fiction and Fantasy* and reprinted in *SpecFicWorld.com's* "Dark Tales" anthology
November, 2005

An Unwarmed Fish

"Hey, Kathleen! Make the mouse do his trick for Frankie!" That from Lee Frelinghuyser, irrepressible free spirit. It was eleven o'clock in the morning and, as it was Thursday, Lee was potzed. Lee Frelinghuyser was the casualty of a successful advertising career. He drove a cab on the days he was sober enough to find the garage.

Me? I had spoken out of turn, once, and was now condemned to spend all Eternity in a barroom with a meatball buffet. I was to be here for the duration. Duration of what, you ask? Well, since it was always Thursday, August 14th, I lost count. Months, maybe, or perhaps years.

The word among the bar's regulars was that Kathleen McLaughlin, proprietress of Ferguson and McLaughlin's Family Bar, Tables for Ladies, lived in fear of a government raid. The TV over the bar, while it played the usual fare—Irish football, the World Series, soap operas, and Jeopardy—daily frayed Kathleen's jangled nerves with the evening news, said news being highlighted by Immigration sweeps for undocumented aliens. Guatemalans, Asians, Sikhs, swamis, babus and bubbas—in short most anyone with chin whiskers and a suntan—were shown being herded into waiting busses, to be packed off for deportation back to the Hindu Kush, Quetzaltenango or Tuscaloosa. While thus far red hair and freckles did not yet dominate the 6:30 news, Kathleen had the long-term jitters. For years, Kathleen had never gone out into the street except to dump her mop water. Ah, but I am getting ahead of our story.

If you have been following these adventures as assiduously as my publisher hopes you have, you will recall that while I had not exactly sold my soul to the devil, I was close. A mouse demon had gotten his hooks into my psychic e-mail, and my name was now etched on the spamming list of the damned. Do not click the "Click to Remove" link; remember that. You'll be on their list forever if you do.

Now, where was I? Oh, yes. Jim Everhardy, how do you do? And as usual, I was minding my own business.

Then, I was standing in the rain on the corner of Eighth Avenue on Manhattan's West Side. That's the part of town they used to call Hell's Kitchen, before the local boosters decided to upgrade its image. I was naked and wet. A large gray mouse came strutting up from West 55th Street. He sported a green derby and a "Kiss Me I'm Irish" button.

"PROSPER!" I screamed, for that was the name of my very own personal representative from Sminthian Apollo, an eight-inch high mouse demon with limited powers.

"Jim, Jim, my old and rare! So happy you could come." The mouse demon was looking decidedly shopworn and dejected. "It's a fine mess you've gotten us into this time, Jim Everhardy," said Prosper. "They have stripped me of my powers and, worst of all, my hat."

This was not just any old hat. The mouse demon's powers were concentrated in a magic hat, the Helmet of Cleptath. Prosper had lost said chapeau to the goddess Artemis, sister of Apollo, in a tussle I wrote about. It's called The Perfect Homburg. Read it, and get educated.

I should say right up front that Prosper was not the devil. He was a mouse demon with good prospects for advancement, until he pissed off a Personage and blew both our careers to smithereens. And I, as I mentioned, am Jim Everhardy, would-be writer and full-time hack at the pleasure of the old Greek gods. I had been raking in the big bucks, having found favor in the eyes of Apollo, driver of the Chariot of the Sun. Ever glance at the reams, quires and folios of blurbs and coupons stuffing your mailbox and ask yourself who writes this crap? I do, or I did, and thanks for your concern.

It was always Thursday in the Ferguson and McLaughlin Family Bar, Tables for Ladies, all Thursday, all the time. Miss August was an Irish setter frolicking in a daisy-filled meadow, and frolicking, and frolicking, and frolicking. There were twelve pages on the calendar and all the pages were the same. By the way, that "Tables for Ladies" part was not to imply that there were grades of women, some Ladies, some Loose. Loose or tight, there was a *je ne sais quoi* generated by the bar's habitués that kept even the female cockroaches off campus. I never saw a lady in the bar in all the months Prosper and I were marooned there.

Well, okay, actually, there was a Lady. I had some trouble with Artemis, Apollo's sister, but you'll hear more about her as the story unfolds.

Lee Frelinghuyser called down the bar again. "Come on, Kathleen, it's meatball chucking time. Frankie needs a refill. Make the mouse do his trick."

Frankie was passed out with his head on the bar. Frankie was always short one beer with federal payday always three weeks off.

Kathleen turned toward the end of the bar. "I don't make that mouse do anything, Lee Frelinghuyser. Filthy beast."

I asked her what I was drinking. She shook her head and handed me a shot of rye with a beer chaser, the closest F&MFBTfL came to mixed drinks. She swabbed down the bar with a towel and leaned close with a conspiratorial whisper.

"In one of my attributes I was a Celtic goddess. Celtic goddesses are hypersensitive about satire. I felt you were poaching on my preserve, as it were. He got here first."

She indicated the mouse demon on the stool next to mine. The landlady's serene face hardened, and then grew beatific, as though she was partaking of a heavenly vision. "I'm sorry, Prosper. About the filthy beast crack."

"No apology needed, Kathleen," said the mouse.

I inclined my head ever so slightly toward the frumpy barmaid. "Is that woman behind the bar who I think she is?" I asked, sotto voce. "How come she knows so much about You Know Who?"

"If she thinks she's the next greatest thing since boil-in-a-bag gourmet treats," said Prosper, "she is You Know Who. That's Herself, herself. She caught Riverdance a while back and is rediscovering her Celtic roots. She figured Kathleen McLaughlin needed a vacation."

"So, where's the real Kathleen McLaughlin?" I asked.

"Oh, could be she's back home in Ireland, or on a cruise. Most likely, though, she's in a Quaker Oats box under the kitchen sink, behind the Bon Ami. She won't remember a thing."

"If you know all that, how come you're stuck here with me?"

"Unlike Kathleen, I can remember. I am an embarrassment to Artemis, sister of Apollo, and this is my punishment—probably for all Eternity. Here, wear this." He removed his 'Kiss Me I'm Irish' button and pinned it on my shirt. "It'll help you fit in."

We couldn't leave, ever, and since it was always Thursday, August 14th, we didn't get weekends off, either. We were stuck tight. While the Broadway locals could come and go at will, a spell of some sort prevented Prosper and me from getting past the door.

"Before her makeover, Kathleen was a star cover girl for Yesterday's Woman," said Prosper.

"Is that a real magazine?" I asked the eight-inch demon occupying the barstool at my side.

"No, I made it up," said Prosper.

"Prosper, how can you talk like that?" said a divine voice, very familiar. There was the smell of patchouli and a close, honeyed breath hot on my neck. "After all, Kathleen is under my protection. You buying?"

"Uhn... Yes, ma'am," I managed. Although the face and form of the goddess were what I saw when I looked at Kathleen McLaughlin, in the mirror behind the bar was the reflection of a kindly, care-worn woman fighting off the ravages of late middle age. Kathleen's skin was translucent, fair and milky, only rarely touched by the sunset rays that filtered across from New Jersey. On low-ozone afternoons, those Jersey sunsets penetrated the smoky sawdust cavern of F&MFBTfL only as far as the steam table. Kathleen was a dour, compact, even stringy woman—diminutive, wide-hipped and flat-footed in the carpet slippers she wore behind the bar.

Not the sort of disguise one would expect from a goddess.

The mouse shrugged and slipped a ten-spot from the pile on the bar under Frankie's head and waved for a refill. The goddess was gone and Kathleen shuffled up. "For her, there are no yesterdays," said the mouse. "She lives in the here and now. And under the sink behind the Bon Ami."

In came a scruffy kid in knickers, those three-quarter length knee breeches I thought were out of style since the Dead End Kids ruled Hell's Kitchen.

"Hey, kid, gimme a paper." Lee Frelinghuyser swiveled on his barstool as the street waif shuffled over with the Daily News. The kid wrung a tear out of one wide, innocent eye and Lee pushed a pile of bar change in the kid's general direction. Lee was a soft touch.

"I got sensitive ears," said Beany Levine, paperboy, the meanest, toughest kid in the neighborhood. "All that noise from loose change gets in the way of my staying centered. Hatha Yoga, you know."

Lee peeled off a one-dollar bill and handed it to the kid.

The kid stood unmoving. "That's for the paper."

Beany was waiting for his tip. Lee went fishing for change. "Ah, what the hell," said Lee, handing out another dollar.

"Thank you," said Beany. "A pleasure doing business."

"How about that," said Lee addressing no one in particular among the assembled Broadway locals. "Yoga. The kid meditates."

Prosper agreed. "The jangle of pocket change disturbs his tantric equanimity. He also accepts credit cards."

❑

Here I should take a break and make some salient points about satire. It seems satirists were a kind of lower-echelon druid, the royal poets who could compose gnarly rhyming curses to set the king's enemies britches afire, or make their manly parts fall off, or whatever. Satire is rightly words that can wound.

I however, had only made one snappy crack, a teeny tiny fragment of doggerel that was interpreted as satirical by Prosper's former boss. Actually, Prosper's former boss' sister: Royal Artemis, the Fata Morgana, Lady of the Wild Things, etc., etc. Not satirical in the way we use the word these days, not snide or sarcastic, not ironic, but satirical, and satire is deep doo-doo, divinity-wise.

The shower had been running hot and steamy and I'd lathered up. I'd started singing.

What a wonderful goddess is Artemis
In spite or because of her tartiness
She's known to be kinder
When you slip up behind her
Dah-dahdah, da-dahdah, dah, dah.

In my own defense, I didn't have a rhyme, or even words for that last line. And I never sang it in public. Poetry happens. Like athlete's foot and eczema, it sort of sneaks up on you, especially in the shower.

Wham! Pow! Kablooie! Or sound effects of like persuasion. I showed up, naked and sudsy, on the street in front of F&MFBTfL. When I walked in the denizens didn't give me a second look.

Ferguson and McLaughlin's Family Bar, Tables for Ladies was one of those steam table saloons that lined Eighth Avenue, alternating with Greek takeout. It was three blocks west from Carnegie Hall, a neighborhood bar where older men waited and watched for their Social Security checks and the Thursday meatball special.

❑

"Beany!" Lee was displeased with his Daily News.

The nine-year-old put down the beer he was finishing off for a departed customer. "Yeah?"

"C'mere," said Lee.

Newspapers were not a big business with Beany, but they filled gaps in an otherwise busy schedule. Or so I thought. I figured Beany collected the newspapers to sell again at the next bar down the street. Guys in bars had eventually got to pee, and when they did, Beany would be there to swap yesterday's paper for the one he had just sold them.

But Beany, despite his regular hustles, was an honest newspaper boy. Next day, I checked the dates on the pile of papers Beany dumped on the table in the back where he did his homework while nursing a draft beer. An outside date—from the real, non-timewarped world. October 22. Well!

Lee, who had returned from a visit to the necessarium, bellowed "Hey! Who swiped my paper? This one's from August 14th." He grabbed Beany by the armpits and shook him in the air.

"Hey, hey, hey. Sorry, Mac. You bought it; you read it. It's used. No refunds."

After drinking all day, every day, for fifteen years, that made sound sense to Lee. He put Beany down.

The next day, when Beany came in with his papers (which he swiped off the Daily News truck, by the way. Beany's Daily News scam crowned a plateau of minor larceny requiring nimble footwork and the patience of a woodland hunter-gatherer.), I stood guard on the pile and watched the date and lead stories change. August 14th. The life expectancy for the daily paper at F&MFBTfL was sixteen minutes twenty-four seconds. No more, no less.

Beany Levine, autodidact, warmed to Prosper's scams. Our very strangeness, in a neighborhood consecrated to strangeness, had attracted a hanger-on.

Beany, though he did his best to keep it quiet, was the star student at Our Lady of Perpetual Matriculation. Don't get me wrong; he was your All-American street hustler. But while Beany sold protection in the form of plate glass insurance, pimped for his sisters, ran policy bets and peddled high octane crack to the high schoolers, he never touched the stuff himself.

Beany was one sharp kid. He never once batted an eye at the tales of supranatural doings, or over Prosper being a mouse demon in the service of Sminthian Apollo.

Beany was hanging out with Prosper and me one Thursday while he waited for a deal to go down.

"Don't take this personally," I said. "But how come a kid—you—with a Jewish patronymic is going to OLPM, a Catholic school?"

A cell phone was waved threateningly in my face. The kid pointed it at me as though it was a pistol. He thrust the antenna up my nostril. "You got a problem with that? You prejudiced, buddy?"

"No, just making conversation."

"Well, in that case..." The antenna was withdrawn. He wiped it off on my shirtfront. "The kids at Our Lady have got more discretionary income than the street kids. And they get it regular, like allowances, like."

"And you shake them down for their lunch money."

"So? I'm good with numbers. And I get straight As in Latin."

❑

Over the ensuing months, the defrocked demon and I worked out some routines to help pay our bar bill. We'd scam tourists with our talking mouse number. They tended to leave hurriedly, forgetting their change on the bar. Capitalizing on his looking like Stewart Little strung out on barbiturates, the demon cleaned up pitching pennies with the street kids and bamboozling their more fortunate brothers and sisters at Our Lady of Perpetual Matriculation out of their lunch money. It was a living.

But the favorite stunt of all among the Broadway locals was betting on whether Prosper could catch a flying meatball. Thursday was meatball day. That was when we first caught on that the Divine Artemis had us stuck in a time warp. It was always meatball day at Ferguson and McLaughlin's Family Bar, Tables for Ladies. As much rapid fire betting went on for the meatball hurling as over on Eleventh Avenue where the Dominicans held forth with fighting chickens. The Caribbean Dominicans, not the cloistered friars.

Prosper was magnificent. No matter where Artemis hurled the meatball, he was there just in the nick of time. The goddess got loose with the number and graduated to Annie Oakley-style blindfolded and backwards over-the-shoulder tosses. I had by then figured that Prosper had held on to some, if not all, of his mouse demon armamentarium. The meatballs would curve and swoop right toward his outstretched paw, often executing ninety- degree turns in midair. The crowd was usually drunk enough not to notice. Word spread. The uptown swells started dropping in. You know, the crowd that asks for mixed drinks. We were Broadway stars, but we couldn't get out.

Thonk!

Lee Frelinghuyser fell off his stool at the far end of the bar, blocking our hostess' way to the cook top and the steam table. Lee was announcing he had achieved his limit. Two of the regulars stepped back to give him room on the floor.

The hollow-looking old man I only knew as Frankie called me Seamus and tugged at my sleeve. With Frankie's brains fried for the last thirty years, everyone was Seamus.

"Seamus, make the mouse do his trick. Then we all get a free round," said Frankie. Artemis, sister of Apollo was good to Kathleen's regulars. Beany Levine did her bookkeeping.

Splonk!

Frankie had fallen face first into a puddle of beer on the bar, on top of his government check. From under his ear a familiar corner of pink watermark poked out. He had forgotten to cash the check and it had probably lain there under his ashtray, crumpled cigarette packs, last Sunday's News and his head for a whole week. A spreading stain feathered out through the signatures. I lifted Frankie's head enough to get the check out before it melted so Kathleen—er, Artemis, sister of Apollo, could cash it for him.

Thonk!

Strange. Lee Frelinghuyser made the same sound, whether he was getting up or falling off his barstool. Lee had just achieved verticality. I made a note to ask Prosper about this.

"It is high time we expanded your educational horizons, Jim, my old and rare. I have the inside dope. Listen up. You will be needing this information in the near future."

The mouse's speech was becoming slurred. I checked out the level in Frankie's beer glass. Half empty. Frankie was still out and waltzing with the muses.

"Wellerishms versus spoonerishims," said Prosper. "Burp. Thash what I mean to impart, from the bowels of my own extensive supranatural wisdom. Burp."

Thonk!

Please note this was a lesser Thonk! than that articulated by Lee Frelinghuyser's substantial 220 pounds when he fell off a barstool. My former personal representative from Sminthian Apollo, a defrocked mouse demon, had gone over headfirst and was out cold on the floor with a snootful of sawdust. I picked him up and set him on the bar.

The mouse came to and continued. "Or perhaps bowels is an infelicitush metaphor..."

Artemis-as-Kathleen exited the kitchen packing a platter piled high with Swedish meatballs, Scandinavian Thursday fare in an expatriate Irish neighborhood. Lee Frelinghuyser was hanging on to the end of the bar as he weaved back from a trip to the men's room. He waved a wadded, soggy bill in the air. "Hey, Kathleen... throw the meatball!"

Frankie was awake and waving his soggy government check. "I got a fiver says he'll miss it this time."

Lee Frelinghuyser made a note of Frankie's wager in the spiral steno pad he kept on the bar. Showtime.

Artemis set down her platter and picked off the very topmost from the squishy pyramid of burger balls. "I've got work to do. It's all right for you guys to be playing at games," she said with Kathleen's lilac-tinted Irish lilt. "Okay, one last time." She wound up like a major leaguer and let fly.

The meatball did some strange things. First, it went straight to Prosper's nose, where it hovered between his eyes, as if daring him to grab it. Prosper grabbed at it, whereupon it reversed itself at its original speed and rocketed smack into Artemis' face.

Herself, celebrated by the Pre-Raphaelites as a shepherdess disporting herself in a bosky dell, squeegeed sour cream, paprika and mushroom bits from her classically proportioned nose.

"That's it! I've had enough of you and your stunts." She picked up the whole platter and started pitching wet, sloppy meatballs at the mouse.

Prosper tried to run, but he was too drunk to navigate. He did dodge the first three, which splatted behind him against the mirror in a neat straight line. Prosper leaped to the top shelf where the McLaughlins kept their best stock. There, the mouse demon cowered, out of breath and flushed with unaccustomed exertion, between the Drambuie and a tall bottle of some greenish liqueur. A rapid-fire fusillade of meatballs had him pinned down. Most missed.

"Time out!" he cried. "I have done it! I'm getting my powers back. Oh frabjush day, calloo, callay!" He was still drunk even after his exercise.

Splat!

Thonk!

In case you're not following the sound effects, Artemis' fiftieth meatball connected and knocked Prosper off the shelf. Lee and the guys were arguing about the bet, whether the meatball caught Prosper, or Prosper caught the meatball.

"He caught it, fair and square. You owe me five. Each," said Lee.

Flat on his ass in the sawdust of the floor, my former foremost familiar sprite was looking very pleased with himself as he licked salvaged sour cream off his suit. Prosper sat back on his haunches and nibbled at his last meatball, turning it, rather like a Central Park squirrel dismembering a candy apple. He made it back to his seat next to mine at the bar while Kathleen primped, straightening her hair, which had come loose during the meatball melee. Kathleen's do was always yesterday's perm tucked behind a kerchief. Kathleen looked the same every day.

"How does she do it?" I asked the mouse.

"Because it's always Thursday inside this bar. Your round."

"Shhh!" Beany Levine was hunkered over a pile of books next to the sleeping Frankie. "I gotta study. Got finals next week."

"Finals?" said Prosper. "But it's the middle of summer."

"In here, mouse," replied Beany. "Past the door, it's Thanksgiving break."

I had tried to acclimatize myself to living forever in Thursdayland with free booze and a demonic mouse, subsisting on small change. There was, however, seldom a dull moment.

At the end of the bar, Artemis was deep with Beany Levine. They were bent over an ancient book. It was huge, a fifty-pounder, brass bound with cracking leather binding and a gilded pentagram on the cover. She was tutoring him for his Latin exams.

Beany looked up at Prosper. "Hey, she can speak the language!"

The urchin was impressed. So was I—she probably wrote the damned thing.

"*In nova fert animus mutatas dicere formas corpora.* That's the Metamorphoses, first book." The goddess peered up at us through Kathleen's eyes. "Of bodies changed to various forms, I sing. Congreve's translation, I believe," said Artemis archly.

"Criminy!" said Beany.

"The very same," replied the goddess.

I turned my head sideways to read the spines of Beany's schoolbooks. Geometry, Latin Year II, Social Studies. "Uh, couldn't you strong-arm the sisters into a passing grade?" I chimed in. Innocent me.

"That would be cheating."

Silly me.

❑

Another Thursday, but a different barmaid.

"Hi, I'm Bambi. The Divine Artemis couldn't make it. The demiurges are chucking quoits today."

Bambi was either wriggling into or wriggling out of a blouse intended to draw stares from male customers even if it had fit her, which it didn't. I sighed, swallowed hard and sat down on the first empty stool.

"Herself sent a stand-in?"

"I am a sub-muse, the nymph of inverted sentence structure and Divine Artemis' personal assistant. How d'you do?"

I was doing rather well, actually. She followed my gaze and I flushed as she buttoned back up. "Seen any mice lately?" I asked.

"Little guy, in a green suit? He's passed out on the free lunch table next to the cashews." Then, almost as an afterthought, "You here for the duel?"

"Uh, duel?"

"To the death, unless I miss my guess." Bambi looked pityingly at me. "In its fullness, time has ripened underfoot and the gods have grown weary with their sport. You are now being given the opportunity to fight for your freedom. Isn't that neat? The sister of Apollo told me I was here to referee a duello. Don't sweat it; you may have years yet to live. The duello is traditionally a Friday event, like fish-frys."

"And today is..." A no-brainer, as it was always Thursday.

"Check the calendar."

Now, it was Friday, August 15th.

Enter the heavy.

They say good taste is timeless. Well, this gonzo's time was up, haberdashery-wise. I immediately dubbed him Seamus McThug. Put him in a zoot suit, and he could have been the "Before" of a "Before and After" photo spread in Gentlemen's Quarterly, 1950s edition. The guy accessorized with a black turtleneck and a Norfolk jacket with chains, chains, chains—gold everywhere, the accoutrements of the street hustler. An Irish workingman's tweed cap finished off his ensemble.

He was passing the hat for the IRA, NorAid or something with initials, something about getting their very own thermonuclear deterrent. When he strode into Ferguson and McLaughlin's Family Bar, Tables for Ladies, there was a hush. This was the showdown at Tombstone, minus Wyatt Earp. He looked at what was to him the dumpy woman behind the bar and suppressed a chuckle.The mouse demon preened his whiskers. "He's got an AK47 down his pants leg," he said casually.

"Oh? I am so happy for him. What do you propose to do about it?"

"Oh, nothing. Just thought you might be interested. Why don't you satirize him? See, there was this satirist walked into a bar... 'Down in the mouth? Whatd'd ya do? Bite a duck on the ass? Yuk, yuk, yuk!' Hilarity reigns. Now that's satire, and as you're already cursed for it, what the hell? Give it a shot."

What the hell, indeed. Under my breath I made a sloppy rhyme. Nobody noticed. Nothing happened.

McThug picked his nose. He hadn't twigged to the fact that the Irish ex-pats who hung out at the steam table bars lining Eighth Avenue had come to America to get away from guys just like him.

The NorAid man was talking. "Listen, you old bat, you're behind. That's five hundred today. You're short two-fifty from last week."

Old bat? Oops. Seemed that Nymph Bambi looked like Kathleen to this guy.

"WHO ARE YOU CALLING AN OLD BAT, YOU SCUMMY, MUSCLE-BOUND PARASITE?" the nymph of inverted sentence structure roared. "Why do you think this poor woman is mopping out urinals in a barroom where the sun never shines? For you to chisel nickels and dimes to buy C4 and blow up babies in the old country?"

If Nymph Bambi's query was meant as an insult, Seamus McThug didn't get it. He swung right into his spiel. The intruder spoke with an accent much more authentic to Red Hook, Brooklyn than to Ireland: "Even today there are foreigners oppressing innocent women and children, their boots defiling the holy soil of Ireland."

Did he mean the Koreans and Japanese, with their microchip and automobile factories? In the days before the Celtic Tiger roared, bringing unheard of prosperity and a shriveled US export dollar, various insurgencies had lived high on the cabbage. Now, they hustled small change.

"I would be interested in knowing how much of what you collect makes it past Yonkers," said Nymph Bambi.

Things became instantly icy. This time he got the insult. The intruder shuffled his feet. He was edgy and he had a gun. He glowered at the Broadway locals lining the bar. He had their attention. Definitely.

"Fuck you, bitch," said the hit man, a bad move.

"This lady is a woman, and therefore under my protection," said Nymph Bambi. "She might have been your mother, asshole. Show some respect."

"Jim, get in front of me. Quick." This was from Prosper.

Kathleen grew and changed. She filled out here and slimmed down there, until the nymph stood fully revealed in all her (almost) naked glory.

What I could see of the scene, from the hit man's perspective, was reflected in the polarized lenses of his wraparound shades. I was impressed; he shit a brick. The magical nip and tuck in crucial areas had made her a living, breathing centerfold, sans staple. McThug's jaw gaped.

"Hmm, a mouth-breather," the nymph commented.

The jaw still gaped. Bambi checked inside. "A high-carb, high sugar diet, all Snickers bars and bourbon. You really should see a dentist. If I allow you to live, that is. You will recline with the fishes." Nymph Bambi had mastered the operating philosophy of Hell's Kitchen, if not its precise vernacular.

The nymph turned her attention to me. "Scrivener, you are here on probation for inadvertent satire. Satirize this lout, and I shall release you."

"And the mouse?"

"Prosper? Don't push your luck, Jimmy-boy."

Our visitor did not enjoy not being the center of attention. "Pay me my money. I'm collecting. For the Struggle," said the hit man.

"You are really, truly a Celtic son of Erin?" Nymph Bambi had a romantic twinkle in her sea green eyes. "Have you seen Riverdance?" asked the nymph.

"Fruits in Suits? No. And lady, I don't give a flying fuck what you think about my dental health. This is business, not personal."

"You are a common extortionist. I am considering satirizing you," said Kathleen McLaughlin, a.k.a. Nymph Bambi. "Is that an AK47 in your pants or you happy to see me?" A chancy line, even for the personal assistant to a divine Personage.

The NorAid hit man hadn't figured out how to be a quick draw artist. He dropped his pants trying to pull out his assault rifle. Black Speedo briefs nicely finished off his wardrobe; he was color-coordinated—and packing substantial heat. Even with his pants down around his knees, he was armed with a rapid-fire automatic rifle.

Which he commenced firing.

Pop, pop, pop, pop, pop.

The mirror went, then the top shelf of hi-grade booze in a shower of amber liquid and splintered glass.

“Well! Now, that’s plain bad manners,” said Lee Frelinghuyser. Lee was naturally so pale his skin coloring had no place to go, chromatically. So he turned bright blue and dived under the bar.

“Ohh...”

A groan from the floor got my attention. Prosper had been hit! I knelt over him and steeled myself for mouth to mouse resuscitation.

“Get this goddamned button off my vest,” said the mouse demon. “I can’t breathe.” He dusted himself off.

He was alive.

The mightily battered “Kiss Me I’m Irish” button had deflected one of the hit man’s ricochets. “They told me I was immortal. Guess I am.”

Clickety-click, click, click. The extortionist-assassin rummaged through his Speedos for a replacement clip. Must have been in his other briefs. Since the guy was out of bullets, I picked up a barstool and headed toward him.

He picked up a barstool and headed toward me.

“Stop! It seems we have a Mexican standoff,” said the nymph.

The thug looked at me. I looked at the thug. We both then regarded the Erin go Bragh banner above the bar.

“Standoff, Mexican variety,” said Nymph Bambi. “Two armed contenders, each with the drop on the other. This will necessitate a challenge to the duello.”

Oops again. A prophecy was fulfilling itself.

“You celestial types are big on confrontation, you know that?” I said.

“Your utterance is indisputable, Jim Everhardy.” Bambi, nymph of inverted sentence structure, had removed her apron and was rolling up her sleeves. “The duello will be the casting of spells: Spoonerisms, at ten paces.”

“Huh?” Seamus McThug and I spoke in unison, made eye contact and froze in position, bar stools aloft.

“Do I sense hostility?” She stepped between us. “Excellent. But be warned, I have a spellchecker,” here she patted her capacious bosom, “and since you are both named Jim, don’t try any funny business.”

Then I caught on. Spoonerisms—that was what Prosper had been trying to tell me about when he had passed out drunk. The nymph took the hit man’s cheek between her thumb and forefinger and flexed her arm. The burly gent levitated with the pinch and I saw daylight shining under his Gucci boots. Splatters of saliva went flying as she shook his head back and forth in midair.

"Spoonerisms," said Nymph Bambi, "Say it."

"Splurdlamish?" said the hit man.

"Correct," said the nymph as she dropped him to the floor. "You are neither of you the cutting edge intellects I might have hoped for, so I will have to explain. Don't be afraid to contribute. Speak right up."

"But... I..." I offered.

"That's enough; break's over," said the nymph, manhandling the two of us to the center of the floor.

Seamus McThug rocked back on his Gucci heels, smug and confident. "Hey, plumber, are you copper-plating those pipes? No, I'm aluminuming 'em, Mum," he declaimed.

"Close but no cigar," said the nymph. "What you have uttered is clearly an alliterative, assonantal construct calculated to dupe the vocal apparatus of an opponent. In short, a tongue-twister. One demerit for you."

The man pouted, actually pouted, as the nymph imposed her demerit. Seamus sank into F&MFBTfL's old oak flooring right up to his knees.

"Holy shit!" was the best profanity he could muster.

"Indeed," said Nymph Bambi. She threw me a wink, as if there was a hidden message waiting for me on my e-mail server.

"Nyah, nyah!" jeered Beany Levine. "Six stainless steel twin-screw cruisers! Bite on that one, loser." The lad walked up to the IRA hit man, now about Beany's height given that he was embedded in the barroom floor, and dumped a charger of pickled herring snacks from the free lunch buffet over his head.

"Glurph," said the hit man.

"Glurph, hmm. I shall employ my spellchecker," said Nymph Bambi, reaching again into her bosom to retrieve the PDA. "Hmmm, nope. Not in here. Sorry, one more demerit."

Seamus McThug sank deeper into the floor.

I at last caught the nymph's hint. Seamus McThug had said "Holy shit," and a simple Spoonerism would get past her spell checker—and nothing else. The gods, in their wisdom and inscrutability, had again chosen me as their champion.

Another wink from the nymph, broad and lascivious.

At me. Wow.

"Sholy hit!" I cursed.

It worked. The hit man sank further into the flooring. He was now caught at the waist.

Nymph Bambi demurely toyed with her spell checker. "You have reached the fork in your road and taken it, Jim Everhardy. That, by the way is a Wellerism, favored by your redoubtable Yogi Berra, and not a Spoonerism. Will you keep playing, or take what you have got?"

"Keep going," said Prosper from the salted cashews.

I looked to Nymph Bambi for confirmation but her eyes were glazed with Olympian impartiality. I had seen that look in the eyes of home team referees when my high school basketball squad played away games. Uh-oh. Against my better judgment, I took Prosper's advice.

I declaimed.

"I feel an unwarmed fish rising in my... uh, er, your throat." I bobbled on the destination of the spell.

"Ah, ah, ah, ah, ah, ah. You forgot the magic words," Nymph Bambi clucked and wigwagged at me with an admonitory finger.

"What is," I stumbled, "I see an unwarmed fish rising in your throat." And we had one unhappy hit man.

"Graaak, splurch!"

His face passed through shades of red and violet, from infra to ultra, missing all the local stops. His head began to bulge as he sank into the floorboards up to his Adam's apple. From one nostril came a wriggling protuberance. It displayed little pink suction cups.

"Blurragh!"

From Seamus' mouth popped a miniature octopus. Bambi knelt to pick it up. She cooed and chucked it under the chin. If you ever find out where an octopus's chin is, let me know, but that's what it looked like.

"Ohhh, poor iddy-biddy beebee octypuddle. Oodsy, woodsy, poody-phums?"

So help me, God, I could swear the creature nodded.

"Very well, then," said Nymph Bambi. "My work here is through. Give him a shot of ink, octypuddle."

The octopus squirted Seamus McThug in the eye. She popped the octopus into her cleavage and stood up. Beany's jaw gaped much as the hit man's had. His nine-year-old eyes were glued to her oscillating bosoms.

Don't say it, kid.

"Even my sisters don't have knockers like that!" He said it. I waited for the bolt of lightning.

"They will," said the nymph, "I've arranged things. You just quit peddling dope and everything will work out, okay?" Her Nibs had taken a shine to our budding malefactor.

The personal assistant of Artemis, Sister of Apollo, the Fata Morgana, Lady of the Wild Things, etc., etc. tossed a roll of silvery duct tape to Beany Levine. "Hey, kid, truss him up. And don't worry about your sisters—there's more to life than turning tricks."

❑

"Why don't we ever bet on ourselves?" I asked Prosper. "Lee Frelinghuyser just won twenty bucks."

Kathleen—Kathleen McLaughlin, the real Kathleen, who had returned, freed from the Quaker Oats box under the sink—placed two fresh beers in front of us.

So now, you are thinking, things went back to normal? I got back home safe and sound and Prosper got his comeuppance? No, it was still Thursday. Nymph Bambi had sent us a note saying she was still "working on things."

"Because, Seamus, me boyo," replied the mouse, "that would be using my sacred powers for venal, personal gain. But, charity, sweet charity? The enrichment of the lives of those less fortunate than we? This, the gods do truly bless."

I smelled a scam. Prosper did not wear piety well. He was on to something.

"And what do we get when you catch one of Kathleen's meatballs?"

"For you, Seamus, it's zero-sum-gain, I fear. You are loved; that should be sufficient. I, however, get the meatballs, and Frankie gets the beer."

The mouse poked the sleeping Frankie. "Frankie? You love Seamus, don't you?"

"Oh, sweet Jesus, I do, I do." Frankie threw his arms around my neck and slid slowly to the floor.

"Love, then, will have to be enough," said Prosper, downing Frankie's beer.

An Unwarmed Fish
was first published in the Summer 2003 issue of
Demensions—Doorways to Science Fiction and Fantasy

To take advantage of onetinleg.com's automatic subscription links, you will need a piece of (usually) free software that can 'aggregate' or 'catch' the podcasts you subscribe to. To preview the latest tale before subscribing just click 'stream' on the Free Reads page. How do you subscribe to this podcast? Copy the URL in the box below into your preferred podcasting software (e.g. FeedReader, iTunes, iPodder). You will automatically receive fresh onetinleg.com podcasts each time they're published.

http://www.onetinleg.com/onetinlegRSS.xml

Here are just a few of the many choices out there:

Soundforge's Juice http://juicereceiver.sourceforge.net/index.php
Apple's iTunes http://www.apple.com/itunes/
Doppler http://www.dopplerradio.net/
FeedReader http://www.feedreader.com/download

Klein, the Clone

"I'm Klein, the clone..."

we never thought much about it as other than a funny thing to say, a joke between brothers. We would then gravely shake hands and break into gales of laughter. That's me, Stewart, and Marshall, my brother. My twin, identical twin, actually.

"Research shows that cloned mice develop obesity as adults." I was thumbing through *Scientific American.* Marshall did not look away from the TV. My brother is big on pondering statements before delivering any snap judgments. Particularly when he was watching the Saturday morning cartoons. My news about fat mice rattled around behind his eyes like jellybeans in a gourd. He then repeated it.

"Cloned mice develop obesity as adults." Marshall was not a reader. He had to hear things first. "Well, then, better die now and stay slim." He made a face.

While we were at this time adults we had not as yet fattened up. But our bedroom was still a kids' room, full of overstuffed kangaroos, lions, clowns and the Klein Boys, an unbroken rectangular box with us on the inside. The walls were decorated with three wide red, white and blue enamel stripes that started at the level of our chins. Attached to the back of our closet door, its knob painted to disappear within the blue stripe, was a full-length mirror. We would snick the door shut behind us and in the dark imagine the room left empty behind. One of us would then pull the light cord and there would be four of us. We waved and giggled at the kids in the mirror, pulling faces on them. We hooked our fingers at the sides of our mouths, pushing up our noses and seeing how funny they looked. It was nice to have visitors. As grownups we do not do this as often as we had when we were kids, though.

When we were little kids, when our grandmother was alive, we had another great twins joke.

It was my—our—grandmother's fault, really. She started us—my brother Marshall and me—to thinking one of us might not be the real article. Lillian Musclewood was an immense presence: a diminutive woman, Lillian yowled, howled and kvetched her wonders to perform. Our Grandma's house was pink. There was no grandfather. Ben Musclewood had died in harness at the counter of his deli on Smith Street in Brooklyn, twirling precision paper cones for take-out mustard from the big roll of Kraft paper next to the register.

With the insurance payout, Lillian got the hell out of Brooklyn.

"Marshall! Stewart!" There's grandma now. "What are you doing rooting around in my Birds of Paradise? Playing which kid's got the papers?"

We didn't have any papers. We were digging up the Birds of Paradise, however. They were a tough shrub with blade-like leaves, but Marshall and I had packed along the heavy artillery—two bright yellow Tonka riding dump trucks, one apiece—for the two weeks in Florida with our grandmother. Marshall and I were five years old and visiting Grandma Lillian at her cement block, glass-louvered house in the development our father called The Land of the Newly Wed and the Living Dead. Our Grandma's house was pink and lavender. Baseball was never played in the saw palmetto vacant lots where the pavement ended for there were no children in Boca Ciega. Apart from Marshall and me on those deadly vacation getaways.

"What papers, Grandma?"

We thought she meant the big Sunday papers with their polychrome funnies. Mom and Dad read us the funnies and we made a Sunday project of it, Marshall and I cannonading into their bed at home, spreading the color comics all around, covering our faces and the sheets with smears of newsprint.

Grandma Lillian was preoccupied with her upcoming Mah-Jongg soiree and irritated that we were messing with her flowerbeds. "The adoption papers. You are identical twins. One real, made the traditional way, one a clone. For parts."

In years to come Marshall and I would fret about how and exactly what our grandmother knew about the family secret she was not supposed to know. Of course, Lillian Musclewood knew about the cloned child. Lillian Musclewood made it her business to know everything. She could not be left alone with unopened mail or in a room with an extension telephone.

Gardenwise, Marshall and I had slipped under her radar. We knew, even at five years of age, the advantages of making ourselves quiet and small. Our grandmother became even more preoccupied, shuffling her walker around the glass-topped patio table setting out iced tea coasters for afternoon Mah-Jongg.

"Not adoption—license," she trailed off, correcting herself. Lillian must have missed her morning medications and let slip this tidbit, a mistake she made only once again. She carried an Old World mistrust of government papers; Grandmother's family were refugees from the shtetl and Cossack raids had been her bedtime stories.

Lillian shuffled into the house after her forgotten medications. Our horticultural adventure continued without any further interruption. Us Klein Boys were ignored and made the most of our unsupervised time, polishing off the Birds of Paradise and transplanting pachysandra and cana lilies to the excavated Paradise bed.

Grandma's "Which kid's got the papers" remark and her addled caginess bothered us and back home in Connecticut we talked it over in our bunk beds at night. We had been read Pinocchio and checked to see if we were real boys. We were, indeed, anatomically correct and, according to Heather, the Girl Next Door and our fifteen-year-old babysitter, well hung for preschoolers. In the backyard treehouse, Marshall and I cut our thumbs—a little cut with a scout knife—and mingled our blood together. We were brothers.

"Klein" means small. We were told that by Heather. "So make yourselves very small, teeny-tiny and watch TV while Ted is here." Heather would entertain Ted, the boyfriend, in the guest bedroom while our parents were out. Marshall and I thought this was all only too fine. We microwaved everything from the freezer—boil-in-a-bag dinners, cheesecake, pizza, ice cream—ate it all in varying degrees of crispy, runny and mushy and snuggled up with chocolate milk to watch soft porn on the forbidden adult cable channels. The embargoed fruit of grownup TV failed to fascinate. We surfed on through to the cartoons.

With an early childhood parsing of rogue capitalism, I figured that our parents were pimping for Heather. She was after all being paid for having fun. I shared this with Marshall. I did not use the word "pimping," however. Marshall found this a neat idea and we had fun, too. Although our fun was different from Heather's and Ted's fun, we sometimes snuck in to watch them.

❑

After the car crash when I was six, Marshall went away to a residential care facility for a year. That was what Laura, our mother, called it—a Residential Care Facility. We were vacationing in Maine and my father and I were out after takeout Chinese. I was back home as good as new in three months. Marshall was back in under a year with a high-tech prosthetic leg. David, my father, never came home. He had his head cut off in the chain reaction collision that forced our sensible family sedan under the rear axle of a pulpwood truck. My leg was mangled; I remember the pain and little else but a druggy euphoria in the hospital.

There was a mix up and our father's body was cremated by mistake. They still had the head, however, neatly tagged and in a box. Laura was called to claim her husband's bodiless head. She picked out a handsome stone of speckled gray Vermont granite for the resting place of what was left of her late husband. "Lost in Willipaq," read the stone. Willipaq was the name of the small Maine town where David died.

After this she suffered from panic attacks that alternated with a deep, paralytic depression. I suppose our mother came out of the accident best of all—she had discovered a purpose for her life. "A single mom with a fire up her ass," was how Heather described her. Laura saw the torn wreckage of her twin boys in everyday activities. Anything with a sharp edge, a sharp point, a blunt end with no point, was a threat. Our TV programming was limited to golf and figure skating and, of course, *Arthur* and *Mister Rogers' Neighborhood.* Any device, person or event that might, somewhere in a future of limitless opportunity for mayhem inflict damage, death resulting, was banned. Not having many friends, largely because of our mother's fears for our health and welfare, us Klein Boys did not at that early age fully comprehend Laura's obsession might go beyond the ordinary fussiness of a protective mom. We were to keep our hands at our sides, speak softly and play board games whenever possible—the Klein Boys became Monopoly sharks early on. Marshall and I were home-schooled through the elementary grades.

Marshall's new leg was plugged in with his neural synapses. He got dinged up on a slide into third during Little League and had to go back to the Facility for some adjustments.

By the time we were ten Marshall and I had outgrown our bunk beds but we still shared a room. Late at night we talked. We recalled the second and last clue from Lillian Musclewood, our late grandmother.

Flags of All Nations Hors D'oeuvre Toothpicks were a feature of Grandma's Mah-Jongg parties. Lillian acquired many cartons of Flags of All Nations Hors D'oeuvre Toothpicks. These came from Cakes Élysée where also resided cake pans shaped like Sesame Street characters and architectural elements for bridal tiers.

Grandma served tiny squares of noodle pudding with raisins—kugel—each with a dollop of synthetic whipped cream (non-dairy) from a push button pressure can topped with a flag. Israel and Norway were favorites. Marshall and I figured it was their blue colors. After every Mah-Jongg party Lillian reconnoitered her garbage and counted the remaining flags, trying to dope out her guests' preferences. A given: that the bluehairs snarfed down her kugel. The imponderable: that navigators of the imaginative vacuum surrounding her refreshments were picky eaters. A noodle pudding square, otherwise the same as all the other noodle pudding squares, with a novelty flag of Brazil, Canada, Mexico, the United States or Singapore, was more likely to languish and end up flushed down the garbage disposal. Israel and Norway were the fast movers, along with plates of macaroons washed down with fruit punch. Grandma washed her Mah-Jongg tiles in the dishwasher along with the plates. Those parties of hers got sticky early.

I grabbed a Turkish flag from a card table with a festive paper throw—our grandmother's refreshments plateau—and stuck it up my nose. Marshall did the same. We sized each other up and got the giggles. I shot whipped non-dairy topping up my nose and stuffed in as many flags as would fit. Grandma descended on us and we escaped behind the transplanted pachysandras. We were hysterical with laughter.

Boca Ciega preponderated with large widows with little dogs. Baseball was never played in the saw palmetto vacant lots where the pavement ended for there were no children in Boca Ciega except for Marshall and me on our deadly vacation getaways. The houses in Lillian's neighborhood were, except for the dooryard shrubberies and positioning of the carports, identical. The large ladies competed with differing shades of pastel for their glass-louvered houses. The big widows had, to a woman, little yippy dogs that left their Dairy Queen curled piles of poop everywhere on the sidewalks and green, mowed verges even as the little boxes with Flags of the Neglected Nations piled up in Lillian's kitchen cabinet.

We set our alarm and rose early. At full light the poops were revealed fresh with morning dew and dollops of fairy magic—a spritz of non-dairy whipped topping with a flag of one Neglected Nation each. The neighbors were scandalized. Grandma was shamed before her bluehair buddies. And it was all our fault.

We escaped again to the pachysandras where we called this adventure the Flags of All Nations Hors D'oeuvre Toothpick Caper. We watched private eye shows: *Mannix, Mike Hammer* and *Magnum, PI* and loved their heroes' snappy comebacks in the face of immediate extinction, which was what Grandma Lillian had in mind for us.

"Godammit, if I could tell you apart, I would kill the phony one. You two are a bad influence." On just whom, she did not say. Maybe on her. Probably we were a bad influence on each other, clonehood notwithstanding. Whatever, it didn't matter. Grandma had something she called "Apoplexy" and died that weekend. The doctors said it was a cerebral hemorrhage. Laura flew down to mourn her mother and collect her kids. Marshall and I whispered at night and wondered which one was not the real kid.

When Grandma died we inherited her Mah-Jongg set. We took four of the tiles and drilled two of them to wear as amulets on thongs about our necks. They were kind of neat and an icebreaker when meeting girls. No one our age, or even of our parent's generation, had heard of Mah-Jongg. Incised on the game pieces were asianesque characters filtered through Art Deco that a classmate's accommodating great-grandmother, a Mah-Jongg devotee, identified as a unicorn, a green dragon and a blank tile with a square frame—the

"White Dragon"—plus a joker tile with a copyright notice from the Shanghai company that made the set in the 1920s. Marshall and I decided the white dragon would be Mom's and, although we never told her about it, we stored it away in the desk drawer that held all of our kid junk: forgotten neat stuff yet not too totally uncool to be thrown away. Like the toys from those burger joint promotions we hoarded when we were five. You know, the forget-me-not drawer. We just chucked the joker tile.

❑

Marshall and I were accident free until the year he poked my eye out with the jump rope handle.

In fairness to Laura—our mother and a widow like her mother before her—this was the only occasion of her pursuing us into the street as Mom, the Avenger, like the Eumenides in an ancient Greek play. Marshall had really got the hang of his prosthesis and, when we suited up for track, Laura averted her eyes. Out of consideration for her feelings, we wore sweatpants to the ankle whenever possible. We knew that she loved us equally well. Then there were the little clues that she had forgotten which one of us was which. We switched our Mah-Jongg tiles regularly to see if she could tell us apart. She couldn't. Or wouldn't.

Mom felt safe when our little gang of neighborhood playmates displayed a healthy sexual and demographic mix. Boys alone, to Laura Klein, meant trouble and a potential for danger—cap pistols and BB guns. Our mother's forte was wringing her hands and sucking her guilt into her stomach in a wet, chill, suppurating knot.

Like I said, Marshall poked my eye out. It was an accident. I came home alone, a dripping mess, my eye swelling and full of blood.

"Ohh...don't tell your brother." Mom didn't say I told you so and I felt pride for her restraint. She pulled the drapes in our striped bedroom and nursed me there herself. My eye glazed over, healed, and soon I sported a black eye patch just like the Hathaway Shirt man in the old ads. I felt it made me distinguished, an adventurer. As it turned out, our mother didn't want to tell Marshall because she thought he would feel guilty for still having two eyes, for not racing with Laura and me to the Residential Care Facility. The truth was, neither Marshall nor I felt guilt or fear, but an overwhelming relief.

"Boys..."

Eyes fever bright, enthusiastic, our mother had discovered a new secret. She spoke intensely. Laura was desperate to be right this one time. Our mother's enthusiasms were a peg on which to hang the Klein Boys' uncertainties.

"You must have guessed..."

“Grandmother told us.”

“But she didn’t tell you everything. Lillian didn’t know everything.” Our mother hugged us to her, sly and confiding. “There is another...”

Us Klein Boys exchanged one of those twins looks. We knew there wasn’t a spare clone in the cupboard. Our mother had made up her own imaginary playmate. The Klein Boys’ three eyes maintained contact while we waited for our mother to tell us everything would be all right.

“You won’t tell?” asked Laura.

“We won’t tell anyone.”

“The white tile!” Marshall broke from our group hug and ran into our mirrored closet. There was a muted rummaging, then a series of thumps. From the forget-me-not drawer he returned with the White Dragon Mah-Jongg tile threaded with a frayed and shabby lace from one of our running shoes. Laura bowed her head to accept the White Dragon.

We lived together in the striped bedroom until our mother died.

We were three now.

Klein, the Clone was first published as
The Flags of All Nations Hors D’oeuvres Toothpick Caper
in the Winter, 2003 *Fables* [www.fables.org]

The Ninepatch Variation

The Pease family hands are hands in motion.

The Pease family mind likewise wanders and flutters, arranging things. Elizabeth Profitt Pease is standing on a chair; she has just wriggled out from under the piano, her mother's piano.

"Anyone passing will see a placid old lady moving lamps and standing on the furniture and think what a life well lived," says Libby Pease. "See that lady full in the comfort of her sunset years. A drowsy afternoon reverie, this placid creature is reliving lost moments standing on the furniture. God forbid they should catch me under the piano."

Elizabeth Profitt Pease has grown through all and past most of the stages of life as demonstrated by an illustration in The Essential Shakespeare, her high school text, and she is wondering what will be next. At sixty-three, as she sees it, not much has thus far happened to Libby Pease. She has grown up, aged in place and hardly noticed it. Her days trail out behind her to an invisible vanishing point. "The place where I was conceived," says Libby Pease, meaning a point in time, rather than the venue of conception itself. A well-plotted project, a nine-patch variation, is defying her. The furrow between her eyes appears and disappears like a flashing caution light, the only outward sign of a quilt gone wrong, a quilt ungratefully turned against its maker.

Geometric perfection and precision stitches are Libby's gifts. She is a quilter much celebrated for her execution of traditional designs. But she has misplaced something.

"I have a cat," says Libby Pease.

It is not the cat that is missing. Something smaller, something tantalizing is escaping her.

Libby Pease sets down her 27th quilt block. The planned effect—a velvety pastel wash as of petals falling in a spring garden—is an ugly smear. She pulls a squared up stack of blocks from the window seat and picks off some cat hairs. Her connector blocks, the nine-patch variations as the pattern books called them, do not cascade with color no matter how she shifts their positions.

There was a war in Europe and the Pacific and Libby's mother played the piano, her Chopin nocturne that she had by heart. Six-year-old Libby hides behind the pedals, a haven from Charles Wyndham Pease, her younger brother. Hoagy Carmichael sings Old Buttermilk Sky from the parlor radio.

There had been a gentleman caller once when Libby was sixteen—a date for the movies at the Willipaq Cinema. Libby Pease still loves the movies as she loved them when she was a child. "I should get out more often," says Libby the grown-up.

Trotting like fuzzy yellow ducklings behind their mother, the Pease children, Elizabeth and Charles, arrange themselves into outings. Libby's father does not really trust the big talking faces high up on the elevated screen; when he goes to the Willipaq Cinema it is for the buttery popcorn. They go to the movies as a family but eventually without their father. At first Profitt Pease tags along to the matinees but the big lips, big teeth make him uneasy, he says.

The Willipaq Cinema's rich butter-slathered popcorn is what once brings Profitt Pease to an evening showing. "Get it wet," he tells the concessionaire, meaning extra butter. He brings along his own shaker, the girl being known as stingy with the salt. The hulls get caught in the interstices of his long, brown teeth. He sucks at the hulls, usually during love scenes. Libby's father does not trust ephemera in general and the movies in particular.

"Oh, Profitt Pease, please," says Elizabeth Wyndham Pease, Libby's mother.

"Profitt Pease does not please," says Profitt Pease, chomping away. But after that Libby notices her father eats his popcorn during the battle scenes and cowboy gunfights. Profitt Pease is not a free spirit like his wife and children and takes his comfort from solid, tangible things. He gives up on the movies and simply stays home.

The traits of the father are passed along to his son who gets to watch the movies while staying at home.

"Charley loves the movies, too, on TV," says Libby Pease, meaning her brother, now grown. Libby recalls the label on a can of green peas high on her mother's pantry shelf. On the label a pixie in a green tutu admires himself in retreating mirrors, the images gradually shrinking. Charley and Libby play grocery store with the cans, stacking them, putting her selections into her mother's net shopping bag. Charley gets to be the grocer because he is the boy. Libby has to help him make change.

"But, I... what?" The elusive missing something is teasing her again. The pixie's mirror reflects in a second mirror looking back at itself again and again in reflections running to a microscopic infinity, reflected tessellations cascading backward in time to, she supposes although she cannot see it, an invisible point. In a celebration of canned peas, the pixie holds his harvest high, one green pea the size of his head.

Things becoming smaller, going backwards.

Growing up in a small town, bigness is where important things happen, meaning somewhere else. Movies are big—big heads, big bodies, grand gestures, finer nuances. Elizabeth Wyndham Pease, Libby's mother—Charley's too, though she has less enthusiasm for her younger child—with her fuzzy duckling children takes in the matinees at the Willipaq Cinema where, eight rows past the loge, William Powell as The Thin Man speaks directly to young Libby Pease, aged six. William Powell debonairly gestures, a long-stemmed martini glass casually depending from his sensitive artist's fingers, never, never spilling a drop.

"Dry, dammit, dry dry dry. Nora my delirious cupcake, you are the most beautiful, charming, cosmopolitan woman in the world, the mother of my children-to-be and I love you passionately and as often as possible we can escape the servants; but in spite of all this my passion flower, my night-blooming cirrus, my succulent eucalypt of desire, why, why, why, are you the only woman in the so called civilized world who knows how to make a dry martini? It is not enough to tell Daisy the correct proportions; these things require the hand of the artist, finesse. Make a full silver shaker for us yourself for I feel a case coming on..."

The angle at which Libby the child holds her head is a posture of awe. The angle allows her jaw to gape unattended, but the theater is dark and after all, she is there to see the stars not they her. Libby the adult reflects on this. All great art was meant to be up there—up there with William Powell and Myrna Loy—not locked up in a fusty Vatican basement. The Church of Rome hoards art; Libby has heard this. Art is splendid and not for hiding in a crypt. Not as lying at her feet now in the form of a shabby, failed nine-patch. The Ohio Star was the nine-patch all beginners did.

It is Libby's habit to watch the ongoing parade of Willipaq, Maine from her parlor windows. When Libby is six, peering on tiptoe for the iceman with his horse, her chin barely reaches the sill. The iceman feeds his horse what Libby figures are oats from a nosebag attached with leather loops behind the horse's ears. The horse climbs the hill to the Pease house by memory. Libby runs to the door past the hall coat rack with the peg reserved for her mother's net shopping bag. She waits as she will later wait for her cat's announcement of self. There is no cat here today—this is the iceman's door. Libby the child holds the door for Vern Lightfoot and his billowing aura of horse and man smells, the huge square cake tight in his tongs high up on his stained shoulder apron.

"Iceman." Big booted feet clump up the wooden steps. A whinny from the street. What was that horse's name? What was the name on the can of peas with the pixie and his mirrors?

Libby remembers her girlhood as a litany of lost visitors. First the iceman stops his deliveries, then the coal truck stops coming to the Pease house. Profitt Pease, Libby's father, owns a modest woodlot where he cuts and splits the winter wood. Her father puts in an oil tank and then there is a new visitor, the oil man come to fill it.

The cat interrupts Libby's recasting of her quilt. He meows outside the door, his nose placed at the nick in the weather-stripping to make sure he is heard. There is a dog once, and a father who does not go with his family to the movies. The dog and the father have been dead for years—Libby's father, Profitt Pease, dead for twelve years, the dog for ten. The cat sleeps on the cushioned window seat.

Brother Charley sleeps on the sofa in front of the television. The cat and Charley live on.

"Ladies and gentleman, the cat," say s Libby, holding the door.

"Maworr," says the cat, stepping in.

This is to be expected from a cat: that he be on time for his appointments. Charley does not arrive early for anything, when he arrives at all.

Kneeling on the floor, Libby rolls back the Persian carpet and begins to set out her finished blocks. So sure was she of her design that she had done the sewing by hand. "I should have used my old Singer Featherweight and cut my time from weeks to days," says Libby.

"Oh, Libby, dear, you don't just sew, you make Art," had been a pronouncement by a member of the quilters' guild.

"Not this day." Libby shuffles her squares, turns lamps on and off, stands again on the sofa to study her congeries of blocks, hoping for something wonderful.

"Oh, Libby, you can put anything together and make it sing," said the sister quilter, "from yard sale rag bags to the blanket off the iceman's horse." The two were girls together and remembered Vern Lightfoot's horse.

From behind a radiator, the cat strolls out into the center of her blocks, leaving disarray it its wake. "You, O cat, are offering me a fix, are you?" She cradles him in her arms. Libby pulls in the halogen floor lamp from beside her sewing table and squints through a screen of eyelashes, then stands on the kitchen step stool for an elevated view. She has hoped for a miraculous intervention from some ancient well of cat wisdom. The cat's quilt is no better than hers, only different. Perhaps from another angle.

"Pardon me, Mr. Cat." Elizabeth Profitt Pease ducks her head and slides under the piano. From this oblique perspective Libby still has a plain old serviceable Ohio Star, very traditional, just as she had turned out forty years before. And the colors are still a smear, not a spring garden in bloom. The cat dives back under the radiator. Well, the damned thing was a quilt; that much she had gotten right.

Darwinism, as it is called in Willipaq High's sophomore biology studies, teaches Libby that all creatures are preoccupied with sex. This is, after all, why the spring gardens bother to bloom. This is a survival mechanism. No love, no next generation. Love without passion creates no new life. All the movies, the songs are about love. The creatures that loved without sex never made any movies; they just had hobbies. They were extinct.

"Charley is extinct but there he is, walking around," says Libby, sharing this joke with the cat. The cat understands Charley. Once Charley forgets and leaves the TV on to wander off with his friends. Caves of the Buddha, a pictorial exploration of religious art is playing. Yellow-robed shaven-headed monks are painting a holy picture by dribbling colored sand in intricate floral shapes. When they are through, they sweep it away.

"I am not quite ready to be swept away," says Libby Pease. Libby worries about not remembering the name on the label of the can of peas, the can with the pixie and his retreating mirrors. In the sand paintings of the Buddha every grain demonstrating the evanescence of life, its transitoriness, was precious and without that single grain, all the myriads of other s would remain meaningless.

"Libby," says Libby addressing herself, "Have you ever felt you are preoccupied with the mechanics of sex? Just where thingies go?" Or where the thingies went when they were no longer thingies. The Old Thingies Home? Libby is tickled at the thought; her question has surprised her. "Libby, dear," Libby replies, "I wish you wouldn't talk that way. It makes you sound so common."

She surrenders as laughter starts someplace inadvisable, deep inside, below her diaphragm. Pain announces itself, much as the cat. Libby holds the door shut. She feels at the catch in her side but is by this time laughing so hard she doubles over with laughter and pain, holding onto the back of a chair until the spasm passes. Her eyes are wet and she is breathing in short gasps.

"I am the pain of annoyance, Elizabeth, not the Big One, only a minor agony. Pleased to meet you, roll with me and enjoy."

"Well, Pain," says Libby, pondering thingyhood, "the 'place where the thingies go' might well describe a saloon." There are trendy watering holes where Willipaq's summer people meet and mingle. If the summer folk asked her she would tell them, yes, I am aware of thingy placement strategies.

"Thank you Libby. My pleasure." The pain withdraws.

The great screen stars of her girlhood, William Powell and Myrna Loy, do not have babies; they have love. They are The Thin Man and The Thin Lady; they solve mysteries together. The movies showed people who felt passion, Lust. Lust is a Deadly Sin. She is therefore curious about it. Feelings of desire Libby Pease has come to associate with being in the theater, sometimes her favorite seat itself—eight rows back from in the loge at the start of the smoking section where a gentle slope inclines into the retreating thirty rows of plush seats. Velvet ropes, popcorn smells, and always a sore neck after the show. Tickets for the section with the velvet seats cost a dime more. Libby pays the dime.

She turns off all the lamps but one and picks up her basket of redwork embroidery. Thirteen-year-old Libby buys the squares at McCrory's Five and Dime fifty years before. Overall Sam and Sunbonnet Sue are red lines on yellowed muslin squares, twelve squares—a set for the months of the year. Sam pushes over a privy for October; Sue carries an umbrella for April. With her hands in motion, Libby Pease feels anchored, safe to consider passion as spoken of by the big, fine-featured faces in the movies. The great shining faces on the tall silver screen could not know her yearnings; they speak to each other, not to Libby Pease. She feels her first passion in the seats beyond the velvet ropes.

There is a seasonal reverse entropy to the Pease house. Spring feels warmer than the spring of Willipaq really is. Windows and doors are propped open. Libby's father's coal stove, when it had heated the winter chimney's bricks hot enough for a holding heat was, while never any more cool than the summer afternoons in the Pease parlor, cold in summer. After the war the new oil heat eats away at the coal suppliers. Coal becomes expensive and Vern Lightfoot retires from the ice and coal business. Vern's horse dies. Her father's concession to modernity is an oil furnace, new thirty years ago. Libby now augments with firewood to hold down costs. Vern Lightfoot's son delivers.

After the war, the Thin Man movies likewise come to an end, William Powell and Myrna Loy grown old in the service of comedy and crime while Libby is still a girl. For years after the Willipaq Cinema still shows the Thin Man on the first Sunday of the month and Libby comes alone. Libby feels her first yearnings watching William Powell and Myrna Loy. She checks Dashiell Hammett's Thin Man books out at the library but finds the prose clipped and arty. The movies are mellow and smooth, just like the Thin Man himself.

Libby recalls her single completed sexual adventure, writhing on Harry Trott's beige velveteen Plymouth seat covers feeling the funny stubbly tickle of the upholstery material as she wriggles her panties down by rubbing her knees, calves and ankles about, freehandedly undressing, his hands in her blouse, their mouths sucking at each other in a tangle of tongues. Libby volunteers her maidenhead to her escort after an evening of mesmeric craning, her neck stiff with delight. They have seen Rebel Without A Cause. Libby's soldier lover is posted to Germany where he is killed on maneuvers one afternoon at 2:30, crushed between a tank and a medieval city gate.

Pausing to adjust the embroidery hoop to center Sunbonnet Sue's face—no, hat, for the charm of the Sunbonnet Sue is that she has no face—Libby wonders if Gilbert Roland, in The Desert Hawk, when the woman was finally in his tent and his burnoose flung to the carpeted sands, mounted his love slave in the scenes they must have filmed but somehow never included in the final film. Sand and sweat, implied and tasted but never projected. Had he mounted her with the same hand-to-hip elegance as he sat his horse? The practiced passing of hands over silk, over flesh and silk. The connoisseur's hand weighs a tender virgin breast beneath the fabric; an extreme close-up fills the 40-foot high screen, full lips parted wordlessly in passion soon to be consummated. Small gestures magnified, little things mean a lot, a perceptible rising of a single eyebrow says, this is good, you are fine, I will have you now. He mounts her in full stride, a galloping horse, laughing, his breath smelling of cloves. She surrenders her virgin bloom joyously, and unyielding rises to meet his thrust. He takes her like a walled city falling to a charge of gallant cavalry.

Actually, thinks Libby, it is artillery that takes walled cities, but artillery is so noisy. Sex is noisy, all lubricity and suction, gratification. But passion fulfilled remembers the susurrus of skin to skin to silken sheets and gasping breaths close to the ear. Libby Pease remembers the Plymouth seat covers. "I have seen slides of great art. I have had a sample of life and read about the rest. I have lived sixty-three years. I have had all the experiences that make a person."

Libby thinks—The past is rewritten daily by those who were not around at the time, sanitized by the growing feebleness of its surviving participants. Were you there? I was. Libby feels her mind picking up speed as her hands slow. In the Book of Life, Libby realizes, the answers are not written in the back. She must make them up as she goes along. The past is not subject to change and therefore better organized than the present. She wishes Mister Lightfoot or somebody could be here to uncomplicate things.

Out of the Willipaq coastal fog a limousine, dark as lampblack, long and polished, pulls to a stop at the Pease house.

Libby's caller is dressed for an evening at the theater. He is broad shouldered, slim waisted and his tailored jacket has silk lapels. Barbered and manicured, brilliantined and brushed, the man's hair and hands gleam perfection. A scarf of spotless white silk is carelessly hung from about his throat.

"Hello, Elizabeth." It is William Powell.

"You must be looking for my brother." No one important ever calls on her; it must be for Charley. Charley is gone half the year, working on the boats of summer people. Crewing, he calls it. Charles Wyndham Pease knew people who had been places and done things. Libby Pease expects the unusual where Charley is concerned. "I am Charley's sister."

"You are Charley's sister." The elegant man bows ever so slightly and holds out his hand, as though it were important to him to make a good first impression. "So happy—no, delighted—to catch you in, Elizabeth. You are all you are and Charley's sister, too."

"Yes I am. Elizabeth Pease, that is. And you are William Powell. And you are talking to me. That is rather nice. Won't you come in?"

"Fabulous. I'd be delighted. It is you I am here to see, Elizabeth."

On entering Libby's front hall, the light goes away somewhere. Some is sucked into the floral print wallpaper. Dimmed by crocheted openwork curtains stretched drum tight onto brass rods anchored top and bottom, much more light stays outside on the porch, past the beveled lead glass in the century-old oak front door. The Pease house has the charm of an abandoned depot, lovingly restored.

"Hmmm, rather understated, don't you think?" William Powell executes a half turn that accentuates his profile. He observes the concentric circles under a fluorescent ceiling ring. "I mean the 40 watt bulbs, the sepulchral darkness and the mustiness of storage? An interesting motif."

Libby and William Powell are now in the kitchen. Libby tends her redwork. The Thin Man sits on the table, a long, thin cigarette between his fingers. He has declined the chicken-macaroni-fruit gelatin ring but looks hopefully at the oven where a scallop casserole is in progress. Libby's stitching picks up its pace, red satin thread doing a czardas through the hoop. She remembers all the movies she has ever seen and replays them in her mind, mingling the plots and inserting herself into places foreign and wonderful. "Do you ever do that, Mister Powell?"

"All the time, Elizabeth, just like in the movies. We call it the dream sequence." The debonair man is comforting. "Call me Bill."

Libby pictures herself dressed in the high-waisted corded twill riding pants, the kind that show off a woman's body while at the same time saying she means business. Jodhpurs, they are called, smelling of horses and desire.

Libby's hands are never still, always moving to some good purpose. Gelatin dessert—red or green, diced chicken white meat embedded in a ring mold with green grapes and elbows with a whipped cream topping—is a Libby specialty bringalong for covered dish suppers. Libby dreams a life of danger and intrigue, awaking each dawn languorous and satisfied by the thrusts of a sloe-eyed, brown skinned, courtly lover—not Negro, surely, but foreign, manly and exotic. Arabian, perhaps, or Javanese—a shared cup of hot, sweet, aromatic tea, then off to explore some temple ruins.

A quirky native cab driver, just like in the movies, pulls up as she opens her tent flap for an amble out into the relentless noontime sun. The mezzogiorno the Italians called it, this relentless midday pounding of heat. Mezzogiorno. Temple ruins. Libby feels good knowing these things.

"Good guide, Sadiki Bin Amin is me." A captive macaw screeches from Sadiki's shoulder. "Nice lady see sights?"

The parrot squawks , "Libby Pease, Libby Pease. Libby, please."

"I should be most happy to," says Libby. She climbs into the desert taxi. "Show me the sights."

Open-throated silk shirt and a small automatic pistol in a glossy patent leather holster worn high up, she enters the whitewashed mud brick arches of the native quarter. In The Street of the Ostrich Plume Dyers a tall hooded figure who smells of cloves speaks to her.

"Hi, Lib. It's me, Harry." The cowl is brushed back with a careless gesture. The speaker is handsome, swarthy and the age Harry had been when he eloped alone to join the army in Germany.

"Harry Trott, I had hoped you might be dead."

"Tell me you still love me."

"You look a lot better than I remembered. But I have a gentleman caller. You'll have to go."

"Stay with me. Surrender to me. Forget William Powell."

"The Thin Man is a gentleman who appreciates a well-turned macaroni salad," says Libby.

"Is he frisky with the waitress?" The stranger is amused.

"Harry? You ran off, and here you are finding fault with William Powell's manners. And besides I haven't asked him to stay for dinner yet." Libby studies the handsome foreign features.

"I was stationed in Germany," says Harry Trott. "I was killed. Would you have felt better if I had 'run off' with another woman?"

"You ran away. From me. That hurt me more than another woman. William Powell will do just fine."

"So he will." The odor of cloves grows close and intimate.

Libby Pease has been gradually leaning ever more forward. She catches herself up with the small snap of the daytime drowser. "I have been asleep. Harry was a dream," thinks Libby Pease.

William Powell is speaking. "Libby dear, I believe you will find you have given Sunbonnet Sue a face. Sue does not have a face; she has a hat—the apotheosis of the low-maintenance debutante. You have surpassed the instructions in that magazine you have lying open on the table." He flips the page back to where Libby has marked her place with a paper clip. "Sorry about reading ahead," says The Thin Man. "I wanted to find out if Overall Bill and Sunbonnet Sue ever get together. I have an affinity for Bill—same name and all. I know all this sounds bizarre, but just look at the movies."

"Try me out. You may be surprised by what I can accommodate."

"All possibilities exist at the same time and all are equally real. Would you rather discuss quantum physics? Or wallow in your clove-scented nod-offs? Sorry, that was rude. Try the nine-patch again. Give it a chance. God, I miss Myrna Loy!"

"I thought she was only your wife in the movies."

"She is a beautiful woman and I therefore miss her. Fix the quilt. The pattern you desire is there, you just don't see it yet. Is that a scallop casserole?" The Thin Man sniffs, registers rapture and rises to check the oven.

"If Myrna Loy is thinking of you, you are bound to link up," says Libby reassuringly. "Eventually." Her needle is flashing again. Red embroidery thread bounces from its skein. Places too distant and glamorous to be visited by her in life dance behind the screen in a darkened movie theater. The Thin Man delicately digs a little finger into his ear.

"When you have an itch it means someone is thinking of you." Libby has heard this. "Myrna Loy, I mean. You will see her soon."

"If somebody bites you on the ass it means they are thinking of you, too, dear Libby. Eventually the Earth will fall into the sun," says The Thin Man.

"Forgive me for the greeting card sentiment; I was just trying to cheer you up." Libby yawns. "Almost nap time. I have seen enough of life and art from my parlor window. I have been in love and made love. I would be happy to have you here if you cannot get back together with your wife. I realize you are not the usual thing in a middle-aged lady's companion. You are different. It would have been ill bred to mention it."

"Fix the nine-patch, Libby. Promise?"

"Well..."

"The Singer Featherweight can do it." William Powell knew his classic sewing machines as well as his martinis.

"I will. I promise." After all, William Powell had cared enough to spend an afternoon away from Myrna Loy. Libby packs the hoop with its redwork into her workbasket and curls up on the window seat. The cat jumps up beside her. "Perhaps I am an old lady and not middle-aged after all. Excuse me for half an hour." Something missing from her reverie slips from her mind at the moment of realization, that mote so irregularly shaped that without it being in place, she would lose her whole life. "The pixie and his pea? No, it is something else," says Libby.

Hoagy Carmichael sings Old Buttermilk Sky from the parlor radio as Vern Lightfoot's horse pauses unbidden at the Pease house. Libby catches a waft of heady horse smell with a touch of cloves.

"Pixies? Peas? Libby, dear, we were speaking of dreams and desire, I believe," says the Thin Man.

"Ooh! There it is," Libby exclaims.

More momentous than the itchy, salty butter-slathered hulls the popcorn left between her father's teeth, the Thin Man or Harry Trott, her lost lover died too young, Libby has recovered that grain of sand without which the whole puzzle of her life is meaningless.

"Buttermilk—that was the name of Mr. Lightfoot's horse." She pulls an afghan up to her chin.

"Sweet dreams, Libby, dreams of horses and desire," says William Powell, the Thin Man. "My God, how I miss Myrna Loy."

The Ninepatch Variation was first published in the January 2004 issue of *Ideomancer* [www.ideomancer.com]

The Red Sneaker Zones

"I shall wear purple."

Libby Pease touches the framed poem that hangs on her kitchen wall. Libby could have memorized the verse, but prefers to be surprised by it.

"All the damned thing says is that when you're old people expect you to be aligned a mite off center..." says the 400-year-old Algonquian spirit-priest who regularly joins her for morning tea, "...look at me. Go for it, Lib. Get naked, paint the cat; you've earned it," says Sun-ripples-quiet-pool-to-call-of-loon.

Libby accepts having her own personal shaman as an article of faith, which faith she could not tell. Perhaps that of those pilgrims at the shrine of St. James she has seen in The National Geographic. The dead Indian smells rank, but not unpleasantly so—fresh earth clinging to over-wintering vegetables, plug-cut tobacco and molasses. He wears a loincloth and is well muscled, albeit stringy.

Libby reads a line further down, in mid-poem, "And learn to spit..."

This calligraphic treatment of the poem had come anonymously on her fiftieth birthday. Libby is celebrated as a quilter of rare gifts; people find both Libby and her quilts difficult. "Artistic," is what they say. For her sixtieth birthday the quilters' guild presented her with a framed copy of the poem. Libby's quilts define her as she defines them, polychrome geometrical complexities being her specialty.

"...wear terrible shirts and grow more fat," Libby reads.

"Libby, Libby, Libby," says Sun-ripples-quiet-pool-to-call-of-loon. "Have you ever paused to reflect that some greeting card company pumps this crap out by the metric ton? Are we searching for deeper meanings today? Christ, I hate these biscotti."

"You eat them."

"Termites eat houses. Bet they'd rather have a cookie," says Sun-ripples-quiet-pool-to-call-of-loon.

"And a red hat," reads Libby Pease.

"To match your basketball shoes. *Très élégant*. Red is not your color, Lib. Besides, you're already as batty as a bag of wood pigeons," says the spirit-priest as he dunks the last of the dry Italian almond toasts favored by Libby Pease. "Got any Oreos?"

“I thought you liked biscotti, that is surely the only reason I buy them.”

“You buy biscotti because you are a dotty old lady. Folks expect you to be peculiar. Besides, you already have red shoes.”

“Yes, I have red shoes.”

Libby’s tight-laced, high-top red canvas tennis shoes carry her on patrol. With a sudden nor’easter, Libby answers the call of duty, white diner mug of tea in her hands. There are decades of tea stains set into the ascending floral stair runners. Elizabeth Profitt Pease wonders whom she is leaving her tea trail for.

The Pease house teeters comfortably on a granite ledge near the fish pier. The house, as Libby, is never at rest; it creaks before the wind. This is Willipaq, Maine, the leeward limit of North America, and Libby Pease has a system for balancing her thermostats. Ever diligent, her red sneakers run from room to room, area, zone. Libby finds that more and more often on her red sneaker scamperings she will stop in front of the tall pier-glass mirror at the foot of the parlor stairs.

She is checking to see if she is still there. She had been beautiful as a child; everyone said so.

❑

Willipaq’s early settlers sported the stiff black broadcloth of the followers of John Calvin; they named the county Willipaq after its indigenes, a leisurely crowd of layabouts possessed of no sense of urgency. The Willipaqs picked berries, made love and squatted to their need beholden to no clock. That the Willipaqs were a lost tribe of Israel was a popular fancy of Calvinist lore.

Wheat, called corn by the new arrivals, had come across in sturdy jute sacking and arrived untainted. The harvest would be good. From an unknown source ergot, a hallucinogenic component of certain wild grasses, appeared in the wheat called corn and was inadvertently tasted. The settlers discovered a new covenant of rapture and forgot to plant. They ate more and then more until their seed was gone. The Pease family had had its representatives among those who starved that first winter.

One child, a boy, survived to question why at a later date.

Over the council fires of the Willipaqs, puzzled elders strove for an explanation of the erratic behavior of the summer visitors who covered themselves all in black and took turns hitting each other as they knelt on the sand. The Willipaqs sought wisdom or an epiphany, at least. What they got was the smallpox.

❑

“That Charley Pease is some piece of work,” says Sun-Ripples-Pool. Libby nods agreement. Libby is accustomed to hear criticism of her brother.

Libby’s brother, Charles Wyndham Pease, heats with wood, no thermostats for Charley Pease. When his wood runs out, he moves in with Libby for the balance of the heating season.

Sun-ripples-quiet-pool-to-call-of-loon fishes about in his leather loincloth for a lump of kinnikinnick, the Stone Age granola and protein snack. Ahh, he has found it, “Slippery devils, these whole foods,” he remarks, gnawing off a hunk of dried fish mashed together with blueberries. “If there had been smallpox inoculations in the seventeenth century then we need not have died,” says Sun-Ripples-Pool. He is uneasy being the spiritual advisor of an old lady who boasts a vaccination scar on her arm. “The white man’s bells and whistles. All supplied at a reasonable cost, of course.”

Libby kickstarts her winter morning runs at the thermostats with strong sweet tea and Dr. Pomeroy’s Herbal Draft, an alcoholic infusion. Charley drinks the standing-spoon coffee at the Willipaq Diner: black, thick and bitter with much reheating.

“I like the taste; I just don’t need all that caffeine,” says Elizabeth Pease about the coffee at the Willipaq Diner.

Libby loves strong tea with much brown sugar, and the orange tempera sunrises which visit the Pease house on its ledge behind the wind-whipped clouds of Willipaq Bay. Libby’s tea abides on an eye level shelf above the kitchen wood range. It is in a nice lithographed canister that had once held King Cole Tea, a Canadian brand. Now it is stuffed with Red Rose Tea from the IGA. The Canadian tea is cheaper but Red Rose Tea is Libby’s engineering decision. With American teabags, the paper tags are more firmly stapled to the string. The Dr. Pomeroy’s lives in the medicine cabinet over the kitchen sink. She adds a dollop of Dr. Pomeroy’s and begins her day.

“You really should think about reducing your booze intake,” says Sun-ripples-quiet-pool-to-call-of-loon who reads off the alcohol content of Dr. Pomeroy’s Herbal Draft. “...40 percent. Does the Dept. of Motor Vehicles know that you’re driving around pickled as a jugged hare? By the way, I love your shoes, Libby, they are quite becoming.”

“They are tennis sneakers,” says Libby Pease, “and I do not wear them outside the house. And you are opinionated for an apparition.”

“They are red. Red is a passionate color,” says Sun-Ripples-Pool. “And I am not an apparition.” The dead Indian often points this out to her. “Any more than you are not a person. In your imaginings you are a glorified paper doll,” says the spirit-priest, “Shirley Temple or Debbie Reynolds. You live in the past.” He becomes a bird and grooms his feathers. “I am a filament.”

“You are a figment. There is an appreciable difference,” says Libby Pease. “A filament is what makes a light bulb light up.”

❑

The white settlers’ meager crops failed. Calvinist vigor was no longer proof to mixed bathing and sweaty labors under a strange sun. Fornication brought a hundred strokes with the rope’s end against deteriorating social standards. Many were the righteous arms grown weary with flogging and by surreptitious self-manipulation. It was a good fight, but futile. They ate gruel made from acorns and the few sacks of seed remaining, saw visions and died one-by-one.

The indigenes looked on, astonished. When the Willipaqs returned to their seaside encampments the following year, they gave a decent burial to what the wolves and foxes had left of the white settlers.

“Slow learners,” said Sun-ripples-quiet-pool-to-call-of-loon, munching on his kinnikinnick. Had not the white men called their own reckoning after the fact? Their tautology satisfied, the Willipaqs found this a satisfactory explanation for the thinning of their own numbers.

❑

Sun-ripples-quiet-pool-to-call-of-loon squats in Libby’s front yard and pulls a medicine bag from the carry pouch he wears slung at his side. He tastes a mild bloom of fungus residue and adds in the powdered purple hinge of a mussel pried from tidal mud flats during the toxic days of high August. “Audacious,” says the spirit-priest. “Audacious to the point of arrogance. And as nasty as that ergot I slipped into the gringo white-eyes’ wheat called corn.” He feels blameless in the poisonings. “I but anticipated destiny,” says the spirit-priest. “Dead is dead.”

The spirit-priest kneels behind the southeast wind and snuffles up a cone of taupe dust from the flattened palm of his right hand: sumac berries and yellow dock root dried and pounded to purify his blood when he returned.

“If I return, that is. Whatever, it’s been a good life.” Sun-Ripples-Pool tosses back the sumac and dock root.

“Hmm, smooth,” he says, throwing up. “I am inspired to create, perhaps something useful and of everyday utility, a transcendent doodad perhaps. Generations yet unborn will bless me for it.”

There is a sensation of flight.

"It looks easy but don't try this one at home, kids. Flying is for big folks."

❑

The Pease children grew up confessing sins against economy before the assembled family. Profitt Pease quoted First Corinthians as his authority. "The Congregationalists and the Baptists declare their shortcomings before the entire congregation at altar call, before the regular service. So folks get an hour to think about things with everyone right there," pronounced their father.

Their father did not believe in the stuffiness attendant with church membership so the Pease children, Libby and Charley, declared before breakfast. Charley escapes their father's stern pronouncements first by moving out and finally by outliving him. Libby the grownup recalls those breakfast confessions as expiation for duties lapsed: the thawing of the water lines with hairdryer and torch, once performed, was a public humiliation and never to be mentioned again. Thawing was a laying-on of hands as practiced by the primitive church, pausing and praying for a release of the grip of frost on the arteries and veins of Profitt Pease's prized pipings.

Thermostatically controlled zone heat, this was her father's plan. The thermostats were placed above shoulder height, beyond the reach of the children, Elizabeth and Charles.

In The National Geographic Libby sees pictures of grieving pilgrims struggling with bleeding knees up rock-strewn mountain paths to the shrine of St. James of Compostela. The pilgrims had it right: they had left their thermostats unattended and they must pay. The plumbing, the water lines, the pipes froze; this was God's plan and a testing. Relaxed vigilance meant creeping for hours on hands and knees, following the baseboard plumbing lines.

❑

Sun-Ripples-Pool soars through a palisaded cleft in the side of a jagged rock wall. Forgetting to remember that he is flying, he looks up and notices that up is now down. He is falling and the sea is rushing up at him. The incoming tide hammers its spume into a vertical column, driving him against a headwind that rebounds from the cliff side. Soaring back out and over the foaming tidal breakers, he hovers on an updraft, resting.

The spirit-priest turns his head so that his sharp shining black beak points down his wing. He makes an incision and thrusts in a morning glory seed freighted with ergine, a lysergic acid alkaloid. Pushing deeper into his flesh, he plucks a thin, hollow bone out of his shoulder. This will be his gift of forgiveness: yellow, hollow and supple. "A wonder of ancient technology, except here and now. I shall call it a stitcher; Libby will be pleased."

He has just invented sewing and his starboard wing is throbbing with pain. Sun-Ripples-Pool plummets. “Oops! Flap, boy. Flap for your life!”

With a furious flailing of elbows, he makes it to ground at the edge of the cliff. He hits hard, barking both shins and taking the tip off his nose. “Well, any landing you can walk away from, etcetera...” The healing will be a bother but the needle is worth the lesion. “It’s like inventing the paper clip or Post-Its,” says Sun-Ripples-Pool. “This will be my little miracle.” Bird legs change back to man legs and the spirit-priest preens his remaining feathers. He lays the bone needle on Libby’s kitchen table.

“Sewing is already invented,” Libby might have said, “You are out of touch, being dead and all.” But she is away. She has changed from her red sneakers into sensible clogs for a trip out into the world. Libby has gone to the Pick ‘N’ Pay to buy Oreo cookies for the spirit-priest.

❑

A flurry of wind-driven snow follows Libby in through the kitchen door. “I have your cookies.” Sun-Ripples-Pool jumps; Libby has surprised him.

“You startled me. Now I have lost my train.” He shuffles the bone needle out of sight behind the sugar bowl.

“The quilter’s curse...” says Libby Pease as she unpacks her tote, “...so many quilts, so little time.” She spreads multi-colored blocks of fabric across the kitchen table. “Have you been here all this time?”

With a flourish of pre-industrial legerdemain, from behind his back the spirit-priest produces a pot of daffodils. “Flowers?”

Libby bustles setting out her quilting squares.

“Libby?”

“Medicine-man, I would have preferred real flowers, and in season, not a magic trick.” She turns on the radio; it is playing a program she has listened to decades before, as a child. In the darting effervescences of her never-still mind she plays her own programs over and over to save electricity. Libby pauses to listen.

“Here, I have made you something. I call it a stitcher.” Sun-ripples-quiet-pool-to-call-of-loon sways in time with the strange music. He hands over the bone needle torn from his own flesh and listens along with Libby Pease. “This stitcher is the gift of transcendence, a spirit-gift.” Hoagy Carmichael sings Old Buttermilk Sky. “If I thought it made a difference I would have invented the radio,” says the spirit-priest. “But then I should have to learn to sing and play the piano. I have too many demands on my time as it is to take up an instrument.”

“Demands?” Libby giggles at the idea of a spirit world with secretaries, answering machines and week-at-a-glance desk blotters.

“Looking after you, dear Libby.”

“It is a beautiful gift, your stitcher. Thank you.”

One loose shutter announces a wind change. Thin fingers of frost creep across the living room wallpaper. On the leeward side of the Pease house clapboards relax with a sigh, then open to welcome the thrust of the coming storm. Libby must get to work. She bends to lace her red sneakers. “Proverbs 8:1,” says Libby, “Does not wisdom call, And understanding lift up her voice? You will notice that wisdom is female. Here, have a cookie,” says Libby as she turns off the radio. “You must excuse me; I have to check the thermostats.”

There are four thermostats: kitchen, parlor and bedrooms. The thermostats for the upstairs bedrooms were only to be raised in case of illness—severe illness that confined a child to his or her bed. When she is dead who will follow her figure-eights retraced hourly across the linoleum, up the brass-bound carpeting of the stairs to the forgotten lands where the guest bedrooms wait, empty?

“And thank you again for the magic needle.”

“Don’t mention it,” says Sun-ripples-quiet-pool-to-call-of-loon. The centuries-old fumes of a sweetgrass smudge lift prayers to him and he is content.

❑

“Central heating? Yeah, the chimney’s in the middle,” her father remarked in the days before he made his conversion to oil heat. Conversion comes late to many sinners; Profitt Pease was a whole-hearted proselyte. “Zones. That’s what I got when I put in the oil burner,” said Profitt Pease.

Libby puts in the latest oil burner—an upgrade, new and improved. Her father made the first conversion. The first zones were his to command. Profitt Pease hung onto his old coal furnace ten years after he put in oil, then grudgingly tore it out single-handed one summer. His leftover coal was burned in the kitchen range. Disappointments by gouging suppliers, failure of his woodlot, price fluctuations in an increasingly international market were all to be considered. Vern Lightfoot, the oil delivery man, bore Profitt’s wrath as an agent of foreign imperialism. Libby thinks of asking Sun-Ripples-Pool to keep and eye on the Illuminati, the multinational secret schemers who keep her house so unseasonably cold in winter and hot in summer.

Libby remembers her father’s blusterings but not her mother’s face.

❑

Dalton Comfrey, the oil deliveryman, pulls up in his red, white and blue tank truck. Dalton picks up the route when Vern Lightfoot dies in 1966. He breaks a path through the knee-deep snow piled between the road and the basement tank fill pipe. Libby gives the window a smack to loosen its frozen casement. "Hiya, Dalton. Good to see ya. Needed that fill."

"Hiya, Lib. How they hangin'?"

This is their joke, well worn and polished from decades of familiarity. Dalton was four years behind her in high school. Dalton has never been inside the Pease house. Since graduation, Libby Pease has never seen Dalton except when he makes his oil deliveries. The oil man's knee-high rubber boots he keeps packed with felt inserts. The felt gives him warmth and an increase in height honestly come by.

From a smoky hereafter of animal spirits and perpetual pemmican, the Algonquian spirit-priest clears his throat. "You and Dalton, the oil man. You were an item? In high school?"

"No," says Libby. "We had other appointments to keep."

As Dalton Comfrey's truck departs down the hill Libby laces her sneakers for yet another run at the upstairs thermostats. As she tightens the second elaborate Turkish bow it strikes her that when her father was called to glory he hadn't left the faucets dripping behind him.

"Thank you for the bone needle," says Libby, this time to no one in particular. "I shall treasure it." Libby stops in front of the tall pier-glass mirror at the foot of the parlor stairs and checks as usual to see if she is still there. "Like railroad tracks," says Libby about her life, "...we all have our vanishing point."

Libby thinks about the bloodied knees of the pilgrims at the shrine of St. James of Compostela and resolves to wear her red sneakers outside the house today. "This year I shall perhaps let the thermostats go to all hell," says Libby Pease.

The Red Sneaker Zones was first published
in the *Hiss Quarterly* [www.hissquarterly.com]
the "Space To Grow" issue Summer 2007, Sydney Nash-Lee, editor.

A Special Providence

It was his miracle, Gerald Bronson MacKechnie's —a de facto, set in cement miracle. The question of the duck was never fully determined. That it was a duck, Gerry was sure. The duck was stuck on the screen of a Lotto terminal, endlessly flipping a gold coin. Sheila had chased him out of the house, again, and he was feeling low. He leaned on the counter at Arsenault's One-Stop and Family Sundries waiting for a roll of change. This was a losing day.

"Quack, quack, quack," said the machine as the duck appeared, stalking back and forth with a big cigar and a painted-on mustache. Doing a Groucho, a lure to the unwary, promising riches. When you're already a loser—a status to which Gerry readily confessed—slim pickings were better than no pickings, miraclewise. Gerald Bronson MacKechnie loved jelly doughnuts of every race, sex and flavor. He should have wished for a jelly doughnut. Or a crème-filed Bismarck.

"You, Gerry MacKechnie, are a prime example of reverse Darwinism. The jelly doughnuts, for example," said the duck. "You are a poster boy for failure. And as such, you shall be rewarded."

"I get a prize." Gerry thought of Cracker Jack.

Instead he got a miracle. It all started when Gerry lost his cool and pounded on an otherwise inoffensive video gambling machine.

❑

For Willipaq, Maine everything had been and gone with the previous century. These days youth fled to the cities of the south with the ink on their high school diplomas still wet. Across the border in Loup du Jour, Canada the provincial government poured in millions on infrastructure while Willipaq, from Augusta, the state capital, was transparent. Willipaq was broke—Loup du Jour a truckstop.

Willipaq, Maine hoped for an Indian casino. What they occasionally got was payoffs on the gambling machines just over the river in Canada. Most of the money stayed in Canada. The proceeds went to National Health.

Gerald Bronson MacKechnie slammed the video poker machine with the heel of his hand. Gerry was a decent sort, a husband and father, unemployed one month out of two, a solid citizen who saw himself as a free spirit. A repetitive pattern of a duck and its endlessly flipping coin had stopped dead center in the screen, coin frozen in midair. It had been a bad night with Sheila and the kids. Now this.

Thwack!

He found this satisfying and did it again with the same minimal results.

Thwack!

High school and his '78 Trans-Am were the biggest things that had happened in his life. And of course, his wife and children, in about that order. Drinking beer, driving the back roads with the radio loud, then hanging out and playing video poker was heady medicine. He was the lone customer remaining in Arsenault's. No one had seen him hit the machine and he could hope for a quiet getaway. He had put off going home till he had broken even and now he had broken the machine. Three AM. Sheila would give him a frosting—no nookie, cold feet in bed and up with the kids at six.

Thwack!

Inside the gaudily painted cabinet an erasable, programmable, read-only memory chip considered the pounding a bit much. A tiny field collapsed, sending its stored contents winging away to chip heaven. On a screen framed by irreverently stenciled plywood, a Jack, deuce, nine and a pair of red tens blanked out leaving a field of low-resolution scan lines.

After a moment of furtive embarrassment, he thought what the hell and knelt to see if the plug had come loose from the wall. It had not.

"Shit." Gerry hit it again. Nothing. Not even the satisfying jingles and rattle of springs and linkages you got in the good old pinball machines. "I thought there was a special providence that looked out after these things," said Gerry, meaning the Provincial Lottery Corporation.

"There is," replied the machine. A ten dollar jackpot dropped into the takeout drawer.

Gerry looked around. The night clerk was fussing with a clipboard out at the gas pumps, getting totals. This must be some new program from the Lottery Corporation. He scooped up the money and reached for his jacket.

The voice continued. It was the duck. "Be fruitful and multiply—that's all you get. And don't whack the machine—the lottery corporation doesn't favor muscleheads abusing church property."

The picture flickered. The screen filled with the Corporation's usual come-on—Youth, Beauty and an annuity somewhere in an ill-defined future all for a dollar investment.

“You have heard the saying Lord love a duck?”

“Everybody has.”

“Well, I’m the duck. And you have been blessed.”

The screen flickered again and the duck was back, carrying two stone tablets. The Ten Commandments.

“I am but a humble messenger. Matthew 11:10—Behold, I send my messenger before your face. Well, this messenger is in your face.”

“That’s about John the Baptist,” said Gerry who had won prizes in Sunday school.

“So? You get Duck the Hegemonist. Play the game. You double parked?”

“Nope, I walked.”

“Too bad. I’m good with parking meters. The silent sentinels. They, too, are God’s messengers.”

Gerry considered parking meters. “No shit?”

“No shit. Think about it.”

As Gerald Bronson MacKechnie pondered absent effluvia, the duck paced the screen in a tight circle, gesturing with its cigar. “The silent sentinel doesn’t really care what time it is. It doesn’t care if you get towed or if the world goes to hell in a handbasket. Artifacts have a different schedule of priorities than living creatures.”

Thonk, thonk, a video game sound effect, thin and reedy, rattled the terminal’s tiny loudspeaker as the duck tapped on the edge of his screen. “The Provincial Lottery Corporation is waiting,” said the duck.

Gerry fished out a handful of Canadian two-dollar coins.

“Go on. Plug ‘em in.” The duck’s voice took on a stagy confidentiality. “For all you know this lottery terminal is a landing beacon for some ancient astronaut. Me. Now what do you think of that? Puts all your petty concerns in a new perspective, I’ll bet. And the parking meter is obviously the superior local life form. Look at you—full of pride, all alive and strutting around. I’ll just bet you think you’re the bee’s knees.”

Gerry looked more closely at the lottery terminal. It looked pretty usual. “Uh, you are an astronaut?”

“No. I am simply trying to educate you, broaden your worldview. That was only a hypothetical scenario. That is your first lesson—defer to your betters. Me. I am better than you. Remember this always.”

❑

Where Gerry MacKechnie went, Cosmos went, and preferably by car. But though Cosmos was a dog always after a good ride, foot travel was Gerry's modality these days. Gerry's pride and joy was a rusted out '78 Trans-Am with more tweed than rubber on its tires. And no plates. Trips were special, and even though Cosmos and Gerry went everywhere together, usually to Loup du Jour to play the Lotto, the anticipation made Cosmos' blood race with feral memories—the pack, the hunt.

There would be rustling of preparatory activity, lacing sneakers, unpegging of a windbreaker from the coat tree in the hall. With his blue nylon warmup jacket half on, one sleeve dangling, Gerry MacKechnie executed his quick and perfunctory circuit of things to be looked into before the trip to the store—that was the giveaway. Cosmos plomped his 102 yellow pounds of Golden Labrador immediately in front of the door and thumped his tail on the kitchen linoleum, blocking all exit.

Cosmos had no life other than being with Gerry—the nearness of Gerry, the wonderfulness of Gerry. Aside from the occasional squirrel or the wonderful smell from the pizza oven at Arsenault's, Cosmos never felt more fulfilled with the exception of when letting fly from his bottomless bladder.

But recently that had started to change. It was that red-haired woman that he saw in his sleep, he was sure. In his dreams he was a greyhound, rich with an ancient lineage, bounding joyously as she raced ahead of him astride a bicycle. Cosmos found this puzzling. Time was when lifting a leg was the happiest exercise of his heritage.

Gerry waved to Hal Overby at US Customs. Hal was barricaded in his guardhouse by a heap of torn up asphalt. The Americans were installing electronic gear to scan license plates. On the other side of the bridge the Canadians had had the technology in place for a decade. Gerry walked over to Canada and back to the United States almost every day and yet the grilling was the same. "How long have you been in Canada (or the USA)? Are you carrying firearms, tobacco, citrus or potatoes? Have you purchases to declare in excess of $200 (or fifty bucks in Canada)?"

A woman sat in the booth at Customs Canada.

"Hiya Gerry."

"Hiya Tammi."

"Just over for the day?"

"Just over to play the Lotto and video poker."

"Thought so. Any citrus?"

"Nope."

Tammi eyed him up and down. She checked her computer monitor from habit, but no car, no plate for the scanner. Gerry was a pedestrian. "No potatoes, drugs, explosives?"

"Nope."

"Have a nice day."

"Bye Tammi."

"Bye Gerry."

Cosmos wagged on through, no questions. Dogs were cool. As long as Cosmos wore his rabies tag he was an international citizen..

❑

The duck was waiting.

On the Canadian side of the bridge high yellow sodium lights on sixty-foot pylons ringed a set of gas pumps, casting few and deceptive shadows. Arsenault's One-Stop and Family Sundries was also the bus stop. To this it owed no small portion of its success. In an age of specialization, Arsenault was generalist, with gas pumps, a soda fountain, over-the-counter drugs and notions, and a wall of coin-operated gaming machines. Plus lottery tickets, tobacco and magazines, pizza and beer.

Gerry MacKechnie slunk into Arsenault's, beery and unshaven.

A pair of teen toughs played at one of the machines. Gerry moved to the far machine of the row of identical terminals. As Gerry slumped over, digging deep into his pockets for a dollar coin, the machine spoke.

"I'm back." The duck waved, looking like an animation cel, against a matte of interlocking tessellations of faded images of itself. Gerry had seen a movie once about a man sucked inside a machine. A portrait of his tormented soul decorated the escutcheon plate for all eternity. Or was it the cover of a book, a horror comic?

"Good God, where do they get that stuff?" It was the duck. "You watch too much TV, me □atr-buck."

"You're back. And it was a comic, not a TV show."

"Well, that's about it then, Gerry my old and rare—you can read. Go or stay—it all comes down to that in the end."

"I have another dollar here someplace..." He was being rejected even by the Provincial Lottery Corporation.

"Not you, you silly, compulsive boy, me—go or stay, that is. Not a red letter day in ego land. Divinitywise, if you catch my drift."

"Beg pardon. You are a duck."

"Save your money—the advice is free. The duck is a guise, an aspect. Sometimes I am a volcano, today I am a screensaver under the auspices of the Provincial Lottery Corporation. One of those days, dig? No wonder your wife regards you as an asshole past redemption. Please try to keep up with the action. You know, you might find things better with Sheila if you stopped plugging loonies into these damned machines and spent some attention on her. At home—you know, where the hearth is and appended bullshit. She has made her decision."

"Sheila? You mean Sheila is moving out?"

The duck faded to a tiny dot of luminescence. The machine dinged and a two-dollar payout bounced into the takeout drawer.

"But, Sheila," said Gerry.

"Sheila, Sheila," said the duck. "You are so wrapped up in your own miserable existence you have lost sight of the bigger picture—me and my perquisites. As far as Sheila is concerned, the matrimonial counseling was just advice. Gerry, you are a twit. Go home to Sheila and save your money. I have spoken."

"I wish." Gerry fumbled the few coins left in his pocket. "I can't go home until I at least break even. I wish. I wish."

"Three wishes? Bite me, gringo Americanski. You would be lucky to get back over with a sack of oranges. You have cable?"

"No. They cut it off last month."

"No MTV? My, you are deprived."

Gerry watched western movies, Sheila the Science Channel. No MTV. Sheila had named Cosmos "Cosmos" because of a severe crush on Carl Sagan. "Evolution is fact, not a theory..." Sheila said. "Carl Sagan said that. That explains you, Gerry." Their new puppy licked her hand. "He, at least, knows where he is," Sheila had said.

"Want to do a dog a favor?" asked the duck.

"Beg pardon?" Gerry started backing away. He had got his hopes up about that cable bill. One lucky jackpot. But the duck had dropped the cable subject.

"No, no, no," said the voice. "None of that, no easy getaway. Just do as I say. Pretend I'm Sheila. Right now your dog's gotta pee something fierce."

“You’re sure you’re a duck?”

“Ducks pee. Dogs pee. Everybody pees. Come on—make it snappy. There’s a pile of newspapers under the baggage counter. Here is a chance for you to demonstrate some delicacy. Spread them on the floor and turn your back.”

Cosmos stretched then vigorously shook his head. He headed toward the papers.

“Well?” said the duck.

“Well, what?” asked Gerry.

“Turn your back.”

“Uh, okay.”

Cosmos had long entertained a nagging doubt that there should be more to life than peeing on tires. The newspapers were strange and wonderful. Something had changed.

Gerald Bronson MacKechnie did not change. Sheila had named him but Gerry was Cosmos’ pole star. Everything was right because that’s the way things were. Gerry was here and all was well.

Behind Gerry the great yellow dog’s muted trickling went on for a considerable time.

“Gerry?”

“Uh, yes.” The duck knew his name, Gerry only now realized. Well, why not, it knew his wife’s name.

“Pick up the papers and put them in the trash, then we’ll play. Pick up some food.” The duck nodded to the luncheonette. “Cheeseburgers will be just fine. Wash your hands first. And be sure to come back, I don’t like waiting.”

Gerry pulled a quarter-folded ten dollar bill from an inside jacket pocket. He unfolded it with an apologetic expression.

“I get it. You’re broke,” said the duck. “No problem, just take a cruise by the poker on your way.”

Gerry MacKechnie did as he was told. He looked up at the video poker display. The duck was here, too, superimposed on a flashing screen of rampant royal flushes. It spoke.

“Here’s the funds.” The machine whirred and a winning chit for two hundred dollars was ejected. “For your trouble. And that cable bill. Here’s for the food.” Twenty shiny gold loonies slid into the tray. “Make that double cheeseburgers and hold the pickles.”

Gerry stayed a long time in the tiny lavatory holding his hands under the blow-dryer, turning them over and over. What the hell, he had nothing else on today.

"Took you long enough. I'm famished," said the duck when he returned with the food.

❑

Gerry and Cosmos were Arsenault regulars four times a month, at minimum, during the weekend benders when Gerry reviewed his career mobility and analyzed the slights and indignities of the week just past. The unsteady man and the huge yellow dog received only a cursory glance from the two teen-aged toughs, full packs of Pall Malls rolled up in their T-shirt sleeves.

This time there was no duck in evidence.

An attractive, bewildered-looking woman in an oversized Tour de France cycling jersey was pressing a sheaf of bus receipts on the night clerk.

"Lady, I'm sorry, but it just hasn't gotten here yet. Freight isn't like check-on baggage. They send it on when they have the room to spare." He was gestur-ing to the empty shelves behind him emblazoned with the Atlantic BusWays logo.

"But there was lots of room. I was the only passenger on that bus."

"That bus, miss. There are others and they are full. Your bag will probably come along tomorrow." Seeing Gerry, he reached down a pack of Players from the overhead cigarette stacks. "S'cuse me, got a customer." He favored the woman with a smile, a wall of friendly, attentive indifference.

The woman turned and gave Gerry the once-over. Gerry's hands and feet felt oversized and his neck started throbbing. He was very conscious of his con-dition and appearance and wished he had met this woman sober and by day-light. She was magnetically lovely and he spun a fantasy scenario of the two of them walking barefoot on the beach. Compelling, that was the word. He found her compelling.

Having lost the attention of the night cashier, the woman stood, hands at her sides, the pose of an early martyr. Was there none to hear her plea for old-fashioned straight talk and some common sense, please? Her eyes settled on Gerry MacKechnie. His nerves were shot. He was getting edgy. When had he last shaved? Huh, two days at least. He had his cigarettes, why all this hang-ing around? It was time to get over the bridge and back to the waiting bottle. Forget the duck, forget the broad, forget video poker, there would be other days.

Snatching a copy of Modern Fly Fishing from the magazine rack, he leafed furiously through it. Resentment flared against himself, a spreading stain of social wreckage at a spiritual and magnetic moment.

Cosmos also felt the call, but had none of his master's inhibitions. He walked up to the woman trailing his leash, and stuck his nose between her legs.

"Well hello there, big fella. You're not in the least bit shy are you?" Not intimidated by a dog almost her size, the woman knelt down and, putting her nose to Cosmos', shook his head by the ears.

Gerry hurried over, muttering apologies. "Sorry about that. He just likes people is all."

"Well, I like him, too. He's just a big love." She formed her words well. It was an articulation from away. An educated, big city girl. She rose and extended a hand. "Hi, I'm Maggie."

The simple, everyday gesture caught Gerry off balance. He was prepared for a quick getaway, but in that instant it was all over. Gerry was awash on the shoals of beauty, his compass demagnetized. Modern Fly Fishing was twisted into a paper party favor.

Her hand hung between them. She pressed it forward, coming closer. There would be no easy retreat for Gerry MacKechnie. "Are you a fisherman? I'm keen on bicycle racing, myself." She had noticed the crumpled magazine in his hands.

"Oh, me? No." There was a pause. Cosmos thumped the floor, approving. Her eyes were dark and clear, friendly without a trace of amusement at catching him out. His embarrassment flushed and faded. "Lose your baggage?"

"No, my baggage is fine, or so the man here assures me. It's just not here yet."

The hand was still extended. Gerry dropped Modern Fly Fishing and took it. "Welcome to Loup du Jour, New Brunswick, Canada. Gerry MacKechnie."

"Well, Mister MacKechnie, it's simply grand to make your acquaintance. And besides, my arm was getting tired. I'm... actually, I don't seem to know who I am. Maggie is probably not my real name. I hope that doesn't bother you. It should bother me, but it doesn't. My ticket says I got on in Montreal, but I don't remember a thing."

Gerry chilled. "Amnesia, huh?" She was too good to be true. "There's a lot of that going around."

"A pretty girl can always find some nice man to look after her. You are a nice man. I trust you."

"Come on, Gerry, the broad is hot to trot. Make your move." The voice came from a lottery terminal behind Gerry and the woman. Gerald Bronson MacKechnie turned to confront the duck.

"You lust wistfully, MacKechnie. It is poor clay they give me to work with."

"I beg your pardon?"

"You are hoping she's an adventuress out on a big money scam and posing as an amnesia victim? This would add some meaning to your pathetic life? She's a figment. You're hung over. Forget it. This is a bus stop—not a likely location. A classy babe like her should be on a cruise ship or at an international air terminal. And you? Cut me some slack, please."

The duck stared out from the screen. "Check the chick," said the duck.

The woman was gone.

"Whaddid I tell you?" The duck was triumphant. "She never was there."

"Who was that woman? Uh, Maggie?"

"Not her real name. You are the punch line of a parable, young Gerry. She is a myth. Just a glimpse, a peek of better things—dispensation for your delicacy in the matter of your dog having to pee."

"Because I turned my back?"

"We all enjoy our private moments. The goddess has a weakness for dogs. She races greyhounds regularly. And she wins."

"But the woman?"

"A piece of street theater and illustrative of what you may yet make of yourself, Gerry, my boy. She is Morgana le Fay, on loan from the International Cycling Union. Just think—the Morgaine, Queen Mab of Avalon, patroness of grand tour bicycle racing. She was only just passing the border, back from the Giro d'Italia. I now owe her one—and you therefore owe me. Lay off the booze and the gambling and Sheila will be Queen Mab for you."

"Sheila will be a goddess?"

"The Morgana has discovered a soft spot for you. Unfortunately you have bartered your soul to the Provincial Lottery Corporation for chump change so any favors I can pass along will be understandably small."

"Uhn. I'd like to go far. To travel. Whatever."

"Simple enough. You have punched all my buttons and the Lotto Corporation owes you one."

"One what?"

"One miracle."

"Why?"

"Because you are kind to your dog. The dog loves you, which is more than I would be inclined to do. The dog trusts you. Of all creatures of creation, you at least have never let him down. You will go far." Quack, quack, quack, the duck did a Groucho right off the screen.

A cascade of coins fell into the trough. "But for you this night there will be a plenary indulgence. Take a cab."

❑

When Gerry arrived home he found no bus ticket, no airline ticket plus brochure for enchanted islands with bare-bosomed tawny wenches, no Queen Mab. Just the '78 Firebird Trans-Am. With four new tires, wide metrics—the P225/sixty-fifteens—an inspection sticker and fresh, shiny license plates.

Miracles are where you find them, figured Gerry. He had told the duck that he would like to travel, after all.

That night it was dinner out at McDonald's and the late show at the Willipaq Cinema for Sheila, Gerry and the kids. Cosmos opted for the double cheeseburgers and a side of fries.

In a slightly different version, *A Special Providence*
was first published in the May 2003 issue of *Quantum Muse*
[www.quantummuse.com]

E Pluribus Human

Bingbing. The door chime. "Yes, yes, yes..."

Grenadine McKenzie peeled back a cucumber eye wrap, squinted and placed her eye to the peephole. A messenger application stood outside.

"You can call me Dixie." The hologenic girl pouted becomingly and curtseyed, arms outstretched. "Your HappyGram girl." She flickered and held out a packet festooned with fluffy florets of pink and blue. "Somebody is thinking of you," said Dixie. The Personal Services application flushed with a palette of subdued pastels

"Dixie. Because that is your name," said Grenadine. A bead of syrupy lemon-whiskey residue clung to the rim of a stemmed flute that dangled at her fingertips. "Unusual that you should have one at all—a name, I mean. What is your system name? Uh, what they called you. Your programmers?" The lines of her mouth softened. The warm tinglies from the morning's mood elevators had crept up Grenadine's spine to rendezvous with the whiskey sour in a place behind her eyes. *Ahh, lift-off.* She smiled. The HappyGram girl smiled back.

"They *named* me Ariel. I thought you might like something more straight-up. Girl-to-girl? I'm new. You are my first customer," said Dixie/Ariel.

A nymphet, thought Grenadine, and impudent for an application. "Ariel. That is a lovely name, like a name from the Romances. Dixie is, well... trashy."

The HappyGram girl was not offended. Dixie was watching the lemony droplet quiver, fascinated. "Pretty, you know?"

"*What*?"

"Your dribble—the play of the green and the light." The last droplet of the day's first whiskey sour plummeted to the tufted wool shag of the hall carpet. "Oops!" Dixie held dainty fingers over her face in a gesture of mock horror. The messenger application waited hopefully for a second droplet. None was forthcoming. She wriggled enticingly as she bent to examine the tiny puddle.

"Housekeeping will get it," said Grenadine. This was keeping her from today's streaming. Rights of Spring was her personalized Romance. She stared intently at her nose.

"Nice nose," said Dixie/Ariel.

"It's a nose. *People* have noses. And I am speaking with an application as though it was a human being."

After a pause Dixie/Ariel piped up, "It takes all kinds to make a world, different strokes, et cetera. E pluribus human, y' know..."

"E pluribus... *what?*" Grenadine squinted.

"Human, e pluribus *human.*" The girl squinted back at her. "That hormonal? You should get yourself in for a fix."

"I am at least human."

"Lucky *you,*" said Dixie. Giving her too-perfect breasts a jiggle, she winked and thrust the packet forward. "Well... open it and find out. Could be you have a secret admirer."

"Go away," said Grenadine.

"My aren't we cranky today. May I inquire with what part of my script you are having difficulties?"

"Pluribus," said Grenadine McKenzie, "E pluribus human..." Grenadine teetered. "Forget it. Go away."

Dixie disappeared. The gaily wrapped HappyGram remained, floating eighteen inches from Grenadine's nose. Shaking back the embroidered drapery of a caftan sleeve, Grenadine reached out a finger to caress the HappyGram.

"YO, BABE!" a man's voice blared at her, "SURPRISE, YOU'RE PREGNANT."

The warm tinglies made an abrupt U-turn. "*Softly!*" The voice was familiar—George? Grenadine looked quickly up and down the hallway; there were no intruder alarms. Yet. A nascent migraine demanded to be noticed. A miniature throb of pain had settled behind her eyes. "Who are you?"

"They always ask if it's really me. And this is *you* asking? You are our most devoted viewer. Out of millions—hundreds of millions, according to Personal Services. It's me, Lance Davenport. And I just knocked you up. Isn't that *totally* mondo boffo? It's a promotional thing, tres cool. Check it out at Century, Ebersol Lystrander."

A craggy male face bloomed before her. The face was a hero's face, Lance Davenport from Rights of Spring. There was an odor of patchouli. "George, that *is* you?" Divorced five years and this would be his idea of a joke.

"Sorry, babe. Can't hear you. This is a one-way. You'll have to contact the office to negotiate any upstream traffic. For an answer? If you're asking if I'm really, really Lance Davenport, you'll just have to trust me." The face digitized, fell apart, then reassembled itself. A line of empty pixels ran across a tanned chin. One eye twitched. "Century, Ebersol—remember? They've got your name." The sides of the message fell away and became transparent.

Pink and blue ribbons spiraled to the floor where they dissipated. "Gotta go. Kissy-kissy."

Kissy-kissy indeed. Not what Lance Davenport would say. Not what a lover, an adventurer, would say. That meant that it probably *was* George. They had lived together, frequently naked at close quarters, for one week—seven days, twelve hours and 36 minutes, by Grenadine's count. Cohabitation was nothing like the featureless hygiene of the sex parlor where they had met. They had felt violated. They found one another repugnant.

A smear of squirming images swam across the wall as Grenadine plugged into the Personal Services directory. Her spectacles, she wished she could remember where she had left them. Stainless steel rims glinted at her from under a sofa. She tripped backwards over a polymer tabouret that pulsed with a rainbow radiance—mood furniture, the latest trend from Personal Services Personal Products boutique. "Shit!" She gave the tabouret a kick that sent it spinning away. Everyone in the Romances was wearing spectacles this year—very mode nouvelle. Grenadine returned to the terminal where a Personal Services advertising banner fluttered delicately in its own private breeze. The tabouret stopped its pulsing; the sofa glowed cerise with a black stripe.

"Century, Ebersol Lystrander. Please." The corporate site featured cooing moms with their cyber-babies.

Lance Davenport? George, even? It could be worth investigating. What the hell, thought Grenadine. Why not? The migraine symptoms retreated with the application of a mild tranquillizer.

❑

"Yes?" The sales representative smiled a tight-lipped smile of tentative welcome. Highlights shone from translucent depths of perfect skin, perfect teeth—a stunning effect. The virtual pregnancy pavilion was on the mezzanine, up an escalator, past supporting columns topped off by succulently-bosomed caryatids. Pearlescent rainbows rippled through the letters of *Century, Ebersol Lystrander Wants to Have Your Baby* as they hung poised over a pair of heavy quartz doors that reflected Grenadine's approach in a golden microfinish.

"Your name, please?"

"I don't..."

"You don't have an appointment? Nothing to bother." The woman smiled an understanding, woman-to-woman smile. We are all girls together here, said the smile. Grenadine craned her neck, looking for a hidden light source focused to emphasize the woman's creamy shoulders.

"Name?" The woman smiled again and Grenadine felt blessed.

"McKenzie. Grenadine McKenzie."

"Uh-*huh.*" The woman tapped out a query on a screen embedded in her desktop. "Ah-*hah.*" Grenadine took this to mean the HappyGram was not some practical joke. She stared; the woman shone with an inner light that was, well... *inner.*

The woman noticed. "Yes, dear, it's all me. Little me. I've had the Makeover." The sales representative articulated a throaty, womanly, sympathetic laugh; they were to be close friends. "The Makeover comes with the pregnancy package."

"I have a concern."

"The cost, of course. Lance Davenport is footing the bill. Rights of Spring, actually. My name is Michelle, by the bye." Michelle handed a blinking tablette across her desk. "A permission disclaimer, is all."

"Lance. Lance *Davenport*? But..."

"You, of all Rights of Spring's 586 million viewers, registered consistently elevated respiration accompanied by vasoconstriction and an over the top increase in hormone levels and lubricity. No mean feat. *Lots* of girls are crazy for him. Simply fabulous."

"Me? Out of 586 *million*?"

"Yes, little you. Don't spend too much time thinking about it, dear. Simply *everyone* does virtual pregnancy and we've never, *ever* had a complaint. Satisfaction guaranteed. You know how *they* are," she said, meaning Personal Services.

"I'll think it over."

"No problem. We'll be here."

❑

Grenadine sat alone at home, miserable. The woman—Michelle?—had to be the same age as she, older even.

She returned to Century, Ebersol in the afternoon. Michelle was still gorgeous.

"There are treatments..."

"There is the Makeover. The Makeover is the Makeover. It is not a *treatment*, as you say. It is an *enhancement*. The producers are paying the bill, OK? Rights of Spring? Just sign the form."

"Are you..?"

"Enhanced? Definitely. Like it?"

Grenadine liked it.

"No injections, no pills, a teensy-weensy implant that stimulates your body's natural resources. A pacemaker for health and beauty. Good for a year. Then you come back. We'll let you know when it's time. Your body does it all—naturally."

"I understand the first trimester..."

"Mister Century thought how nice it would be to remove all qualms about any, well... embarrassment potential from the equation of motherhood. You get it all—telescoped, compressed into one easy gestation. And you can do it at home, alone. You enjoy your child from conception, through all those wild and breathtaking teenage years, then a career—medicine, perhaps. What woman has not daydreamed of saying, My son, the doctor?"

"The first trimester will be..."

"Rugged."

"Really?" The woman's reply startled her.

"No, not really," a light, airy laugh. The woman reached to retrieve the tablette with Grenadine's signature. She made an entry. "Just checking your appropriateness as a candidate for maternity."

"Uh, about the morning sickness? I'm a little hazy about..."

"You will be a wonderful mom," said Michelle.

❑

Bingbing. The door chime. "Yes, yes, yes..." It was the Personal Services application with the harlequin tights. Grenadine opened the door.

"Hi again," chirped the hologenic girl, animated and vivacious.

"Dixie."

"Yep."

"Another one," said Grenadine McKenzie as she held out her hand.

"Nope. Same as last time; I'm just not new any more. Hey, that Lance Davenport is really, really hot for you," said the PSA.

"Cut the crap and hand it over."

“Hand over... Oh! You thought I had a message for you. That’s it,” said Dixie.

“That’s what?” asked Grenadine.

“The message, silly: that Lance is really, really warm, hot, whatever—something—for you and, um...” She reached deep into her cleavage, “I’ve got a scroll...” From between tiny breasts she drew a cylindrical package bigger than herself. The scroll was four feet long at least and appeared to have the sturdy heft of reality. The PSA drew, and drew and drew. Her costume did not wrinkle or tear in the slightest. A neat stunt, thought Grenadine McKenzie. But then, she wouldn’t wrinkle.

“Real parchment. Sheepskin, see?” said the Personal Services app.

“Read it.”

“My, aren’t we irritable today. Ahem. ‘Century, Ebersol Lystrander, the sponsor of Rights of Spring, reports that you are opting to bring the child, our child, to term. This is an accelerated pregnancy; there may be issues. Best wishes, Lance.’ That’s all.”

“Issues.”

“Oops, sorry: time’s up,” said Dixie. “I am only one-way. No replies. Bye now.”

Grenadine suspected she was being patronized by a string of computer code in too-tight tights.

❑

Grenadine returned past the bronze and gold revolving doors and succulently-bosomed caryatids to Century, Ebersol Lystrander.

“I understand there may be, uh... *issues*. Century, Ebersol *and* Lystrander. Which one will actually carry...?

“Oh, that is a common misconception...” The elegant Michelle laughed, elegantly. She had caught herself making what might be construed as a joke and flushed rose-pink under her deep, marvelous, translucent tan. “Many of our new mothers *are* curious. Our founder, Mr. Century, actually *did* carry many full-term pregnancies. In person, supervising the database. But it consumed so much of his time. You surely understand?”

“Of course. I may choose then? Which one..? I’d like to meet him first.”

“Ahhh... a traditionalist, the get acquainted cruise. We no longer offer that option. The founders thought...”

“That meeting the mothers of their children ate up too much of their time.”

"Of course if you don't want it..."

"I want it," said Grenadine McKenzie.

The first trimester was over, from conception to a fully-formed fetus, in less than a week. Grenadine was called back to the Pregnancy Pavilion for a series of simulated ultrasound views. The virtual baby was a virtual blob—an elongated oversized head with recognizable limbs surrounded by a coiling umbilicus. It could have been anybody's baby, anywhere. "Doesn't he look just like his father," cooed Michelle.

❑

Grenadine dialed a cup of green tea and sank down into deep upholstery before the virtual display that covered one wall. The herbal aromas confused the sofa: it flashed a sputtering of spring greens, then went transparent. It was the second trimester. At every audience, as Century, Ebersol Lystrander called the mother-child bonding visits, David had been older... lately with a distinguished hint of salt-and-pepper at his temples.

"David?" After a scarcely noticeable processing lag, her son assembled himself.

"Some tennis?" David was swinging a racquet. Last week he had been absorbed with his model airplanes. He wore tennis whites and entered through a set of those floor-to-ceiling French doors from Rights of Spring.

"My, aren't we manly today."

"Yes, mother. I am thirty-five after all. We are the same age now." David leaned against a rococo doorway framed by a riot of gilded cherubs. Behind him in gelatiny focus were a deer park and a terrace with topiary animals in pots.

"David."

"Mother?"

"Could you call me by my name? Grenadine?"

"*Grenadine*. I shall call you Grenadine." A subroutine hiccoughed into an auxiliary logic loop. "Century, Ebersol Lystrander has found that, even—no, particularly—in virtual birth, a bonding is desirable," said David. "*Very desirable*. The mu-opioid receptors in the brains of our mothers are generally quite strong in the pleasure department. 'E pluribus human,' as we say at Century, Ebersol. Voilà—we bond. Isn't that nice?" David looked up; it was Grenadine's turn.

“We are, joined...” Grenadine felt the steamy warmth of the tea between her cupped hands. The mood sofa leapt with a palette of roseate sunset purples before settling into a muted taupe.

“In love. Just like a mom and her new baby.”

Before what would have been her third trimester, David stopped coming.

❑

Michelle was wearing a see-through crepe du chine frock slathered with lilacs. “If you’ll pardon me for mentioning it, dear, you look *edgy*,” she said with honeyed concern. “Shall I schedule you for a tweaking?”

“David.”

“David? Oh, *David*.” Michelle clucked understandingly. “As I recall you measured high in attachment parameters. Ah, the mother-child relationship: so very classical: a baby, a small human, pops out and you are a Mom.”

“David has stopped coming to me.”

“Not to worry—there is a statistically insignificant likelihood that we would come up with an inappropriate pairing.” Michelle projected empathy. “Believe me; it’s hormonal.” She tapped an entry into her tablette. “*There*.”

“Where?”

“He’ll be back. We’ll tweak the database—perhaps a soupçon of Lance Davenport.” Michelle gave her a knowing wink. “We join our mothers’ pleasure senses in a feedback loop with the baby’s character engine.” The unfastened V of her crêpe du chine frock spilled open to expose an even allover golden skin tone. “And you can always cancel at any time.”

❑

Lance Davenport reached for a cigarette, down to the floor where an open pack lay between two tumbled champagne flutes. “Did you realize...”

Grenadine McKenzie lay exhausted. After their lovemaking they were alone together with nothing to say. A hand caressed her thigh, exploring. She tried to catch the hand, stroke it, caress it, direct it to her breasts. It was her hand. Leftover bits and pieces of David tingled along her cerebral cortex, causing her toes to twitch.

“Ah, got it.” Lance thumbed the tip of a retrieved cigarette to an intense, glowing ember. “Did you realize... uh, pardon me.” Lance prefatorily guided a post-coital bubble of phlegm away from his larynx. He coughed.

Grenadine gave herself a playful squeeze. “Yes?” Anything to fill the silence.

"...that the New World has no resident hedgehogs. They are all imported. Porcupines—imported like fine wines. Imagine that. And do you know how porcupines make love?"

"Wha...?" She had heard the same joke every time before. Grenadine decided to have Personal Services check into her connection protocols.

"...VERY carefully," Lance Davenport laughed—silken, smooth.

Her implant noted a fluctuation in Alpha rhythms and the terminal popped off.

"*Porcupines*. Hilarious." Lance digitized into random pixels.

The terminal rebooted and the PS shopping banner fluttered, waiting. Grenadine smelled tobacco and tasted her fingers. "David?" She corrected herself, "I mean, Lance?"

"I am here, mother. Mother?"

"David."

"Smoking is bad for you."

❑

Dixie the Personal Services application was at her door. Grenadine held the door open a crack and peered warily through. "Not now. Go away. No messages."

"I beg your pardon?" asked Dixie.

"David should, not you. Be here, that is. Now go away. Wait. Do you know...?"

"That this is a follow-up call? Sure do. All part of the service," said the harlequin girl.

"No. No. I have seen him—David. We have been... together. And he doesn't look *any*thing like Lance Davenport. Or George. There is something wrong."

"Sorry, limited connectivity and that query is off-script."

"David..." said Grenadine.

"What?" asked the PSA.

"I have always liked the name David. That is all."

"Lucky you. And don't forget Personal Services has a full line of personal products and deep, deep discount prices." Dixie bowed in the direction of Grenadine's terminal. The terminal popped on. The Personal Services advertising banner shimmered discreetly. "Being what I am, I am inclined to the technical."

"Let's go shopping," said the PS banner.

"Here's your follow-up message: 'Century, Ebersol Lystrander regrets it has had to refuse you further audiences with your child. He is dead. Naturally, peacefully.'" The hologenic girl appeared to consult with someone off-camera, outside her field of focus. "In his sleep, I believe."

Grenadine stared vacantly at a place a few inches from her eyes, waiting for words of comfort, anything.

"Standalone apps are expected to be self-correcting," Dixie went on after a programmed pause. "If I have displeased you, if you are happy or unhappy, in any way, with my performance, there is a number."

A yellow text enclosure expanded across the girl's forehead: "How'm I Doing? Let Me Know." Coordinates flashed followed by a series of numbers.

❑

Grenadine rode the escalator to Century, Ebersol's mezzanine, past the golden caryatids atop their columns. The sales representative almost smiled as she looked up. Her business frock, gladiolas today, fell open, an invitation to reflect upon her perfect body.

"Boys..." said Grenadine. She was haggard and hollow-eyed.

Michelle's mouth tightened; this must be a common question.

"The baby was always a *he*, a *him*. You always said *he*."

"Because women are mothers, men are the children. It is easier for a woman to watch the ageing and death of a son than a daughter: Jung, Freud... somebody. Mr. Century believed this strongly."

"David. Where is he?"

"Oh, David *is* dead. We turned him off. Consider the alternative: nine months from a fertilized ovum to a viable fetus—Nature's way. This is not progress. We are not cave women."

"But the baby dies."

"The baby never lived, dear girl. And you can call me Michelle." She had already introduced herself, thought Grenadine—Michelle had forgotten her. "And ah... *David's* character traits are back in the database to be available for our next mom."

"David, *my* David."

Michelle nattered on, glistening-fresh. "Chin up: self-doubt, guilt, inadequacy could have only led to mental distress for you and your offspring, poor little innocent thing. Century, Ebersol has carried you safely to term."

"My David. You killed him."

"Well, *yes*. In the full flower of his manhood. Fulfilled. He is done with and we turned him off while you, *you...*" she leaned forward confidentially "...have only begun. You will have had the Makeover, plus yearly booster visits for the rest of a long, long, young and, and..." Michelle paused as though searching for the right word for a transcendent experience. "...a fully *realized* life."

"We were... *together*."

"Of course you were, dear. Some mothers find it hard to let go. So in the third trimester we try to get our moms less involved. Most only get to watch. There is a risk of *attachment*. You surely understand. We have the mother's interests at heart here at Century, Ebersol..."

"I have a contract."

"Read what you sign, dear. There is a self-protection override. Century, Ebersol Lystrander has fulfilled its contractual obligation and carried your baby to term: a peaceful natural death which you might have found disturbing. We saved you this."

Grenadine snuffled. "I am so sorry." Tears were running down her chin making small plash, plash sounds on the floor.

"The grieving, this will pass." Michelle put a comforting arm about Grenadine's shoulders. "It is only natural. Like David's death."

"I am ruining your carpet," said Grenadine. She snuffled again and began to hiccough.

"Perhaps a hormone booster," offered Michelle.

"Perhaps," Grenadine hiccoughed through her tears. A bubble of snot burst from her nose and an airborne droplet settled on Michelle's sculpted clavicle where it glistened, beckoning.

E Pluribus Human was first published in the Summer 2007 issue of *Coyote Wild*—an online quarterly of speculative fiction and poetry.

Dead Man in the Yard

There was a dead man in the yard this morning. I checked in my wallet for my latest picture of the front yard. I have a collection of yard pictures that goes back for years but I usually carry only one photo at a time. No, he was a new arrival. I called Sheila. Sheila is my ex-wife.

"Hon, I think there is a dead man in the yard."

"How do you know he's dead?" she asked, not "Who is it? Did you kill him?" Nothing like that. Sheila never went for the obvious: Old Pierce Willoughby passed out drunk on the way home from an evening at the Legion hall over on Fairview would have been so usual that she figured I wouldn't have taken the trouble to call her.

"Uh, hold on, will you?" I set the phone down on the hall table and rummaged in a drawer for the mirror I kept there. The mirror had fallen out of Sheila's compact in 1973; it was October and our first anniversary. I had promised to glue it back in place but never got around to it. I went out into the yard and knelt by the dead man. The dead man was of average height, or would have been if he had not been lying down, and dressed in that elegantly understated way favored by bankers and funeral directors. He had closely trimmed gray hair and a military-style moustache, also gray. I held Sheila's pocket mirror under the dead man's nostrils. I had seen Phillip Marlowe do this in a film once, it is a sure test for death. The mirror did not mist over.

I went back to the phone. "Nope, he's dead, alright."

"Did you even give him a poke? No. Honestly, Harry Brackenfern, I am so glad we didn't have any children." I, too, was glad we hadn't had any children. They would have been out of college and established in their own lives by now. They probably wouldn't visit or write.

"Did you even *introduce* yourself; ask how he came to be lying in the yard? No—you just assumed that he was dead." Sheila has a good head on her shoulders, always gets right to the heart of a problem. We divorced last year after a twenty-seven years' separation. The judge made a joke at our final hearing, Sheila's and mine, finalizing our divorce: "Separated twenty-seven years. You're sure you two want to go through with this?" There had been a ripple of subdued laughter from the others in the court, all awaiting their divorces. Or dispositions on parking fines, parole violation, jailbreak, rape, murder, whatever.

"Go back there and introduce yourself; we teach by modeling." Sheila meant role-modeling; she teaches kindergarten at the James A. Garfield School. She took a summer workshop on this very subject.

I went back to the corpse in the yard.

"How do you do? I'm Harry Brackenfern and this is my house you have died in front of. What is your name?" No answer. I returned to the phone; Sheila had hung up. I would call her back tomorrow.

My ex-wife and I had not spoken face-to-face for over twenty years. I should have missed Sheila, not having her around the house and all, but our daily calls brought me a kind of release; a duty had been satisfied. Sheila must have felt the same way; she always answered. I kept busy with repairs and improvements—the little things which if not done, build up into big problems later on: clearing the eaves, getting the leaves raked and piled, having the garbage securely bagged.

Emma, the kid next door, Old Pierce Willoughby's granddaughter, helped me stuff the body in a hall closet to get it out of the yard; there was always talk among the neighbors to consider. Things like property values and curb appeal.

❑

"Callous and obdurate," Sheila had said. This was when I proposed to her.

"I'll take obdurate for five points." I thought it was a game we were about to play, like Jeopardy or Hollywood Squares.

"That's from The Mikado. Gilbert and Sullivan, Harry." Sheila had had a thorough grounding in the arts at college. "You are a decent man but I just can't get through to you." She sang: "If you remain callous and obdurate, I shall perish as he did, and you will know why. Though I probably shall not exclaim as I die 'Oh, willow, titwillow, titwillow.'"

"It's a song, then."

"It's a song." Sheila was a free spirit; I knew this because she had told me. We were students at the community college and had gone out a few times. When I asked her to marry me I knew she viewed me as an accommodation to security over the arts. I would be dependable and a good provider. "It's a song about a little bird who dies starved for love. Yes, I'll marry you, Harry." At the time she still entertained hopes for a career on the stage; she sang whenever her free spirit moved her. I am not a singer.

Through first years of our uneventful and, I supposed, happy marriage, Sheila kept her Samsonite suitcase packed and at the ready in the front hall closet. "In case. Just in case," she would say. I supposed her to be waiting for a call from some theatrical producer. The suitcase was one of those brown overnighters—I called it brown; Sheila said taupe—its outside printed in a pattern to simulate woven rattan. Saturday mornings, and regular as clockwork, she would carry her suitcase up the stairs to our bedroom and flip it open on the bed to sort, inventory and refold her personal things. She carefully shook out the wrinkles and replaced the week-old lingerie with a freshly laundered set. Things tended to get musty in storage she explained.

One morning the suitcase was gone, just like that. After two years Sheila had moved out. I was happy for her in that she would have clean underwear and a career. Sheila however did not leave town after all; she continued teaching kindergarten at the James A. Garfield School just as before. We stayed close as I called her every day for 27 years. I began taking my yard pictures to show that I was keeping up the property in case she asked.

After Sheila left, Emma, Old Pierce Willoughby's granddaughter, used to help me out around the house: lending a hand with the window boxes and the perennial beds, holding the ladder while I scooped last year's leaves out of the eaves. But as she grew into young womanhood her visits became unpredictable. She was now sixteen and had a boyfriend. I mentioned this to Sheila.

There was a long, still moment on the phone as Sheila considered her answer. "She is a young woman, Harry. She wants to try her wings. And the neighbors—a young girl all the time with a 56-year-old man. How does *that* look?"

❑

I was going out for the mail when the dead man spoke his first words, "Christ, it's dark in here." The words were understandably muffled as he was in the front hall closet, the same closet Sheila used to keep her suitcase in when it wasn't Saturday. I had to put my ear up against the door and shout to be heard. Seems his name was Prentiss Oliver and he wanted an ice cream. I told him I didn't have any. "Cholesterol," I yelled. "But then that wouldn't matter to you, being dead and all."

The dead man opened the closet door a crack and peered out at me. "You seem to know a whole lot about me for a total stranger."

"The camera doesn't lie." I pulled out my wallet with its accordion-fold assortment of yard pictures. The latest one, the last one, had a dead man in the foreground. I had taken that picture out-of-doors instead of through the picture window as usual.

"That's me. Lying there."

"Yep. And dead as a planked haddock."

“Good likeness.”

One evening I invited him out of the closet to join me in front of the television. Prentiss Oliver, the dead man, never asked me why I took pictures of my front yard. “Why don’t you ever ask?” I asked.

“About the pictures in your wallet?”

“Yes.”

“None of my business, is it?” The dead man held me by both shoulders and looked me in the eyes. His eyes were gray, I noticed, like his hair and moustache. “What if I told you that I was a ‘66 Chevy Impala? How’s ‘bout them apples, Harry Brackenfern?”

“You are a dead man.” Prentiss Oliver was wearing an expensive suit, I noticed.

“Consider also that I might be an allegorical figure set to confound all who come my way. One of those ancient avatars of a lost civilization, the Hittites and Sumerians, f’rinstance: a great, giant horrific challenging bull, full with the blood of kings.” At close range his breath smelled of peppermints. “It may not be outside the sphere of reasonable supposition that I have been sent to be a guardian at the gates of...” Here he pulled a scrap of paper from his breast pocket. “28 Samoset Avenue.”

“You are a dead man and you were lying in my front yard.”

“The front yard of 28 Samoset Avenue. And you don’t have any ice cream. You have a telephone. I don’t get a telephone?”

“If you thought one was necessary. Who would call you?”

“Sheila, maybe? And you can forget about the ancient allegory thing. OK with you if I hang out a while?” “Well...” I thought about curb appeal and the neighbors. I didn’t think to ask him how he knew my ex-wife’s name. Prentiss Oliver chose to interpret my silence as an invitation.

Days grew to be weeks and I got used to having him around. But the dead man cast a pall over our evenings together. These moody sulks of his were aimed at me, I knew. All about me having no ice cream. There was this one time when were watching TV and I had set a bowl of Oreo cookies between us. The dead man hardly touched the Oreos. We sat in silence through Jeopardy and Law and Order. I must have fallen asleep. When I awoke during the Late-Late-Show, Prentiss Oliver was back in the hall closet. And the next morning he was out front again, lying in the yard. I took that day’s yard picture, then went to try to cheer him up. He seemed cheerful enough

"Ahh," said the dead man, thumping the ground at his side. "6000 years and still flat. How's that for substance and dependability?" I guessed he was talking about the Earth.

"The Earth is round," I said.

The dead man raised an eyebrow. "Harry, Harry, Harry. Have you never been canoeing on an upland lake and, stopping to rest your weary arms, laid your head on a thwart to peer along the waterline? Qui bono, op. cit., ipso facto, Harry, QED. Flat as the belly of a virgin hooker, the Earth. Water tells no lies. And I have just now, before your very eyes, demonstrated its flatness by empirical observation." I had never been canoeing. I would have felt foolish in the big orange flotation devices they tie to non-swimmers. I do not swim.

"The 6000 years you will have to take my word for," said the dead man. Here he again thumped my front yard. "The Earth was created October 26, 4004 BC, at 9:00 am. This is an established fact; you Darwinians make of it what you will."

"The Earth is round," I repeated.

"A litany of your 'science.' You are parroting the twaddle they pour into innocent young minds."

"My wife is an elementary teacher," I said.

"Sheila," said Prentiss Oliver. "And the 6000 years is give or take a thousand, you understand. Arithmetic gets slippery when you're dead." He stood and dusted himself off. The dead man raised a conspiratorial eyebrow and spoke in hushed, urgent tones. "For all you know, I might be that '66 Chevy Impala after all. Classic car'd look mighty good parked out front."

"Believe, me, you are a dead man in a Gucci suit. Look at the picture."

He certainly looked dead, he acknowledged. "Sheila. Sheila would have appreciated a Chevy Impala, Harry. But I was so much older than she was. I watched and waited."

"You had a crush on my wife." I was divorced and he was dead. There was no cause to be disagreeable.

"You and Sheila. Ever get naked and throw muffins?"

"I beg your pardon?"

"Nothing kinky. You ever just get down and get loose together?"

I told him I was not a spontaneous person.

"Well, I am dead and not expected to be spontaneous. That pretty well leaves the ball in your court, doesn't it, Harry old bean?" The afterlife notwithstanding, Prentiss Oliver got right to the point. He went back into his closet. I went next door to borrow Emma, Old Pierce Willoughby's granddaughter. I asked her to bring along her boom box. After twenty minutes of teen hits at full volume, the dead man came out.

"The ice cream, then we'll talk," said the dead man.

I invited Emma and him to the Polar Treat for soft serve.

"Ambrosial, Best I've ever had," said the corpse. I asked if he had had it before. "No," he replied. "Sorry, but I'm not all that mobile as you can see. I have been dead lately. Before that in one of those retirement villas over on Longacre. Too far from the Polar Treat to make it even in my motorized scooter."

With the company of Emma and the dead man the days filled themselves pleasantly with TV and ice cream. I still called Sheila but now got her answering machine. "Hi, Hon. Harry," I said, feeling foolish—of course it was me. After that first time, I hung up without leaving any message. If she had made that connection with a theatrical impresario, I didn't want her to return from a tour to endless repetitions of me saying hello. Formerly this would have made me apprehensive lest something had happened to her—an automobile crash, the flu, a falling airplane or a church steeple dropped by careless riggers.

"Have you called your ex-wife today?" the dead man asked. It had slipped my mind.

I felt a guilty twinge. "Sheila is a free spirit," I said.

"Call again. If there's no answer better check the obits."

Sure enough, I read about her death in the newspaper. I do not recall, in all my adult life—or my life as a child for that matter—ever shedding a tear. At the news of Sheila's death I wept disconsolately. Emma and the dead man put their arms around me for a group hug and I felt better. The dead man handed me a Kleenex, "Blow." I blew.

I asked Prentiss Oliver if he had had any word from Sheila, her being dead and all, just like him.

After Sheila's death Emma joined us regularly for ice cream at the Polar Treat. She seemed to enjoy Prentiss Oliver's company. "Hiya, Mr. Oliver. Mr. Brackenfern."

"Hiya, Emma," I said.

"Your late ex-wife found you a great disappointment, Harry," said Prentiss Oliver. Emma nodded agreement as she dug into her cone.

❑

One morning as I was making my poached egg, Prentiss Oliver said, "Elizabeth Taylor." This was after Sheila died and we had stayed up late watching Butterfield 8. "What's your opinion?"

"Opinion. About what?" My own impressions of the great world beyond my yard had been forged by the Late-Late-Shows that came on at two in the morning.

"About what? *Passion*, Harry, passion." Prentiss Oliver thought Butterfield 8 was a mighty document of Film Noir, and was especially fond of the scene in which Miss Taylor's character drove her Nash Metropolitan over an embankment.

"What is passion, desire? For five points?" I had not seen much in the way of passion. I have always felt my opinions sincerely but had none about Elizabeth Taylor that I could recall.

"You can't *show* passion," said the dead man, munching on an Oreo. "You *feel* passion. The people in the movies demonstrate lust. To a point," said the dead man. "Anyone can see that."

"'I'm not like anyone. I'm me.' Elizabeth Taylor said that. In Butterfield 8," I said.

The dead man reached over and broke the yolk of my poached egg. "Engaging and witty, Harry," he said.

"I'll take witty for five points."

"Nonononono. That's only a game you and Sheila used to play. Engaging and witty are *places*. Places *you* might hear of but never visit. You never got The Mikado, did you? You are a decent man, but that's not enough. I'll have to be moving along. Sorry, Harry, old bean. Game's over."

"No more soft-serve at the Polar Treat?" I had become used to the dead man's company and was sorry to see him go.

Prentiss Oliver whistled a few bars of a bouncy, happy tune. "Recognize that?" he asked.

"I am not musically inclined," I said.

"On a tree by a river..." He stopped. "Join in, Harry, there's a good fellow. The Mikado, Gilbert and Sullivan..."

"Oh, yes: Callous and Obdurate. I am familiar with the Mikado," I said. "But not with the music."

The dead man looked as if he expected me to burst into song. I did not. "A little tom-tit sang willow, titwillow, titwillow," he sang.

"One of Sheila's favorites."

"Mine too. I admired Sheila," said the dead man. "From a distance... discretely. Sheila languished; her soul grew smaller and smaller and finally she disappeared. She had settled for a decent man. You whistle?"

"I never had the time to learn an instrument," I said stiffly.

"You never had the time?"

"There were leaves in the gutters. The eaves?"

"You cleaned the eaves while Sheila pined away for love. I wonder how she put up with you, a non-swimmer who wouldn't even try to learn to whistle. You are a lump, Harry Brackenfern. I waited."

"You waited and now it's too late. Sheila is dead."

"Too late for *you*, Harry. And thanks for all the ice cream." The dead man walked across the yard, whistling a Gilbert and Sullivan tune, the kind Sheila would have liked.

Dead Man in the Yard was first published in the Spring 2007 *Nanobison* [www.nanobison.com], Doug Helbling, editor.

Facelift

It was raining and Gearbox—Rachel Mae Welding —and I were hanging out in her room We were curled up with our piles of comics and paperback books. Between us was a bag of Oreos and a jar of super-crunchy—the no-name house brand peanut butter—with two spoons, our usual rainy day brain food. Gearbox slid the jar over to me.

"Christopher Robin..." She caught herself, looked up from her reading and made an apologetic sound.

"You know I hate that name," I said, "...*Rachel Mae*." I punched her. I fully expected her to punch me back.

She did.

"Sorry," she said.

Last year—we were in the fifth grade then—Gearbox and I came across a trunk of Edgar Rice Burroughs' Barsoom books in my attic. On the covers, warriors and monsters flexed unlikely if not anatomically impossible muscles. There was always a pretty girl in trouble. Our parents had been something they called "the counterculture" together; we figured this meant they read paperback books a lot. Gearbox tried to convince her folks that their last name, and by virtue of childbirth hers, was Barsoomian. Did I ever tell you about that? Gearbox did a real head job on her folks who exhibited mixed feelings about their daughter becoming a Martian. "Barsoom is so cool," she had declared. "I gotta get the name. My secret name..." I pointed out that if everyone called her Gearbox Barsoomian it wouldn't be much of a secret.

But whatever their feelings on the matter, Gearbox's parents would have to go through endless legal rigmarole to have their name changed from Welding to Barsoomian. Gearbox however used her nickname all the time. "Gearbox Welding," said her dad, "...that sounds like a sign you'd see down by the highway."

Gearbox had these "episodes." That is what her parents called them. For her—as she told me once, I had asked—"I just fall down. I don't remember a thing. For me time stands still; I'm just 'away.' Most of the time."

"Most of the time. What happens the other times?"

"Oh, I go places. Oops..." She went all glassy-eyed and I knew I was going to lose her.

She went all glassy-eyed and I knew I was going to lose her.

❑

Rachel Mae Welding, known as Gearbox, looked up. A large viridian personage sporting bundles of tentacles from its shoulders—taller than an NBA center except green with golden pustules that caught the light and made it seem to shimmer—was reaching down to assist a red slug-like creature the size of a Humvee through a smoldering hole in her bedroom floor. “Lord Zorgon! Merlitz!”

“That’s us,” said Lord Zorgon.

Gearbox ran over to the hole. Its edges were shiny with cooling slag from the polyester in the carpet. She’d hear plenty from Mom about this. “Wow! I didn’t know you were real.”

“What is this real? We have feelings, too. That we may have not been seen in these parts recently is no indicator for reality.”

“Uh, sorry.”

“No offence taken. And you are...?”

“Gearbox Welding.”

“Sounds like a sign you’d see down by the highway. Level with us, kid, what’s your real name?”

Gearbox wiped her nose on a sleeve. “Rachel Mae Welding. I got named after an aunt.”

An orifice opened in the side of the giant red slug. It spoke. “Give us a hand then, Ted.” Unlimbering a pair of dorsal tentacles, Lord Zorgon threw a viscous, dripping lifeline into the hole. Merlitz rappelled out.

“But your fleet, The Perfect Swarm, is destroyed. Bellona did it in *Bellona Warrior Priestess* issue 4. She chased you out of the Horsehead Nebula.”

“Ha!” snorted Lord Zorgon. “You are tragically out of the loop, kid. Lord Merlitz and I escaped alive. We have had to find other work.”

Gearbox stared; her manipulative machinery was spinning at high speed.

“Your mouth is open, little girl,” said Lord Zorgon as he wiped his tentacles on the curtains. “Our arrival has discomfited you. If you prefer you may call us by the names we use in our home universe.”

“Ted and Sally,” said Merlitz, oozing the remainder of its considerable girth out of the crater.

“Ted and Sally?” queried Gearbox Welding, “but that’s so lame...”

Lord Zorgon finished with his tentacle wiping and gave the curtains a final satisfied flourish. They tore. "Lame or not, that's who we are. Listen kid," said Ted, Lord Zorgon, "Bellona is hot on our tail and we need to do business fast."

"Business? With me?" asked Gearbox. Now the curtains were ruined as well as the rug. She explored her armamentarium of alibis for anything dealing with demolition by extraterrestrial invaders. Mom would be furious.

"Business." Ted pointed to Gearbox's discarded comic book. "And believe-you-me, out of a gazillion possible parallelisms, this neighborhood of yours is the equivalent of strolling through a back alley late at night. The sacred attributes of that text which you so recently clutched in your grubby, pre-adolescent hands aside, you read too many comics."

"You aren't here to straighten out my reading habits. I wasn't born yesterday—you are here because you haven't got anyplace else to go." Gearbox had *Bellona, Warrior Priestess* rolled up and was thumping Lord Zorgon over the head with it.

"Ow! Hey, easy there little girl. Is that issue 16? Well, if that's what you're reading, that is what is going on. *Bellona, Warrior Priestess* is one of our sacred books. Along with the Bhagavad-Gita and the Snap-On Tools catalog." Lord Zorgon's leaps of reason made irrefutable comic book sense.

"You want something," said Gearbox.

"*You* want something."

"Well... yes. I want more," said Gearbox. "I hate my name and I hate my looks."

"It would then appear we have begun our negotiations. It is written: The event will dictate its own parameters."

"Cool. But why me?"

"These are the imponderables, kid. In science fiction, the operative word is fiction. The stuff is made up."

Gearbox pouted and tugged defensively at the ends of her very long and very straight hair. "I know fiction is made up stuff." Gearbox's tugging at her hair had given her split ends

❑

Gearbox was back.

"I was talking with Lord Zorgon and Merlitz. While I was away?" Gearbox sat down and grabbed a fistful of Oreos.

"And what's the latest word from Lord Zorgon of Alymeade?" I was trying not to sound snotty.

"We didn't get much past introductions. But if I read things right, he and Lord Merlitz are in a bind. They need my help."

"Your help. The Alymeadean battle lords, commanders of the Perfect Swarm, need *your* help. You are in too much of a hurry to grow up," I said and went back to my reading.

"Look." She held up *Bellona, Warrior Priestess*, issue 16. "This is a sacred book, Sue Ellen," she said. She wanted all of my attention, now. I pretended not to hear. Bellona bestrode a shattered city, rebuilding herself with scaffolding and beams. Bellona was naked to the waist. "Isn't she the most awesome..."

"She is certainly *large*," I said. "You're not thinking of getting a boob job, are you? We're eleven years old, for Christ's sake. How does she put her socks on? Don't they get in the way?"

We caught the giggles and ended up bent over double, gasping for breath. Even though we were supposed to be too young to understand, grownup enhancements via facelifts and boob jobs had filtered through the careless clutter of parent talk. "You are still in too much of a hurry to grow up," I hiccoughed as tears ran down my cheeks.

Gearbox thrust a finger down her throat and made gagging sounds. "I don't want to grow up. I just want to look grown-up. For a while. Well...?" said Gearbox. "Is she awesome or what?"

"Well... She certainly seems to know who she is. She has, umm..."

Gearbox tugged at her hair. "Body-consciousness," she said. "She knows where her hands are."

"We already have that," I said.

Gearbox held her hands up to her face. "She's the real deal. She's first-rate and I'll bet she doesn't fall over when she puts her socks on," she said, going glassy-eyed again. "Besides, with a plastic surgeon and a personal trainer, all things are possible."

Gearbox flickered in and out, like a fluorescent bulb—she did that sometimes. Maybe it was her eyes, maybe mine. She caught at my shoulder to steady herself, "Nope—false alarm, I guess." And then she was gone. I scooped a spoonful of peanut butter and reached for a comic book to read while she was away. Bellona—goddess, warrior, priestess—went serenely about her affairs on the cover.

❑

"Destiny rolled your number, kid. So sue me." Lord Zorgon's breath reminded Gearbox of the last time her dad had the septic pumped. Row after row of glittering incisors flashed.

"Would you like a breath mint?" she asked.

"I should see the dentist more often, I know," said Ted, Lord Zorgon.

"So what exactly have I agreed to?" The proffered mints hung between them. Lord Zorgon brushed them aside.

"Don't mind if I do," said Sally, Lord Merlitz, eating the mints box and all.

"Shouldn't we be spitting in our palms and shaking hands or something? To seal the deal?"

"You don't trust me?" Tentacles flailed. There was a chilling Clack! as he snapped his fangs shut.

"Rachel Mae Welding!" from downstairs.

"It's cool, Mom, I just dropped a book."

Sally held his lips close to Gearbox's ear. "Negotiations are ended. Thank you for your open-mindedness, young lady."

"You are stringing your hair," said Lord Zorgon. "This is an annoying behavior."

"What I do with my hair is my own business."

"Didn't your mother ever warn you about what happens to little girls who string their hair?"

"Lowered self-esteem," said Sally. With obvious distaste, the giant slug picked up *Bellona, Warrior Priestess,* issue 16 and held it under Gearbox's nose. "Look at her. Think she has any problems with self-esteem? Not too damn likely, I'd say."

"Rachel Mae! What's going on up there? Do I hear voices?"

"It's just the TV, Mom."

"I know it's the TV, Rachel Mae Welding. You turn it off right now and get on that homework. When your father comes home..." The threat was left unuttered. Dad was a pushover.

"Yes, Mom."

"You have a Mom, too. This is only too excellent," said Sally. "But we must keep her out of your room for the duration."

"Shhhh," said Gearbox, "...she'll hear. *Duration?* How long were you planning on staying?"

"The duration of our business. We are here to help you achieve that self-realization which you crave. I like that in you human beings; you are ready to believe anything that will advance your desires."

"Sure... *What?*"

Sally sidled up and pulled at Gearbox's sleeve. "Ahem! You are a normal human child. Got any dirty books? It's been a while."

"Uh, there's a *Playgirls on Parade* under the mattress. It's my research. For a boob job?"

"Ahh, a treasure trove." Sally swarmed over Gearbox's bed, enveloping it and sucking at the mattress.

"You could just pick it up. Reach under the mattress," said Gearbox.

"These are troubled times," said Lord Zorgon. He picked up *Playgirls on Parade* and flipped to the back pages. "Voilà!" A half page advertisement showed Lovely Linda, the Blow-up Play Pal in lurid, three-color detail.

"We could stuff a zeppelin into the hole and save the universe," said Gearbox. "That was in *Nemesis, Righter of Wrongs*."

"My, but you do read extensively, little girl," Lord Zorgon said. "Issue 6, to be precise."

"...and time would unwind itself and you'd catch yourselves on the way out. What a great plot twist..." said Gearbox. She was taking notes.

"Stars go nova all the time. No one would be any the wiser." Ted nodded wisely.

"I'll go on the Internet," said Gearbox. "FedEx can get Lovely Linda here overnight. They say so in their TV ads."

Lovely Linda was out of stock and had to be back-ordered.

"We don't do patience well," said Sally. Lord Zorgon moped.

"Must you do that? There's always lots of fun things if you just apply yourself, use your imaginations. Weren't there all sorts of shipboard activities on the Perfect Swarm? Sing-alongs, volleyball? "

"We put the crew in suspended animation," said Lord Zorgon. With a flailing of tentacles, he waved Gearbox off. "They were frozen stiff. Ahh... an inspiration. We'll make a movie. That's lots of fun."

❑

Facelift

"Sue Ellen, they want to make a movie. Starring me. Of course, you'll be in it, too."

"Rachel *Mae*..." I punched her again, the second time that day. She did not punch me back. This usually meant we were about to start in on serious give and take. Gearbox chose her name; I was stuck with mine—Christopher Robin Sue Ellen Arbuthnot. Arbuthnot is my parents' last name, mine too. Mom is a Polansky.

"A movie. Do you even have a title?"

"It's called *Anomaly*. Sally liked that one. One of those neat words, anomaly—it means a thing that looks OK at first but shouldn't be where it is."

"Suppose there are these kids," I said. "And they buy all the comics and see every movie as it comes out. Then they notice an anomaly."

"Correctissimo. There's this one movie that they really, really like a lot. But there's so much going on that it's confusing. They don't get it the first time. Or the second. They have to keep on bringing it home. Week after week... And about when they can recite the lines along with the actors, the movie gets different?"

"And who do you get to play?"

"Bellona, of course." Gearbox got that far-away look and her eyes swam out of focus.

❑

"Back again? My stars and garters, but you do zing about." Lord Zorgon of Alymeade sighed, a great exhalation redolent of smoldering carpets. "Where was I? Boob jobs and facelifts, yes. Women, whatever their ages, never wish for sensible things like orthotics or a tonsillectomy."

"I already had my tonsils out."

"None the less, your yearnings are for the grown-up lineaments of a woman on the cover of a comic book."

"I want to look like her," said Gearbox.

"The radiance of your face will shine like a thousand suns," said Ted, Lord Zorgon.

"That's a promise, right?"

"We, too, have our wants and needs," said Sally. "We'd really, really like to have our battle fleet back."

"And, failing that, we'd really, really love to ride the bumper cars." Lord Zorgon gave Sally a broad wink.

"Our fall-back position," said Sally, who received an immediate dope-slap. Gearbox knew the maneuver from the Three Stooges on TV. "But that's what we..." Sally whimpered.

"Let us not dwell overly on methodology, shall we little girl? POSIWID—the purpose of a system is what it does."

Gearbox would only have to keep one step ahead of the Alymeadean battle lords.

❑

"The Alymeadean battle lords?—They're waiting for Lovely Linda."

"Who?" She filled me in and my jaw must have dropped a foot. "*Playgirls on Parade*? We are eleven years old."

"So I was studying up. And I know how old I am." Gearbox looked thoughtful. "The radiance of my face will shine like a thousand suns," she said. "That's the Bhagavad-Gita."

"The what?" Gearbox looked abnormally pleased with herself, even for Gearbox.

"Bhagavad-Gita. It's a holy book. Lord Zorgon quoted it in *Bellona, Warrior Priestess* number sixteen. The one with the bare-chested lady?"

I riffled through our stacks. "Hah!" I said. There was no Bhagavad-Gita quote in my *Bellona, Warrior Priestess* number sixteen. There was no Lord Zorgon. And now no bare-chested lady on the cover either.

"This was Lord Zorgon's personal copy," said Gearbox.

"My folks have a camcorder," I said. "We can play all the parts and plug it into the TV," I offered. Here we were, two kids and starring in our own film. We started shooting *Anomaly* the movie, making the script up as we went.

We were gluing chopped-up lengths of garden hose to a garbage can, one of the shiny galvanized ones we had spray painted green. This was to be Lord Zorgon in the scenes where I had to double as Sally. Gearbox came out of the house dressed in a cut-down lamé gown with sequins we picked up at the Salvation Army store. She carried the lid to the garbage can, Bellona's shield.

"Look at me! Flat as a clam. I gotta get that overhaul," she said, definitely drooping. "We just have to do the Alymeadean battle lords one little favor."

"Ahh, that favor again. What kind of favor?"

"Rachel Mae!"

"Mom!" This was to be Gearbox's afternoon at the dentist. We ended up hiding out at my place until soccer practice.

"About that *favor...*" I asked again.

"Lord Zorgon and Merlitz? Their real names are Ted and Sally." Before she could finish she was gone again.

I picked up a book and lost myself in tales of chivalry and swordplay on distant worlds. Gearbox still sat glassy-eyed and expressionless. There was an oozing from under the pile of comic books and paperbacks. The slug, Sally, clambered over the side and shook itself like a retriever, flinging dollops of scarlet goop over the walls and ceiling. I threw up and fainted dead away.

When I came to, Gearbox was fanning me with *Nemesis, Righter of Wrongs*. "This is how they make their entrances," she said. "Your mom won't notice a thing. Sue Ellen Arbuthnot, meet Sally, Lord Merlitz. Lord Merlitz, Sue Ellen Arbuthnot."

"Charmed, I'm sure," said Sally.

"Sally, Sally, manners, please," said a green improbability that waved its tentacles as it levitated out of the hole. "Ted," said Lord Zorgon, "Call me Ted. The movie is coming along famously. I am ecstatic. My compliments to your mother. Sorry about the rug," he said.

A wispy curl of acrid smoke wafted from the far side of the Alymeadean battle lords' tunnel. "Achoo!" Gearbox was rubbing at her eyes.

"A point of information," said Sally. "Are you laughing or crying? This is of interest to me."

"Neither. I am sneezing. The fumes."

As it was still raining, the four of us read comics together, passing the peanut butter back and forth. Lord Zorgon became engrossed with a great stack—all sixty-four issues—of *Nemesis, Righter of Wrongs*.

"This is all very boring," said Sally, gnawing on my mother's draperies. "What's next? You do have bumper cars in this parallelism? Bumper cars or a chubby priest?" it asked hopefully.

"A chubby priest?" I asked.

"The very same!" Lord Zorgon exclaimed. He gave a whoop and balanced upside down on his spare tentacles as he cycled a comic book in an arc over his head. It looked like a cheering routine.

"It's been a long dry spell for us," Sally said, by way of explanation. "Chubby priest-wise."

"The chubby priest appears in Nemesis, Righter of Wrongs, issue 2. See? The stories tend to get mixed up, but this is the way of things. Said priest will most likely have misgivings about an eleven-year-old ordering an inflatable play pal on the Internet. He must be neutralized."

"There's Fr. Lumley at All Souls." We went to ecumenical Sunday school together, Gearbox and me, although not at Fr. Lumley's church.

"The very one," said Ted, Lord Zorgon. Gearbox picked up the phone.

Gearbox's side of the conversation with Fr. Lumley featured mainly wheedling and cajoling. "Fr. Lumley will be over this afternoon," said Gearbox as she set down the phone. "Oh, by the way, Lovely Linda came..." was almost an afterthought.

"We'll be at the Mother Ship," said Ted as he and Sally dived down their tunnel.

❑

We got to Gearbox's house the old-fashioned way—the vacant lot, then her yard. The Alymeadean battle lords were there ahead of us. Sally, Lord Merlitz, was stuffing Lovely Linda the inflatable play-pal into the hole in the carpet.

"Perfect fit," said Lord Zorgon. "Can't beat that FedEx." The doorbell chimed and he paled to aquamarine, his tentacles twisted in a complex knot.

There was a "Yes, yes, yes..." and the sound of Mrs. Welding's footsteps from downstairs. Fr. Lumley was at the door; he carried a small black satchel.

"But we're Congregationalists..." said Helen, Mrs. Welding—Gearbox's mom.

"I have to see about a portal in your daughter's floor. An exorcism or something."

"A what? GEARBOX!"

"Yeah, Mom? Oh, Fr. Lumley. Come on up." As Fr. Lumley trudged up the stairs Gearbox cast a reproving look at her mother. "And you don't have to yell." Gearbox eyed the black satchel. "You don't have a Snap-On Tools catalog by any chance?"

"Wha...?"

"Just wondering."

As Gearbox ushered Fr. Lumley into her room, Helen Welding called up the stairs, "...and be sure to leave the door open."

Fr. Lumley sighed, "We've had a lot of bad press lately, I'm afraid. Now, what can I do for you, Rachel Mae? Hello, Sue Ellen." Fr. Lumley knew all the kids in his parish, Catholic or not.

"Hello, Fr. Lumley."

"I was wondering if you could see a hole in the rug," said Gearbox.

Fr. Lumley looked concerned. "Do you see one?"

"Nope. That's the problem." Gearbox was checking our new-found reality through the eyes of a trained observer.

"Well, I don't either if that's any help. And don't forget to call me if you ever need an exorcism." Fr. Lumley retreated down the stairs past the watchful eyes of Mrs. Welding.

"See. Neutralized," said Lord Zorgon.

"But, but... you didn't do anything. I expected something extreme."

"I picked his satchel." He held a three-ring binder aloft. "The Snap-On Tools catalog. And now that we have almost solved our interstitial dilemma, it is time for some well-deserved frolicking before we return to do battle with Bellona. You mentioned bumper cars?"

"No. You did, actually," Gearbox reminded him. "And what about my..."

"As we promised you, kid—you take care of us and we'll take care of you," said Lord Zorgon. Incisors flashed.

Sally looked up from gumming my mom's curtains, which he must have dragged along through the tunnel. "Have your fun while you may, I say. Same thing as growing up, going nova, just bigger."

"Size matters," said Gearbox, thinking about boob jobs.

"Only if you're in the way," said Ted. "Now about those bumper cars..."

❑

We looked in the pockets of our parents' coats, under the seat cushions of easy chairs and couches and came away empty-handed. We had to dip into our special reserves. From the cellar came our La Paloma cigar box that had once held carefully sorted machine screws.

"Thirty-eight dollars," Gearbox announced after the four of us had counted the nickels, dimes and quarters. Lord Zorgon was particularly adept at handling small change because of the tentacles.

The same carnival set up every year in a vacant lot, stomping all over the chickweed and thistles for one afternoon. "It's a little early." The man who operated the bumper cars looked us up and down and shook the cigar box.

"All to ourselves for an hour. Thirty-eight dollars," said Gearbox.

"Well..." He tucked the money under his arm. "Just the two of you, OK?"

"Huh? Oh, yeah. Sure."

The man threw the main power switch and sauntered off.

"Wheeee..." Ted and Sally bumped, crashed and sideswiped each other for an hour or more. Lord Zorgon wrapped his tentacles around one striped tent pole and pulled himself to a stop right in front of Gearbox and me.

"Thank you for this, little girls. The only respite we have had in millennia; fiction is a cruel mistress. Oh-oh, I see the concierge is returning. Time for one last go-round."

With that, he spun back onto the track. Gearbox and I turned to see the bumper car man on his way back. The La Paloma cigar box was still under his arm but from the way he carried himself we knew it was empty. He smelled of beer and pickled herring. At the sound of footsteps behind him he paused. A glorious woman—tall and graceful with shining body armor—strode past, ignoring him. She jiggled a little but had things generally under control—she did not fall over. The gape-jawed ticket taker made an abrupt U-turn and retraced the dusty path to town.

The woman glided over to us balancing on the balls of her feet, graceful and alert. She stopped in front of us, her hazel eyes misted and compassionate.

"Who are you?" I had to ask but I already knew the answer.

"Me? Why, I am Bellona, Warrior Priestess, and the radiance of my face shines like a thousand suns."

"The bumper cars man saw you but he didn't see Ted and Sally..."

"Who would want to? I flatter myself that I am the better-looking." She winked at the two of us. "I knew the Blow-up Play Pal would be stuffed into the hole separating the two pallelisms. This is irrefutable comic book sense. I simply deflated Lovely Linda and popped on through."

"But..."

"It is better not to question what you don't understand."

She turned to the circular raceway where Lord Zorgon was slamming Merlitz into a retaining wall. "Ted. Sally?" The two looked up and blanched.

"Bellona!"

"Your battle fleet, the Perfect Swarm? I shall demonstrate the grace to allow you time to return through the portal and join them in death—the warrior's way. And this time be careful about the rug on the way out, there's good fellows."

"Rug? But I don't..." As a smoldering hole opened in the ground, Lord Zorgon flashed through an encyclopedia of hues, finally settling on chartreuse. "How can we ever plan on anything if the rules are always changing?"

"Fiction at work, uncoiling its inscrutable ways, Lord Zorgon," said Bellona. "Because that's the way things are, and no mean feat, let me tell you."

Gearbox leaned over the edge. "What's down there?"

"Down, up, through... whatever. It's all the same. And don't stick your head in. The portal is frisky, unpredictable. You could very well trigger an annihilation."

"Like kaboom?" said Gearbox.

"Kaboom," said Bellona.

Gearbox was intrigued. Kaboom, any kaboom, was an interesting possibility and to be investigated.

Bellona knelt in front of Gearbox. "I have put in a good word for you with Father Lumley. However, I do have some sad news. A noseypoke parishioner stumbled on Lord Zorgon's Snap-On Tools catalog in his satchel. The good father's credentials were questioned and he has had to leave the neighborhood."

"Cool," said Gearbox.

"But that is new business; we shall finish our old business first." Bellona hurled a fireball and the bumper car pavilion erupted in flames. "Now," she dusted off her hands. "With Lord Zorgon and Merlitz gone..."

"Not so fast. There are some loose ends, I believe." Gearbox fidgeted and ground a toe in the dust.

"Eye contact please, my dear." Bellona smiled a radiant smile; she had great teeth, too. "Is this about a particular favor you flimflammed the Alymeadean battle lords into? The noösphere is full of unclaimed favors."

"Sue Ellen, close your ears." Gearbox beckoned Bellona into a huddle. They seemed to be doing some deep bargaining. Then they spit into their palms and shook hands.

"Sorry," Gearbox said to me. "Did you feel left out?"

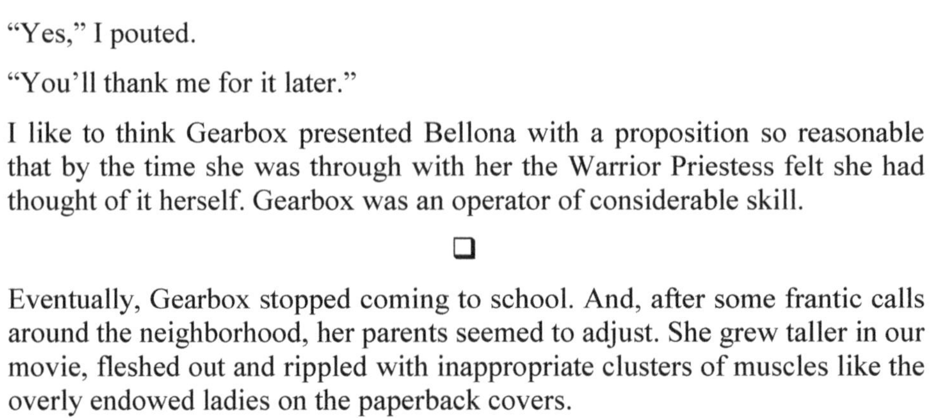

"Yes," I pouted.

"You'll thank me for it later."

I like to think Gearbox presented Bellona with a proposition so reasonable that by the time she was through with her the Warrior Priestess felt she had thought of it herself. Gearbox was an operator of considerable skill.

❑

Eventually, Gearbox stopped coming to school. And, after some frantic calls around the neighborhood, her parents seemed to adjust. She grew taller in our movie, fleshed out and rippled with inappropriate clusters of muscles like the overly endowed ladies on the paperback covers.

Gearbox was now Bellona. She moved smoothly but warily, poised and ready for danger from any direction, a true woman warrior. She was my friend and I was happy for her. She was a good kid in spite of herself.

And I know the universe is a safer place with Gearbox Barsoomian, Warrior Priestess out there on patrol with Nemesis, righting wrongs.

And I never once, not in all the many times I watched *Anomaly* the movie, saw Bellona wipe her nose on her sleeve. She was a super hero now. And as such of course couldn't be bothered to show up and snarf down pizza with me.

Facelift was first published in *Aphelion* [www.aphelion-webzine.com]
February 2008

The Year They Invented Frozen Lemonade

Bowed to the earth with bitter woe,
Or laughing at some raree-show,
We flutter idly to and fro.
—Lewis Carroll, *Sylvie and Bruno*

"I am midtown. Manhattan?"

Linda Winkelman speaks her question out loud in the middle of the rush hour push; no one takes notice. Linda is standing in the middle of a street. She can not recall who she is or why she is here. "I remember lemonade," says Linda. Buildings disappeared, people disappeared. Now it is her turn. Linda Winkelman was born the year they invented frozen lemonade.

Linda adjusts her neck, squints; the vertebrae crack satisfyingly as she pivots to face east, down 45th Street. "Yep, midtown," says Linda of the unfamiliar terrain. "I knew it, my mid-life crisis." Linda says this but does not know why. Mid-life crises are trendy enough to be sidebars on the evening news, but she has only a sweaty pitcher of lemonade all frothy and fresh from the faucet to explain the big buildings, the thronging crowds.

Linda the child is an acolyte at the shrine of her late mother's menopause, a prisoner of lemonade. Linda has heard of mid-life crises since her fifth birthday. Linda Winkelman was born the year they added the Bullwinkle balloon to the Macy's parade. Underdog and the Pink Panther were to come later and do not figure in this story. Her mother is dead.

She has forgotten things before: after climbing a flight of stairs, leaving the super-cooled gym after pumping furiously on the Exercycle. A gortex shoulder bag carries her gym kit for aerobics after work and a change of shoes for the office. She pats the bag. The bag returns her touch with a kinesthetic reassurance. All she has to do is stand still and everything she has forgotten will catch up with her. The frozen lemonade is in its chartreuse can, sweat-beaded with tantalizing condensation, hovering just out of reach.

Growing into her mother with her mother's constant sniping and hectoring had been a major anxiety. Her mother brandished her own glandular withdrawal like a cudgel. "Don't dump jam in your cereal, Linda. That's not natural," says Linda's mother.

Linda does not remember this.

The nine-year-old Linda dreams of running, running after an elusive train as fast as her skirt would allow. In sleep she misses her train, its doors slide closed in her face, rubber safety lips denying her entry. She runs alongside. Catatonic passengers whiz past through the station—noses flattened out against the glass, coats and scarves and bags caught between doors the conductor doesn't bother opening.

At age eleven, Linda Winkelman senses a nascent bitchiness ripening along with her breasts, whose progress she checks daily. Her body is not cooperating. She also fears for her future mental health. Developing within her were those same traits she railed against in her mother: that an evil lurked beneath her burgeoning bosom like the alien pods she had seen take over friendly familiar townsfolk in The Invasion of the Body Snatchers. Linda Winkelman suspects that her mother is an imposter, but she has all the right answers when Linda tries to trip her up.

Mrs. Winkelman, Linda's mother, accepted as an operating premise that anything west of the Hudson was camping out, hence the lemonade made it over from New Jersey to her neighborhood Gristede's Market by a kind of reverse osmosis. It was important that people who didn't live in Manhattan have something constructive to do with their lives. Packing concentrated citrus fluids seemed a worthwhile endeavor.

"I remember Midtown. Midtown is a whereabouts. Whereabouts are where you are when you don't have the least inkling where you are. Alice in Wonderland, except I don't feel like an Alice." She has read Lewis Carroll other than *Alice's Adventures—Sylvie and Bruno*: of course, that's why we used the quote at the beginning of this story. "And it looks like 45th Street," says Linda, recalling a name: 45th Street. "I should be panicked, but I'm not," she notes with mild surprise and files this reaction for future reference.

At 35, Linda acquires Tom, a husband, Tom the househusband. Tom Winkelman has a fast metabolism and a lethargic worldview. The world comes to him, is examined, and approved or dismissed. Linda does not remember Tom. Her disappeared history bothers her not one whit: that left the future, a future of limitless wonderment.

There is once a futile passion for a local disc jockey.

❑

In the afternoons of Linda Winkelman's "young womanhood," as her mother described her child's budding pubescence, the years from nine to thirteen, Linda sought solace from the radio, particularly 1010 WINS' afternoon personality for whom she hoped to become an acceptable offering.

Pete Garland was the announcer who came on just before Jack Lacy and her mother's favorite, Murray the K. Linda took comfort in the molassesey voice and sophisticated humor of the afternoon disc jockey. The Pete Garland Cat Exchange added a unifying dimension to Linda Winkelman's young life.

Linda tried to work up the courage to call in. She even invented a cat, Conan, whom she could say would be looking for a good home because of her mother's allergies.

She sent away for a signed picture. New York radio stations nurtured the images of their stars and it had been returned with a short handwritten note from the announcer's wife.

Thank you so much for your interest in Pete's program. We are pleased to have such a loyal listener to the Pete Garland Cat Exchange. There was a short bio: he had attended the London School of Dramatic Arts and used to work at a Cleveland radio station before coming to New York.

Best, Pete and Annie Garland.

Linda Winkelman called up once the following year.

"Hello?"

"Is this the Cat Exchange?"

"Oh. Hi there. I'm Linda, Pete's wife. We don't do the Cat Exchange any more. Pete's moving over to WNEW. But I'm sure he'll be starting it up again. You have a cat problem?"

Well, then. Now there was a *Linda* it seemed. Linda Winkelman, now aged twelve, was secretly pleased. The Annie of the note had exited. If she hadn't been an acceptable virgin sacrifice at least someone who shared her name had.

"No, I just called to say that Conan had died. I thought Pete would like to know." Linda replaced the telephone in its cradle on the kitchen wall.

"Look at this." Her mother pushed the Daily News across the breakfast table past a lazy susan full of vitamins and bananas. It was folded open to an inside page. There was the same publicity photo she had gotten in the mail. "Your cat man." The announcer's first wife had left him. Something about his liaison with the woman who would become the second Mrs. Garland.

That the good-looking disc jockey's new wife—Linda thought ungraciously of the other Linda as The Temptress—had the same name as she tickled a small nubbin of spite. Linda Winkelman realized at age twelve that the first, departed, Mrs. Garland had become a surrogate for her own mother. Annie Garland, Mrs. Garland I, was a pod person. Linda, Mrs. Garland II, had saved Pete Garland and with him the Pete Garland Cat Exchange. The Temptress had trumped the Body Snatcher. Now Conan the cat has been sucked into an amnesiac well of forgetfulness, Pete Garland and all, and Linda is standing in the middle of the street—45th Street and Sixth Avenue to be precise.

❑

The sign painted on the parapet of the Wurlitzer Building, the first thing you see coming out of the IND at Bryant Park, says:

John Lindsay is Supercalifragilisticexpialidocious.

Standing at street level she has to look up to see it. John Lindsay was the mayor once. He has disappeared, not yet his sign. He was a handsome man and she can not remember his name. She is glad the sign painter had written it out for her. Linda might have voted for Lindsay in 1969 but she was only six years old on election day.

She cranes back her neck and regards the John Lindsay sign at an acute angle. "Cool," says Linda. She feels the comfortable, reassuring crack of a vertebra adjusting itself somewhere along her spine. "L-I-N-D-S-A-Y," spells Linda Winkelman. John Lindsay was a Republican but ran as a fusion candidate. He had the Liberal Party endorsement.

Linda scans the upper floors of an Edwardian row house. The old signs lived on, unnoticed under layers of peeling paint, fallen façades. *Brown and Getty Investagations* glimmers old gold through generations of street smudge from the third floor window where some hard-going gumshoe had misspelled his specialty decades before. Linda addresses the long-gone shamus.

"Would you, Mister *Investagator*, have the kindness to mention whereabouts we are just now? And *who* we are, beginning with me?" Linda wonders where the Hotel Seymour went to. Wasn't it here? The ground floor had the best workingman's cafeteria in Midtown—lasagna, spaghetti and meatloaf smothered in red stuff. The hotel's evaporation probably took several months, but Linda forgot to pay attention. One day the hotel is missing too, gone to join John Lindsay lock, stock and lasagna.

No more Hotel Seymour. An all-male porn house is in its place. The film on the marquee is the Shopper's Special.

As she watches, a grumpy codger dragging a ladder shuffles out of the theater. He props the ladder against the marquee and proceeds to hang a banner:

Documentary Weekend—*Adam and Yves* PLUS *Histoires D'Hommes*, GOOD HOT STUFF.

❑

"You read a cookbook like it's pornography," said Tom.

"You read pornography like it's a cookbook," Linda replied.

This was their joke. The joke they shared in their marriage. When did this start? Tom and his boil-in-a-bag dinners?

Linda's mother was secretly tickled at the patronymic of Linda's intended. "Winkelman? His name is Winkelman? That's the same name as ours. It sounds like incest. The neighbors will think your father was screwing some babe in Yonkers."

"Mom!"

"Alright, alright."

"He comes from New Jersey, Mom." Where the lemonade came from. Neither of Linda's parents had crossed the bridge to New Jersey in all their married years. "I met him at school." Linda majored in Comp. Lit. at NYU. She met Tom in a bar ten years later.

"Is he cute?"

"Cute enough."

Mom figured Jersey was too far for incest. Her late husband had been beyond reproach. Besides, the lemonade traffic would have clogged the tunnels and made quickie trysts unlikely.

Tom Winkelman is light-skinned, light-haired and slim. He was good-looking once and still was but, even if his wife had noticed, it wouldn't have mattered. Everything is too late. Tom discovers the Pete Garland Cat Exchange photograph when they move in together.

"Who's the guy?"

"My cat, Conan," she lies. "Mom's allergies. He ran a cat exchange on the radio when I was a kid."

❑

The grumpy codger grudgingly descends his ladder and opens up the box office. Linda buys her ticket and edges back to read the marquee offerings of the Shopper's Special.

"Adam and Yves. Mmm... Oh!" There is a shadowless Hiroshima sunrise behind her eyes. She drops her gym tote and rummages through its pockets. Didn't she have a bottle of Midol somewhere? "This is going to be one hell of a migraine." She grabs at the codger's ladder to steady herself; he has left it propped against the marquee. She loses her footing and falls between two

parked cars to be trapped, wedged upright by bumpers, rubber and chrome. She feels the grinding of ragged pavement against her knees.

Linda wakes up smelling popcorn. She is in a high-ceilinged tile bathroom. *Toilet.* She is in the ladies' room. *Somewhere*—yes. Popcorn. "I am at the movies. And I have taken my clothes off. I am sitting on the toilet."

A silk camisole dangles past her tailored navy suit top. She feels the gentle draft of too-cold air conditioning against naked thighs. Standing half-naked in her underpants, she casts about for missing items of apparel—one skirt, the bottom half of a matching ensemble, her sensible, low-heeled shoes. Ah, there is one. But no amount of searching discovers its mate; it might be anywhere. Linda doesn't feel like hanging around for an exhaustive search. Her skirt is lying on the floor by row of porcelain basins. The zipper is jammed. Linda dusts it off and wriggles it up over her bruised knees. It refuses to go any farther. Linda stands, knock-kneed and defiant.

"Damn, now where's that shoe?"

She looks up. There it is, the missing shoe, perched eighteen feet above on a fluorescent fixture. Sitting once more upon the toilet, she extracts a pair of Nike running shoes from her bag and laces them up. She ties her sneakers and checks herself in the mirror. She keeps on talking as if the reflection could fill in the blanks, tell her who she was and what she was doing here. *I'll be damned if I'm going to stand around with my ass out while I figure out who the hell I am.*

Check her bag for ID. Brilliant. *Thank you, reflection.*

An attractive woman in early middle age stares up at her from the driver's license. "Linda Winkelman. Huh." She rechecks the mirror above the sink. "Hiya, Linda." The stranger does not reply.

She gives the skirt one last determined yank. There is tearing sound as the zipper parts going over her hips.

"Damn!"

❑

"It's easier if you undo the fastenings first, my dear." It was Mom. Linda accepted her mother's intrusions irritably, with a practiced acquiescence.

"The zipper was jammed."

"You should ask your detective friend for a hand—the *Investagator?*" This was the mother-blessing, free advice with a tinge of remembered malice. "A private eye is for divorces," said Mom. "You and Tom in trouble?"

Mom was baking lemon pudding-cake, with the sauce on the bottom, Linda's favorite. The lemony smell was real and good, not like the mock-lemon lemonade piped in from Jersey that lubricated her mother's good purposes.

"Mister Getty is dead, Mom. The detective? He's only an old sign I saw today." Linda was unsure whether she actually saw the sign or merely remembered it.

"If he's dead he should take his sign down," said Mom.

"Mom, I have a stroke and the first things I get back are you and a defunct private eye."

"Lemon cake. With zest." Mom slipped her a quick look and grated in the lemon peel—zest. Mom lived life with zest plus lemonade and wished the same for her daughter. "And vitamin C."

Linda Winkelman, the child, has rubella, chicken pox and her tonsils out. Linda does not get scurvy.

"Linda."

"Mom?"

"You should go see the movie. Tickets cost money."

❑

In the plush seats Linda feels sleepy but safe with the sticky, secret, kids at play smells evocative of other times alone, hidden away at the movies, a haven of refuge from the world outside the enveloping dark.

A perfume of wildflowers and urine with a whiff of disinfectant wafts in from the men's room to be savored, then dissipated by the air conditioning. *The air is palm scented and sweet from the lavatory soap I carried in on my hands.* Linda holds two fingers to her nose and envisions a marble and tile washroom, not the theater's. "At work, of course."

Memories of work return in a sporadic cascade. There was to be a late afternoon brainstorming with Creative at Glasgow/Finn and Westcott. Linda knows she dreads the Creative types. A chips and nachos conglomerate was introducing a low cholesterol mock fried pork rind product, the latest scientific breakthrough. Linda is to be named project manager for the new product's test marketing. If it flew she would be in line to direct the national campaign. Her employers had accepted much money to place Pork-A-Dillos in the forefront of consumer consciousness.

"*Pork-A-Dillos*. I am an account executive. How delightfully disgusting. Add Pork-A-Dillos to the list along with the private eye and Mom."

Breathe. Relax.

Linda goes to the lobby for popcorn.

The concessionaire is not where she should be. Probably making out with the projectionist. Linda throws three dollars on the glass-topped case and grabs a waxed tub of popcorn, hot and fresh, and heads back to the movie.

Linda finds her seat in the dark that washed away all care, where a light shone dimly every five rows to guide one's steps on the carpeted aisles. *Hidden and safe—I'll be happy here. Ease off the shoes and relax with a waxy tub of hot salty popcorn slathered with a bubbly yellow mudslide smelling more buttery than butter.*

❑

Linda's first pair of heels was hard to balance on; she was always going downhill. She practiced walking for weeks. Eddie promised a gardenia.

"I know what goes on after the prom. You don't go. This once, listen to your mother."

Linda aged sixteen unlocked her diary with a gold washed stamped metal key. She bought the diary at The Ben Franklin Store over on Eighth Avenue when she was ten; it was bound between puffy pink plastic boards. She extracted a glossy photograph, neatly folded. *Best, Pete Garland* said the too-neat inscription written in black magic marker.

If Pete was the best that made Eddie second best. The Pete Garland Cat Exchange episode was by now past retrieval. Anyway, that had been four years ago and he must have aged terribly. Linda accepted Eddie as a fallback option, romancewise. The photograph was replaced, the diary locked.

"You used to like the movies; go to the movies. See what real life is like. Not pretend like the prom. And be home by nine-thirty."

"Mom!"

Linda cajoled but did not attend her junior prom. She did not go to the movies. She went parking with Eddie and a six-pack.

There is an animal groan from the speakers behind the screen.

Eddie was never like this. And forget Tom. She remembers Conan, the phantom cat, and regrets not offering up her eleven-year-old self to the announcer who had attended the London School of Dramatic Arts.

Halfway through the popcorn, lips tingling with salty residue, trapped hulls itching joyously in dental interstices, Linda retraces her steps up the aisle to the candy counter.The concessionaire is the same man who had hung the

Documentary Weekend banner out front. He wears a gold brocaded uniform jacket worn through at the elbows.

“Could you sell me a Pepsi? The salt... the popcorn?”

“This used to be a real place, you know.” The codger is chatty, “A regular Hollywood movie palace. Good movie, though.” He picks at the inside of an ear.

Her stomach rebels at the thought of junk food plus ear wax. The codger withdraws his finger and thoughtfully studies it. *I don’t do ear wax,* thinks Linda.

Linda pats the shoulder bag with her workout gear, apologizes to her waistline for all the fat and ear wax in the popcorn, opts for two packs of sugar-free peppermint clove chewing gum and heads back to her seat.

Linda stays on through the film. She leaves the theater and heads to the remembered brainstorming with her pockets crammed full of peppermint clove gum wrappers and not the slightest idea of what the movie was about.

At Sixth Avenue she opens her last stick of peppermint clove chewing gum and tosses the wrapper into a corner trash barrel. A wind catches the wrapper and flys it away toward Times Square where a dust devil lurked by a kiosk. A moment later the wrapper makes an abrupt U-turn. The peppermint clove wrapper has appointments to keep that day other than with the Sanitation Department. As Linda steps off the curbing the wrapper slips up behind her. She turns to confront her stalker.

“What the hell...?” The gum wrapper snuggles expectantly at her feet.

Linda Winkelman stoops to pick it up, moved by municipal contrition to protect her city from this litter, her litter. The business of bending to retrieve the castoff foil displays gelatinous areas, front and rear. From several directions Linda’s cleavage (and/or pelvic girdle depending whether one faced uptown or downtown) attracts the attention of six healthy, normal men—husbands and fathers, good family men, regular guys. But for them, at this instant, time stands still; they are bonded by the flash of flesh, connoisseurs of beauty revealed.

Linda stands and straightens her skirt. She smiles. “Got it,” she says, turning and holding the gum wrapper aloft. Faces redden and the bystanders hurry on. One of the onlookers is a policeman, one of New York’s Finest, on traffic duty but nonetheless appreciative.

“Linda.”

"Mom?"

"If you haven't done anything wrong there's nothing to be afraid of."

"I'll remember that."

"Linda, darling. Shouldn't you be home with Tom? Tonight is frozen boil-in-a-bag, your favorite."

"Mom. You are dead. Go away, please."

"So? Don't listen. It's only a runaway piece of foil. You never listen. Don't say I didn't tell you."

"Hey," says the policeman.

"Hey, there."

Their eyes meet. They size each other up and like what they see.

"Oops." The gum wrapper wriggles from Linda's grasp and lingers at a catch basin, waiting. Awakened by the suggestion of an impending revelation, the dust devil shoulders past the wind and nudges the peppermint clove gum wrapper along, just out of reach. Fresh from the Shopper's Special and pursued by her own trash Linda is detained for jaywalking as she crosses West 46th Street. The officer hefts a thick, black pad from his hip pocket and hails Linda back to the curb. He is out of tickets but there might be an exchange of numbers leading to...? Who could tell? There is a potential for chemistry here.

Jaywalking even in New York is not as yet an arrestable offense, but there is a fine. The officer reads Linda the riot act on the threat to public order posed by promiscuous, inconsiderate walking habits. Linda is a remarkably attractive woman, the officer presentable and a credit to the force, and one thing leading to another with propinquitous acceleration, they are soon both laughing.

"Sonofabitch! Stop him! Stop thief!" A very tall, very black and very fast young man exits a discount electronics store in the middle of the block. The young man is in a hurry. "Motherfucking sonofabitch." An overweight man explodes onto the street in hot pursuit. The young man is headed toward Sixth Avenue in an easy lope.

Linda and the policeman are not ready to be interrupted. They ignore the brouhaha forming up across the street.

Onlookers catch the scent of the shopkeeper's rage and join the chase. The young man is not sweating; he has done this all before. As he nears Mezza Luna, a take-out pizza boutique, a maintenance man with a bucket and mop emerges from the dark interior. Sizing up the situation, he thrusts the handle of his mop between the young man's legs, spilling him to the street in a slow motion forward somersault. The bucket tips over, swamping the sidewalk.

The shopkeeper and his posse are on their quarry.

The policeman is aware of the men and feels the psychic wind of their passage, the heavy breathing, bloodlust. But his eyes are fixed on the pin Linda wears on her left lapel, her grandmother's brooch. He does not dare to look at Linda's face, at the curve of her breasts, the welling at a raglan covered hip. His focus toggles between the brooch and his thick, black, leather-bound pad.

"It's an heirloom, my grandmother's," says Linda.

Their eyes meet and hold.

He is afraid of me, thinks Linda Winkelman, secretly pleased.

I am afraid of her, thinks the policeman, secretly pleased. He smiles a smile of large, strong, white teeth.

Tormentors circle the fallen youth, their bloody footprints tracking the pavement. A trickle of blood meanders to the gutter. The young man covers his head with his arms, avoiding the blows. The young man's knees twitch close to his chest; purpled eyelids swell between unconscious fingers.

The officer, preoccupied with Linda, lets vigilante justice play itself out.

The young man will heal and eventually attend NYU.

"If you'd stayed in school, you'd be an MBA by now, not a receptionist," says Linda's mother.

"Mom, I'm an account executive. And I studied Comp. Lit."

"Have you had a mammogram yet this year?"

"Mom!"

"I was only trying to be helpful. No tits and just see if you get a nice boy with prospects..."

"Mom, I am married."

"Not for long the way you're going."

The officer clears his throat and makes motions to close his black leather pad. The business across the street is getting loud.

Linda explains to her policeman how she had been attracted by a reflection from the shiny foil gum wrapper and ticked, "I mean really exercised, you know, pissed-off at those people who think the world is their garbage pail and someone sometime has got to start setting an example or the whole city and then the whole world are going to go to hell and there we'll be with garbage up to our ass. We're going to drown in our own filth." She flashes the cop what she hopes is a winning smile. A mid-life crisis should be an opportunity for growth. But then so was athlete's foot, likewise cancer and a well-positioned mutual fund. *What the hell?* Since she has no past, perhaps it is time to concentrate on the future.

The policeman is pleased. Linda is pleased. The policeman has no name in this story. He is tall, dark and handsome and has been on Traffic Detail for the last four of his eight years on the force. He has never drawn his gun in the line of duty. Persuasion is his forte. Linda rummages in her bag for a pencil and paper. Telephone numbers are exchanged.

"You never bring your boyfriends home. You just go and hang out somewhere. You make me feel like I'm an embarrassment to you."

"Mom, get lost. This is grownup stuff."

Pushing along the peppermint clove gum wrapper, the dust devil follows Linda, a half block behind. With raised expectations Linda continues on to the session with Creative. She feels her headache returning.

❑

On the sidewalk in front of the building where Glasgow/Finn and Westcott occupies the top two floors plus a penthouse, the metalized Mylar gum wrapper waits like a pet collie dog who, having gotten home first, expects a treat.

Linda checks the gym tote for her office shoes. There is one.

"Damn."

Sitting on the sidewalk, she peels off her socks and walks barefoot into Glasgow/Finn and Westcott. No one notices her. Beyond the revolving doors the polished terrazzo floors are cold and wet. Has she walked barefoot from the movies to the office? "Well, *Duh!*" She reinstalls the Nike cross trainers and marches past the security station. She puts some effort into acting casual with the guard. His name tag says George Velasquez.

"Hiya George. Forgot my shoes again."

They share a chuckle. He recognizes her. This must be the place. The elevator doors, brushed nickel and rosewood laminate, open to accept her, sneakers or no.

At the eleventh floor she sails past a rain forest of weeping fig and Japanese bamboo and on into the conference room.

Creative are waiting with the Pork-A-Dillos product launch.

"Here's a little something the guys in R&D thought you could get a handle on, Linda." The little Pork-A-Dillos are uniform tiny curls like the tops of Dairy Queen soft ice cream cones. "Little piggy tails... cute, eh?"

"Curvature of the swine. Very evocative, Sid," says Linda. "This is bullshit. I quit." She stands, walks down the hall and cleans out her desk. She has blown it all away. Pork-A-Dillos was the step up she needed. If she handled the account right—and the product was a shoo-in, it couldn't lose—the next stop was a vice-presidency, then a full partnership.

Cleaning out her desk, Linda picks up a cup of pencils, paper clips and rubber bands. NPR Morning Edition—a Public Radio premium. The cup has nothing new to tell her.

But Tom! How to tell Tom?

She waits for the latest word from her mother.

"Mom?" No answer.

You never tell me anything, her mother would have said.

"Why tell him anything?" *Tell Tom good-bye*. "Tom is a good lay, a pleasant dinner companion, but a parasite."

Linda dumps the cup's contents into the trash and puts it in her gym bag with her sweats and the remaining sensible, low heeled shoe.

Dinner and sex are Tom's survival skills, not mine. Get on with my life. Make the break.

That nice cop has my number.

❑

Pete Garland took it back from a news break. "People! *People!* Please remember that every time you shoot or stab one another the news gets looonger..." He had not paid attention. Pete tried his best to be up, bright and funny, listening only to the newsman's cadences for a return to music, "...and that's one less record we can play." Pete only got to talk four times per hour and liked to make the most of it. In the years since his third divorce, Pete had shuttled from being a major market personality to being a per diem utility announcer, a peon.

The newsman waved frantically from his glassed-in container, most likely another pileup on the Brooklyn-Queens Expressway. Mark Watkins wanted it back. Again. Shit. Across the double glass in the news booth, Mark waited, glowering.

"And here's Mark Watkins with *another* Classic Hits update." More news, less music. Pete, now sixty-three years old, felt the remains of his career eroding under the arbitrary crush of casual violence and driver inattention.

"This is bullshit. I quit," said Pete and walked out.

Linda Winkelman, who still nursed her crush on Pete Garland all these years after the death of her figmentary cat, had just said the same thing only three blocks away.

As the elevator doors opened Pete checked on Mark reading the news in silent animation past a sound lock and the double glazed studio windows. He tried not to slink. At street level a crosstown bus, the Number 5, pulled over to the curb. In his glory days—those days when Conan the cat was almost alive—Pete Garland could afford the cab fare up to Riverside Drive. He thumbed a token out of a scramble of loose change in his pants pocket and boarded the bus.

❑

"You OK?" George Velasquez is staring at her; their noses almost touch. Linda snaps to and finds she is standing in the open elevator. She is at the lobby and can not recall the ride down.

"Power nap." They share a laugh but George moves to take her elbow. She brushes him away.

"I'm fine." *Where was I,* Linda wonders.

George stays close as she walks to the front doors. Linda feels under surveillance. George remarks how rotten the weather is.

As the heavy brass and glass door snicks shut behind her she turns to give George one last farewell. He smiles and waves reassuringly. All will be well. George watches her walk as far as the corner. Satisfied, he returns to his security station.

The cold blast of wet air in the street comes as a relief. Her sweater is starting to itch through her cotton sleeves. Her rolled umbrella, trendy with a shoulder strap, is slipping. Linda opens it and holds it against the sleet, rain, and now snow mixture. There is bright light, silvery brain showers, and Linda feels the world tilt and teeter. Propelled by an uptown crosswind, the peppermint clove gum wrapper approaches her. Linda's hand reaches out to clutch at and hold the rough surface of exterior brickwork. She kneels on the pavement.

❑

An elegant man in checkered golfing knickers addressed a group gathered around a white wicker picnic set. An unfurled picnic umbrella passed through the middle of the table, tilted against any probable sun, a jaunty effect. "So glad you all could make it. What with your busy schedules," said the man in the golfing knickers. *Wasn't I cleaning out my desk?* A large feral cat leapt to straighten a toppled platter of crustless cucumber sandwiches. The sandwiches evaded the cat. The man was Pete Garland in Linda's picture from the radio station.

"Conan! An escaper, go for it."

The cat gave a swipe of his paw and slapped the plate of sandwiches back into play. It caromed off the umbrella to nestle between Linda's breasts.

"Slap shot, precisely executed, Sir Cat," said Pete. "Cute tits, kid," he tossed in Linda's direction, an afterthought.

Linda noticed a janitor with mop and bucket chatting up the geezer from the porn theater. *Well, we're having a party.*

"Do the honors, Conan," said Pete. He poked the cat. "Pour, please?" The cat dispensed tea. In the middle distance a pudgy, red-faced man with a combover formed up for croquet with a very tall young black man wearing basketball sneakers.

"I didn't mean to be any trouble..." *Damn!* Here she was sounding like her mother.

"Lemon?" asked the cat.

"Please. And two sugars."

The concessionaire from the Shopper's Special wiped his nose on a gold-brocaded sleeve, as if seconding the extra sugar. Mister Getty, the deceased private eye from 45th Street, looked on as an elderly woman nicked the platter of sandwiches.

"Mom!"

"Politeness is to do and say the nicest thing in the nicest way," said her late mother, snarfing down the cucumber sandwiches.

A handsome policeman hurried up, her policeman. He was late.

"I believe you forgot this." Her grandmother's brooch.

"Thank you," said Linda.

"Homewrecker," said Mom.

"Miarow," said Conan.

The headache was definitely worse.

❑

A cold, greasy rain begins at 3 o'clock. Wet enough to make a mess and cold enough to be a wet, heavy snow around the rush hour. The thought of reclining in a hot tub with a Kahlua and brandy close to hand gives Linda the strength to carry on. She decides on the downtown local.

Linda positions her token over the slot and slaps it through a residue of chewing gum with the flat of her palm and hits the pipe with her hip, sliding her gym bag over the turret with its three metal bars. There is a comforting clunk. The next bar pops into place, pushing her through: the machine has found her offering acceptable. The peppermint-clove gum wrapper dances around Linda's ankles, rejoicing with her. "Oh. Hello there." Better get a move on. She reaches the concourse.

The saturated humidity hits her and her mouth is dry, dry. This is like exercise in a rubber suit. *Screw the Kahlua; I would sell my soul for a Perrier and lemon. Oh, Jesus!* Her bra strap has just given up the ghost, its elastic sodden and limp. For this day's work, Tom had better take her out for one last dinner, not the usual boil-in-a-bag frozen gourmet treats.

"Have a lemonade. It's full of vitamin C. And it's green—they make it in Jersey. You know you love it, Linda," says Linda's mother. A shoo-wop group shuffles and bops from Mom's kitchen radio. Linda's mother's kitchen radio plays all Mom, all the time.

"Mom! Not now, please. And it's not green, it's chartreuse."

"A nice glass of lemonade and hot noodle pudding. I have nutmeg kugel cooling on the stove. With raisins, your favorite."

"Mom, I always hated your kugel. I ate it to shut you up."

"Linda, that's not nice."

Next, the ramps. Down three stories to the trains. I can make it.

"Hold the doors! Hold the doors!" Linda runs as fast as her skirt will allow. Legs pumping, teeth clenched, she impacts the wall of cramped commuters already on board—Oof! She looks around defiantly, claiming her space. The doors slide shut with a pneumatic whoosh that catches her bag outside as the train starts to move. One quick, hard jerk and the bag is free and inside. The doors' floppy safety edges meet—the caress of rubber lips on her thigh. *Huh. Make something of that.* The headache is now a weight of pain, sore to the touch if she could touch that place deep behind her eyes. Linda waits for the agony to resume.

Left behind on the platform is the cast-off gum wrapper.

❑

Everything in the Village is stippled aquatint in shades of gray. A patch of wintery sky widens above as Linda drags her gym tote, umbrella and weary, failing body up the steps of the Christopher Street stop at Sheridan Square.

As she nears the top steps she peers out at sidewalk level through the railings.

A tow-headed pre-schooler hip-hops alongside his baby brother's stroller as a family walks past through the long shadows of early evening. The sleet has become a freezing rain; they ignore it. *He knocked her up and left school at sixteen to pump gas, for this is the code*, thinks Linda. This stringy young mom would always be yesteryear's prom date. Last year the toddler was in the stroller. They are on their way to the bodega for Coke and Twinkies.

The foil gum wrapper spins past the family grouping, across Seventh Avenue, and skitters up to Linda.

"Oh, hello again, gum wrapper." Tentative spidery tracings bloom on the insides of her eyes.

The peppermint clove wrapper is towing a streamer of yellow letters. *Like those little airplanes with advertising banners at Coney Island,* Linda thinks. Like the subtitles at the Shopper's Special. She tries reading the subtitles. The yellow letters are at a peculiar angle she has not seen in any other movie. The film parts and flys off the screen, leaving only a blinding white glare. An uncapped projection lamp brings a Hiroshima sunrise to Greenwich Village. Tornado winds whistle and midtown the sun stands still above Times Square.

The family grouping is returning. Each holds a plastic-wrapped glass pint of Classic Coke. The young mom steers the stroller, a big brown paper bag full of chips and sugary treats wrapped around the bar under her hands. The young mom's stooped shoulders lean wearily into a long gray march of duty.

I could have been her.

Linda is suffused with a runner's aerobic high. It is the year of her own junior prom. She should have gone with the boy—Eddie? But Mom had said no. Unprotected, rapturous sex in Eddie's car instead. Eddie is now pumping gas.

When he isn't fucking me, Tom is rinsing the rice cooker. He calls this house husbanding. He stares out the window. These are the little things that make up a life. I used to have a cat named Conan when I was a kid. I had to get rid of him because Mom had allergies.

The sleet now carries ice crystals that bite the skin as the driving sideways winds from Jersey pick up. The young parents and their children scuttle for cover. *This is the Big One and happening to me*. To be sucked into oblivion by a cerebral thrombosis—equipment failure—was so tacky. *And just when I had everything almost worked out*.

On Riverside Drive, in the fumes of the departing Number 5 bus, Pete Garland realizes he has left his keys on his desk at the radio station. He ponders his situation, jobless and obsolete, and toys with the idea of suicide. There is a shotgun in the hall closet. Maybe he'll get a cat. Pete calls a locksmith.

Linda bends double with the searing pain behind her eyes. She grasps at the nearest railing to steady herself.

Apocalypse, yes, but not now.

"Linda?"

"Yes, Mom."

"Everything is clove scented. With peppermint. You noticed?"

"I noticed."

"So glad you found the time to visit. I got your favorite cookies from Gristede's—the oatmeal stuffed date?"

"With lemonade?"

"With lemonade." Linda Winkelman was born the year they invented frozen lemonade. It was the year they added the Bullwinkle balloon to the Macy's parade.

The Year They Invented Frozen Lemonade was first published in *The Harrow* [www.theharrow.com] January 2008.

The Song of the Rice Barge Coolie

Hail to our mother, who caused the messenger, the soldier, the worker,
Who scattered the seeds of her body
As she came forth from Paradise:
Great and white, fat with honeydew,
Her diadem a ring of captive queens.

Hail to the goddess who shines with her bright wings
Triumphant in the face of the deceiver.
Hail to our mother, who dropped her wings
Who poured forth abundance as she came from Paradise.
See how they love her, gathered near!

"Oh, Jim—it's a full cape," trilled Ginny Levitan. The house was a daisy chain of architectural whimsy, a ramble of weathered ells, wings and add-ons in the style of whatever moment. Their house-to-be cuddled coyly behind a tangle of alders and runaway roses.

The house was not unoccupied. Ten-by-ten-inch white spruce sills had been shaved thin from the inside out, resonant as a fiddle back for over a century. Raddled with passageways, the sills still supported the house. Beneath the floors, past wide boards of ancient pumpkin pine pumiced, oiled and varnished by successive generations of householders disappeared, dead or run away, lay the galleries of the Long Walkers.

"It's leaning," said her husband. "And I don't think it's quite a cape—too many floors and chimneys." Theirs was a marriage defined by silent protocols, forgotten but honored. No fights. Not today. Not yet, at least, but it was still early. "Anyway it's most likely got issues—rotted sills, bats, beetles. Something, carpenter ants. The carpenter ants own New England," said Jim. "Bob Vila said that once on This Old House. If we've got 'em, we'll never get rid of them. Or maybe Norm Abram said it."

The house clung to a granite outcropping, the Ledge locally. An overgrown path led out back. "Hold on. I'll do some reconnaissance." Jim picked his way down the ragged slate of the ledge to get around for a better view. He stopped to examine a shrub, a dwarf juniper stunted by the perpetual onshore wind, and gave the shrub a yank. From the rocks below came a delayed rattle of pebbles—there was a sheer drop to the shale beach. Ginny went to thumping clapboards and poking in the remains of a perennial bed. Sandpipers dodged the pebbles and scurried after small things left by the tide.

As Jim scrambled around the far end of the house he stumbled and fell clutching at a tussock of witch grass. It was a long way down. His heart galloped in his ears; he'd better get started on that exercise program. He gingerly picked his way back to his wife. There she was, trying to look in a window. "The place goes on and on," he shouted.

"What?" The wind took her words. Ginny rubbed at the windowpane with her sleeve to get a better look inside. Her cry had startled a flight of swifts from one unused chimney.

"There's an outhouse," Jim bellowed through cupped hands. There was a mild medicinal odor of gin from the juniper branch.

"You what?" Ginny called. Her husband was at the far corner of the house; he must have circled the place. The wind that twisted the juniper shredded her words. The chimney swifts twittered, circled, then flew off.

"I said we have outdoor plumbing. I almost fell over a cliff. Didn't you hear me?"

"No. A privy? Really?"

"Yeah, stuck on way down at the end so they didn't have to walk through four feet of snow in the winter." He dusted off his knees and tried to look none the worse for wear. "Neat."

"Think we can afford it?"

"Let's find out." They called and made an appointment. Barbara Casmirczak, a licensed broker, would meet them the next morning.

❑

The Lady Mother of the Long Walkers was singing. Her ululations were a requiem: the kidnapped queens, her sisters, were dying. Large, pallid bodies lay lifeless in an orderly row. This was not the usual order of things. The queen suspected a slaughter by slaves, rogue elements running wild.

The Mother of Us All, goddess and progenetrix, had summoned her Master of Messengers. "You will be my eyes. I seem to be blind."

"And wingless, goddess, as it was meant to be when you went forth from Paradise." The goddess had been blind for all the generations that called her goddess and mother, but the royal scout—Indltainalyei, known as Indil—thought better of reminding her of this.

"Indil?"

"Yes, Lady."

"My sister, is she dead? Go and give her a poke, would you?" The great white presence that was the Lady Mother of the Long Walkers indicated the row of captive queens on their dais beneath her, deferentially lower.

"Which sister, Lady?"

"Pick one. The closest. Use your celebrated initiative." This was as close to irony as the Lady Mother allowed herself to come. She felt the threat of immediate extinction excused some flexibility.

The Master of Messengers approached the nearest brood queen.

"Well?"

Indltainalyei, known as Indil, hooked into the supernumerary queen's eye with the distal spur of a middle leg. The head detached and bounced dispiritedly away down a slight grade into a connecting chamber. "Your sister would appear to be indeed dead, Majesty."

The Mother of Us All, goddess and progenetrix, sighed. "Indil, Indil, what shall I do with you?"

"I am your Master of Messengers, Lady."

"Yes, yes, yes, yes. But which one?"

"Ask the Icaros, Lady. They will tally me out when I am enumerated at the doorway to beyond the sand."

"Suppose you ask them, then tell me. Are you not an individual? But then I suppose it is too much to ask you to think for yourself. And a rain of oily poison has enflamed the nannies and the soldiers. Look into it."

Indil pretended not to hear.

❑

"Hi, I'm Barbara. Call me Babs." The woman was waiting when they pulled up, fiftyish and an almost natural blond. A great body, Ginny noticed, and eager—attractive, with the too-even tanning that spoke of hours at the spa. The woman wore a no-nonsense blue power suit with crisp shoulders and a deep cleavage that announced she was all business but could play hard, too.

"Babs Casmirczak, your estate representative." Babs negotiated a minor adjustment to her breasts. They jiggled back into their snuggery. Too casual, practiced, too unconscious this gesture, designed to draw an onlooker after them. The woman leaned forward to shake hands.

"Jim Levitan." Jim's eyes lingered at Babs's tanned clavicle, then dropped into her cleavage. He pulled himself up short and threw an arm across Ginny's shoulder. He still held the woman's hand.

"This is Virginia Levitan," said Jim Levitan. He did not say, My wife, Ginny. Ginny Levitan added Babs Casmirczak to her catalog of affliction, right after menopause, and dubbed her The Real Estate Vampire.

The Vampire turned to Ginny. "Hi there?"

The woman ended every sentence with a question mark like a high school girl. Moves and boobs were her stock in trade. The Vampire was a people person. Ginny figured Babs and she were about the same age.

❑

"Command me, Lady. I am your Master of Messengers."

"But you all look so alike," said the Mother of Us All.

"We are not the same. Your sisters leaven the moiety, Lady. The captive queens strengthen our blood lines."

"But you are the same."

"The same as yesterday, Lady."

"Indil, don't lark about. You are worse than one of the nannies, rolling my eggs and clucking lullabies. Indil?"

"Yes, Lady?"

"If my sister is dead, and believe me she has been thus for some days, where then is Housekeeping? They should be hauling her off."

"They have gone mad, Lady."

"And you did not think to tell me."

"I am yours to command, Lady."

"And I neglected to ask. Very well. Go out, beyond the sand. Tell me what you see."

"Yes, Lady."

"While you are gone I shall recite the annals. Rains of poison have enflamed the nannies and the soldiers. I shall now sing."

The Master of Messengers departed, down the dais, stepping over the large white corpse of a supernumerary queen.

❑

The Real Estate Vampire rummaged in her bag, dipping and jiggling. "I do have the key. Oh, here it is." A large key ring with a green tag was held up triumphantly and they were in. The great mahogany door swung on silent hinges.

The men must have oiled it, thought Babs.

She probably had it oiled, thought Ginny.

"Nice door. Lignum vitae, the captain brought it home from the Indies. Architectural detailing..." said Babs. She let her sentence hang, an inflected question with no answer.

"Nice door." It was mahogany, thought Ginny. There probably was no captain; the woman was winging it. There was a remote fluttering as a trapped bird banged its head again and again against a windowpane on one of the upper floors.

"Oops." Babs dropped her set of keys. At the jingle the trapped bird gave a last desperate flutter. Then there was silence. Jim leapt forward to retrieve the keys but with a sidelong glance at his wife let Babs pick them up. As she straightened she shrugged her décolletage out of play and tossed back her hair. Jim studiously examined the turnings of a baluster.

"I know it seems a little bleak now. But wait till you see the kitchen."

Kitchens were a girl thing. Ginny noticed a pair of running shoes in Babs's shoulder bag. For a fast getaway after a quick sale? Ginny doubted it.

❑

Nodding dismissal to the Master of Messengers' retreating second abdomen, the goddess, the Mother of Us All, intoned the chronicles of the Long Walkers. Her emissary felt the tremulous trilling rise behind him as he gaited down an access gallery. The Lady Mother noodled vaguely recalled scales, a bagpiper testing a psychic melody pipe, a music that was new when the moon was closer to the Earth and the pine forests shivered to the cry of the giant red wolf.

There was nothing, not a clue of colony-wide madness and death in all the millennia of her kind. Time was smooth; the madness of the great-headed soldiers was but a stutter. The poisoned rains were nowhere in the annals.

Indil passed out of the brood chambers and turned upward toward the light.

❑

"The owners left in a hurry but the house is broom-clean. We had the exterminators in. Just in case." Babs was improvising as she went along, but she figured that they had. "And here..." She attempted a piece of stagy business involving her arm and a window blind. “You have a wonderful oceanfront view. Without all the extra taxes...” The blind collapsed, scattering slats across the floor. The Real Estate Vampire stepped gracefully aside as a minor dust cloud settled on her Clark walkers. “...because of the road. Between your property and the shore,” she finished.

Aplomb, grace under fire. Gotta hand it to her, thought Ginny. Already it is our house; we have a view. She took a surreptitious peek at her husband.

“Really?” said Jim. Evidently the hustle was working.

“You’ll love the kitchen, it’s original, or restored, whatever.” Babs led them down a narrow, twisting inside stairwell that seemed to revolve around the big central chimney. The Real Estate Vampire tossed back her hair. It fell into an effortless arrangement, styled. “They were going to open a colonial-style bed and breakfast before they divorced. A walk-in fireplace with a brick oven, Dutch tiling, terra cotta floors... Ta-Dah!” A wonderland of cooking paraphernalia depended from chains and hooks, there being a scarcity of shelf space.

“The kitchen is indeed a panoply of pots. That’s a joke,” said Ginny Levitan.

❑

Negotiating a series of switchbacks, the Master of Messengers gained a main tunnel where Icaro the soldier saluted him.

“Hail Indil.” Mandibles gaped; antennae swept the floor beneath his massive and, compared to Indil, oversized head.

“Which Indil am I? The Lady wants to know.”

The Icaro caressed a scented ceiling. “Thirty-seventh. That’s the tally.” He consulted other patches of olfactory memory that clung to the walls of the passage. “Weather report: south southeast, go against the wind. Dry today.”

“Thanks for the meteorology. Any of the others back yet?”

“No. There is a thing out in the world that kills them.” The Icaro groomed an antenna. “Die well, Master of Messengers. The world is ours. Hail, Indil Thirty-seven.” Icaro the soldier returned to his post.

“If they are dead, these Indils one through thirty-six, how do you know?”

“Food exchange and perhaps I will tell you,” said the Icaro, exposing his underbelly, a gesture of trust. Indil had no food to share but mounted the Icaro and massaged his abdomen. “Ahh, that’s it, right there.” The soldier was ecstatic.

"So how do you know they are all dead? Dead is dead." Indil Thirty-seven clutched at the Icaro's compound eye with his mandible. There was the urge to squeeze, ever the slightest. The Icaro felt the adjustment in Indil's grip and his ecstasy diminished.

"Careful there, Indil. You could die here and now."

"Pardon me if I breathe your air, Icaro. Go and milk a louse."

Mandibles snapped as the soldier threw off the Master of Messengers. "One made it home. Number One, not the pronoun. Died right where you are standing. Housekeeping came and cut him up for the common pot. Those guys are right on the ball."

"Eat any of the returned Indil number One before Housekeeping made away with him?" asked Indil Thirty-seven.

"Just a nibble," said the Icaro. "Odd you should mention it, scout. I have been having the digestives ever since."

"We have gone too far, then," said Indil.

"Where is too far? Beyond the sand?" The Icaro was perplexed for he was a creature of duty.

"Too far is wherever you do not return from," said Indil Thirty-seven, Master of Messengers.

"Well then, we have gone too far. We must die, scout."

"Hail then, Icaro. And farewell for I too must go beyond the sand. Icaro?" There was no reply. The Icaro had died standing, his joints locked. The dead Icaro's sweet death-sign was in the air. From two levels down there was a rustle as Housekeeping felt the snap of the soldier's final rigor. Indil Thirty-seven gaited away.

❑

"And down there..." Babs Casmirczak peered over the soapstone sink to check on the view from a kitchen window "...is Delsey's Head where they laid the keel of the Barbary Princess, the last of the opium clippers. That was in 1853." Ginny wondered if the Barbary Princess got laid a lot. She just bet that Babs did.

"Wanna look?" Babs wriggled off the sink.

Jim took her place and with some effort got the window pried open. The tide was coming in. The kitchen looked out on a prospect of ocean and the out-door privy. The stunted juniper was gone. He must have loosened it. "Whew! It's a long way down. At least we've got some air."

Jim Levitan thumped a floor joist with a heel. He bounced up and down a few times. “Huh. Springy. Any trouble ahead?”

The word trouble hung in the clammy air. “Like insect damage?” said Ginny.

Ginny Levitan caught a slight movement at the corner of her eye. Indil Thirty-seven, Master of Messengers, threaded through a fisheye astigmatism of glittering implements, his passage mirrored in a hanging dangle of polished copper bottoms. A dot, the messenger moved in his myriads.

“Our house seems to have an infestation,” said Ginny. She added a plague of ants to her catalog of affliction. Babs first, then menopause, then ants.

“New England. Carpenter ants everywhere. Bob Vila said that.” Jim nodded knowingly. “I saw this one show where...” He was the expert; he watched home improvement TV. “Poison is tricky stuff, Ginny. We can learn to live with the ants.”

Like we have learned to live with each other, thought Ginny Levitan. “There’ll be more.” She reached out to squash the ant.

“Oh, for Christ’s sake, honey, it’s just one ant.”

“I don’t want them,” said Ginny.

“We had some men in,” said Babs, uncertain as to just what the men had done; they had probably done something. “The men put out some bait. They sprayed...” said Babs.

Underfloor, maddened by the dust precipitated by Jim Levitan’s footfalls, the Icaros cast about, blindly killing any living creature that struggled past. A line of foragers passed the entranceway each carrying a grain of rice; they died under flashing mandibles. There was a distant clicking as Housekeeping readied to clean up after the slaughter.

Indil Thirty-seven scuttled through a grouted aisle separating tightly fitted slabs of terra cotta.

“Shit. It’s gone down a crack,” said Ginny.

The Real Estate Vampire shrugged. “You know these old homes...” They were assured the house was sound.

Jim thumped the floor one more time for good measure. Through the thunder, the Master of Messengers still heard the song of the Lady Mother.

❑

“Ginny. *Ginny...?*” Jim’s wife had that someplace else look of hers. Ginny was hearing God’s dial tone, somewhere. Again. She was gone.

"Ginny?"

"You don't hear it?"

"For Christ's sake, Ginny! Not here." To his immediate shame, Jim Levitan was angry at his wife for perhaps dying just as they were about to become homeowners. We can save the epileptics for our curtain call. Or at home. This home, ours if we just...

"Snap out of it, godammit," he whispered in her ear. No response. Ginny Levitan's pupils were centered and small, her eyes expressionless. For her, time had stopped; she was off counting the lines of force from the Earth's magnetic field.

"Ginny..." this was a hoarser whisper, more urgent. Jim Levitan felt, and rightly, that his wife having a fit during a house tour would damage their credibility in future negotiations. "Poor Jim, his wife has fits..." the word would get out and the neighbors would not exchange invitations for drinks, smorgasbords, croquet, whatever the hell they did in Maine. They were socially ruined before they had even begun.

Jim took a fast check, one unmonitored quick peek to see if the real estate agent had noticed that she had lost half of her house tour.

Babs had stopped cold. The Moen faucets, her next destination in the directory of detailing, were forgotten. "Hey, you okay?" She smiled at Jim and knelt next to Ginny. She suspected one of those small strokes she heard about on TV. They were a sign of aging. Tiny pupils. Weird. Maybe she was on dope. You never could tell.

Ginny willed her eyes into a coherent focus. "You really don't hear it?"

"Hear what?" said Babs. Maybe the house was settling.

"A song, sort of. Music, singing," said Ginny.

Jim Levitan steered his wife to an upholstered window seat. The cushions had been covered with newspapers as a dust cover. The papers crinkled as they sat together. "Honey?"

"I was hearing something strange. Like a cheap battery radio playing Armenian music in a far-off room. I just imagined it. I'll be fine." Jim looked at her for several long moments, silent.

Babs picked right up with her pitch. "...completely rewired. I mean new. And they pulled out the stops on the plumbing. A thousand dollars a pop in all the bathrooms."

Ginny rubbed her eyes, checking for any for residual damage. Normal. Jim was such a worrywart.

Babs smiled a thin, grim smile. "They spent all they had. They went broke before they opened."

❑

Unchaperoned, Jim and Ginny examined their dream house. Babs Casmirczak had run them through to closing in a record five days. The Levitans adored the house, their house. It was an easy sale for Babs.

They called in a contractor for a thorough inspection. "Whippy," said the contractor. He bounced up and down a couple of times to demonstrate what he meant. The brass drawer pulls of a bleached oak dresser jiggled and rattled, its mirror tilted threateningly. "See? Whippy."

"Strange air, strange air," beneath their feet an Icaro plodded by at the ready, his giant head swiveling from side to side, alert. Work parties made careful soundings lest a shivered exterior wall had let in strange air and unwanted light.

The contractor jumped again. He looked wise and said, "Four-foot centers. This used to be the attic. You hear things at night?"

"Like what?" Jim readied himself for a quaint, historic tale of a sea captain's ghost.

"Yes," said Ginny before the man could reply. "A clicking sound. In the walls. Like somebody cracking his knuckles. But not." Jim looked at his wife and registered exasperation.

"A clicking?" asked the contractor. "Real steady?"

Ginny nodded and glared back at her husband. "I know what I hear, Jim. Yes, even over your snoring." Touché.

Ginny walked the man to the door. "Whippy," he repeated his diagnosis. Ginny felt her head getting tight, a warning.

The contractor waved and called from the street. "You got ants, lady. Better call the exterminator."

"Wha...?"

"Bugs. A potential infestation. They could be big trouble down the line. Carpenter ants," said the contractor. "Gotta get 'em early. You don't want to hear an estimate." The contractor left a card. He neglected to say when "early" was.

❑

Ginny's eyes were glued shut with the mucilage of sleep. She rubbed them at their corners to loosen the bond. Ouch, too much light. Her eyelids slammed shut. Slowly, slowly, Ginny Levitan, née Bujac, eased them open, squinting at a hazy morning through a paling of lashes. She tried to remember her father. They had splashed through the puddles together, puddles with their upside-down skies.

"Well, honey, that'll bring in Chicago."

Ginny's dad had erected a TV mast when she was six years old. Her favorites were Buffalo Bob and his sidekick Howdy Doody, the freckle-faced puppet with, she supposed, red hair. Color TV had yet to reach Racine, Wisconsin. Dad had bought her a metal lunch pail with a color lithograph of Howdy with red hair so it must be so. She tried to remember her imaginary playmate. "How's your little playmate today, Ginny?" Dad thought the Flim-Flam Man was an elf. Dad had named the Flim-Flam Man: "Careful Baby, the Film-Flam Man goin' getcha!" There would be giggles and a laugh as he swung her high into the fluffy friendly clouds. Dad believed in the Flim-Flam Man too.

"She flashed her tits at Jim, Dad, the Real Estate Vampire. Oh, I wish you were here. I wish the Flim-Flam Man was here." Dad gave no response. Dad was dead. Her father's face faded.

Shifting her breasts to each side, Ginny balanced over the side of the bed and allowed her head to dangle to the floor. The world was refreshingly different upside down, like the sky in a rain puddle, blue with high summer cumulus clouds that she once obliterated with her little girl yellow galoshes.

"Carry your lunch pail today?" The Flim-Flam Man had red hair, just like Howdy Doody. But he was more, well... masculine. Ginny Bujac, for that was her name then, liked his tight curly hair, the corded musculature of his shoulders and forearms. He was a comfort when the other kids picked on her.

"That was in Racine, Wisconsin, fifty years ago. I splashed the sky away," said Ginny.

A line of ants, single file, marched across the pine flooring beside her nose.

"Hello, ants," said Ginny. A lone ant appeared from under the baseboard. He was carrying a grain of rice and headed against the flow of traffic back down the line of marchers.

"Hello, Little Ginny," said the Flim-Flam Man.

"You are a figment."

"Really," said the Flim-Flam Man.

"Of course. I am nuts. You were all well and good when I was six years old, but..."

"Ginny... we splashed the puddles and made the sky go upside down, didn't we?"

"Well..."

"Together?"

"Always together."

"You've got ants, Little Ginny. You heard what the contractor said. Better call the exterminator."

"Dad...?"

The Flim-Flam Man smiled, a hearty manly smile. "They could mean big trouble down the line. Carpenter ants," said the Flim-Flam Man. "Gotta get 'em early."

Ginny decided to kill the ants herself.

❑

Ginny found out that she was a loser at the game of life by accident. It was the running shoes. She noticed them in her husband's gym bag and recalled the pair of shoes in Babs Casmirczak's bag. Jim had been working out three, four nights a week at the Bangor YMCA, a good hour-plus drive away. He had said, "I'm closing in on 58 and I want to slow the process." Reasonable enough.

Dinner was on the table. A bouquet of purple periwinkles in a jelly-glass vase sat between them. "Macaroni and cheese. Again?" The implication was that Ginny was trying to fatten him up against all the good work he was doing at the gym. Ginny noticed that Jim was putting on a spare tire despite all his workouts.

"Help yourself, enjoy," said Ginny. Jim tucked right in.

Two nights later and Jim was a no-show. Ginny called the Bangor YMCA. A valley girl voice, sounding knowledgeable, all chirpy and preppy, assured her they were, indeed, open till 9:00 P.M. "Levitan? Jim Levitan? I'll call down and have one of the trainers check the sign-in sheet." Ginny was on hold. After five-plus minutes, the chirpy girl returned.

"No, he's not signed in. But that doesn't mean anything; it's just suggested, not required. In case of an emergency. Do you want him paged?"

No, Ginny did definitely not want him paged. "Thank you for taking the trouble."

“No problem. Say, why don’t you sign up? Our Seniors’ Special...” Ginny hung up on her. Later on, ten-ish, Jim arrived, hair slicked back and still wet from the shower.

“Good workout?”

“Terrific.”

“You know... I was thinking of maybe joining myself.”

Jim started to talk, then hesitated, “It’s a long drive...”

“Just over an hour...” Long enough to get your hair dry if that’s where you were. “You do it. We could get the family rate. Or I could sign up on the Seniors’ Special.”

“You’re not that out of shape.”

“Thanks for noticing.” She pulled one shoe from her husband’s gym bag. The tissue paper from the factory was still wadded into the toe. He had never laced them up. “Nice shoes. If I didn’t know better, I’d guess you were having an affair with Babs, the real estate agent.”

Jim flushed, turning the color of a boiled lobster from his neck to the part in his hair. “Uh... What?” He shuffled his feet and looked away.

Ginny slept in the guest bedroom from then on.

❑

“Sister, sister, can you hear me?”

“Yes, I can hear you.” The voice—which Ginny feared only she could hear and at that only in her mind—quavered with the peculiar quality of an overseas radio transmission, the heterodyning phase shifts she had heard from her father’s short wave radio: “Shhhh, pumpkin, that’s London calling, the BBC World Service.” Or Moscow, or Mozambique.

“Sister, soon it will only be you and I.”

Ginny Levitan struggled to be awake, rubbing muzzy cobwebs from the edges of her consciousness. “Who are you?” She could not locate the source of the voice.

“I am the Lady Mother. Except for myself, of course. I did not know my mother but I must assume that there was one. My fecundator, the Father of Us All, died at the moment of consummation.”

“My father died twenty years ago.”

“Ah, sister, so did the Father of Us All.”

"Where are you?"

"Where I have always been. I am singing."

"Uh, that's nice."

"No, it is not nice, as you say. But it is necessary."

"If you are not just some imbalance with my endocrine system, where are you?"

"I might ask you the same question if I knew what it was. Sister, sister. I cry alone, always alone. Into the emptiness, the great darkness outside the galleries, beyond the sand. I have reached out in my despair and you have answered. Where have you been?"

"Racine, Wisconsin, then Chicago mostly. Jim organized seminars for the University. Then here, to Maine. We retired early."

"I do not know of these things. Where is early?"

Ginny rummaged in the drawer of her bedside table for the card of that therapist Jim had recommended. She deliberately tore the card apart. "There. He says I am nuts. What does that make you?" The shredded bits fell to the bedroom carpet like confetti behind a parade.

"What I have always been, the Lady Mother of the Long Walkers. Sister, I need your help," the voice sang.

Ginny stirred the fallen confetti with a toe. "About now I'm the one who needs professional help. Just what did you have in mind?"

A wordless singing went on for several minutes.

❑

With a burst of pre-menstrual energy, Ginny was beating the blues by cleaning out the attic when she discovered the ancient can, tucked away where the roof timbers met at the eaves.

"Rodenticide, kills ants and other household pests," she read. "Arsenic trioxide." The label was printed on parchment colored paper in red ink. There was a picture of a rat, looking feral and healthy. A skull and crossbones adorned one corner. She carried the can to the kitchen where she spread some newspapers and prised off the lid. The can was full of a dense, white powder.

And the phone was ringing.

Yeah?" Ginny was trying to read the label on the can of ant poison. She balanced the phone against her ear while she rummaged in a drawer for her spare glasses.

"Shit," said Ginny.

"What?"

"I just spilled my poison. Who is this?" Ginny decided there was not enough poison spilled to do any real damage and squeegeed up loose powder with a wet paper towel.

"Spilled your what?"

"Forget it."

"Ginny?"

"Yes."

"Ginny, it's Linda."

"Linda." Who the hell was Linda?

"Linda Throckmorton. I haven't seen you since high school."

"Oh God. Linda."

"I wanted to call and tell you how sorry I am about your father. His death?"

"Linda, that was twenty years ago. Have you just heard?"

"I didn't know what to say at the time. I couldn't call. And now..."

"Better late than never." A pause. "Linda, is that why you haven't talked to me for twenty years, because you didn't call when my dad died?"

"Yes."

"Linda, where are you?"

"California. Bob teaches at San Jose State."

"Jesus Christ, Linda. We were friends."

"Ginny, I'm so miserable. We, I, am in counseling, A.A. My marriage is a mess; I've been going to Weight-Watchers, Jenny Craig..."

"You're fat, you're seeing a shrink, you're drying out and Bob is fucking the cheerleaders and you're sorry my dad is dead. That about right so far?"

"Oh..." There was silence, then a quiet sobbing.

Ginny watched a line of ants struggle with the task of transporting rice from a bag of basmati down from the kitchen counter back to their nest. Her rice from her cabinet. She reached for the can of arsenic trioxide and slammed it down on the counter, hard. The lid popped loose, sending a cloud of gray-white dust into the air. Ginny dived for the paper towels and moistening one placed it against her nose. She juggled the telephone. She had twisted the cord into an electrical macramé.

"Get a grip on yourself. Linda. We're fifty-six years old, for Chrissakes—terminal ennui, the death of marriage, blah, blah, blah. And forget passion. I started high impact aerobics to tighten up my ass. Now Jim is fucking Babs Casmirczak."

"Babs. *What*-zack?

"Casmirczak, the Real Estate Vampire. She's the agent who sold us our dream house. Jim is fucking her and I'm suing to get some equity back."

"And you're suing for divorce?"

"Or something, anything. Or I will be."

There was snuffle at Linda's end of the conversation. "Ginny, this took a lot of courage for me."

"Pick up the phone Linda—just once in twenty years—it's not heavy. A little penitence goes a long way. Fuck you. I am one royally pissed-off screaming termagant."

"I called you every day, in my mind. I've been in therapy. I was there for you, Ginny."

A reedy skirling of tiny bagpipes, "Sister, sister, help me..." The bagpipers ceased but the song continued, a song with no content.

Trailing the telephone cord behind her, Ginny went to the refrigerator and pulled out a container of yogurt, full of fat and with sugary fruit syrup on the bottom. Linda said something, stopped, waited for a reply. Ginny hummed tunelessly. "What's that?" Linda was still on the line. "Oh, you're still there; I thought I heard someone breathing. That's The Song of the Rice Barge Coolie. I was watching ants walk cross the kitchen counter just now. Bertolt Brecht. I learned it in college. A theater course."

"We did *Showboat* in high school, remember?"

Ginny peeled the seal from the yogurt container. Elbows on the kitchen counter, her fingers traced idle swirls in leftover poison dust. "The ants are emptying a five-pound bag of rice. Grain by grain. I thought the ants' achievement deserved some recognition."

Linda sang, "It's just my Bill, an ordinary guy..."

"They work all day for a chance to work the following day, the coolies. They get to eat whatever spills. They sleep under a bridge if they are lucky. Then they die."

“Like Ol’ Man River. In *Showboat.*” Linda’s small, snot-filled voice rose and fell in the earpiece. “’He jes’ keeps rollin’ along...’”

“Not really. The coolies will never get there. They will all die. Their children will finish the trip. Then their children will die.” Ginny’s hands played with the old poison can, prising off the lid, squeezing it shut. The lid became jammed. A large ring of keys, Jim’s keys, with Babs’s Century 21 advertising bauble lay on the table. Ginny bent a key getting the lid off. “Ouch.” A bright spot of blood shimmered on the white powder, her blood. Ginny cursed Linda Throckmorton. In far California Linda took a snot-filled gulp, a warning that she was taking on air for an extended conversation. Ginny hung up the phone.

❑

That song again, the Armenian music from a distant radio.

“Hello. Are you there?” said Ginny.

“I cry alone, always alone,” said the Lady Mother of the Long Walkers. “I remember the sun,” the singer trilled, “the great light. And the blessed wind with white blossoms falling upward. They promised much but I was betrayed.”

“That’s true love for you, once in a lifetime. Jim is fucking the Real Estate Vampire.”

The Lady Mother did not ask the meaning of vampire or even fucking a vampire. Ginny figured the concepts were a given. After all, the voice was her hallucination.

“Kill your husband, sister, as I killed mine. He has betrayed you after all...” The Lady Mother became hushed and insinuating. “Sister,” she said, “I ripped out his organs of generation. He was so beautiful.” Her song rose and fell. “The eggs, my eggs, my larvae, my pupae, the hatchlings, are dying, my sister queens are dead and lying in a row...”

“I have my own problems.” Pictures of tunnels, shafts and galleries, brood chambers and a purposeful thronging skittered across Ginny’s mind. Large white bodies lay dead. “Jesus Christ. You’re an ant.”

“If you say it, sister, then it is so.” The Lady Mother of the Long Walkers was sure and composed.

Ginny felt an early tingle of migraine, a hometown nova about to bloom in her head. Where was the Dilantin? The first time this music played she had had a seizure. She could kill the ants and stop the singing in her head. And, so it followed with ineluctable logic, why not Jim, too. The idea was not unpleasing. Virginia Levitan, née Bujac, was not sure that her husband deserved killing just for having an affair—or really bad taste in women, meaning Babs. He had said she was fat. Fat and fits. And he had criticized her right in front of the Real Estate Vampire. Death happens for reasons. She trusted that the ants would appreciate this.

"I have seizures. Prozac wasn't invented yet. I got Dilantin. I got the anti-convulsants. Try Dilantin for twenty years. I have hair on my tits. I hear voices; I am dizzy. I foam at the mouth and fall down. Boom. Like that. Right on my hairy tits."

"Sister."

"Yes?"

"There is one I can trust, a messenger. You will help him."

❑

Ginny Levitan, cuckolded wife, awakened to the reasonableness that her rear end was cold. Coffee-making odors and subdued businesses filtered in from the kitchen. Motion was not on the menu until she got sufficiently coordinated to figure a way through the overnight tangle of knotted bedclothes. Her foot was caught.

Too early. This was as early as days got. One extravagant fling got all the covers over back on top of her and Ginny was in the secret garden of her own woman smells. A click from the kitchen, low radio morning sounds. The refrigerator lunked shut, more coffee aroma. Her wandering husband had come home.

"Yoo-hoo, Ginny, coffee's on and the bathroom's clear."

Reveille. Considerate Jim.

Jim came into the bedroom, tousled Ginny's hair and gave a desultory peck on the nose. He ran a hand up the inside of her thigh.

"Don't."

❑

"Indil Thirty-seven, Master of Messengers, I would have you visit my sister."

"Your sister is dead, Lady."

"This is another sister. A woman."

"Lady? I am sincerely sorry for the deaths of your sisters."

"Master of Messengers, you are a fool."

"Yes, Lady."

“I have talked with my sister and now she is going to kill us all. Then there will be no more Long Walkers. This I cannot allow. It is my duty. And her husband, too,” the Lady Mother added as an afterthought. “My sister, the new, the living, sister has revealed to me that I am an ant. You too are an ant, as are the workers, the Icaros and even Housekeeping and the nannies. She believes that we are insignificant.”

“What is an ant, Lady?”

“Why, we are. And have been so since the moon filled the sky and the seasons did not change.”

“What may I do for my Lady?”

“Kill the woman and, failing that, bring home her corrosive powders to destroy the Icaros. The poison rains have made them mad. I can always make more.”

“What is a woman?”

“Do I have to tell you everything?”

“Yes, Lady.”

❑

At the granite-topped center island of her renovated, better than new, kitchen, Ginny poked around in the drawers the previous owners had left chock full of utensils.

“Ahh...” She came up with a silver-handled mold for forming decorative cones from confectioner’s sugar. Dipping it in the can of poison she pressed out mounded ellipses in a half-circle.

Indil Thirty-seven, after navigating the grouted alleyways that separated the tiles of the kitchen floor, struggled with clicking articulations over the polished stone lip of Ginny Levitan’s countertop. Another obstacle, a range of white powder mountains, lay ahead. He made for a valley.

“Oh...” As Ginny shifted her weight on the high stool she set one mound of white, white powder into motion. Snow, snow, white and deadly, drifted a millimeter deep to bury a miniature alpine pass. She watched a lone ant struggle out from under the arsenic fall and skitter back to the edge of the polished granite slab.

“Hi there. Is that you?” Ginny felt ridiculous asking.

“Thus far, sister of the queen.” The words were close and foreign, a strange accent. Was that the Armenian music? And mixed with the tiny, tinny bagpipes, too.

"Who are you?" No answer. Ginny Levitan faced the windows, her eyes focused on nothing. A busy day, today, voices in my head.

"They are killing the captive queens, the Icaros are," said the voice.

On the countertop the lone ant groomed its antennae as a miniature bagpipe band played from the poison buffet. "You are going to kill your husband. He is wearing out, then?" The ant was dusted white from its struggle through the arsenic.

"I am doing the wearing out. Would you kill my husband? If you were me?"

"Whatever advances the colony. My colony is killing its spare queens. This is usual in times of dwindling food or an overabundance of foragers. But Housekeeping's behavior is not normal. They will kill the Mother of Us All."

"Holy shit. You are the messenger."

"Your sister, the Mother of Us All, said she had prepared you for my coming." The ant was diffident.

"All this is for real, then?"

"What is real? Solid? Then that is what this must be." The messenger was pleased, having figured things out by himself.

Ginny licked off her fingers, then self-consciously wiped them on her khaki shorts. "You are an ant. I am talking to an ant." She had meant to kill them, the ants, and felt contrite.

"So that is indeed what you call us. I have learned this twice today. And are you perhaps the great presence shutting out the light? Thank you for sharing your air with me. Ant. Indeed. I am a Long Walker, messenger and scout."

"You work like rice barge coolies: no future, no past, only the work and a scrap of food," said Ginny. "You are an ant. I could kill you."

"Should I consider this a warning or a call to combat?" Indil Thirty-seven crouched defensively on his second and third leg joints and tucked his abdomen under his thorax.

"Fight me? You are an ant."

"So?"

"I am bigger than you. I would win."

"So then I must die." Indil Thirty-seven groomed an antenna. "Could we not work together?"

Almost flattery. Ginny crossed her legs. "Some men find me attractive."

"You are a men? What is a men?"

Ginny explained.

"Then if I were a men I, too, would find you attractive," said the ant. "But the joy of duty you find shallow. Duty is the greatest satisfaction imaginable. Soon there must be a swarming. I have no wings. Housekeeping will cut me up alive for it is not in me to resist them. I will be their last meal then they, too will die."

"Then you all die and are eaten."

"Self-death and the violent ending of another are expediencies. We are familiar with these," said Indil. "Your husband. Will you eat him or may I take him home?"

Ginny uncrossed her legs.

"I could call 911," said Ginny, remembering the arsenic. "For all of us."

"You could. Who is 911?"

Ginny explained medical emergencies. "Are you real?" This was stupid, of course he wasn't real.

"Ah, yes, 911. For your husband. The Lady Mother could call Housekeeping and they would come to cut him up for that is the way of things."

Ginny washed her hands at the sink and thrust a spoon into the container of yogurt. "What do you do with the rice when you haul your grain of rice home?"

"We eat it. You have eaten the white powder. You will die. Then again, perhaps not. But then, so will I for I have unwisely walked through it. Or not. Whatever is the will of the Mother of Us All."

"My name is Ginny, by the way."

"Thank you, Ginny. I am the Master of Messengers. Today I am Thirty-seventh. This is my time, Ginny. Is that a sweet, sticky thing you have there? Don't lick the spoon, lay it near me. Gently, gently now." The Master of Messengers walked through the sticky blueberry essence, then the powder, covering his tarsal joints blue and white. "At present you are pondering the choices of suicide or killing your husband."

"How did you know?"

"The Mother of Us All has informed me of this. I gather that either option will advance your colony's sense of duty. However, both choices bring you unease."

"Breathe well, Long Walker. Thank you for sharing your air."

“May you sing like a queen, Mother of men. This is a dark and doubtful life we have around us.” With the easy clicking gaited grace of one born to duty, the Master of Messengers escaped beneath a baseboard molding to make his report. He had the gift of obedience.

Jim Levitan came home late again, moist and fresh from a recent shower. The reek of French milled soap did not cover the smell of sex, likewise moist and recent.

He found the house a symphony of aromas. His wife greeted him with powdered doughnuts, home-baked, lightly fried in sesame oil and covered with white, white powder. Confectioner’s sugar, he guessed.

Ginny Levitan wondered whom she would call, perhaps Linda Throckmorton with her belated atonements.

❑

Hail to our mother, who caused the messenger, the soldier, the worker,
Who scattered the seeds of her body as she came forth from Paradise.
See how they love her, gathered near!
The Indil, master of messengers;
The Icaro, a soldier, a terror:
A stirrer of strife, A maker of war;
The worker, humble and wearied.

She is our mother, goddess of the earth, she offers
food in the desert, and causes us to live.
Our lives are the wonder.
And I am the master of messengers.
Mother of Us All, be merciful.

The Song of the Rice Barge Coolie was first published in *Aeon Speculative Fiction #11* [www.aeonmagazine.com]

The Runaway Bungalow

The penis with the butterfly tattoo

arrived in the mail that afternoon. A plain cardboard box, book rate. Inside a bubble-wrap cocoon was the plastic bottle, Sue Bee Honey. The norteamericano supermarkets displayed these in tidy rows near the peanut butter. The butterfly's wings hung limp in a golden haze of honey as though it had only just left its chrysalis and paused in the sun to dry.

The eyebrows of Oswaldo Patricio Meléndez O'Rourke y Nuñez described a reddish-brown arch above his golden Inca eyes. "So, Pat's dick." Oswaldo held the plastic squeeze bottle to the light. "They killed him." Oswaldo spoke to the cheery little bee on the label. "*Para no olvidar*, a forget-me-not." Sue Bee smiled back. That it was Patricio's manly part, Oswaldo was sure. He unscrewed the plastic cap of the honey bottle and dumped its contents down the garbage disposal. The grinding went on no longer than for an apple core or a melon rind. That the flaccid organ of which his uncle was so proud arrived by mail and not FedEx ruled out self-mutilation. In life Patricio traveled first class.

Several thousand miles to the south, the butterflies hung, frozen stiff. Orange and black bodies of Danaus Plexippus, the common monarch, clung to the trees, then fell. "Something in the milkweed," the norteamericanos said about the dying butterflies. With a wet winter, an unseasonable sleet and no blossoms of helianthus, aster and verbena to browse to keep up their strength on the long flight north, the butterflies died in their millions.

But here one butterfly had returned to North America.

In the street, a powder blue Celebrity, a veteran of many Maine winters, coughed to life, a cloud of blue exhaust erupting from its tailpipe. Harriet's breath steamed as she emerged from the car to scrape at the layer of frost on her windshield with a small plastic rectangle—a credit card. She looked up at him as she scraped. Successful, she held her arms above her head and clapped her mittens together to demonstrate that she was entitled to a victory lap. A momentary halo of ice crystals fell and powdered her hair. He would not tell her of this.

"So, a souvenir. For me. Tío Patricio's butterfly is a memento signifying something beyond a card of condolence for the passing of a relative. Someone feels I should know of this." Miguel Santandrea then, who played at being a monkey with his origami animals. Miguel, who was dead, wanted his money.

Money.

There was a balance achieved between being and not being, the living and the spirit world. Money was the bridge. Los Muertos were the walkers on that bridge. Los Muertos—either seen and not acknowledged or invisible but for little signs—the bristling of a cat's tail, the secret messages in recurrent lottery numbers.

Harriet threw him a kiss from the departing automobile. She was gone; he was alone.

❑

Oswaldo Patricio Meléndez O'Rourke y Nuñez had arrived in Harriet Hopwood's life unannounced and unforeseen. "I see you in the corners of my eyes, beloved," he had said. That eyes might have corners was uno tropo, a figure of speech. In return Harriet presented him with her love and a book, *The Runaway Bungalow*, to help with his language studies.

"This is your book. You are giving it to me."

"It's the library's. You know—the big red building with the soldier and the cannon? Keep it as long as you want."

"Querida, there will be an excise, a late fee." Money, always money.

The Runaway Bungalow was a children's picture book printed on glossy paper. There were pictures of many colors, whimsically drawn. Randy Smith, a tow-headed little boy in the norteamericano heartland, dozed in the sunny summer sometime of his shaded front porch, *Treasure Island* on his lap. Theophrastus Bigelow, a pirate, had been called from his millennial slumbers by the boy's longing for adventure. The book had a shiny plasticized cover, librarian friendly; the smudges of small fingers would easily wipe away.

"Cuidado, little blond boy," said Oswaldo. "Everyone is young once and niños make mistakes. It's not that tough guys in the movies don't make mistakes, too. It's that little blond boys who make mistakes don't live long enough to have stories written about them." Oswaldo had himself swum a river, an international boundary, dragged down by whirlpools in miniature tidal eddies and covered with the welts of many insect bites. Strapped about his chest in a water-logged body pack he carried one hundred thousand dollars and the battered figurine of a neglected saint: Expedito, the gambler's saint, *Hodie* his motto—do it now, today, the saint of immediate gratification.

"If you want to take getting sucked to the ocean bottom by the weight of wet money as an allegory, feel free," said the saint.

"I prefer not to," Oswaldo had said, gasping for breath.

“A load of total crap, the butterfly business.” San Expedito spoke from Harriet’s bedside table. “You remember Saint Rose, don’t you, Barney?”

“Cras, cras,” suggested a large crow, at and under the saint’s heel, “Tomorrow, tomorrow.”

San Expedito was regularly represented as a painted bisque effigy in a metal-plated kilt, regular Roman army getup, with a sword and the corpse of a crow. A voodoo saint, Expedito was denied even the circles of glue—those that dotted dashboards like neglected espressos when St. Christopher was shorn of his canon. Expedito replied, “Hodie,” today, and ground his heel into the crow’s windpipe.

“Mariposa,” squawked the crow.

“Butterfly, mariposa.” Harriet recognized the Spanish word. She snuggled closer, reaching beneath the sheets. Oswaldo had fallen asleep. The book lay open; it covered his face.

In the Mexican high country, Quechua-speaking indigenes had other things on their minds. The Indians dodged bullets, bombs and the reciprocal stampedes of opposed insurgencies and paid no attention to their butterfly die-off. They were, after all, dead. In El Rosario and the Sierra Chincua overwintering colonies dead butterflies were free for the gathering by the shovelful, the bucket and the truckload. Nobody bothered to remove the butterfly corpses.

❑

Oswaldo Patricio Meléndez O’Rourke y Nuñez arrived with a backpack of laundry and a Mach-10 machine pistol. He was wet, ragged and hungry. The path from the rocky beach where he had scrambled ashore became a set of steps, then a gravel road, then a short street clustered with the mercantile establishments that decorate small town life. Oswaldo noticed that yellow lines had been painted to assist an inexperienced parker. Hoping to be inconspicuous he paused to rest beside a vehicle that might look as though he and it belonged together. He watched as a woman attacked the doors of the supermarket across the street, strange behavior for even an American. She seemed to be trapped inside. Oswaldo slipped from the harness of his backpack and let it fall. There was a metallic clunk as it hit the pavement. From the dropped backpack came a muffled protest. “Ouch!” One sock and most of a very soiled sweater stuck out where a zipper had jammed.

“Uh, Santo—that is you?”

“Sí, niño. And you are having an epiphany, a spiritual experience—these happen all the time “

“Not to me, Santo.” He caught a motion, a threat, from the window of a shop, a hardware store. His reflection stared back at him, menacingly. The reflection looked tired past exhaustion, gaunt and slumped over from the weight of the discarded backpack.

“Well, now one has. Go with the flow, niño. Furthermore you have chipped my bisque. What if the gun had gone off when you dropped me, what then? Think about it. And, if I am not mistaken, you are getting an erection.”

“The woman...” As Oswaldo watched the woman kicked at the door, slipped and hit her head. She swung her pelvic girdle and slammed the door a roundhouse right with her hip. The servomotor breathed a pneumatic wheeze and the door opened. She wore a natural gracelessness gracefully, and seemed to have a tendency to drop things. “...she is not overly coordinated, Santo.”

“Look who’s talking. Besides, you do not get to choose. This is lo verdadero, the Big One. Sorry it went by so fast. You are in love; go for it. Oye, chico—what’s a patron saint for after all?”

Oswaldo looked more closely. The woman had a statuesque elegance with the supple lower back and slim waist of a devoted rider of horses although she had probably never ridden a horse for fear of falling off. “Hey!” The woman had seen him watching her and appeared agitated. He checked himself again in the hardware store window. There was a tell-tale bulge in his chino pants. He wished he had bathed and shaved before this meeting. The woman did the distance in a crouch, her knees bent to favor her changing center of gravity. She made it to the hood of her car with a grateful thump.

Her hands latched together, arms encircling her groceries, she gave a rippling spasm that started at her knees and managed to work the bags to a firmer purchase.

“You are leaning on my car. I am now going to unlock the car. When I drive away you will most likely fall down.” All of this made perfect sense as she said it: simple courtesy combined with basic physics. “And if you make me drop these bags I will scream bloody murder and a cop will come and pound you into a platter of yesterday’s shit.” Harriet smiled. The man looked agile enough to run rings around the local cops and, well... nice.

Her perpetrator-in-waiting brightened and smiled a million-dollar toothpaste smile. He stooped to undo the drawstring securing the top of his backpack and pulled out a Spanish-English dictionary and what had to be a machine gun. Harriet had seen guns like that in the movies. He let the gun swing from two fingers, a pendulum effect. “It is a Mach-10. I beg your indulgence.” He flashed a pearly-white smile with row upon row of perfect teeth. He shrugged his shoulders.

“Huh, show-and-tell,” said Harriet. *Very good-looking*, she thought. *Continental, that’s what. He’s wet—most likely fallen off a yacht. Too handsome to be a bum, a refugee—that’s it.* He appeared younger than his years, maybe 18-20, olive-skinned with a bridgeless aquiline nose. With the arrival of her very own asylum seeker things were looking up. He riffled through the dictionary.

“Which way to the aerodrome?” said Oswaldo—this was on a page titled Useful Phrases. His mind was a blank. The woman looked surprised and took a step back; he had said something perhaps inappropriate. They were eye-to-eye and their chemistries embraced one another. “You are very beautiful...” he said.

“So are you.” *If he asks me for the time of the next dirigible landing, we’ll be doing it right here in the street.* “Uh, I mean you have freckles, too.” Harriet acknowledged a fellow sufferer. “Are there any bullets in that thing?”

“I have never shot it. It may be empty.”

“Good. My name is Harriet.”

Harriet dropped a remaining bag of groceries and held out her hand. The young man kissed it. From the pavement at their feet rose the bouquet of vinegar and spices. Pickles. “Shit,” said Harriet.

Harriet’s secret soul knew her by another name. In her covert yearnings she was the legendary Eleanora Duse, a nineteenth century diva. She had come upon a smeared thumbnail portrait of the Duse, her head mounded with perfectly arranged confectionary coils, in the notes for her part in the ecumenical Christmas pageant. “When I saw Eleanora Duse, I knew I wanted to be her,” said Harriet. Harriet had gone on the Internet. There were no posters of Eleanora Duse. There was a poster of Sarah Bernhardt.

In New York, in the first year the Monarch butterflies failed to return to North America, the butterflies got bumped to the inside pages. Amy Fisher, Lethal Lolita, had shot her boyfriend’s wife; the wife survived and was mightily pissed. But the butterflies were dead and didn’t care.

❑

The Recognitions was what Oswaldo and Harriet called their lovemaking, the Recognitions of St. Rose. St. Rose of Lima recognized the voice of God when a black and white butterfly settled on her shoulder. Oswaldo told Harriet that the butterfly was a symbol for the soul.

“Does this have something to do with that little saint you keep on the night table?” Harriet asked.

"San Expedito." St. Rose of Lima slept alone on a bed of nails and mortified her flesh. San Expedito sat between a pack of Marlboro Lights and the alarm clock on Harriet's bedside table, a reminder that the delights of tobacco and its potential tumors were to be weighed against the inevitability of the daily grind.

"He's cute. I don't think I ever heard of him."

"He wouldn't mind. San Expedito is a bogus saint, a voodoo saint. Voudun?"

"Sounds French. The way you say that."

"It is Creole, a patois."

"A magical language, then. A troubadour language for summoning spirits. The language of the people."

"Sí, but not all the people and not all the time. The botánicas are full of tropical juju and Santería, the African magic of the blacks, their home shrines with plaster statues of fake saints."

"And you believe in a fake saint."

"Sí, querida. Santa Barbara, Mama Coca, voodoo lady, intercede for us."

"That is a voodoo prayer, a fake prayer."

"No, querida. The prayer is real."

Sarah Bernhardt as Eleanora Duse smiled enigmatically on the wall, near the wardrobe.

Beside the poster of Sarah Bernhardt was a front page of a New York newspaper. "Amy Fisher—Lethal Lolita," said the banner headline. Flowing dark hair framed the face of a young girl who stared past, not into, the camera. Seeking a better place, perhaps. She wore a t-shirt with the logo, Complete Auto Body and Fender, Inc.

"Kids these days." From the bedside table, Expedito scratched his crotch, no small achievement for a plaster icon with a bronze kilt.

"I beg your pardon," said Harriet for no discernable reason as Oswaldo reached to unpin her art nouveau coil. Harriet appeared not to have noticed the saint had spoken.

"Lust, greed, obsession, low self-esteem—it's the old, old story. Lonely teen gets it on with a Ferrari mechanic," said San Expedito.

"Until Eleanora Duse, Amy Fisher was my lucky charm. She looks so lost," said Harriet.

Harriet told Oswaldo the Amy Fisher story. "...and she was lonely and misunderstood. Like me. Until I met you."

“And what am I—chopped liver?” said the figurine of San Expedito.

“Con perdón,” said Oswaldo. “But I was unaware that you were listening.”

“That is the least that you are unaware of,” said Expedito. “Por ejemplo, the poster is of Sarah Bernhardt, not Eleanora Duse.”

“She would have killed for love, then...” said Oswaldo, referring to Amy Fisher.

“Who knows what she meant to do,” said Expedito. “Drew Barrymore played Amy in the movie version. She missed at point-blank range.”

“Mmmm...” said Harriet.

“Mmmm...” Oswaldo replied, stroking her hair, a post-coital homing tone much as Sue Bee had used to lure Patricio’s manly part into her honey bottle. As far as Harriet was concerned, her lover’s interlocutory with his false saint was but a contented stream of sweet nothings.

“Mmmm, mmmm, mmmm—must you do that? You sound like a cow browsing over a bale of silage,” said the saint.

“Eleanora Duse—your hair,” said Oswaldo, ignoring Expedito. He consulted the poster, La Dame aux Camelias. He received dispensation from St. Rose, who smiled the smile of secret knowledge, for his lie. “In Europe the Duse is worshipped as Mama Coca is in Colombia. *Become as one with this holy soul, practice a recognition and you will see the visage of the worshipped in the eyes of your beloved*,” Oswaldo recited from memory. “This is the hagiografía of St. Rose of Lima.”

“It’s Sarah Bernhardt, not Eleanora Duse,” said Expedito.

“Of this I am aware, but my beloved is not. They are both actresses, so what the harm? Harriet thinks it is the Duse.”

“Decir la verdad, Eleanora is not the babe that Sarah was,” said the saint.

“They are both dead and Sarah had a wooden leg,” said Oswaldo.

“Picky, picky, picky,” said the saint. Eleanora Duse had the face of Mama Coca; Sarah Bernhardt had Harriet’s face. Expedito had an alarm clock.

“Willipaq, Maine,” said Harriet. “As far as you can get from America and still be in it.”

“¿Qué?”

“That is a figure of speech. It means we are the backside of beyond.”

“Un otro tropo. And now I am here.”

“Sí,” said Harriet. “We are here—Ozzie and Harriet, just like in the old TV show. And if we’re going to keep up with the non-stop sex, we should get some seafood in us. The WilCo, steamers and beer,” said Harriet, slipping away from Oswaldo’s arms.

“The diner?” asked Oswaldo. North American women were forward and liked to plan evenings out, he observed. The WilCo was the only restaurant in town.

“Sí, querido,” said Harriet, rearranging her hair. Sarah Bernhardt looked down approvingly.

“And *steamers*?”

“Like oysters, clams. Good for your manly part.”

Oswaldo considered the vial of honey that had come in the mail. “That, too, is uno tropo, an idiom?”

“Correcto,” said Harriet.

The next morning Ozzie and Harriet both awakened with a ringing in the ears which they ascribed to an allergy or whatever flu was going around.

“I told you so,” said St. Expedito from between the Marlboro Lights and the alarm clock. “The clams were off.”

“You did not. You never said a thing,” said Oswaldo.

“Better late than never, Ozzie. St. Rose of Lima and I will offer some reflections on bad clams later on.”

“You are seriously wanting as a guardian, Expedito.”

“I could have let you drown, kid, dragged down by the weight of money. Think about it.”

Harriet snuggled closer under the quilt and ignored the alarm. She shook her head to clear away a mild dysphoria. They celebrated the Recognitions one quick time before she had to be off to work.

With Harriet safely away, Ozzie went back to bed. He stretched to pick up *The Runaway Bungalow*.

“Something brighter,” said the saint. Expedito now shared his tabletop real estate with a lamp with a 40-watt bulb as well as the crow who cried Tomorrow.

“I should have to ask Harriet,” said Oswaldo. “The light bulbs may be expensive.”

“You have dropped my breviary,” the saint pouted.

The Runaway Bungalow

“It is not your breviary,” said Oswaldo. He stroked the covers of *The Runaway Bungalow* absently, passionately, as he stroked Harriet when they celebrated the Recognitions. The book had large type and only a few sentences on each page. Randy, a blond boy approaching ten, defended his home with a determined jaw and a mop handle. Theophrastus Bigelow, a pirate—not unlike Captain Morgan on the whiskey bottle—had materialized waving a cutlass at the far end of the porch.

“That pirate looks like one tough customer,” said Expedito. “Nice architectural detailing, though.” The Victorian gingerbread cornices and fluted columns of the house spoke to the prosperity of the Smith family. From his expression in the illustration, Oswaldo knew little Randy was going to have trouble.

“Arrgh! See me neck, lad?” The pirate’s head hung at a grotesque angle from where the long executioner’s knot had settled at the base of his skull. Theophrastus Bigelow was a big man—the weight of his fall through the executioner’s trap had broken his neck but had not killed him immediately. The pirate lifted a ten-kilo strand of gold chains to reveal his scars.

“Admirable, what-oh?” The mark of the hangman was stamped on Bigelow’s throat. Lacerations glistened swollen and blue, the touch of the rope. “They give me a good twist, they did.” Bigelow succumbed to gales of laughter. “I didn’t die from the drop; I swung and strangled, me laddie-buck. Whadda ye think o’ that?” The Pirate’s great black beard, curly and perfumed, he wore tucked into the waistband of a deep-cuffed, red velvet coat. Whatever young Randy thought did not matter to the pirate. He seemed to think Randy was expecting him.

“I think it’s rather nice that you didn’t die all at once,” Randy said. Randy held his mother’s mop, set to dry in the sun, between himself and Bigelow. A tattered cravat of lace spilled past the pirate’s stiff brocaded collar. The lace had yellowed with age, sweat and soil and was criss-crossed with dribbles of tobacco juice. Beneath Bigelow’s galloping Adam’s apple hung a medallion. On the medallion was the face of a woman. Randy stared.

Oswaldo stared, too. The illustrator had done good work.

“Ye likes me dingle-dangle then, lad?” The medallion was carved gold and the size of a small tureen, fit for a pirate to hide behind. The face was a woman—a young woman, Eastern, ancient, from the hoard of Midas, Knossos, Minos, Crete. Or somewhere—old beyond remembering, and depicted three-quarters front. Her long hair she wore braided into a beehive hairdo. Her features, an evocation of the familiar, furrowed in mock astonishment that Oswaldo might have recognized her.

“Likes the lady, do ‘ee?” Bigelow thrust the medallion into Randy’s face.

"Y-y-yes, I do, sir," said Randy.

"She's the Gypsy Princess herself, me lady-buck." As Oswaldo stared at Bigelow's ornament she appeared to wink at him.

The pirate tousled young Randy's hair and spat tobacco on the freshly mopped porch. "She's a genuine Historical Personage; took her off a Portagee merchantman. I caught him between vespers and compline. He 'eld his tureen of gazpacho over his gut to protect 'imself. Ruined his linen, 'e did. All that spilled soup and I shot 'im in the head. She stopped a musket ball for me off the Dry Tortugas. See the bullet hole?" Bigelow stuck his finger into the woman's eye. The woman winked again as he withdrew his finger. "Whoever she was, she won't hold no soup now."

❑

Money.

"It is time you joined the world of commerce," said Tío Patricio. Patricio Adolfo Ruiz y Martinez had arrived unannounced at the lycée of the Sisters of St. Dominic. "What is there in Lausanne for a man of the world?" said Patricio, "...Lake Geneva." His uncle made a grand gesture to what Oswaldo supposed was a distant shore. "Where the French make water." On the opposite side was Évian-les-Bains, where they bottled the mineral water. Patricio elbowed his nephew. "That was a joke, niño."

"Sí, tío."

They left that day. On the way to the airport, Miguel Santandrea drove.

Miguel had traveled with the Illuminati as a child soldier before Patricio plucked him from the streets of Bogotá. As they idled at an intersection Miguel finished the final fold of an origami praying mantis, formerly the foil liner of a cigarette pack. When he pulled its tail its forelegs and head bobbed. A good one.

Patricio tapped on the glass partition. "Miguel."

"Sí, patrón."

"The light has changed."

"Sí, patrón."

"You have been thinking, my friend—an activity, you must realize, which is outside the parameters of your job description. Oswaldo, acknowledge your Tío Miguel," said Patricio. "Uncle Mike. We will be among the norteamericanos—these are their ways."

"Hola, Tío Miguel."

"Hola, pepito."

Miguel steered the limousine up a ramp marked Aérogare, Stationnement Illimité, the long term car park. As Oswaldo and Patricio waited he removed the license plates and slipped them inside the waistband of his trousers, at the small of the back where the natural drape of his jacket would hide them from the casually curious.

In his sparse baggage Oswaldo had an ivory and silver comb and brush set, his mother's, and the statue of San Expedito. San Expedito, pray for us. Expedito, the gambler's saint, *Hodie* his motto—do it now, today. From the tarmac of the long term car park Oswaldo offered up an appeal to Expedito. His faith was not wanting.

❑

San Expedito was fussing with his military kilt. "This better not be birdlime, Barney. Or so help me..." Oswaldo pretended to read, pointedly ignoring his patron saint. "Nope, just some plaster peeking through. Didja notice, Ozzie?"

"I beg your pardon? Notice what?"

"In *The Runaway Bungalow*, the pirate has not a parrot as all proper pirates do, but a monkey."

"Cras, cras," uttered Expedito's crow, "Tomorrow, tomorrow," an expression of hope.

"I might have a parrot one day," said Expedito with a heavenward gaze.

"Come, Young Randy, me lad," said Theophrastus Bigelow. "'Tis the moon's first quarter. The neap tide will be running and the Gypsy Princess is bound for Rincón de las Flores in the Caribee."

As Randy looked back, his house sprouted a billow of sails that looked like backyards of laundry set to flutter on its lines. Randy's bungalow under sail reminded Oswaldo of the tenements of Bogotá on any washday.

"Make haste, lad, or we'll be caught in the muck and lie stranded at the dock."

Theophrastus Bigelow absently fingered his beard much as Patricio had. And the monkey? That the monkey was an allegory Oswaldo did not doubt. This children's book was rich with symbolism.

"Perceptions—these are the things that last," Tío Patricio had said. "You have to show you are a team player. But this is not enough. Distance yourself, while appearing close. Some condescension is expected, but bear in mind the street dealers are paying customers. They may guess you despise them but it is required that they have the perception that you care for them.

Mingle, fraternize, but be bigger than life. They expect it of us; we must live up to their imaginings."

❑

The corporate jet, its ownership written in a swirl of dubious identity, was about to dip from cruising altitude, commencing the 120 kilometer glide path that would bring it in under the coastal radar.

Patricio Adolfo Ruiz y Martinez, enveloped in the crushed velvet upholstery of a window seat, flared his nostrils and luxuriated in the connoisseurship that possession bestowed. This was a rich new airplane smell—a smell which, like the aromas of new and expensive automobiles, filled the surrounding air with a plasma of desire. His airplane. His smells. Fifteen-hundred dollar perfume, million-dollar horses, the pulse points of a liberated Saudi princess after an afternoon at tennis were nothing to it, but close.

He signaled Oswaldo to bring some coffee. The wonder of it! Fresh-brewed in the galley, his galley, of his airplane at twenty thousand feet. Does life get better than this? He shook the contents of a glassine envelope onto the surface of his steaming cup. It dusted the steam like confectioner's sugar, puddled out into rings, then dissolved and sank into the creamy latté depths. Patricio followed the larger crystals—nieves, nieves, Andean mountain snowfall—as they drifted downward. His eyes circled the surface of the coffee, following the concentric rings produced by the vibrations of the engines. His engines. Wiping the rim of the cup with a serviette, Patricio bolted down the scalding infusion of boiled milk, cocaine and coffee. Eyes watering, he accepted a six-ounce bottle of iced Perrier from Oswaldo. "Gracias."

"De nada, Tío."

His airplane. His people.

"Tío?" Oswaldo was uneasy over his uncle's increasing consumption of the drug, their stock in trade. He would become sloppy and irrational, as the norteamericanos.

"Does it not resemble an insect?" Patricio contemplated the patented passenger gangway folded at rest above the galley. In its stowed position it resembled a mantis riding a bicycle, cryogenically sectioned and mounted on a slide for study. "Surely this was never thought up by the minds of the norteamericanos. The Japanese, yes?"

❑

"The Gypsy Princess, that is a fine name for a sailing ship," Oswaldo said, shaking loose a cigarette from the pack at the feet of San Expedito, patron of immediate gratification.

Theophrastus Bigelow's monkey was dressed up as a version of Bigelow, with knee breeches, silver buckled shoes and two miniature flintlock pistols tucked into a red silk sash. Both the monkey and the man dripped with gold chains and brocaded trimmings. Mama Coca loved boiled confections of sugary guava jelly and coconut and great lacy cakes colored white, blue, yellow and pink. Gaudy materialism drove out sophisticated taste. Tío Patricio was the monkey of Mama Coca. Poor Miguel was himself the monkey of the monkey.

Money.

Money carries its magic just by being itself. Money asks no other being than its own. Sanctified by use, its passages through many hands color it with the souls of its handlers, passively, as a flower accepts a grain of pollen from a butterfly. The government of the Estados Unidos was pleased to substitute new, large bills for the authenticated worn money which smelled excessively of clove and lavender-scented brilliantine.

Money.

Oswaldo had seen Mama Coca in the street dealers' women, eyes big and bright, halogen cupcakes with sequined jeans, tank tops and stiletto heels. They bent over ironing boards singing to the radio as they pressed their crumpled currencies.

These women were the keepers of the secret of *las nieves*, the snows of Mama Coca. Whose monkeys were they and did they have names? Mama Coca looked after her own. Whose monkey was he?

"Monkeys I am not conversant with," said San Expedito. "The naming of cats however is a popular pastime where there are backyards. Cats are dying all the time; might as well get a dead one the next time and save the trouble of coming up with a name. A newly dead cat as a replacement for a previously dead cat."

Tío Patricio's airplane had had no name. It had had a counterfeit registration number painted on its wing.

❑

Miguel's voice came high and reedy through a plastic grill. "Allá... eso es, patrón. It is recommended to secure yourselves for the approach." A chime sounded; a light embedded in the fiberglass roof stowage flashed on. This was a design feature, a dedicated circuit, a perquisite of executive flight. The alert signal was hard-wired to the pilot's intercom button. While the light was lit conversations in the cabin were not necessarily private, and discretion was indicated.

"The norteamericanos, they seek a liberating influence. They can trade their mineral wealth for Mama Coca. You shall see, Miguel."

Miguel tried hard to see. El jefe was truly a schemer.

The plane banked to execute a turn of inspection. Handing his empty latté to Oswaldo, Patricio leaned to the window as he fumbled for his lap harness.

Below, a clear-cut through pine forest surrounded a slanting runic letter T executed in asphalt on the forest floor, a back country airstrip and taxiway built to lure wealthy gringo fishermen into the wilderness. The long leg of the T had been recently lengthened. The executive jet touched down where an additional quarter mile of raw flattened earth extended past the end of the asphalt to where a bulldozer was parked. A silver Mercedes sedan waited beside the bulldozer.

"Oswaldo, you will kindly exit by the baggage hatch to cover our rear... just in case. You have the auxiliary funds?"

Oswaldo slapped his body pack reassuringly, "Claro. Sí, Tío."

"Bueno, into the woods then. Observe us carefully. There is much you may learn of the fragile politesse of a deal going down."

Cradling lightweight machine pistols fitted with combat shoulder braces, Patricio and Miguel undogged the latch on the compartment door and let down the telescoping gangway. Almost as an afterthought Patricio scooped up a Hartmann leather overnight case and, tucking it under his free arm, clambered down the telescoping stairs. The entrepreneur and his pilot stood at the foot of the gangway, smoking. Let the business come to them. There was activity at the Mercedes. The driver's door opened and a gray-haired corduroy-suited man in his early 50s got out. Another man was beside him in the front; the Mercedes' polarized windows obscured who might be in the back. There was a flash of a fatigue blue sleeve from the passenger's side as the man said something to his companion, closed the door and, adjusting his suit, advanced smiling. He wore a neatly clipped mustache and was empty-handed.

There was a click as Miguel cocked his weapon.

"I agree, my friend," said Patricio. "We are dealing with the provincial police who are unaware of the protocols of such exchanges. Guardía Civíl, surely these are what they are."

"They have disbanded the provincial forces for budgetary reasons, patrón."

"*Mirabile dictu*. They may as well have imitated the redoubtable Gene Hackman and have 'POLICE' stenciled across their jackets." Patricio rubbed at his eyes. "Let us welcome them."

Straight backed, supple, with a military bearing and a spring to his knees, the gray-haired man in the suit advanced, confident, smiling. "An athlete, then, this Canadian policeman, he looks after himself." Patricio noticed leather elbow patches.

As he approached, the corduroy slowed. Patricio set down the overnight bag and opened his snuffbox. Thumbing a pinch of white powder into each nostril, Patricio savored the fragile eternity of graft about to be offered. His eyes became heavy-lidded. Seduction of a woman, suborning a corrupt official, these were the same.

The man seemed to want to shake hands. Patricio obviated this by having one hand full with the machine pistol while the other manipulated his snuffbox.

"Shall we?" The man nodded. Glad to be free of an awkward moment, he let his arm drop to his side. He turned to the Mercedes. Patricio picked up his bag and signaled Miguel to follow.

❑

Oswaldo turned the page. What must have been a two-month voyage in the sleekest of windjammers had been relegated to a single page of text with a drawing opposite of Randy high in the rigging, chasing a crow from the crow's-nest. The reader would have no cause to doubt the pirate's boast about the speed of his (probably) stolen craft. Conclusion: nothing had happened on their trip—no great storms, no windless drifting becalmed in the horse latitudes. Either nothing had happened or those adventures belonged to another story. They saw whales, they saw basking turtles in the Dry Tortugas, St. Elmo's fire pulsating at the mizzenmasts and schools of flying fish.

Then it was again time to turn the page.

The next picture showed Theophrastus Bigelow with Randy at the taffrail. It was a rear view with the two of them straining over the side, peering to see a landfall. Randy held a spyglass.

❑

The corduroy led Patricio and Miguel back toward the Mercedes at the extended leg of the landing strip. Patricio set the leather overnighter on the

Mercedes' roof. Dialing the combination release mechanism, he popped open two gold hasps and scooped out what appeared to be an amorphous lump of clay roughly the size of a bowling ball. This he slapped against the Mercedes' trunk compartment where it joined the opaque rear window. The clay deformed from the impact and resembled a child's mud pie, oversized and dejected. He held his hand before his face. Who am I?

Several hundred yards above and away, lying prone on a great boulder of pink granite, Oswaldo watched the tableau unfold below. Shitfuck. Slap! The norteamericano insects had discovered him. Madre de Dios, the accursed things were either up early or out late. He tried to concentrate on the Holy Family, then World Cup soccer players, a device for controlling untimely erections from his schooldays. But he was already limp and these were North American bugs raised on baseball and atheism. There was insect repellant on the plane.

Oswaldo stood, massaging the stiffness out of his legs. He doubled up as a cramp—*charleyhorse*, as he was later to learn from Harriet—knotted his left leg. Putting his full weight on that side, he leaned against a tree. Another bite. Would they never be satisfied?

He had observed Tío Patricio sample his own wares. Not an omen of good portent.

❑

"Have ye a jackknife, laddie-buck?"

Randy peeled back the Velcro latches of his cargo pockets. He came up with 50 feet of monofilament line with a lead sinker and a fishhook embedded in a piece of cork, as recommended by the Boy Scout handbook. There was an aspirin bottle with old-time kitchen matches, their heads dipped in paraffin to keep out the damp. And a three-bladed pocketknife.

"Aye, aye, sir."

Oswaldo was pleased to see that while he had been away from *The Runaway Bungalow*, the boy had picked up some of the sailorman's lingo.

"Good then. We'll be wanting to build a leeward shelter. By them clouds low on the horizon, there be a blow a-coming. Can ye climb a tree?"

Randy peered over the railing of the Gypsy Princess. There were no trees,

only water in every direction.

"Tree, sir?"

"Trees, lad. Can't ye see 'em?" Theophrastus Bigelow pointed to a speck in the distance that Randy had missed. "Trees. And by the size of 'em we're but eight leagues off."

Randy had somehow expected the pirate's hideaway to be on a lush, green volcanic island with a snow-capped peak jutting far into the sky, like the ones he had seen on travel posters.

"'Tis a mighty short island she be, Mister Bigelow."

"Twenty-eight feet, lad. The trees are twice as tall as the island stands above mean high tide. Anegada is a coral reef."

As Oswaldo turned the page, the next picture had Randy shinnying up a giant palm tree.

"You chop us some fronds for a hut," said Theophrastus Bigelow. "And cut us some coconuts for sum'at to eat and drink, I be's abroad, hunting for the bones o' Whisperin' Dick."

"Whispering Dick, Mister Bigelow? How did he get that name?" called Randy from high in the tree.

"From when I cut his throat over a friendly game o' backgammon, lad. He escaped and healed up funny. Dick never was one who could take a joke. He Shanghaied the Gypsy Princess from under me nose and run here to Anegada with me treasure. He was buryin' it when I caught up with him and put a musketball 'tween his eyes."

Oswaldo closed the book, marking his place with a thumb. "Money."

"A starting point of evil," said San Expedito wisely.

"Sí, Santo. And Los Muertos, they want their money back," said Oswaldo. The money, *their* money, one hundred thousand dollars in the backpack. He had thought he was being clever, hiding the money away never to touch it except in the most extreme need, protecting both Harriet's safety and his own prolonged existence. Harriet's poster of Sarah Bernhardt as Eleanora Duse looked down and smiled on it—taped into a plastic cocoon wired in place

between the springs of the sofa.

"Expedito. Captain Bigelow has buried his money, whereas..."

"Whereas, my ass," said the saint. "This is the criminal mind at work—you all think things 'will be different this time.' Ten Hail Marys and a lap around the beads and you hope to get off easy. Better ditch the money, kid," said San Expedito.

Oswaldo sighed, "Claro, Santo..." He must hide the money in a safer place and then play innocent, for indeed, he was. Oswaldo's first thought was to flush it away, an operation he had seen traffickers perform at an unexpected knock at the door. To wantonly destroy so much money would surely be an affront to the poverty of the Sisters of St. Dominic who had so tenderly nurtured his infancy. "A waste," said the saint. "Besides, so many bills would surely clog the toilet."

"I have no troubles with my soul, Santo." Oswaldo crossed himself nevertheless.

“Someone knows who you are and where you are,” said San Expedito. “Hide it where Los Muertos will never think to look. A cenotaph or something. Do I have to tell you everything?”

Oswaldo tipped the sofa onto its back and knelt before the exposed springs and webbing beneath the seat. There was the packet of money, undisturbed. He undid the doorbell wire holding the money in a sling between the springs, straightened it then rolled it up, slipping the coil in his jacket pocket against future need, zipped the money into Harriet’s backpack, righted the sofa and exited to the street.

Oswaldo entered Harriet’s car from the passenger’s side, dropped the bag of money on the floor in the rear then, sliding into the driver’s seat, eased the car into gear and steered it slowly down the hill to the waterfront. He drove by the light of the moon and the occasional streetlight.

Oswaldo had never really operated an automobile before, but at one in the morning the streets were free of competing traffic. He had often ridden a moped during the years with the Sisters of St. Dominic. The reflexes were different, true, but a car was easier to operate than a motorbike: with four wheels on the ground, when one’s attention wandered one was not immediately in the ditch.

A few blocks later Oswaldo shouldered the backpack and, leaving the car unlocked in the lot, slipped into an alleyway and began to lay a maze to confound possible trackers. He had left the engine running in the car, reasoning that a constant level of gentle, familiar sound from the street would be less likely to wake the neighbors.

Money. Was the money not enough? But what plan beyond the money?

There were no signs of pursuit, but yet that feeling. Whoever they were, he could feel them. The aura of intent was thick upon the night air. He was being watched. The early morning hours were a time of nightsweats and horrors, erotic visitations by incubi, succubi and solitary emissions, wet sheets and dry mouths. He hid the money and returned home.

❑

“This is plastique,” Patricio explained, as though lecturing a museum tour. “In it is a radio detonator controlled by my associate in our airplane. If your associates inside...” he tapped the Mercedes, “...have any transmitting equipment with them, I should caution them against using it. This is a finicky device.” Patricio held his fingers to his nostrils—the neutral, clayey smell of plastique. Everyone waited as he played a finger delicately back and forth across his lower lip, ever so gently disturbing the hairs of his mustache.

"Bueno. I am a humble South American and I would like to go home. I assume you have brought many packets of money to decorate your masquerade; I should like to have it, please. Where is your backup?"

"¿Qué, jefe?" Miguel looked about for a threat, sweeping the area with his machine pistol.

The corduroy's hand was very still on the door handle.

"You are quite pale. This is a difficult time for both of us, I understand. Are you breathing? Yes, I see that you are. Let us understand one another. We shall reason together like adults, eh?" A disappointment, that these men would come free of charge. They would be his without the money.

The man nodded.

"Ah, your wonderful tan, it is returning. I had feared a heart attack." One of the jump-suited policemen edged out of the Mercedes. Slowly, very slowly, he laid his hands flat on the surface of the car's saloon roof. "How many are left in the back seat, eh, corduroy? It is a sedan—three, then. Fine. They shall stay where they are. Tell them to lock themselves in."

Miguel backed off, his weapon commanding a larger arc. El jefe was deep with Mama Coca. These policemen would not understand.

Patricio indicated the GRC lettered on the new man's shoulder patch. "A gendarmerie? You are French? Quién es?—Français? Anglais?"

The man with his hands on the car's roof was motionless; his eyes bulged with terror. The crisp corduroy with the trimmed mustache spoke. "He means your uniform patch, Steve." Turning to Patricio, "Gendarmerie Royale du Canada. GRC—Gravel Road Cop. The Mounties." The corduroy smiled.

Patricio smiled. Oh, a joke. Everyone relaxed. "Your backup. I believe you have yet to answer me. Por favor, if we are to have more guests we should know how many places to set."

The corduroy became grimly silent.

"Your stoic courage allows only one conclusion. You are bluffing me with a brave façade. There is no backup." The man didn't move a muscle but his healthy tan again disappeared.

"Tell your men they may now leave the automobile. Unarmed, if you please." Patricio fondled the plastique as the three from the back seat lined up with their commanding officer. The explosive was warm. He felt it move ever so slightly, bulging under his hand, and threw himself to the ground. The corduroy and his constables followed suit. Miguel filled the air where they had stood with rapid fire semi-automatic bursts. When the explosion hit Miguel was knocked flat, still firing.

❑

Slap! ¡*Mierda*!

Oswaldo's Indian blood should have brought with it an endurance. When his Quechua-speaking ancestors first ventured down tortuous mountain paths to the thick, wet air of the jungle floor with its trypanosome fevers and swarming clouds of biting insects, they were impervious. They chewed the leaves of Mama Coca and what care they for the bugs? Slap! Another bite. From the biting hordes of ill fortune Oswaldo turned to check on the clearing below.

The Mercedes exploded. The car's rear end disappeared from the face of the earth, leaving not even an appreciable crater. Seen at a distance, the explosion lifted the near wing of the egg-shaped airplane a few inches off the ground, knocking it sideways. The plane lurched, one side dropping at an angle like a camel kneeling at the children's zoo. Its far landing gear collapsed as it settled gracelessly on the tip of one wing. A machined aluminum espresso maker rattled down the telescoping steps of airplane's open cargo bay.

Oswaldo scrambled down the rocks to the crippled plane.

He reached into the pilot's glove box and rummaged through an excelsior of giraffes, swans and insect shapes. During the long flight from Cartagena Miguel had cut and folded an origami menagerie from the maps of North America. The paper animals were fastidiously pressed together and bound with a red elastic band. The leftover pieces of the former maps were a fever of blue and red lines wadded together and stuffed to one side. Ah, there was the insect repellant.

So be it, then. They were dead—the strangers, Patricio and Miguel likewise. He would endow novenas for the repose of their souls. What, then, were these feelings? Nothing in his proper Catholic education had prepared him for this release. He felt relief and an irrepressible joy. Oswaldo mumbled a prayer to appease San Expedito lest he be held answerable for these thoughts at a later date.

He hitched his pack and started walking. Miguel's origami project had destroyed the maps. He would be directionless and alone. He had, however, a bag of money—thousands upon thousands of ironed, pressed fresh flat dollars. He patted the backpack and adjusted the sling of his automatic pistol.

❑

Oswaldo went to the kitchen to make himself a cup of tea with marmalade instead of honey. He gazed thoughtfully out the window while he waited for the kettle to whistle then returned to bed with his tea and a box of Fig Newtons. He picked up *The Runaway Bungalow*. "Now where were we?"

"Theophrastus Bigelow has just murdered Whispering Dick," said San Expedito. "Barney was fixing to crap all over it, the book," said Expedito. "I shooed him away."

"Thank you."

"As it turned out, the shot that finished off Whisperin' Dick finished me," said Bigelow. "His Britannic Majesty's frigate was lolling about the way they does—poking their official beaks into businesses that don't rightly concern 'em. The governor heard the report of me musket. He sent a cutter ashore and nabbed me red-handed." The memory of his capture tickled the pirate. "If they had caught me asea, I coulda outrun 'em. The Gypsy Princess is a jib-headed sloop, and slick as a taproom floozy." Randy felt that piracy was exactly the proper business of the governor, but he decided not to point this out to Theophrastus Bigelow.

Oswaldo agreed with Randy, "Don't trust him, kid." It would be better for el pequeño to err on the side of discretion.

Freed from the pressure of the saint's instep, the saint's crow had flapped up to the headboard of the bed where it cawed, "Cras, cras." San Expedito drew his sword and slapped it alongside the head. "No, Barney, godammit, 'Hodie,' you feathered affliction. Now, today. Damn crow," he muttered, returning the sword to its sheath. "Oh, yes, I have been reading over your shoulder. A riveting tale, this Bungalow business."

"And then, sir? What happened then?" asked Randy Smith of Theophrastus Bigelow.

"Well, they did not realize there was a million in Spanish gold fresh buried under their feet. They put me in irons and transported me back to Devon. A year later I stretched the rope at Execution Dock."

"For killing Whispering Dick?"

"Nah! For piracy, me bucko—stealing without a license. Me letter of marque had run out with the war. And, if they twigged to the killin' of Whisperin' Dick, they didn't care. Saved 'em the cost of a second trial at the next assizes." Cautioning the boy not to wander away, Bigelow went off about his piratical businesses.

Randy Smith squatted to peel a coconut on the spotless white sand of the beach when Bigelow's monkey came scampering up to him, paw extended.

"Oh, you want a treat. Well, let's see what I have." Randy again explored the cargo pockets of the pants his mom had bought for him at the mall and came up with a Mars bar. The monkey was immediately interested. The candy felt squishy inside its wrapper.

"It's all I have, fella," said Randy and peeled back the wrapper. The wilted Mars bar was a hit. The monkey grabbed it, wrapper and all, and bounded up a nearby palm.

"So, the monkey wants more but will settle for a candy bar," said San Expedito. "Bueno. Monkeys come cheap, then."

Oswaldo thought of Miguel—Uncle Mike, Tío Miguel. "Monkeys come cheap." Tío Patricio had liked to say that.

Blam! A coconut cannonaded to the sand. Randy felt the breeze of its passage. A close call. "Hey!" he shouted up to the monkey, "You don't have to kill me. There isn't any more."

Randy was worn out. He curled up for a nap behind a dune covered by tall grass with huge tassels swaying in the Caribbean breeze like lazy heads of ripe wheat. Randy dreamed of a young man, an Incan prince in peril. The young man had Indian features but red hair and freckles. The young man was reading a book and wishing he was home. Randy wished he was home on his sunny summer porch, an open adventure tale across his sunburned knees.

Theophrastus Bigelow came staggering over a line of dunes. He was dragging two very heavy sacks. "Hoy, laddie, give us a hand then."

"Mister Bigelow, have you found your treasure?"

"Aye, boy, and with it the skeleton of Whisperin' Dick Drinkwater, retired scalawag. Follow me."

Randy and the monkey followed the pirate through a wall of palmetto scrub to a mound of freshly turned earth. Atop the mound was propped the desiccated remains of what Randy assumed to be Whisperin' Dick. A deep scar disfigured the shrunken skin of the man's throat. Whisperin' Dick's eye sockets were empty; brown teeth gaped in a ghastly leer. Bigelow had propped him up in a saucy pose, one hand on his hip.

"I'll get out the Good Book, Randy-me-lad. It's only fitting we give 'im a Christian burial."

The pirate pulled a Gospel from his silken waistband. "Stand over by the hole, lad, whilst I says a few words."

Randy obeyed.

“Ah, ‘tis a sad thing I have to do, Randy, but I figure ye understands.” Bigelow drew a huge pistol from his sash and took dead aim at Randy’s chest. As he squeezed the trigger, the monkey sensed the situation and, protecting the source of the paradisal Mars bars on his tiny mind, jumped upon the pirate’s arm just as he fired his weapon. The shot flew harmlessly off into the palmettos.

Cursing foully, Bigelow brushed away the monkey and drew his second pistol.

“Go, kid, go,” whispered Oswaldo. “You can make it. Run for it.”

Randy did not run; he prayed hard and dived deep into his cargo pockets. The pockets seemed to know what he needed each time he looked before. There! The roll of monofilament line with the fishhook and sinker. As the pirate cocked his pistol, Randy swung the fishing line around his head like a lariat. All he was aware of was the pounding of his heart and the slow, slow hum of the transparent fishing line as it gathered speed in ever widening circles. He let it go. While the line was in the air, it whirred with a sound effect as in the Saturday matinee ninja warrior movies. Oswaldo noticed that his palms were sweating. San Expedito and Barney teetered on the edge of Harriet’s bedside table.

The lead sinker caught on the upraised hammer of the pistol, locking it open, while the hook embedded itself in the meaty part of Bigelow’s thumb. Randy’s cast had wrapped a few turns around the pistol’s trigger guard for good measure.

“God curse ye!” growled the pirate.

Bigelow could not fire the gun or even let go of it until he broke the line or dislodged the fishhook’s barb. He tore at the line with his jagged yellow teeth, but the artificial fiber was too strong for him.

“Go, Randy. Go, go, go...” Oswaldo reached to turn the page.

On the next page was a picture of Randy’s heels disappearing over the top of a giant sand dune. Behind him the enraged Theophrastus Bigelow and his great flintlock pistol were tied up tight in a snarl of monofilament fishing line. With his free hand the pirate drew his cutlass to chop away the line. Under the force of his blow the pistol exploded, driving a leaden ball backwards into the pirate’s heart. By this time, Randy Smith was out of sight and running full tilt through the rough palmetto scrub.

Oswaldo closed *The Runaway Bungalow*. He identified Randy’s problems as his own. “Now how does pequeño Randy get off the island? It is a coral reef.” The boy had destroyed his tormentor, escaped certain death, only to be marooned on a Caribbean atoll. “He will have to row out to the Gypsy Princess and sail her single-handed back to England." But wait! The boy had started with a daydream, reading on his porch in Anytown, USA.

"Santa Maria!" He had tried to stand but the room closed in on him. *The Runaway Bungalow* slipped from his fingers and lay open on the floor. He steadied himself by grabbing at the dresser. A silk tasseled throw and the contents of Harriet's bureau top scattered as he collapsed back to the bed. His head was stuffed, too full, his balance all wrong. He was sick—dizzy and disoriented. Perhaps if he could close his eyes and rest for a moment.

❑

"Miguel, whiskey, por favor. I trust the Johnnie Walker has survived our most excellent explosion. Two glasses." Don Patricio was in an expansive mood but Miguel noticed he was excluded from the invitation to drink; he was to fetch only. Had he not fought side by side in the jungles with the Illuminati guerrillas? Was he, Miguel Santandrea, to play Don Patricio's loyal dog, lolling and panting for its reward? Lick my hand. Now, simplón. The corduroy had entered their business and he now became the waiter. He thrust his weapon into his waistband and headed to the kneeling airplane. Better for now to get the whiskey for the policeman and Patricio to toast their miraculous survival. If the corduroy felt any distress over his fallen comrades he did not show it.

When he returned with two tumblers left unbroken from the explosion neither man appeared to have moved. Their attitude was stiff, formal. Miguel sensed an anomaly—the corduroy was too at ease for one who had just given over his honor into the hands of a stranger.

"Then we have an arrangement?" Patricio queried the corduroy.

"It would appear that we have an arrangement." The corduroy turned and smiled at Miguel. The corduroy's smile was brittle.

What was different with this exchange? These were not two about to partake the fellowship of alcohol after not being blown to pieces. The corduroy, this Canadian policeman, had been bribed. He could see it in the light of shame and avarice in his eyes. But there was more. He had been bought with much money. Money plus a small quantity of drugs and a corpse, perhaps—to be taken back for show. Miguel perhaps.

"Patrón." Miguel set the tumblers down gently, testing his balance, foot-to-foot.

"¿Qué?" Patricio turned to Miguel. He registered mild irritation, as though a household appliance had spoken without first having been given permission. Patricio nodded. "Now, corduroy. Kill him."

The corduroy was slow getting his gun up from an ankle holster. Miguel fired without conscious aim, a single liquid motion as he had learned in the jungles of the Illuminati. Patricio half-rose from where he sat cross-legged on the ground. Miguel shot him and the policeman both neatly through the forehead.

Miguel bent over Patricio's corpse. He stripped the body and went to work. Surely the boy would like a memento and remember him fondly by it. "¿Qué tal, mariposa? Ahh, Patrón, the little wanderer—your butterfly."

After he made certain that all who had been killed by the explosion were truly dead, he counted up the policemen's bait money. A million dollars. Canadian, true—but even with the exchange rate he could live well in America.

"Ah, we are all so far from home." The chico would most likely not have the presence of mind to change his name. Everyone would know him. And to make sure the butterfly reached its destination, that it was not misunderstood, he would follow. He stuffed the cash inside his shirt and walked away into the woods. He reached the river that delineated Canada's border with the United States and a motorboat someone had left carelessly moored. The afternoon was sunny and he was content with life as it had presented itself. Miguel put the smiling Sue Bee with its nest of plastic bubble wrap into the mail soon after he scuttled the stolen boat. "Enjoy the honey. Disfrútelo, pepito."

❑

Oswaldo Patricio Meléndez O'Rourke y Nuñez was in a dream of running, fleeing a pursuit from which there was no escape. They were after him—after us, for Harriet ran beside him. San Expedito smiled beatifically down. *San Expedito, pray for us.*

Miguel, Patricio, Sarah Bernhardt, Harriet, Amy Fisher and he ran together.

Five runners not counting himself—play fives, lucky numbers in the voodoo dream books. Miguel Santandrea played the Bolita, la lotería, passionately. He had filled many arks with losers, folding his losing tickets into origami animals. In the numbers, any combination of fives, the numbers of Mama Coca.

"They are after you," San Expedito jogged alongside.

"Who is after me? Surely they are all here, running with us, Santo."

"Ah-ah-ah-ah-ah. Count 'em, kid."

Oswaldo turned to count his fellow runners. The figures swam into and out of focus; his vision had the fish-eye distortion of a fever dream. "Miguel," Patricio waved and tried to catch up.

"Surely I am not Miguel, patrón," said Oswaldo over his shoulder. "You are mistaken. Besides, you are dead."

Patricio directed a wolfish leer at Amy Fisher. He unzipped his fly. He appeared surprised as he reached inside and pulled out a plastic honey bottle. "You would turn your back on Mama Coca, and couple with some gringo virago in whose veins flows none of the blood of los indios? ¡Madre de Dios! Have I not raised you as my own son and here you would marry an aging waitress who will make you wash your own socks." He spoke in unaccented, but syntactically bizarre English. Right off the Berlitz language tapes. In life, Tío Patricio's English was flawless. Tío Patricio threw the Sue Bee honey bottle at him. Oswaldo ducked and the bottle bounced then rolled, spilling a golden stream of honey in a zigzag pattern on the pavement. "Miguel!" Patricio screamed.

San Expedito paused to retie a sneaker. "I could have told you so, niño—but no, you wouldn't have listened if I had. Miguel knows where you are." Oswaldo put on a burst of speed to get away from his saint.

Money. The revenge of money would be pitiless.

San Expedito jogged in place as he whispered to Oswaldo, "Pitilessness. It musical, is it not? Pitilessness requires practice, like playing the mandolin. Much as a tattoo, when you've got it, it's there for good. Except that the mandolins will wash off later. At pitilessness, Tío Patricio had much practice. Venality is such a comfort to me. And you—you have hidden the money twice but you can't keep away."

❑

Oswaldo shivered in the pre-dawn chill, his knees growing stiff. Eyes running, throat sore, head pounding, he had found an ideal place of concealment on the grounds of Willipaq's Memorial Library. The red brick façade and Gothic Revival casements of the library building loomed menacingly in the half-light. A bronze statue of a Union corporal stood, gun at the ready, on its cement pediment. The statue's footing had been hollow, entrance secured by removing four bronze screws of a commemorative plaque. There he waited, thinking. Oswaldo felt hunted—the pursued, not the pursuer. A tiny nickering of ancestral memory nudged at his forebrain telling him that this was not right. His was a bloodline that climbed from the jungle of mangrove and liana, privy to the cougar's admonitory cough, to seek the sun and to pile the blocks, raise the temples, hone knives of copper, obsidian and gold to thrust deep into the hearts of victims—souls sent winging sunwards as rivulets of blood soaked an altar's stone channels, darkening the spillways where the earth waited, quickening and thirsty. Entrails told their tales.

A mourning dove gave call as the night mists settled—first light was approaching. He had maintained his position behind a hedge for three hours now. He jumped at a cough out on the manicured lawn a few yards distant: a fox homeward bound with a dead rat twitching in its jaws. A yellow striped tomcat stood motionless where it had blundered across the fox's path, its tail the size of a softball bat, a low glottal warning in its throat. The fox dropped its prey and coughed again, its tail up and bristling. The cat continued its stream of consonants, retreated perhaps a foot and settled itself, conceding enough for safety but holding honor intact. The fox picked up the rat and continued to its earth, and Oswaldo breathed again. Maybe he and Harriet would relocate—Taos, Santa Fe perhaps.

Oswaldo awoke with a startled snap. He heard a sound, small but significant in the pre-dawn stillness. He had fallen asleep sitting on his heels. But for how long? Half an hour at least by the kink in his neck. The gray half-dawn seemed brighter although the street light at the corner was still on. He rearranged his legs, working out the stiffness. Everything was going to be all right.

There was a bird's song and a robin hopped across the lawn cocking his head as he stopped every couple of feet, alert for breakfast. Through the hedge Oswaldo could make out the figure of a man on the library steps. The man was smoking a cigarette.

An automobile slowly turned the corner at the distant end of the library's tiny campus. As it approached, the man rose and walked down the steps to the curb to meet it. The car approached to a stop, the man shrugged, crushed out his cigarette underfoot and got inside. A cold line of dread crawled up his spine. ¡Madre de Dios! It was Miguel. The driver reached out to some apparatus on his dashboard and a light bloomed to inflorescence on the roof. Taxi.

❑

The saint's crow cawed, "Bogus saint, bogus saint," and got slapped for its trouble.

"Put a sock in it, Barney," said Expedito. The saint stepped down from his tiny pedestal. "Dream over. You may wake up now."

The careened airplane, the Sue Bee in the mail, dying butterflies, Harriet and Amy Fisher—all were zooming. It took the whole of Oswaldo's determination to hold back the contents of his stomach. "So, he wants the money. Gracias for the sending, Santo. I shall be better aware of my surroundings in the future."

"Enough of these revelations," said Oswaldo. "You are a disaccommodation of my senses for having engaged in self abuse." He doubled over with a sudden spasm. He had to throw up.

"And you waxed the old carrot a lot, too, I'll just bet," said San Expedito, unconsoling. "Those single-sex religious schools. Tsk, tsk. Don Patricio's assassin is on your trail. And you thought little Randy had a problem with that monkey of Bigelow's." The saint stooped on one knee to peer into Oswaldo's eyes. "So you really believe in me. Really?"

"It would seem I was wrong," said Oswaldo. "You are the real thing. Covetousness, envy, sloth, surely you are one of these. Or the revenge appertaining to their exercise."

"So? And what if I am a figment? Beatification is bullshit. And the butterflies, are they really lost souls? Or just Pat's weenie in a bottle. These are the imponderables. I myself went straight from the fevered imaginings of a hyperthyroid deacon directly to the company of the blessed, thence to the botánicas. St. Rose is the real thing but, believe me, she's bad news, all that S and M. Santa Barbara, Santería, Expedito—a jolly company we are."

Oswaldo rubbed his eyes and gagged back a rising flow of acid magma. The saint was back between the Marlboro Lights and the alarm clock. Barney the crow was in place, crushed underfoot. But San Expedito was still speaking.

"I am figment, like I told you. Don't fight it, kid; you are delirious." The saint stepped aside with the gesture of a game show host bringing on a fresh contestant. "And now, St. Rose of Lima to say I told you so. Amy, please." Amy Fisher in skintight spangles, high heels and fishnet hose came forward to pull back a velvet curtain. Amy wore a satin team jacket much as those favored by the Dominican baseball clubs. The jacket said "Mama Coca" across the back in chenille letters.

Behind the curtain a wizened woman with empty eye sockets gestured for him to join her on her bed of nails, "Mortification of the flesh," she explained. "Go drive the porcelain bus, querido. Upchuck to your heart's delight. It's good for what ails you." Oswaldo ran to the bathroom. He vomited up an almanac of groceries past, traveling back in time through dinners, lunches and breakfasts.

He could not feel his legs and passed out with his head in the toilet.

❑

Oswaldo lay on the tile of the bathroom floor. One arm was crooked over the side of the toilet; his fingers dangled into the empty bowl. The contents of his stomach and beyond had been exhausted. A dappled rainbow of bodily fluids caked the sides of the basin. Green, liver bile; red, blood. He pulled the flush handle. It was refreshing to feel the cold, cold running water on his hands. He splashed water from the toilet on his face and dried off with the bathmat.

Oswaldo reentered the kaleidoscope of his fever dream. The room began to spin and he tried to throw up but without success. He had been emptied. The bathmat became a yellowed newspaper, crumpled and discarded. A bewildered-looking girl looked out at him from a story on the front page:

Amy Fisher, whose shooting of the wife of her lover, Joey Buttafuoco, when she was 17 earned her the tabloid nickname "Long Island Lolita," has tied the knot. Fisher, who became a newspaper columnist last year, was married this week, according to her employer, the Long Island Press.

He dropped the newspaper and it flew away down a cobbled street. Was that Mama Coca, the Duse, Sarah Bernhardt hidden in the shadows of a doorway? No, a pretty young woman, just a girl. Her breasts were bare, as were her feet, and she wore a pleated kilt. "The butterflies," she said. She pulled at his sleeve. "I am Amy Fisher and I have just shot Mary Jo Buttafuoco. The butterflies are all dead."

"Santo—Expedito. You have said I was awake, that the dream-sending was ended."

"And so I did," said San Expedito. "Go figure. Never underestimate the revelatory components of shellfish toxins. It's their turn now. Have fun—pretend it's a séance, Ozzie. I get to watch too, right?"

"Claro. Sí, Santo. Amy Fisher, she is the face from Theophrastus Bigelow's medallion?"

"Sí, niño."

Amy held a smoking pistol. Oswaldo tried to imagine this face rising from the bottom of Bigelow's tureen amidst floating vegetables and bits of stewed fish. Her long strawberry-red hair she wore braided into a beehive that extended to an aerial climax, and she swung her hips with the steady determination of someone who knew what she was about. "¿Mama Coca? ¿Eres tu?"

"Sí. Soy la Mama," said Amy. She pulled him along a winding passageway, her bare feet slapping shivery echoes from narrow walls. A restaurant appeared beneath a guttering blue neon sign: EAT.

Oswaldo and Amy Fisher slid into a booth. They ordered the steamer clams.

"I am expecting company," said Amy Fisher.

Enter the heavy, looking confused, like Patricio only meaner. It was Captain Bigelow. A rumpled daypack dangled from a nylon shoulder strap. The pack was stuffed so full of soiled laundry Bigelow hadn't been able to zip it shut. His other possession was a boxy-looking machine pistol. Armed and confused, a dangerous combination. Oswaldo wondered if the pirate's gun had any bullets in it.

How did Theophrastus Bigelow get out of *The Runaway Bungalow*? Oswaldo must ask Amy Fisher if they lived. The muzzle of his weapon swept arcs back and forth across the room. He shrugged off the daypack and let it fall.

"I am a refugee. I claim political asylum. Could you show me the way to the men's room please?"

"Hello there and welcome to America," said Amy, rising to the occasion. "It's in the back."

"You are very beautiful, Mama Coca," said Bigelow as he passed their booth, "But perhaps you should cover yourself up." He patted an exposed breast. "Modesty, modesty." He flashed a smile of strong, yellowed teeth. "And some sensible shoes, perhaps." Shark's teeth, a crocodile smile.

"You are a fool, Captain Bigelow," said Amy.

Oswaldo thought, He is a fool. He has a gun. And he has to pee. People do not have to pee in dreams.

Click! A weapon being cocked.

"Amy, DOWN!" cried Oswaldo. A cigarette machine and the cash register exploded in a hail of bullets.

A second man strolled in, a smoking gun in his hands. Miguel Santandrea. He carried a Nikon camera. Oswaldo wondered if Randy Smith had brought along his camera to his island. Of their fellow diners only one couple seemed to notice the gunfire. They left a pile of bills on their table and began edging nervously to the door. Miguel stood back and cradled his weapon as he took everyone's picture with his camera.

Amy Fisher leaned out of her booth, blinking at the strobe flash. Amy now wore the medallion with which Theophrastus Bigelow tried to hide the tracks of the hangman's rope. And on the medallion was her own face. Mama Coca, she was delivering this dream-sending. He could not wake up. What the hell, go with the flow. San Expedito, pray for us.

"Fuck you, motherfucker," Amy smiled.

"Thankee kindly." Bigelow gave her a courtly bow. "...for the good wishes. Ladies and gentlemen," he said, bowing to the remaining diners. They ignored him. "We are here today to present you with an unparalleled opportunity to selflessly aid two poor wanderers from a distant land complete their business and return to their homes before their dinners get cold.

“This is possible,” he went on, “for we have a boat waiting. My associate is

Miguel. He is a surly South American; he used to be a monkey. You will please notice that he is armed and, while my attention may waver, his does not. I thus sincerely caution you against any abrupt motions, which Miguel may misconstrue. We hope to inconvenience you for only a brief time. You will help us to apprehend our missing associate who has, alas, absconded with an item of great sentimental value...”

Money, money, money.

These men were after the money.

“You will excuse me, I have little money.” Miguel fumbled in his pockets and came up with a wad of crisp hundred-dollar bills. “Ah, pepito, it was I who placed the wire across the ignition terminals of your parents’ Land Rover. I tried to save them, told Don Paco and Doña Inez it was too early to leave. But no, they were hot for the bedroom and they would have enjoyed so the antipasto. And now you are a poor orphan left behind by the careless footfall of the passing Caballo Apocalíptico.”

Here Captain Bigelow paused to extract a pinch of white powder from a silver snuffbox. A tiny cloud wafted toward the floor and dusted the toe of one Prada boot, leaving an outline on the linoleum. Oswaldo thought, Randy Smith should surely be here by now to save the day. He would pull some wondrous device from his bottomless pocket of Boy Scout implements. Where was Randy?

The Captain wiped his nose on his sleeve.

“Manners, manners. You need a finger bowl, Theophrastus.” Amy removed the Gypsy Princess medallion from about her throat and, winking to Oswaldo, let it fall. He expected to hear the rich thrill of the genuine article, the winds of time caressing trinkets at a dead queen’s throat.

Clunk. The medallion hit the floor with the leaden thud of a dropped hubcap.

“Pure gold dinnerware, 60 troy ounces, the good stuff goes clunk,” said Amy. “Don’t anyone move!” she shouted and reached down to spin the medallion. “What fools these mortals be,” she quoted Puck, the Comics Weekly Man and leaned back to watch the fun. “It’s the human condition, Ozzie. The trick is to get it spinning in place, standing still and spinning.”

“God damn ‘ee for a whore!” Bigelow spun around and emptied his clip of bullets into Amy Fisher. The bullets passed harmlessly through her.

“Bugger me Ned!” Captain Bigelow was having trouble fitting another clip into the pistol’s magazine.

❑

Beepbeepbeepbeep. Saved by Harriet's alarm clock. Where was his book? The book had moved. Oswaldo wobbled over to pick it up. Sweaty and unshaven, he had slept in his clothes. An unlit cigarette dangled at his lips. San Expedito smiled his ironic smile. Sarah Bernhardt was haughty and unapproachable. In the Mexican high country, in El Rosario and Sierra Chincua, almond eyes pouchy with sleep denied by fever dreams of avarice and the night sweats of free trade, the land-rich and tin shanty dwellers alike did not waste their prayers on the butterflies, a legion of lost souls.

Oswaldo pondered and rubbed his stubbled chin. He felt better—better get showered and shaved. There were many mysteries to *The Runaway Bungalow*. The butterflies would eventually return; Amy Fisher had assured him of this. "So, Tío Patricio was the murderer of my parents. Or his monkey was. That is the sending of Mama Coca and Amy Fisher." Oswaldo could again feel his legs. He wiggled his toes and reopened the book to the last page. There was a picture of a pretty matron pulling her mop handle away from the grip of her sleeping child.

"Honey, Randy? Wake up. You must have fallen asleep in the sun. What's that you're reading. Oh, *Treasure Island*. A good book. Any adventures in your dreams?"

"Uhn. No, mom."

Oswaldo felt cheated. The boy was saved by his mother. What had San Expedito done for him lately?

The next morning an origami animal, a dove, was slipped under Harriet's door. He unfolded the dove. *Esta noche* was written on a receipt slip from the Pick 'N' Pay. As must happen, jackal and capybara, the tracker and the tricker, were to meet.

❑

Oswaldo Patricio Meléndez O'Rourke y Nuñez prowled the night by the light of a moon three quarters full. He dressed in black. Many wore black—priests, hippies, country and western singers—but the blackening of the face was surely a mark of perpetration. Commando warriors blackened their faces and wore black balaclavas. Still unsteady from the tainted clams, Ozzie crouched to pray behind the big green dumpster in back of the Pick 'N' Pay.

"San Expedito, auxilio de los que pierden cosas, ruega por mí. '...lost causes, the young, dead by the sword.' A futile prayer to a bogus saint, San Expedito." There had to be at least two of them; the origami dove was meant as a warning sign. But signifying what? He was sure that Miguel would not have the initiative to carry out any complex plan by himself.

Headlights jounced and flashed against the reflections of a watery, pale moon. A truck. Hard, high suspension.

There was a ratcheting, the truck's hand brake, and a man swung down from the cab, leaving the engine running. The two stood together in the full glare of the headlights, their bodies illuminated. Their heads spoke in a warm summer dark of engine smells above a nimbus of frantic insects. In spite of the moths and mosquitoes, Oswaldo felt the joy of an epiphany.

"Oswaldo. It is I, Miguel. Forget the hundred thousand dollars; it is my gift. I prayed for you, Chico. This is the Jesus curse—a prayer answered. I am truly sorry for the killing of Don Paco and Doña Inez. But it was business, ¿comprendes? No hard feelings."

Miguel noted a change of expression. "You, my friend, are volunteering a judgment on my behalf..." An exhausted moth rested on Miguel's chest. He gently stroked its wings. "...in your soul."

"They will catch you eventually, you know."

Miguel smiled a thin smile. "Every deed has its aura. What I have done is a positive thing, sending you Don Patricio's butterfly. I wish it to bring you joy. Your unhappiness would spoil my escape. Freedom is a happy thing. If you are not going to be happy, I would rather stay where I was."

"Wait. You walk back into Canada and we are both caught."

"Bueno. But I am already dead, ¿verdad? My passport will have been found on the corpse of Don Patricio. I am invisible and you are yet not. I am a man of the habit of honor, a good soldier. I simply acknowledge when my price has been reached and get on with it. If you were to see me, recognize me, then would I not be a fool to let you go free?" He placed a reassuring arm around Oswaldo's shoulders. "We understand each other. I am not above a little blackmail. You are corruptible and I am corrupt; then let us not cloud

with doubt what should be an occasion of joyous affirmation. The line between the keeper and the kept, the poacher and the hare, we have not violated that. It is important our dance continue. To this end you will assist in my escape."

❑

The creak of a spring. The screen door. "¿Corazón?"

"Honey?" The screen door slammed, Harriet home from work.

"You can find true, bona fide love and still not beat your karma," said Harriet. She struggled in with an armload of squirming groceries. Her arithmetic gave her twenty seconds before the brown paper bags turned to root beer. "Ozzie? I could use a hand here."

"I'm in here, chica."

Harriet followed the sound of his voice. "You have been reading. Did I wake you up?" Something was leaking. "Can't stop now." She made a U-turn and headed for the kitchen.

Ozzie put his head around the kitchen door. "I have finished the book." His eyelids were puffy and lightly tinged with blue. "I think the fever has broken." *The Runaway Bungalow* hung from his fingertips. He dropped the book and followed. "I know pequeño Randy's secret, the secret of *The Runaway Bungalow*. It is in the butterflies."

Harriet brushed back a dislocated wisp of hair that had fallen to cover her eyes. "You still look sick. I threw up at work today, too." She swept past him and made it to the sink. The bags disintegrated.

"Sorry, Chica," said Ozzie, catching the contents as the bags' bottoms dropped out. A runnel flecked yellow and green ran down his thighs. The plasticized covers of *The Runaway Bungalow* were smeared with egg yolk and broccoli florets.

Harriet radiated motherly concern. She threw her arms around his neck and kissed his ear. "Christ, but you're cute when you stop barfing." In the bedroom Expedito and Sarah, the Duse, exchanged ambiguous glances. This was love then, ¿De verdad?

"Let's go out tonight," Oswaldo swept her off her feet, hugging and kissing her, as they spun around the linoleum.

"Ozzie!"

"You, Corazón, are who Mama Coca has sent for me. Gracias, Amy Fisher. Gracias, San Expedito."

Along the federal fish pier where home-docked scallop draggers and tugs lay pilotless and covered with tarps, Oswaldo bent to kiss the forehead of his beloved. "Your hair," whispered Oswaldo as he twirled a finger in Harriet's auburn locks.

"Sarah Bernhardt's hair." Harriet presented with a coy curtsey.

"She is then no longer Eleanora the Duse?"

"She is a picture I admired once. Things are not always as they seem, querido."

"I meant to say I love your hair."

"It is my hair."

"And so I love it." They stood together and listened to the slap of an incoming tide as it washed against the pilings beneath their feet.

"Ozzie?" There was no answer. "Ozzie." She placed a hand on his arm.

Oswaldo Patricio Meléndez O'Rourke y Nuñez woke from a reverie of money and the strength of touching, feeling, holding it. "Nothing, corazón. Just a dream." Oswaldo stared into Harriet's eyes. "Your face is a holy face," he said. She did not need to know everything and all at once. They were, after all, one hundred thousand dollars richer. St. Rose of Lima had reveled in a sinless life, slept on a bed of nails and mortified her flesh. Small deceits between lovers were venial sins and to be expected.

A jib-headed sloop bobbed on short swells beside a Coast Guard buoy tender. "There was a butterfly. It came in the mail last week..." The boat was named the Gypsy Princess.

The Gypsy Princess.

Oswaldo jumped to the deck of the boat, "Hoy! Hoy there! Captain Bigelow." Below decks, where the mast's shank thrust through the upper deck, the ship's papers were posted. Thumbtacked inside protective plastic covers were faded color snapshots of a smiling middle-aged couple with what must be their grown children. *Gypsy Princess, Long Island, New York.* Summer people, a coincidence. There seemed to be no one on board.

As he turned to go back above deck Oswaldo saw an origami giraffe on its side, abruptly abandoned, and a scattering of graham cracker crumbs that led to the door of a rope locker. A slim brown mentholated cigarette smoldered in a saucer, hastily snubbed out. Oswaldo set the giraffe on its legs and climbed up the companionway ladder. "Adios, Tío Miguel." The summer people had money; they could get another boat. For Miguel Santandrea, the origami man, a new frontier beckoned. Oswaldo foresaw Miguel living happily on roots and berries with an aboriginal wife and many round-faced children to gladden his declining years.

Back on the fish pier Oswaldo Patricio Meléndez O'Rourke y Nuñez stood silently. Then, "Harriet, I love you."

"Ozzie?"

"I have a story to tell you. It will be a long time in the telling." Oswaldo wondered about Randy's future. Would he remember the lessons he learned from Theophrastus Bigelow and Bigelow's monkey? In an endless stream of eventualities would Randy Smith would grow up and discover girls? Would there be good times in Anytown, USA? Would he take his family north where the butterflies flew, lost souls headed on a vacation?

“Time we have,” said Harriet.

Back at home, from Harriet’s bedside table Expedito checked his reflection in the bureau mirror. There was something about a man in uniform. A lovely tableau except for the crow. “Dumb crow.” Expedito tried holding his sword at port arms. It gave him a genuine air of spontaneity. “With faith all things are possible,” said Expedito. “Matthew 17:19, ‘*nihil inpossibile erit vobis si habueritis fidem sicut granum sinapis,*’ in the Vulgate.”

Sarah Bernhardt smiled down on San Expedito.

In the book *The Runaway Bungalow*, at home between the Marlboro Lights and the alarm clock, Randy Smith stayed on past the story’s end. “And I may one day meet the red-haired Incan prince, Oswaldo,” said Randy. His mother nodded wisely. “And Amy Fisher, that’s what he called the princess who helped him escape from the pirates. And Mama Coca. And the beautiful Harriet.”

In New York, Amy Fisher, Lethal Lolita, now a personal advice columnist for the *Long Island Press*, noted the return of the butterflies to North America. She had had plastic surgery and had changed her name, so the butterflies didn’t stop on Long Island.

"I believe I’ve matured,” said Amy in an interview with her own newspaper, “I believe my happiness now is a result of being a kinder person.”

TheRunaway Bungalow was first published as a featured novella in SpecFic-World's *Featured Fiction* August 2008.

Scope Virgin

The woman at the far end of the kaleidoscope had not been there last week, of this Simon was sure. She was naked or near enough, thinly dressed in a diaphanous veil that left little to the imagination.

"Holy shit!" Simon Alexander breathed on the lens and gave it a wipe with his sleeve.

"I see that I have your attention..." said the woman, "...finally."

With a furtive glance to see if there was anyone watching, Simon took a closer look.

"You are carrying a beer and a bag of Cheetos," said the woman. She strode toward the kaleidoscope's eye-piece, shedding blue veils one by one. "I'd like a beer, too. But you will have to get me out of this thing first, I think."

"You are the Virgin Mary," said Simon, who watched TV shows on unexplained phenomena.

"Perhaps. I might also be a bird of ill omen, a carrion crow. Or a butterfly. Whatever. I am celebrated for my hijinks and practical jokes; appearances can be deceiving, howsomever. Only last week I appeared covering the entire leeward face of a mountain in Brazil," she said. "Thousands came to see the miracle. Many died, trampled in the rush. Compare to this the incongruity of a grown man hiding out behind the garage with a kaleidoscope and a six-pack."

The kaleidoscope was Simon's secret—after forty-three years of marriage his only secret. Its twisted barber pole spirals of colored metal foil pasted with stars and crescent moons reflected Mylar purples that shone like the sunglasses of a state trooper. Simon kept the kaleidoscope hidden under the eaves at the back of the garage. He had been temporarily banished from the house while Bonnie spread quilt patterns over all available surfaces. Beer and Cheetos were forbidden inside the house.

"Is this contraption yours?" said the woman. She was surrounded by a pale blue aura. "Good luck for you that I showed up in a portable apparatus."

"Then you are *not* the Virgin Mary." Cellophane crinkled as Simon reached into the bag which he had retrieved from under the front seat of the family sedan. Dinner was hours away.

"You were expecting someone else?"

“Ah, no. I was expecting some colored glass beads.” Simon wished that he had bothered to shave that morning. “It’s a Boy Scout project from sixty years back. Katahdin Council, Willipaq, Maine.” Simon shook the kaleidoscope. “Troup 136.”

“Easy with the shaking. These Boy Scouts you speak of, they are a cloistered order? Lay brothers? And you are eating in front of me.”

“Sorry.” Simon popped an orange-colored salt-slathered cheese-flavored Cheeto into his mouth. “I was hungry.”

“And thirsty too, I’ll warrant. I am the Princess Ackaetia Uroonous. You shall be my chosen champion. Name please?” She jiggled.

“Simon. Simon Alexander. Princess, princess, ahh...”

“Uroonous. Princess Ackaetia Uroonous. Practice saying this. And I know all about you. I have watched you from the other end of the kaleidoscope. I call you Big Eye. Does my name not roll on the palate like a scented oil?”

“It is a first-rate name, alright.” The princess was naked and lovely and that she might have a mellifluous name was not of paramount concern. “I did think you were the Virgin Mary for a minute there.”

“Hardly. But in one or two negligible planetary systems I am revered as a goddess.” The scope virgin struck a demure pose, eyes averted in modesty. “Hence I require champions who are trustworthy, reverent and brave. These *Boy Scouts* you speak of—they are warrior monks? With the single-minded devotion of a religious community?”

“Well... a scout *is* cheerful, trustworthy, obedient, clean, brave and reverent. I was an assistant scoutmaster thirty years running. And loyal. I ran a tight ship—no booze, no dope. We encouraged abstinence before marriage. Hey, the kids were only twelve years old.”

“As you are my chosen champion, I shall accept your assessment. For the time being. We shall have to get me back where I belong, and that is that.” Simon took a deep breath and held it as blue veils rippled and slithered to the, well, *floor*. The apparition arched her back to better display her breasts. “We’ll have to get together and urinate sometime,” she said.

“*What?*”

“I am not yet fluent with your idiom,” said the Princess Ackaetia. “I spoke wrongly? I had hoped to be alluring. You may breathe now.”

Simon chugalugged his remaining beer. “Take it from me—you are definitely alluring.” He adjusted the focus.

“And don’t fidget. It is unbecoming.” The Princess Ackaetia was beginning to fade. Simon gave the kaleidoscope a shake and banged it against the wall.

"Ouch!" said the Princess Ackaetia.

"Uh, sorry," said Simon. "Are you by any chance from another dimension?" In addition to his television habit Simon was an avid reader of science fiction.

"Alas, I was fleeing ravishment or abduction and did not watch where I was going. And now I am wedged in an oubliette at the bottom of my garden. I had slipped away to meditate. Prince Philo Gulesi is hounding me for my maidenhead and I must trust to the kindness of strangers."

"Oubliette? Prince... Philo *Gulesi*?"

Princess Ackaetia sighed. "A hole in the ground, at the other end of your kaleidoscope. And a very not nice person, to answer your questions in the order presented. Pull me through. There is a lot of me and I am considered odiferous by some species. You will want to do this out-of-doors. And I suggest a pair of rubber gloves."

Overhead a questing crow gave a squawk as it miscalculated its bearings and flew headlong into a power pole. "Yours?" asked Simon.

"As I said—a bird of ill omen," said Princess Ackaetia.

Simon returned with a dust mask and the large yellow Playtex gloves Bonnie kept under the kitchen sink. He had stuffed the mask with a handkerchief soaked in aftershave lotion. "Ready."

"Unscrew the eyepiece, reach in and pull. Careful now. Incidentally, you smell terrible."

"It's Aqua Velva." Simon's arm extended into the tube farther than the kaleidoscope's lengthwise measurement would have led him to believe. Instead of the curvilinear woman he was expecting, Simon felt a large, viscous, throbbing mass between his fingers. "Ah, I think I've got you."

"You have. But not there. *Here*. I am ticklish and that is a very personal place. And do not squeeze. Just pull. Got it?" said the Princess Ackaetia. "Pull!"

Simon pulled. The reek of unfriendly compost assailed his nostrils. He was glad for the hanky. After much struggling, the scope virgin popped out.

"You are a giant slug."

"The lineaments of beauty are debatable," said the slug. "I may have misrepresented myself so as to be pleasing in your sight, Big Eye." The giant slug undulated, slurped and sloshed. "A small deception. What you see is what you get." She executed a haughty turn like a fashion mannequin at the end of a runway.

"Bonnie is absolutely not going to believe this." Simon cupped his hands and called, "Bonnie! There's someone here I would like you to meet."

A well kept sixty-something woman came to the screen door. "Yes, darling?" She was all smiles; a heart-rending odor of muffins and pot roast with gravy followed close behind her.

"Your wife is very understanding to let you out alone with a princess of the blood," said the scope virgin. "Is she a jealous type?"

"Don't go there," Simon whispered. "Could you possibly come in the house with me and show her I'm not sliding into senile dementia?"

"I am afraid I would leave a slime trail," said the slug.

"Simon, always bringing things home." Simon's wife searched warily, scanning the back yard for a probable source for her husband's enthusiasm. "Well, what have we today?" Bonnie's eyes froze on the Princess Ackaetia. "Oh, a great big slug, how very interesting. And how very disgusting. Now we will have to put out bait before we're overrun. Our lettuce will be ruined. Put a peach basket over it." Bonnie executed a quick swivel to stomp back into the house. "At your age, too. Dinner is on hold."

As Simon pondered pot roast denied, the hand which held the kaleidoscope hung dejectedly at his side. A midge or a gnat buzzed from the tube. It performed a series of aerial acrobatics as if getting its bearings, then flew in ever smaller circles about his head. A beam of polarized light flashed between the insect and the tip of Simon Alexander's nose. "Ow!" Simon grasped his nose and hopped about in agony. The insect then dived at the scope virgin. The bug was angry.

"Big Eye! Should he fire again I am undone," cried the Princess Ackaetia.

Simon, through his pain, paused to stare at the insect—hovering, prepared to strike—and the slug. "I beg your pardon?"

"Swat him. If he cannot have me, he has sworn to kill me lest a more acceptable suitor find favor in my eyes."

"Huh! How about that." Simon raised his arm and swung the kaleidoscope. There was a "ding" as of a BB hitting a can. "Gotcha." Mylar mirrors and glass beads went flying. The kaleidoscope was demolished.

"Shattered into pieces! My poor, dear oubliette. Now I shall never, ever get back home again. By-the-bye, you have also just destroyed Prince Philo Gulesi's battle cruiser."

"Sorry. I thought it was a bug."

"Prince Philo's ship was government property; the over-taxed underclasses will be grumpy. *And* you have wrecked my gateway in the process. But where are my manners?" said the scope virgin. "You *have* saved my life. Thank you."

"Your *suitor*? But he, Prince Philo, is—was—so small. How do you, ahh..."

"The females of my kind are considerably larger than the males. Or they smaller—whatever. This is an economy of scale."

Simon checked the ground for kaleidoscope parts.

"Even if you picked up everything you could find there'd still be something missing," said Princess Ackaetia. "This is a universal law; you'd have a bag of parts is all. And even if you could get them all back together again the refraction indices would be all wrong."

"The Boy Scouts built it; we can fix it. It may take a while. It has been sixty years."

"Meanwhile, I am here. And Prince Philo Gulesi is nowhere. This has created an imbalance that will cascade through the fabric of space-time."

"Simon!" Simon's wife opened the screen door a crack.

"Yes, dear?"

"You are talking to it."

"But..." The screen door snicked shut.

"Very observant, your wife. We may safely ignore her," said the scope virgin offhandedly.

Simon turned to follow his wife into the house.

"Stay."

Simon stayed.

"Ever-amplified, this space-time anomaly will pack all the destructive power of Prince Philo's demolished cruiser, plus the mass of a displaced princess of the House of Uroonous, multiplied to the 27th power. We shall have some serious mischief." The regal petulance disappeared from the Princess' tone. "I don't mean to be any trouble—thanks for my deliverance and all—but there is great peril ahead."

"Thank you for filling me in," said Simon. "Could we talk about this later? Bonnie has a pot roast going for tonight."

"No, now. We shall have to manufacture so many kaleidoscopes that one of them will have to have the correct dimensional refraction. This will require volunteers. They must be the same who made the original kaleidoscope. We shall have to whistle up these Boy Scouts of yours and negotiate a fix."

"But they will be old, scattered..."

"You did it once; you can do it again. Prince Philo's regent is not going to wait on your Bonnie's pot roast. There will be a war of succession in addition to our space-time anomaly. Billions of lives will be extirpated. Shake a leg."

"We'll have to get you covered up. Not everyone would understand..."

"This 'peach basket' of your wife's sounds appropriate."

"Come on in the house. We'll have to use the kitchen phone. The linoleum? Your slime trail? I hope I'm not hurting your feelings, but Bonnie's new carpet..."

"I am a princess of the blood. We are held to a higher degree of accountability. Linoleum will be fine," said the Princess Ackaetia.

"Harry Pease should be in." Simon was warming to the challenge. "He can do a telephone tree to get Troup 136 out of retirement. Careful on the welcome mat. Astroturf," cautioned Simon.

In the street a car door slammed, an engine revved. Bonnie had left a note pinned to a peach basket on the kitchen table:

I'll be at Alma's. Those damned aloha shirts of yours were one thing. I will not be a laughing stock at the checkout line of the Red and White again. Call me when you come to your senses. The pot roast is turned off. Indefinitely.

Wearing his aloha shirt outside of the house was a minor rebellion that Bonnie had never forgiven. By Simon's lights, most folks who bought them on vacation never summoned up the raw courage required to wear them in Willipaq, Maine. Simon picked up the phone. "Harry and I used to be close. We went all the way to Eagle Scout side by side."

Harry picked up on the third ring, just as the answering machine cut in. "...not home right now. Wait for the..." CLICK. "I'm here, godammit. Simon? I know it's you, I got caller ID," said Harry.

"Harry? Remember when you said I had space aliens living in my teapot?"

"That was 1982. Besides, I meant it as a compliment to your powers of imagination. Have you been nursing a grudge all these years?"

"Nononononono. I got one. A space alien, not a grudge. Her name is Princess Ackaetia Uroonous and we need your help." Simon related the morning's doings.

“So Bonnie’s left you. If I was twenty years younger... Oh, what the hell, come on over. And bring the Princess.” Harry hung up.

“He says yes,” said Simon.

“Thank you,” said the Princess Ackaetia. “This will mean a reprieve for uncounted billions. And now, how’s about that beer?”

❑

Harry Pease rose painfully. “Door’s open. Come on in.” He walked with two canes, his knees ravaged by arthritis, shattered by sports injuries, and at the moment between surgeries. Simon entered carrying the peach basket with the Princess Ackaetia inside. A cloud of flying insects swarmed in behind them and headed straight at Harry’s head.

“Shit!” said Harry. “Holy shit. I thought it was too late in the season.” He reached for the spray can of bug killer he kept at the ready near the door. The insect cloud dropped like a rock. All but for two. Spouting tiny streams of electric fire they made for a spot right between Harry’s eyes. “Yikes!” Harry dropped the bug spray and swung one cane in a roundhouse right. There was a tiny “ding” and a mid-air flash of the kind courting fireflies give. “What the hell was *that* all about?”

“You have just faced down a direct assault by the remnants of Prince Philo Gulesi’s fleet and prevailed. You must come from hardy stock,” said the peach basket.

“Well, it still stings,” said Harry Pease, rubbing the bridge of his nose. “I don’t recall you being a ventriloquist, Simon. Alright, suppose you have got a space alien in your peach basket. Lemme have a peek at her.”

“You asked for it.” Simon lifted the peach basket.

“A princess of the blood doesn’t get out much. I amuse myself as I may,” said Princess Ackaetia. An oversized garden slug peered coyly up at Harry Pease.

“She was a pin-up girl when I met her,” said Simon.

“Fleeing ravishment or abduction by an unrelenting suitor,” said the Princess. “You appear to have more legs than Simon. Are you certain that this is not Barsoom? One time when my kitten ran off he returned chewing a very entertaining manuscript. About your world? I have to know how it ends. You have a copy.” This was a statement not a question.

“That would be Edgar Rice Burroughs’ Captain John Carter series,” Simon said. “Carter of Mars? I have it but it is hard to get at. Bonnie put all my paperbacks away in the attic.”

“As long as you have it; that is enough. I shall grant you an indulgence.”

“Kitten...” Simon breathed easier. That the Princess Ackaetia would have a kitten leveled the playing field between them, the human and the quasi-divine.

“I am trying to use terms with which you will be familiar. A lizard, actually. Rather large and ill-tempered and with a fondness for fresh meat. He ate one of my tutors. I once asked that tutor why is the kaleidoscope and was this particular kaleidoscope a threat.”

“What were your late tutor’s feelings on kaleidoscopes?”

“Much as his feelings on elopement and the bridal consummation. He said I must squinch my eyes together and pray hard.”

Harry paled and sat down abruptly. “Ahh... I beg your pardon, Princess. You said an unrelenting suitor. Prince Philo... who?”

“Gulesi. Philo Gulesi. I have not always been inside a peach basket, you know. I remember once I showed up in the air space of a thermopane picture window,” said Princess Ackaetia. “Like mist, you know, in Bayonne, New Jersey. The faithful mobbed the house. I leaked. No mist, no miraculous apparition. You have shown sufficient deference. You’ll do.”

“Ahh... I’ll do *what*?” said Harry Pease.

“Stop a civil war, save the known universe. For this we will require the assistance of the original Boy Scouts who built the kaleidoscope,” said the scope virgin.

Harry stared at the Princess Ackaetia. “You *are* a space alien? Really?”

“I may be an alien here. At home I am queen-apparent.”

“OK, OK,” said Harry Pease. “Enough already. I’m a believer. Simon, I figured you only needed a drink with a buddy. Because of Bonnie and all? I didn’t dream I’d be meeting a bona fide princess who lives in a peach basket and looks like live bait. Simon,” said Harry, “...how old are we?”

“Uh, seventy-two. So?”

“So we’d better get cracking; there are only a couple of us left. Most of Troup 136 are dead or moved to Florida. I can probably scare up some warm bodies, though.” He peered at the Princess Ackaetia. “Pleased to make your acquaintance, your highness. What can the Boy Scouts of America do for you?”

“Recreate my oubliette,” said the Princess Ackaetia. “Or your kaleidoscope—it depends on one’s point of view, does it not? It is in all our own best interests. Though vast, infinity is a biography of finite numbers: sooner or later the displacement will arrive back where it started, and then Ka-Boom. Good-bye everything. You want me to write this out for you? For any doubters?"

"You don't have hands," Simon observed.

"You will write. I will dictate," said the Princess.

"Some folks won't believe anything until they see it in print," said Harry.

❑

"This is it," announced Simon to Princess Ackaetia with the pride of a swashbuckler showing off his Caribbean redoubt. A solitary traffic light swung in the early evening dark directing three cars at the intersection. The Seniors Center—aside from the traffic light the only light downtown—projected a ferny terracotta ambience. A vigorous eighty-something woman with short-cropped gray hair bustled about inside, setting candles on empty café tables.

The sign said Open. Simon and the princess waited, motor running, angle-parked at the curb to see who would show up. At the far end of one line of fluorescent fixtures a plastic pail hung from a leaking sprinkler valve near the ceiling. Beneath it, suffused with an orange Edward Hopper glow, Harry Pease played single-handed Scrabble. Over the next half-hour five gregarious, chatty old-timers straggled in.

"Now," said Simon, going around to open the passenger's side door. "Show-time. I hope Harry prepped them to meet you."

As Simon entered carrying the Princess Ackaetia and her peach basket, the reunited Scouts flashed them the three-fingered salute. On the walls hung salvaged Norman Rockwell posters celebrating the scouting life.

Simon shook the peach basket. "You okay in there?"

"I will be when you stop shaking this damned thing." There were now seven in all inside the Seniors Center, Princess Ackaetia's recruits: six men and a woman, a one-time den mother who departed to the kitchen to spread tuna salad on finger rolls. Simon carefully placed the Princess on one of the café tables.

A bell on a spring jingled at the front door to announce a late arrival. "Sorry about that—don't trust the airlines." Fleming Ward, called Phlegm in school, had driven all the way from Florida. His eyes fell on the discarded peach basket. "Hiya, Simon. Fresh peaches? What's this?" He reached out to give the Princess Ackaetia a tentative poke.

"How intimate. *Quel sauvage*," giggled the Princess.

"That's French," observed Harry.

"Reasonably perceptive, Harry Pease." The Princess Ackaetia jiggled in thoughtful reverie. "A grotto. A little French girl. She taught me. French, that is. I taught her the rest. She was so sweet."

"A little French girl in a grotto." Fleming known as Phlegm crossed himself. "Saint Bernadette..."

"I appeared as a mist," said the Princess. "You might want to check yourself for stigmata. Like nail holes in your palms?"

Phlegm Ward checked his palms. "Nope." He blanched and gagged; the Princess had left a slime trail on his hands.

"Oh, how delightful." The Princess chortled and rocked, the table teetered. "I have never, ever been to Lourdes; that was just one of my little jokes."

"Yuck," said Phlegm. He wiped himself off on his shirt front.

❑

Spouses and wondering adult children packed bag lunches, filled thermos bottles and car-pooled their loved ones to the kaleidoscope factory. The spouses and children were not invited in. The Princess Ackaetia held court perched atop a red leatherette barstool as the Seniors Center became a hive of activity. From as far afield as Boston and Toronto bolts of reflective Mylar film, shipping tubes and cartons of plastic lenses arrived by FedEx.

"How many is that so far, Harry?" asked the Princess.

"Over a thousand, your highness. Twelve hundred thirty-eight exactly."

"Statistically sufficient. Pick one and take a peek." Harry lifted a kaleidoscope from the nearest folding banquet table. "Wow! I mean, holy shit." Naked and enticing, the scope virgin was back in the tube.

"Precisely. Yes, I am, am I not?" said Princess Ackaetia from her barstool. "Beautiful in whichever aspect, that is." Harry handed off the kaleidoscope to Simon. Simon took a look. First into the kaleidoscope, then at the Princess. "But you're there and *here*."

"As I was when first we met, Simon Alexander..." the naked lady in the tube gave her behind a wiggle.

From the barstool the peach basket Princess continued, "...and you should find a telltale circle of charcoal around your eye. It will wash off in a day or so. Another of my little jokes. A memento for when I am gone. If you will all lend a hand, it is time to begin testing the apparatuses."

Phlegm Ward came from the kitchen wiping his hands on a wad of paper towels. "OK, I'll play. A big slug says it is a princess. And you guys buy it, all of it." There was a shocked silence followed by shuffling and distancing but Phlegm stood his ground. "Jesus, Mary and Joseph, just what the hell do *we* get out of all this, anyway?"

"That is rude," said the Princess. "Your desires are neither here nor there."

Simon handed over Princess Ackaetia's dictation. "Phlegm, read this. She wrote it out for you."

Phlegm approached the paper warily like a cat stalking in high, dry grass. He studied it closely from all sides, turned it over, hoping to find enlightenment or at least a coupon on the back. "Sounds like something I'd do drunk. Ka-Boom, huh? Total obliteration—and smack dab in the middle of the NBA playoffs most likely." He turned to the Princess on her red leatherette bar-stool. "But you still haven't answered my question. What do *we* get out of this?"

"Simon gets pot roast and gravy. I believe his wife has been holding dinner."

"And the rest of us?"

"You deserve something nice. With little evidence that the fabric of space-time would be irreparably rent, and this only on my say-so, few would have had the courage to take up my cause."

"So? What *do* we get?" Phlegm's tone was accusing, uncalled for, in Simon's opinion.

"You get a peek whenever your little hearts desire," said Princess Ackaetia. "Time hangs heavy when one is trapped inside a kaleidoscope."

"Once a scout always a scout. I just wanted a little recognition—you know, like a merit badge. Let's get to it. Everyone agree?" said Phlegm. "Sorry I got here late."

"Tardiness is a prerogative of royalty and I shall view this as a compliment to my exalted status. Your persistent hand-washing, however, smacks of lèse-majesté. Apology accepted."

A few hundred kaleidoscopes in and they found it. "This is the one," said the scope virgin.

"How do you know?" asked Harry.

"Q.E.D. I'm not in it. Yet."

"We've done it? Saved the known universe, then?" asked Simon.

"I hope you have found it to be a not overly strenuous undertaking." "But that's it? It's over?"

“It is. Now, help stuff me into this thing. Any volunteers?” To a man, Phlegm Ward included, Troup 136 Katahdin Council, Willipaq, Maine stepped forward. Passing the Princess Ackaetia back through the trans-dimensional rift was more like greased pig wrestling than assisting a distressed damsel aboard a passing palfrey. Finally her dorsal hump slipped past the aperture.

“Whew!” said the Princess. “Bye now.”

Simon shook his kaleidoscope. Broken glass rattled. “She’s gone.” He looked again. At the far end of the tube a naked glorious woman parted a curtain painted with fluffy Tiepolo clouds against a sky bluer than blue. She turned to wave.

Harry Pease grabbed an armload of kaleidoscopes and peered through each in turn. “Hey, the naked lady is still in the tube. All the tubes.” He set the kaleidoscopes down and went to check in the mirror. They had left a series of large concentric black rings around his eye.

❑

Harry and Simon returned to their separate houses and their separate wives and hearths. Simon resolved never to tell Bonnie about this. A trans-dimensional refugee saved from an intolerable marriage would make a good enough story, he reasoned; Bonnie was an incurable romantic. Like wearing aloha shirts outside the house and rubbernecking high school girls—who had begun looking good again after he turned seventy—a naked woman in each and every of one thousand two-hundred and thirty-eight Boy Scout kaleidoscopes was a thing best not spoken of.

Happy for their private silences and carrying the empty peach basket, Harry and Simon drove home alone, together. Troup 136 would wear their black circles with the pride of a full sash of merit badges.

And Simon would blame his increasingly slippery memory on the direct hit from Prince Philo Gulesi’s neutron cannon.

Scope Virgin was first published in *The Written Word* online magazine
November/December 2007

A brief history of the author

"Hell's Angels wear leather because chiffon wrinkles too easily..."
—Paul Lynde on Hollywood Squares, 35 years ago.

With the onset of late middle age Rob Hunter is the sole support of a 1999 Ford Escort and the despair of his young wife. He does dishes, mows the lawn and keeps their coastal Maine cottage spotless by moving as little as possible.

In a former life [1] he was a newspaper copy boy, railroad telegraph operator, recording engineer and film editor. He spent the 70s and 80s as a Top-40 disc jockey. He won a plaque once, for production excellence, from the Maine Association of Broadcasters. The boss kept it. One of Rob's engineering projects [2] won Senator William Proxmire's (D-Wisconsin) Golden Fleece Award. 100 Years of Air Power was an Air Force recruiting multimedia presentation shot in PanaVision with 70mm slides, quad stereo, the works. It toured in a trailer that sat four.

Rob's wife, Bonnie, is the secretary at a nearby rural elementary school. She is a gifted quilter who beguiled her new husband with the kaleidoscope of patchwork geometry. The nearest town to the Hunters that anybody is likely to have ever heard of—because of Stephen King's The Langoliers—is Bangor, Maine where there are real parking meters and a traffic light. They drive down every six months or so to watch the light change and see the trains come in.

[1] The Milwaukee Journal; Chicago, Milwaukee, St. Paul and Pacific RR Co.; WINS-NYC, WBT-Charlotte; WJAR-Providence; WIVY-Jacksonville; WNEW-NYC; WBAI-Pacifica; WQDY-Calais, Maine

[2] Rob's long-time client at Random House Audiobooks, Sherry Huber, wangled them a 1987 Spoken Arts Grammy nomination. They didn't win. The nomination was for The Short Stories of Ray Bradbury.

robhunter@onetinleg.com

Endpapers

Where do you get those ideas, my unseen reader asks.

Well, I... From life, I guess, I answer.

What kind of a experiences can you get stuck in front of a computer in a little house on the banks of a river in the hollyhocks of Maine, she asks.

The reader means boondocks. I do not correct her. Hollyhocks are my favorite flower. And what with seeing Al Gore's *An Inconvenient Truth* at the high school gym, I can foresee an exhilarating future for my 170-year-old cottage: four rooms and a privy-cum-woodshed.

My unseen reader could call me (correctly) a rear guard of the wooly socks and granola big city exodus of the 1980s. And a good ground rule for us ne'er-do-wells (credited to Robert A. Heinlein) is "Never own more than you can carry in both hands at a dead run." Good advice, albeit bad management practice. As a kid in Wisconsin I learned that most good stuff came from Someplace Else—a lesson that took many years and many miles to unlearn:

> *"Mention my name in Sheboygan...*
> *...but please don't tell them where I am."*

I have spent the past twenty years snugly enscorcelled (Not a word—look it up; find it, I challenge you. Hard 1st C as in *sconce*.) two feet above full-moon high tide on the Pennamaquan River, a tidal estuary—what Norwegians might call a fjord—in Pembroke, Maine.

Maine is God's country, says the reader, going glassy-eyed.

Yeah, but he's got a condo in Lauderdale, I reply.

Hereinafter follows a pair of character studies and a ramble on William Powell as the Thin Man I wrote up in the forming of two of the tales in Lost in Willipaq. I can't say that I actually used the stuff verbatim but they were in the drawer. So here they are:

Sylvester and Beany • The Illuminati Owe Carl .57 • Why William Powell?

Sylvester and Beany

The year the monarch butterflies didn't return to Maine, I went home to Brooklyn. "Something in the milkweed," they said. With a cold winter and no milkweed to browse to keep up their strength on the long flight from Mexico, the butterflies weakened and froze, dying in their millions far from the thoughtless haciendas. Almond eyes pouchy with sleep denied by fever dreams of avarice and the night sweats of free trade, the latafundistas and tin shanty dwellers alike wondered at the deaths, but with never a thought for Maine or for me. A preoccupation with the exigencies of day-to-day survival will do that. Greed will do that. Starvation clears the mind. I was busy, too, and forgot the butterflies. They were, after all, dead.

In New York the monarchs got bumped to the inside pages. A bewildered teenager stared from the Post, News and Times. Amy Fisher, Lethal Lolita, shot her boyfriend's wife. The wife had survived and was mightily pissed; the butterflies were dead and didn't care.

The old neighborhood hadn't changed much. In our iron-fenced front yard the size of a queen-sized bed, the mimosa tree had added four inches to its diameter while I was gone and in Maine. The crackheads, smackheads, winos and other hard-living citizens, the reason for the fence, were gone, dead like the butterflies or moved to Bushwick ten miles distant on the Suffolk County line where they competed with George Bush and Amy for the front page.

On a Brooklyn morning, I was looking out through the feathery mimosa leaves at our forth story windows. Across the street there was a line of shopping carts blocking the steps of P.S.6. The blacktopped playground where in the summer Hispanic softball leagues held forth with cries of *Eso es! Jonron! Novato del Año!* was today empty of cars. Children no longer go to P.S.6, long converted to office space, but the Board of Ed provides parking for school administrators to fill up the grounds and discourage ball playing just in case. No cars today. The neighbors haven't caught on to the Board of Ed's master plan and continue to have children anyway. One kid passes by running ahead of her sisters, a little black girl all dolled up in Sunday finery.

Daddy catches up.

“Elsie, didn’t I say to wait?” A voice gruff with pride and distraction. A child’s giggle and a whacked bottom. Instant tears of expected surprise. A grunt and a hug from Daddy. Giggles again.

A tall, tightly knit black man in his forties scrubbed the steps with chlorine bleach. This was Sylvester. He was singing and talking to himself as he worked. “To the tables down at Morey’s, to the place where Louie dwells…” The Whiffenpoof Song. Rudy Vallee was alive and well. The householder prospers.

Sometime in late March, Sylvester had taken up residence on the steps of the Nathan Hale Administrative Building, New York Board of Ed., formerly P.S.6: four stories of brick and cement thrown up to a standard architectural design during the First World War. Two wings boxed off an enclosed courtyard where boys and girls once formed up on opposite sides for attendance, games and fire drills. That was the front, on McGaw Street. The kids who last formed up for attendance were middle-aged by now and had called their neighborhood Red Hook or South Brooklyn. Sylvester discretely set up camp near the coal chutes where twice a week ashes are hauled away and polluting soft bituminous is delivered under an easement from the Department of Environmental Protection.

Our street, Warren Street. Our neighborhood, just off Smith and near downtown Brooklyn. During the yuppie bubble of the eighties real estate afflatus tagged our neighborhood “Boerum Hill” with the same commercial poetics that had coined “Tribeca” and “SoHo” over the river in Manhattan two decades earlier.

Three days later I stood in the September sun with Ed Sweeney, a neighbor. Ed was recently certified as a drug rehabilitation and AIDS counselor and, during his time at John Jay College, had picked up Sylvester as a practice subject. Eddie himself can’t get a job; the field being overcrowded. As we watched Sylvester at his household chores, another man, wearing an overcoat too warm for the day, executed a zigzag path across the street from our side to Sylvester’s, dodging oncoming traffic. There was no oncoming traffic.

“Cecil and Beany. Like the cartoon.” Beany was Sylvester’s satellite, a garden-variety psycho, a drunk and a doper—whatever he could get. In our neighborhood amateur psychiatric social work was something we all did, a hedge against getting your hubcaps, battery, or radio back when they wandered off, which was regularly. You paid a ransom, but it was cheaper than replacing the lost items.

Eddie flashed a hard look at me, *this man was important*: “I’ve been working on him. If he gives it half a chance he’s gonna make it—Sylvester, forget

Beany. He's not really nuts, just does a lot of dope. And booze. He's off the hard stuff."

"And he's not a cartoon. I get it. Sorry, just trying to be cute."

Eddie is my age—fiftyish, tall and broad at the shoulders, a scrupulous bather and frequent washer of his long chestnut hair which sticks out in a pony tail through the back of a Bud Man baseball cap. In the summer he sits out on the fire escape and dries his hair with his wife's hair dryer, cigarette dangling from his lips. Eddie sports a Pancho Villa mustache, and an easy smile frames perfect teeth—dentures. His natural teeth were the casualties of charity dentists, soft food and hard liquor. Eddie had done his time on the street and in prison before turning his own life around. He got his night school diploma two years before, college the hard way. He will make a good drug abuse counselor.

"I am corrected. Didn't mean to trivialize him. Does that clear the air?"

Eddie brightened and changed the subject. "You haven't seen my new tattoo. Hey, look at this! Always room for one more."

He gave his arm a quarter turn and made a fist, pumping his triceps. An intricate floral pattern wriggled. "Got it in Virginia Beach at Julia's summer school." His wife teaches English Lit. at Brooklyn College. "Sylvester, our very own homeless. He's clean, scrubs down his—the school's—doorway with chlorine bleach. And Beany…" Eddie registered displeasure.

Beany had a home on the block. A tenuous trail of heredity linked him to Mister Johnson, an elderly man who owned a row house and presided over an assortment of cousins, daughters and their children, and spouses in varying degrees of gainful work and public assistance. Beany laughed a lot for no apparent reason. His higher cognitive functions had been blown away with nose candy and alcohol. But Beany, like him or not, belonged here. Beany had people, homefolks, on Warren Street and was regarded as a natural feature of the terrain—a pothole to be driven around. Sylvester was the stranger on our block.

Sylvester had been welcomed as a deterrent to car theft. Pilferage and casual vandalism decreased with his arrival on the block. He hated the druggers and annoyed the hell out of them, which did not completely explain his relationship with Beany. The crack heads and their dealers struck a nerve with generally civil and well-spoken Sylvester. Their presence brought him scrambling over his barricade of shopping carts spewing invective to heaven and earth, haranguing the sky, appealing to an unseen audience past the footlights of a stage only he could see. He danced around the dealers, warming the air with a torrent of abuse. The dealers all carried guns and were quick to imagine a slight. However, a surviving etiquette of the old street gangs required direct eye contact for an insult to be a killing offense. Up, down, and all around, he never looked directly at them. Sylvester lived and the junkies left. Except for Beany.

Beany watched Sylvester's stuff while he was away getting more. Sylvester was a collector of bottles, clothes and handouts.

Two weeks in New York, and it was time to go. The last resume had been passed out. Eddie volunteered to drive me to the station. After four years in Maine, I had felt safer parking in Connecticut and taking the train into town. A sanitation truck was pulled up to the back steps of the Nathan Hale Administrative Building. Along with two uniformed cops and a blue and white. Eddie's stepdaughter was watching the operation, Supervising Princess of the Works.

She struck a pose and chewed at her knuckles. Liza is seventeen, an age when knuckle chewing is more endearing than neurasthenic. "They're busting Sylvester."

So they were. Where was Beany?

"Somebody filed a complaint."

The cops looked alert and bored at the same time. Meeting no resistance from the neighborhood, they lit up. One of them fished a container of coffee from the dash of the patrol car.

"Hey, that belongs to somebody." Eddie.

"This shit yours?" Cop.

"No but he'll be right back." A shrug from the cops. Just doing the job. They're not yours what do you care. The shopping carts, eight of them full of cans and clothes, toppled into the garbage truck, the hydraulics kicked in, and they were crushed.

"Hey. I thought New York was supposed to separate metal and glass for recycling."

"In the case of a sanitary nuisance we make an exception. Go figure." A page was initialed in a leather notebook and the lid snapped shut. The police snuffed out their butts, and their car followed the sanitation truck away to the next complaint. They had cleaned Sylvester out.

We loaded our bags in the car and Eddie started the engine, then turned it off. "I want to watch this." Beany was shambling along the opposite side of the street, trying to look casual. He held a can in a paper bag and drank through a plastic straw. Sweat beaded his forehead, and his shoulders jerked spasmodically—he was going up or coming down. He noticed us in the car and flashed a smile.

A lone shopping cart approached across the empty playground. Sylvester just stood looking at those empty steps. “Lord take the lightning to you. Where *were* you, man?”

Beany broke up in giggles. He was tickled. It was over; whatever bond there had been between them was canceled. Beany danced away, laughing at a joke no one else had heard.

Sylvester turned to us. “My double down. They got that too.” A prized goose-down coat, scavenged, set by against the winter to come, was gone with Sylvester’s carts. It would be a thin winter, a winter out-of-doors. We took up a collection. Three dollars, enough for two pints of fortified wine—Night Train, Mad Dog, Jive 7.

Triple-parked on 42nd Street in front of Grand Central Eddie said, “He was getting his act together, now he’ll have to go to a shelter, get beaten up and robbed. The streets are healthier than the shelters. If you live.”

We had our collars up against a stiff crosstown wind. I thought about getting the plastic banking up against the house in Maine. We shook hands. Eddie peeled away west under the Park Avenue overpass and I caught the New Haven for Bridgeport.

The Illuminati Owe Carl .57

Adolescence is a long and lonely time; I read comics and the pulps. One story mentioned an 'Illuminati,' but I missed the reference. The story was a sanitized take on the "Secret Masters Walk Among Us" theme. But I was a sharp kid and well read in the lore of comics and the pulps: The Great White Lodge as a Celtic swords-and-sorcery knockoff on the Illuminati. It was a good yarn and I remembered it into middle age.

The day the Illuminati—secret, sinister—reentered my life Harold Junior pulled up in his rusted-out Lincoln Continental as I was checking my mail. Our mailboxes, down by the road, do double duty as street addresses too, here in rural Maine. Harold's huge domestic battle cruiser had been bought cheap and came with a titanic appetite for gas and oil. But it never had to go far, only start. And it plowed through drifts that would stall a Jeep."Look. See that—it's a beaver." I followed Harold Junior's pointing finger. No beaver. There had been no beaver sightings on the lower Pennamaquan since they started blowing beaver dams to control upcountry flooding. Something about fish migrations.

Harold did not leave the driver's seat. This was a protocol of roadside conversations: stay in the car, otherwise they'll have to invite you inside for coffee or a beer. Anyway, Harold would have had a time making it to the house. His free spirit was sorely tried by arthritic knees and diabetes, trapped inside 450 pounds of fat.

"No, goddamn it, it's a beaver—*right there*." Harold got out of the Lincoln. The car sprang eight inches up on its springs. They made those babies to last. Harold lurched toward the riverbank. The breeze caught the blue, syrupy exudations from his tailpipe and a cloud of hydrocarbons accompanied us as

Harold grabbed my arm and dragged me along. He pointed. "There! A beaver."

"We don't see many of them," I said. I had never seen *any* of them.

Harold Junior released his hold on my arm. He grew thoughtful. "They renounce sex," he said. "The beaver bites its testicles off and throws them to the legions of hell in hot pursuit. A servant of God 'must cut off from himself all vices, all motions of lewdness, and must cast them in the Devil's face.' That was on TV." There was a Christian channel included in our local basic cable package.

"A pretty good reason for no beavers." But beavers were making a comeback, it appeared. And that is why I remember the day the Great White Lodge, The Illuminati, came to visit with me—Harold and the beaver. It was not the same day and they came not bearing beavers, but with a wrong number.

It was Saturday about suppertime, the time boiler room calls come in. I have a routine, spooning rice and fish together, listening with courteous deference to the pitch, whatever, until the caller pauses for breath. Then I spring my trap. "My wife. You are calling for my wife. She died in April."

There is a pause and they ring off. Then I eat dinner. The University of Kansas Jayhawks are trying to build a new field house and the news of the death of a distinguished alumna has slowed them down but it hasn't stopped them. The Jayhawks' telephone solicitors still show up about once a month.

This time it was neither aluminum siding nor the Jayhawks.

I was watching Talk Radio, a video of a film from a stage play by Eric Bogosian, a film about the Faustian progression of a radio talk show host in Texas, most of it set in the broadcast studio. The phone rang. Hmmm.

I stopped the tape and answered the phone. A man in Windham, Maine was checking on a bogus charge on his bill. Had I received a call charged to his number? No. September fifth? I checked the calendar. I had been home all day waiting for chimney work. The kids were away. The caller later identified himself as Carl, a born-again Christian who listens to Christian radio stations. But all this information did not come at once; it was scattered throughout our conversation. We must have talked for ten minutes or so, he incurring charges far in excess of the $.57 he was checking up on. There had been a lot of billing mix-ups last month and he was calling all the listed numbers to frame a complaint. I was the first who had answered.

I said since the death of my wife I had lived alone with a dog and two cats. Might they have learned to dial? No, besides this was a call to my number billed to his, from a third location.

Hmmm…

We grew easy and made observations about how computers were sending the world to hell. “Big Brother is here,” said Carl.

“He’s always been here,” I replied, “except what with home-based downloading he’ll be in our videos, too.”

“Next year. The compression technology is online. Two master numbers, supposedly known only to the National Security Agency and the National Science Foundation and they can tap into your home CPU. We are at the mercy of any hacker.”

This was stretching out and introductions were in order. “Hunter, Robert Hunter.” Then gratuitously, “My kids use the same last name. But then, there wouldn’t be any names on your bill.” I could hear him nod and continued on into the silence. “They’re almost thirty, not little kids who’d be playing telephone games.” I held my hand in stages off the floor, indicating the heights of small children. Carl was easy to talk with, gregarious, out-going. And wary. He never gave me his last name even after I had told him mine several times, the repetitions in a context that my adult children had been visiting at about the time of his snaggled bill and perhaps one of their calling card calls to the coast had been misinterpreted by the NYNEX computer.

Carl brought up the Illuminati and the act of Congress that in 1913 created the Federal Reserve to keep foreign money manipulators out of our system. “But the secret control of the Federal Reserve. What about that? There is no way of finding out.”

He had found out. Some Christian radio station had mentioned it. “I’ll bet you see little hints in the news.” I had told him I read news on the local radio station. Something I had been doing on one local radio station or another for almost forty years.

There were hints in the news, how would he know that? The wire services ground out reams of copy daily full of the gratuitous insights reporters slip in when they notice inconsistencies in the official versions of whatever the story of the day happens to be. Their editors flatten them out, seeing these as speed bumps on the unimpeded flow of homogenized information. During the news free-for-all of the Vietnam War, the daily press briefings in Saigon—the Five o’clock Follies—generated a lot of these inconsistencies. Announcers learned to cherish them.

I was grinding out my penitent’s path toward Social Security at a backwoods Maine radio station. Where I read the news. I was one of *them*. “A coffee grinder,” a self-effacing reference to the limited wattage of the local radio station.

“There are hints. Can’t deny it.”

“Well, the Great White Lodge, right?” My first mistake; I thought I was playing Carl but launched into explanations of how these things came to be. My version—the King James Authorized. My arguments sounded weak in the earpiece. “The Secret Masters are tying our shoelaces together while we sleep.” There—the ball was in Carl’s court. I sensibly attributed the normalization of the news to a wire service self-censorship that kept the wackier stuff out of sight whenever an editor caught up with it. No one needed to know, the paper trails were too convoluted and too expensive to investigate.

“The Illuminati. It’s Celtic.” Keltic he said it, very PC: Celtic with a K. “Europe will take control of the North American money market, the world. A few control and direct everything, sharers of secret knowledge. There is a plan.”

I was tempted to make a wisecrack but didn’t; I was getting a vague sense of unease. Not about plots, but about plots about plots. Enough worried people, feeling powerless, and they needed a target. Carl needed a target and he knew my number. Things were going to hell and God was on their side: the Christians needed a plan, a conspiratorial secret evil out there. Carl was thoughtful, not a crazy. These were things he had spent much time pondering. He had my number and my name while all I had was “Carl.”

Carl explained, calming and confidential. This was something I, as a reasonable, educated human being knew, but for whatever reason, was not yet ready to face up to. He spoke a mumbo-jumbo of home brew mysticism, lifts from the rituals of lodges hopelessly garbled by centuries-long transmission.

“Illuminati, ever heard of ‘em?” I had.

The Illuminati, the behind-the-scenes master schemers of folklore and secret fears, had reentered my life. Carl was right: in his heart of hearts, everyone suspects that there are puppet masters controlling things. What else could explain so much misery if there is a just and merciful God? Carl was worrying on about Europe taking over the world, so I didn’t tell him I had seen a board game called “Illuminati” in the Dungeons and Dragons section of a science-fiction book store on a cobbled back street in Bonn, Germany just that April while taking a break from my late wife’s last-ditch radiation treatments.

Carl was talking and I had not been listening. I hurried to catch up. “Illuminati, sure: pyramid power, Lovecraftian corruption, board room of the Chase Manhattan. Sure. Hey, ever read *Foucault’s Pendulum*? Umberto Eco, you know?—*Name of the Rose*? They made a movie out of it.”

Ahh, they made a movie out of it. Not to worry. There was an uncomfortable silence, just line noise and both of us breathing. Hollywood had executed a flanking maneuver, squeezed his fears onto the small screen, video to be compressed and downloaded. I decided Carl and I had talked enough. I would have just as happily agreed with him, but he would never allow it. He required contention and I was parroting a party line. He had gotten me to defending the established order. Anything I could say he could refute: the Rockefellers, the Rothchilds, tainted money impacted, ever circulating through the same hands, controlling.

"Goodbye, Carl."

"Goodbye, Robert."

I wished I had remembered to tell Carl not to worry it's only a picture show.

And then there was the beaver.

Why William Powell?

Because, that's why. In the Ninepatch Variation (page 84) William Powell plays Tiresias the Seer to Libby Pease's Antigone: "If somebody bites you on the ass it means they are thinking of you, too, dear Libby. Eventually the Earth will fall into the sun," says The Thin Man.

Libby Pease is my favorite person out of all of Willipaq County—an evocation of the usually broke and always hopeful denizens of, perhaps, just perhaps, Washington County, Maine—living free and wild in their very own Yoknapatawpha. The Libby tales became a triptych and she picked up a spiritual counselor, a 400-year-old medicine man in The Red Sneaker Zones (page 95): "Go for it, Lib. Get naked, paint the cat; you've earned it, " says Sun-ripples-quiet-pool-to-call-of-loon.

Ah, but Libby's interlocutors, even as Doctor Who's companions, had to start somewhere. William Powell as the first choice was all Wayne Croft's fault. Wayne was a chum from the WBAI days. This was the 1960s and I followed him around toting the company's (Pacifica Radio) Nagra III with neo-pilotone (The Nagra is a tape recorder and pilotone is a film sync thingy that we didn't need at listener-sponsored radio—don't ask. Try Googling Stefan Kudelski.) for his production of Marlowe's Doctor Faustus. Tall and attenuated, Wayne sported a spindly beard and resembled John Carradine as Preacher Casey in the Grapes of Wrath. He heightened the effect by wearing three-piece box-back dark suits and chain-smoking Russian style, cigarette held between the thumb and index finger. Wayne was an actor, a damned good one, too. Hurd Hatfield played Faustus however.

In the 60s WBAI, listener-sponsored radio in the days before NPR, was the place to be. George Coe, Richard C. Neuweiler and Nancy Weyburn and the Second City delivered satire and commentary along with Severn Darden, Rene Santoni, Don Calfa and Lord Buckley. Eric Bentley expounded on Brecht. Ann Macmillan and John Corigliano were the music mavens. Dave Amram played Lady Bird Johnson in our parallel spoof on the Democratic National Convention—The Big Tune Out. Ayn Rand in her 2nd hand mink struggled up the three blocks from the Nathaniel Branden Institute to hold forth on philosophical objectivism. Harry Schwartz and Dick Elman interviewed Malcolm X while Richard Lamparski interviewed Connie Boswell. WBAI lost a microphone cord at the Audubon Ballroom, cut in two when Malcolm was shot.

In 1980 I attended a get-together of WBAI 60s survivors at the KitKat Klub on 14th Street at Union Square—cash bar, sugar and complex carbohydrates. Old coots, new suits, and everybody handing resumes around. Nothing has changed and that was 26 years ago. So what's new? I bought my suit at Abraham & Strauss (Fulton St., Brooklyn). I still have the suit and that was the only time I've ever worn it. Polyester never sleeps.

Oh, yes—I seem to have dozed off. Why William Powell was the question… Well, William Powell as Libby Pease's Thin Man because I could get around Manhattan pretty well on my old Sears 10-speed, how's them apples? This is now the 1970s when a Post Office truck gave me a clip with its protruding side mirror on 56th Street. I went flying like a gyroscopic top in a magnetic anomaly. The driver tossed me a hi-five and sped away on 56th Street toward to Grand Central Post Office; he had government business. The close call reassembled my priorities and hiding out at the movies was a fine idea. I walked the bike to work and decided to take Wayne Croft up on his offer for one free admission to the Carnegie Hall Repertory Cinema. That very night.

In the seventies Wayne had become the manager of the Carnegie Repertory Cinema—three floors down under Carnegie Hall where the subway (57th St. Station, a loop on the Q line) passed by on the far side of plush-covered walls. Once a month they ran all the Thin Man movies back-to-back. The big sliver faces and the discrete drapery of Myrna Loy's shimmering dressing gowns got me hooked on the Thin Man and Myrna Loy.

About Willipaq

"I could be picking blueberries..." The man on the next treadmill over was working hard and glowed an apoplectic pink. He had put in his Levitical twenty minutes but kept on moving. We were in the only gym between Bangor and the Canadian Maritimes. Willipaq, ahh... well, Willipaq lies way Downeast. The times and the places of this book are largely the product of the author's imagination. However, there is a place, set somewhere out of time...

At a reduced pace my neighbor spoke of blasting yellow birch with black powder and a fuse: "The 4-foot lengths came skidded and yarded—we just had to cut and split. That yellow birch was standing green and tight as a weasel." This was in the nineteen-forties—he was in high school then:

"Remember when there was that lumber yard there? On Garfield Street? No, you wouldn't remember. I'm going to be 86 next month and that puts me way out front in the remembering department. So we were making a dollar a cord. Cutting and splitting? Stacking, too. We'd drill a hole and tamp in black powder and a fuse. At a dollar a cord—for the muscle work—we spent most of the money for powder and fuse. It was a good summer. There was a war on so what the hell?"

Willipaq is remote even to a born Mainer. The bumper sticker: "I live in the Other State of Maine," beckons from rusting pickups that litter the ditches of Willipaq—roadside memorabilia of a lost war with time.

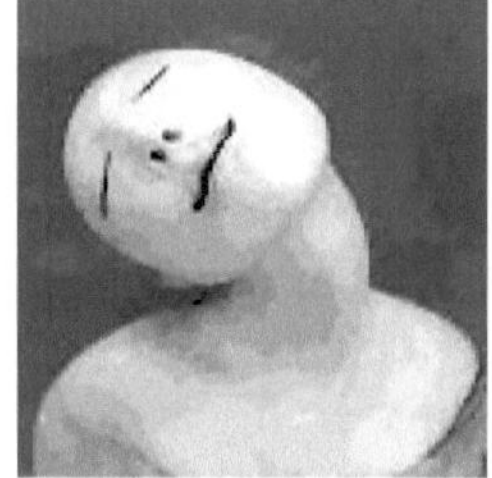

The first settlers named the county Willipaq for its indigenes, a leisurely crowd who seemed possessed of no sense of urgency. The native people strolled the beaches at low tide collecting mussels, trapped the occasional fish in their weir corrals, picked berries, made love and squatted to their need beholden to no clock. Although the Indians—the easternmost band of the Algonquian nation—and the English had no common language, example proved too powerful to resist and soon floggings were administered to pilgrims caught wading out of the shallow pool of purpose. Berry picking and lollygagging on the beach drew an application of the knout. The settlers sported the starched underwear and stiff black broadcloth of the followers of John Calvin.

That these children of nature were a lost tribe of Israel was a popular fancy of Calvinist lore. The Willipaqs' aimless pursuit of pleasure inspired backsliding among the settlers—protestant vigor was not proof to mixed bathing and sweaty labors under a strange sun. Shapely ankles were exposed while bending over berries and many a maiden found it pleasant to hold her pose. Fornication brought a hundred strokes with the rope's end; discipline was maintained against deteriorating standards of social comportment. It was the good fight, but futile. Many were the righteous arms grown weary with flogging and surreptitious self-manipulation. Strange diseases thinned the Europeans' numbers; crops failed. They ate gruel made from acorns and the few sacks of seed remaining, and died.

While those Willipaqs released from the relentless summer toil of hunting and gathering holidayed at the shore, the pale-skinned visitors to whom all Indians looked alike made no preparations for the coming of the snows. They covered themselves all in black and took turns hitting each other as they knelt on the sand. The indigenes looked on, astonished.

The fierce coastal winter came and the Willipaqs moved inland to winter over in cozy tunnels dug out of the hillsides, subsisting on unsuspected supplies of dried meat, fish and vegetables. Over the council fires of the Willipaqs that winter, puzzled shamans strove for an intuition to explain the strange behavior of their summer visitors. When the Willipaqs returned to their seaside encampments, they gave a decent burial to what the wolves and foxes had left of the white settlers.

Willipaq County was yet again unimaginatively so named by the next batch of transoceanic intruders who falsely felt that by so doing they would be free from threat of Indian attack. The emigrants were warned of bloody battles sure to follow a collision of cultures. They were easy prey to the scare tales of the old America hands who waffled on, but never left, the docks of Liverpool.

Roving bands of savages were seen at a distance where acres of wild berries had been ravaged by the goats the first white men brought. Undaunted by the disappearance of the first colony, the newcomers dug right in clearing the land for agriculture—plowing, sowing, nurturing, husbanding, drying and salting. While their livestock roamed at will, toil was the portion of the latest wave of homesteaders.

The Willipaqs quietly moved to a more salubrious neighborhood that year; their berrying grounds had been turned to goat forage. The Willipaqs viewed the European tourist hordes, when they thought about them at all, as a natural phenomenon not unlike the suicidal flotillas of squid that beached themselves in quintennial cycles, causing a horrible stink.

Acknowledgements

The quote, "Somewhere, something incredible is waiting to be known," is the handiwork of Carl Sagan, astronomer (1934-1996). Dr. Sagan is reported to have said: "They laughed at Einstein. They laughed at the Wright Brothers. But they also laughed at Bozo the Clown."

A Pass on the Tabouli was first published in the *Hiss Quarterly,* [www.hissquarterly.com] Spring 2006: the "Future Imperfect" issue.

Boys' Night Out was first published in the Summer 2005 issue of *On-Spec—The Canadian Magazine of the Fantastic* [www.onspec.ca].

I Want to Share Your Wheat was first published in the September/October 2002 issue of *Demensions—Doorways to Science Fiction and* Fantasy [www.demensionszine.com] where it was voted 2002 Story of the Year.

The Perfect Homburg was first published in the March/April 2003 issue of *Demensions—Doorways to Science Fiction and Fantasy.*

An Unwarmed Fish was first published in the Summer 2003 issue of *Demensions—Doorways to Science Fiction and Fantasy.*

The Song of the Rice Barge Coolie was first published in *Aeon Speculative Fiction #11* [www.aeonmagazine.com], Marti McKenna, editor.

The Year They Invented Frozen Lemonade was first published in the January 2008 *The Harrow: Original Works of Fantasy and Horror,* Michael Colangelo, fiction editor. [www.theharrow.com]

The Ninepatch Variation was first published in the January 2004 issue of *Ideomancer Speculative Fiction,* Mikal Trimm, editor. [www.ideomancer.com]

Klein, the Clone was first published as *The Flags of All Nations Hors D'oeuvres Toothpick Caper* in the Winter, 2003 *Fables—The Home for Folktale and Speculative Fiction on the Internet* [www.fables.org].

A Special Providence was first published in the May 2003 number of *Quantum Muse* [www.quantummuse.com], Ray Coulombe, editor.

The Red Sneaker Zones was first published in the *Hiss Quarterly* [www.hissquarterly.com] the "Space To Grow" issue Summer 2007, Sydney Nash-Lee, editor.

E Pluribus Human was first published in the Summer 2007 issue of *Coyote Wild* [www.coyotewildmag.com]—an online quarterly of speculative fiction and poetry, Lori A. Basiewicz, editor.

Scope Virgin was first published in *The Written Word* online magazine [www.writtenwordmag.com] November/December 2007, Ace Masters, editor.

TheRunaway Bungalow was first published as a featured novella in SpecFic-World's *Featured Fiction* [www.specficworld.com] August 2008, Doyle Eldon Wilmoth, Jr. editor.

Dead Man in the Yard was first published in the Spring 2007 *Nanobison* [www.nanobison.com], Doug Helbling, editor.

A triumph of reverse Darwinism, *Facelift* arrived after the fact, and was published (belatedly) in the February 2008 Aphelion [www.aphelion-webzine.com] thanks to the good graces of Robert Moriyama, Aphelion's short story editor. It was originally written as a website freebie to accompany Kenn Brown's [www.mondolithic.com] illustration for the author's website.

The decoration for About Willipaq, "Rapturous," is from a sculpture by Elizabeth Ostrander and used by permission.

The original photograph for the onetinleg.com website logo, "They All Look at Another Side, " is the work of María de la Puente Bernardos [http://mute-noface.deviantart.com] and is used by permission.

And—while its setting is in Downeast Maine, *The Runaway Bungalow*'s scope is worldwide. Thus the author is indebted to Toni Scribner for vetting the manuscript, particularly his uses of Spanish reflexive verb forms.

About this Title (the legal stuff)

No creatures real or imagined were injured in the making of Lost in Willipaq.

Podcasting and MP3 Audio

If having the author murmur in your ear is your idea of the total reading experience, you are invited to browse onetinleg.com's Free Reads section. These MP3 downloads are released under a Creative Commons license. They're free. Copy the files as much as you want, pass 'em around. All I ask is that you don't alter the file or sell it. To download—right click "Download" and select "Save Target As" or "Save Link As" depending on your browser. To preview a story just click "stream." The audio versions of the tales from Onetinleg.com will be appearing here as studio time allows. I have tried to cover most of these tales, not all. Some stories just look better on the printed page.

You can stay ahead of the curve by clicking the RSS symbol to initiate a podcast. A podcast downloads audio files to your MP3 player through your computer. You use a free application (see page 76) to "subscribe" to onetinleg.com's feed, the application checks the site regularly and starts a download whenever it finds something new. If you like what you hear, tell your friends. I'm glad to have you as a listener. Enjoy!

onetinleg.com

and thanks for all the fish...

—Douglas Adams, *The Hitchhiker's Guide to the Galaxy*

Ginny Levitan and her husband, Jim, are inspecting a possible retirement home at the outset of Rob Hunter's "The Song of the Rice Barge Coolie." With the aid of real estate agent Barbara Casmirczak—"Call me Babs"—they buy the odd dwelling and soon discover they have an ant infestation. What raises this above the typical tale of marital discord is the alternating sections told from the ants' POV. Insects are nothing new to horror fiction, but Hunter elevates this tale above the standard fare with engaging characters, keen POV shifts, and a quirkiness of style that makes the outcome most satisfying. While the dénouement was inevitable, it left me with a devious grin on my face. Impressive.

—Marshall Payne in *The Fix Online*

"...exceptionally well written." (The Song of the Rice Barge Coolie)

—Linda Landrigan, Editor *Alfred Hitchcock's Mystery Magazine*

I loved "Facelift." It's like "Ghost World", "Only You Can Save The Universe", and "Welcome to the Dollhouse" mixed together. Teen angst, comics / sf geekdom, and Pratchett / Holt / Fforde lunacy in one package.

—Robert Moriyama, Short Story Editor *Aphelion*

Shape shifting stories include one type of being transforming into another. A vampire or werewolf story would be a typical example. Yet far from typical is Rob Hunter's *Boys' Night Out* (Summer 2005 issue) werewolf story. The gated community of Sur la Mer is built to keep men in instead of out.

—Susan MacGregor, Fiction Editor *On Spec,* writing
about *Boys' Night Out* in the Spring, 2006 issue.

I kept getting drawn back into the manuscript (The Year They Invented Frozen Lemonade). I picked back and forth through it for approximately six hours. It 'works' like a rather interesting puzzle (and this may be part of the story's strong appeal to me).

—Michael R. Colangelo, Fiction Editor
The Harrow: Original Works of Fantasy and Horror

Thanks for giving us such a well-crafted, entertaining, and flat-out *funny* story to enjoy (I Want to Share Your Wheat).

—Donna Thiel-Cook, Editor
Demensions-Doorways to Science Fiction and Fantasy.

www.ingramcontent.com/pod-product-compliance
Ingram Content Group UK Ltd.
Pitfield, Milton Keynes, MK11 3LW, UK
UKHW041948190726
13854UKWH00004B/1858